LET THE HERO BE
THE HUNGRY MAN

By the same author

Non-fiction

The Story of Parkend
Warren James and the Dean Forest Riots
The Industrial Teagues and the Forest of Dean
Around the Forest
Four Personalities from the Forest of Dean
Man of Iron – Man of Steel. The Lives of David and Robert Mushet
Blood on Coal

Edited by Bess and Ralph Anstis

Diary of a Working Man – Bill Williams in the Forest of Dean, 1872/3

Fiction

Dean Forest Stories

The author wishes to thank the artist
Owen James for permission to reproduce on the cover a detail from
his *Image for my Grandfather*

LET THE HERO BE THE HUNGRY MAN

by

RALPH ANSTIS

ALBION HOUSE

Coleford, Gloucestershire

First published in Great Britain in 2000 by

ALBION HOUSE
Parkend Walk, Coalway, Coleford
Gloucestershire, GL16 7JS

ISBN 0 9511371 5 8

Designed and produced by

The Short Run Book Company Ltd
St Stephen's House
Arthur Road
Windsor
Berkshire SL4 1RY

For Bess

'When the history of our time is told,
let the hero be the hungry man.'

Alexander Cordell, *The Fire People*

This novel is set mainly in the Forest of Dean in Gloucestershire in the early 1870s. The characters are fictitious, though the momentous events that shape their lives are a matter of history.

CHAPTER 1

Waldo Evans stretched his arms above his head and regarded Adam coldly. He allowed his gaze to wander over his face and body for a few seconds and then began to ask him questions. This was the first time he had deigned to talk to him since Catrin had brought him to the farm some two months ago. Waldo's voice was loud and accusing. 'You have been in Wales a year now, is it?'

Catrin moved uneasily and her mother put another log on the fire. But her father looked straight ahead. Adam gave an easy smile. 'Yes, about a year.' He was a little older than Waldo, just twenty-two. But Adam, broad and upright, knew he gloried in the ripeness of his youth, whereas Waldo was an undersized fellow with a crumpled face that showed more dissatisfaction than his years would suggest was possible. Adam had tried to be friendly, but had met with no response. Waldo's sneers, his attempts to ridicule him, indeed his refusal to accept any approach of friendship annoyed him. Yet it was important to carry Waldo with him if he wanted to marry his sister.

'Where do you say you come from?'

'Coalway, in the Forest of Dean, in Gloucestershire.'

'Why did you leave there?'

Adam already disliked Waldo, and under the fire of these questions his dislike exploded into hatred, an emotion he had never experienced for anyone before. He realised what it was and noted his curious reaction. It was as though he was sitting calmly, letting it surge up, then setting it apart from himself, as if he were putting a bundle out of the way, but not forgetting where he left it. He shook his head as if to rid himself of his thoughts, and his eyes screwed up slightly as if in pain, as they often did in moments of mental distress. But he was not going to let Waldo upset him.

'Because there was no work there for a miner,' he answered, 'but there is some here.'

'A coalminer you are, then, is it, and working in Erwgoch?' said Waldo with the air of settling some abstruse point.

'You know that, Waldo.' Adam had learnt from Catrin that very day the reason for Waldo's hostility, or at least one of the reasons. It was the farm, which Waldo helped to run. In spite of his young years he already had a big say in running it, and his father, not being in good health, hoped in a few years to hand it over to him completely. Catrin suspected Waldo thought Adam wanted to marry her so he could take it over and dispossess him.

'When are you going back to the Forest of Dean, then?'

'Nosy, is it, Waldo?' said Catrin, annoyed. She added something in Welsh; Waldo replied with what seemed to be a string of invective; and Catrin's mother, who was sitting by the fire, spoke sharply to Waldo in Welsh also. She was a thin, grey-haired woman, tired-looking, but with iron energy.

Adam ignored the family altercation. 'I don't rightly know when I be going back. It do depend, like.'

'On what?'

'On things.' Adam would have liked to take the fellow outside and punch him on the nose. But he disguised his feelings and looked at the fireplace. The kettle, hanging from its rod and easy for tilting, was puffing gently, and he was relieved when Catrin's mother began to make some tea. From the oven came the separate smells of rabbit pie and apple pudding, baking for supper.

Old Mrs Evans, Catrin's grandmother, a solid stick of a woman dressed in black, now entered and made for the settle, an enormous structure that would accommodate six people on the seat and half a dozen hams in the back. She took her place on it nearest the fire, as was her right, accepted a cup of tea, put on her glasses and took up her knitting. Adam, who was sitting near her, tried to be friendly. 'What are you knitting, Mrs Evans?'

She looked up sharply, clearly regarding the question as impertinent. She concentrated on a stitch. Then, having judged that the silence had lasted long enough to punish Adam for his indiscretion, she said, 'I am knitting a jersey, can't you see?' She eyed him over her glasses. 'You look as if you could do with a new jersey.'

'Yes, I be going to buy one when I've saved up a bit of cash, though I don't know when that'll be. My landlady takes most of my wages.' And, he said to himself, the rest goes mainly on beer.

Mrs Evans grunted. 'I hope the rest doesn't go on drink.'

'Oh, no.' He would compromise, but not capitulate. 'Only some. Colliers have to drink a lot of beer, Mrs Evans. It be the dust, you see.'

Mrs Evans grunted. 'You speak funny, young man. Because you come from London, is it?' Adam guessed London was the only place in England she had heard of.

'No. I do come from the Forest of Dean.'

'Never heard of it.' She settled back and her needles clicked with hostility. She eyed him again. 'They tell me you are a coalminer.'

'Yes, Mrs Evans.'

'A coalminer in a forest?' She examined an errant stitch critically. 'Strange it seems to me, coalmines in a forest.' She looked at him suspiciously.

'Yes, but they're small ones,' said Adam patiently. 'All surrounded by trees.'

'Do you want to go back?' pursued Waldo. He was on the attack again. 'What keeps you here?'

Adam was silent. Waldo must know at least one reason why he stayed in Erwgoch and visited the Evans's family every Sunday. Impatience again rose up within him, but he managed to remain calm and polite.

Catrin attempted to steer the conversation into safer channels. 'Adam says that the Forest is small and beautiful.' She enunciated each syllable of her words separately and clearly. 'Beau-ti-ful it is, with hills and lots of trees.'

'Coalway doesn't seem very beautiful to me if you've got coal mines there,' interrupted Waldo. 'Like Erwgoch, is it?'

'No, not like Erwgoch.'

'Erwgoch.' Waldo corrected his pronunciation.

Adam ignored the correction, and looked over at old Mrs Evans. She was concentrating on her knitting, monotonously and relentlessly, but he knew she was listening, picking up every nuance, noting every rejoinder Adam made. The noise from her needles rattled in his head.

He switched his glance to Catrin's father to gauge his reaction to Waldo's onslaught. Mr Evans's square face, unhealthily pale beneath the deceptive brown bestowed on it by the wind and the sun, showed no emotion. Adam realised he had to get this right. If he upset Waldo by belligerent answers, he might also upset his father, and he was the one who had to be won over to agree to Adam's marrying his daughter. But Mr Evans was staring into the fire, his face emotionless. Was he supporting Waldo in his insolent attacks? Did he pamper him in everything, even to allowing him to bait a visitor in this way? If Mr Evans's views of him agreed with Waldo's, why did he invite him to the farm Sunday after Sunday as if he was a prospective son-in-law? He hoped that in spite of the way Waldo was questioning him now and had no doubt been disparaging and vilifying him behind his back, the old man had not dismissed him as a candidate unworthy of marrying his daughter. Perhaps he was still making up his mind on the matter. But his feelings about Mr Evans, he realised, were beginninng to be tinged with dislike. And yet, and yet. He must pause. He could not be sure about Mr Evans.

'Do you like working in a coal pit?'

'Waldo, please,' said his mother, impatiently.

Adam decided there was nothing wrong with the truth. 'Yes, I do. I was brought up to it. Anyway, a man's got to work at what he can do.' He spoke defiantly. 'You need skill to be coalminer, you know.' He paused, weighing up what would be the effect of what he proposed to say next. He decided to say it. 'I reckon it be a more skilled job than rounding up sheep and delivering milk in the village from a cart.' Though his words were biting, he delivered them gently, and he looked Waldo straight in the eye.

Mr Evans laughed, breaking the tension. Waldo looked round at the others uncertainly, then rose and left the room. Adam settled back in his chair; he felt he had won that round at least. But he realised there would be others.

When Waldo came back Catrin was laying the table for supper. The cloth was clean and white, because it was Sunday and there was a visitor for tea. She laid the best cutlery and took down blue-and-white plates from the dresser. Catrin's mother came in with cooked vegetables, and took the rabbit pie, steaming and juicy, from the oven and served it. Twenty minutes later she took out the apple pudding. It was an excellent meal. Much food, little talk. Adam always found the food at the farm good; it contrasted with the greasy grey stew his landlady usually served up. Indeed at first it had been the food that had encouraged him to come every Sunday. As they ate Adam looked across the table at Waldo sitting silent and morose, and decided he was probably the main obstacle in his way to marrying Catrin. He would have to be dealt with. Somehow.

After tea Catrin and her mother cleared the table and retreated into the back kitchen, whilst the others sat around the fire. There was a silence, broken only by the sound of old Mrs Evans's knitting needles. Mr Evans dozed off and Waldo went out. With his departure Adam pushed thoughts of him from his mind. The heat from the fire penetrated through his clothes and warmed his body. He gazed into the fire and recalled the events of that afternoon which he had spent with Catrin in the Welsh hills above Nantyglo. They had walked hand in hand, her touch smooth and gentle in his calloused fingers, her long skirt flapping in the breeze. Across the valley the hills rolled away before them, purple in the distance, mixing with the sky; below, snaking along the valley bottom, was the road to Pen-y-garn, and a few miles away they could make out steam puffing from an engine on the new railway. They stopped. He stood behind her and, pulling her towards him, felt her softness against his belly. 'Will you marry me, Catrin?' he whispered. 'I love you so.' He felt a tremor go through her body, but she did not reply.

'Please, Catrin, will you marry me?'

She turned to look him in the face. Her dark eyes were cheeky. 'Oh, I don't know.' Her Welsh accent, slow and precise, thrilled him as it did every time she spoke. 'You'll have to ask my Da, you know,' she said more seriously.

'I'll ask him this evening, then.'

'No, no. Leave it for now, I think.' Then she had told him about Waldo and his belief that Adam wished to take over her father's farm.

'I'm not after your father's farm. I'm after you. Anyway, I'd never make a farmer. I'm a collier. Mind, I won't always be an ordinary collier. You can tell your dad that. When I gets back home I shall be earning good money. And one of these days I hopes to be a pit deputy, or even an under-manager.' But as he said the words he realised it would not be easy. He was, he knew, uneducated, poor at expressing himself and spoke with an accent that people outside the Forest found comic when they did not find it impossible to understand. Yet he was determined to make something of his life, and knew he was nobody's fool and had more brains and initiative than his fellow colliers.

'Love you I would, whatever you were,' she replied and smoothed back his thick brown hair from his forehead. Then, glorying in his strength, he seized her round her waist and lifted her in the air. His eyes shone into hers. She laughed and demanded to be let down and he let

11

her slither slowly down the front of his body. The contact banished his thoughts about Waldo and quickened his desire for her.

Adam's recollections of the afternoon were brought to a halt when Catrin and her mother returned. Old Mrs Evans started on a new ball of wool and Mr Evans woke up and, reaching for a spill from the mantelpiece, lit his pipe from the fire. 'Aye,' he said in agreement with nothing in particular. 'Aye, Adam, you were telling us about the Forest of Dean, and how lovely it was there.' It was the first time he had had much to say to Adam. 'Beautiful country it was in Erwgoch once, you know. Before they began to dig out the iron-ore and the coal to smelt it with. The end of the eighteenth century, that would be. Then coalmines and ironworks opened up and houses for the workers rose like mushrooms, and soon the valley was stripped of all its beauty. You could no longer hear the bleat of the sheep, only the noise from the ironworks. Instead of our beautiful hills you could only see the muck brought from the bowels of the earth scattered over them. Ugly and frightening it was.'

'Yes,' said old Mrs Evans. 'And Welsh people, always so clean and proud, were forced to work in those places. and it degraded them. Then in the forties the Irish came, thousands of them. Starving they were, fleeing from a famine land. Decent people wouldn't go near them, with their coarse behaviour and their beer shops and low morals. We hated them.' Her voice rose. 'And they weren't the only ones. The English came over the border as well, fighting the Welsh for their jobs.' She glared at Adam.

He was dismayed. Now *she* was attacking him for coming to Wales and finding a job there. He decided to remain silent, comforting himself that in her ignorance she did not know that the inhabitants of the Forest of Dean did not call themselves English and considered themselves a cut above them. He sighed inwardly. He had tried so hard to be polite and pleasant to her and cover up anything he thought she might call coarse behaviour, though he had to admit he had told her he drank beer.

'But Adam is different,' said Catrin, fearful of offence.

There was silence, as if everyone had decided the only way to heal the breach was not to speak. Though the old woman's outburst had upset him, Adam decided she was less of an opponent than Waldo and carried less weight with Mr Evans. He could clearly assess his grievance now. It was that Waldo was putting pressure on Mr Evans to refuse permission for him to marry Catrin, or more likely was trying to persuade him to exclude him from the house altogether. Adam felt sure of it, but was at a loss how to proceed. His usual approach to problems was to face them head on and, if there was an opponent in his way, to fight him; but he could not do so in this case. It would be foolish to force his opponent out into the open and defeat him.

The silence was disturbed by the coal in the grate settling with a crack. Mr Evans, apparently unperturbed by the outburst of his mother, took out his watch, looked at the grandfather clock ticking reluctantly in the corner and said, as he no doubt said every night and as he certainly said every Sunday night when Adam was there, 'Nine o'clock it is, and time for bed.'

He looked round. 'Where is Waldo?'

'Shutting in the chickens, I expect,' said his wife.

'Adam, be a good lad, is it, and ask him to get some logs for morning before he comes in.'

Adam rose willingly and went along the corridor and out of the back door, his heavy boots ringing on the flagstones. In the yard he looked round. There was still some light, though the sun was below the horizon. He was not sure where the henhouse was but he found the barn. Its door was unstapled and flapping in the breeze. He went in, his footsteps silent and soft on the hay strewn over the floor. As he walked the sweet smell of the hay rose. A little light entered from the open door, but the end of the barn was in darkness. He went in further. The sour smell of sheep droppings now rose, warm and moist. It sickened him and he was about to turn back when he heard restrained laughing. He followed it behind some bales of straw.

In the gloom he recognised Waldo's red check shirt. He had his back to him. His trousers were down. So Waldo was here with a girl. Adam had never been with a girl in spite of the incessant talk of his friends of its delights; but, much as he had wanted to, he had never found the opportunity. Waldo, who was younger than him and less of a man, was doing what he had never done. He felt annoyance and envy, his manhood diminished. Waldo had insulted him again. His hatred of him surged up once more.

Waldo heard him and turned, and Adam saw it was not a girl in Waldo's arms. It was a young man, a labourer on the farm who lived nearby. The young man broke away and with a sob pushed past Adam without raising his eyes to him. He had lost his belt and was clutching his trousers round his waist as he ran into the yard.

13

Adam ignored him. He was looking at Waldo. He had heard about this sort of thing from the men in the pit and they had jested about it, but what it was all about he could not be sure. His first reaction was excitement at being present at a mystery, an excitement tinged with disgust. But this reaction, scarcely formed, was pushed aside when he saw that Waldo was looking at him stunned, like one of his sheep awaiting slaughter. Adam's mind raced ahead. Waldo's eyes begged compassion from the man he had decided was his enemy, and Adam could see that Waldo was at his mercy. His earlier mortification turned to triumph. He had Waldo now. He had him like an insect under his thumb.

'You won't tell my Da. Please.'

Adam's heart beat fast. He realised luck had given him power. But he showed no sign of his feelings. He rubbed his nose with the side of his finger. 'Perhaps I will,' he said slowly. 'Perhaps I won't. I don't know. It's up to you.' He moved closer to Waldo. 'I want to marry Catrin, see, and you're going to help me. So you'd better stop pouring poison about me into your father's ear.'

Waldo did not reply.

'You know what I mean, don't you, Waldo? You do your bit and I'll do mine.'

Again Waldo did not reply, but Adam knew that he had given him a lifeline.

'I've come to tell you your father wants you to bring in some logs for morning,' he said. And turning abruptly he left the barn.

CHAPTER 2

As he walked home later that evening the stars in the velvet sky shone out in their beauty. But Adam didn't give them a second glance. They were nothing compared with his thoughts about his beloved. Never before in his life had he felt so alive and at the same time so contented as when he was with Catrin. She induced in him a vitality, a physical vigour that was not destroyed even by a hard shift in the pit. He realised how empty life would be without a mate. But he would soon have one. Catrin would give him a family and provide a home for him.

When he got to his lodgings Emrys his roommate was sitting up in bed reading a newspaper by the light of a candle. 'You'll ruin your eyesight.' Adam's gruff remark concealed his affection for his friend. Emrys worked alongside him in the pit and was the same age as himself, though in the candlelight he seemed older. His body was sinewy, his hair close-cut, sandy and thin, and his face pit-marked with coaldust and taut as parchment.

Emrys put down his paper. 'Was it a good evening you had at the farm, then?' His face looked younger when he smiled.

Adam, still running over with excitement, sat on the bed and with his hands on his friend's shoulders shook him gently in affection. 'I asked her to marry me, and she said yes.'

Emrys sat up with interest.

'But Catrin's brother is being difficult.' He told Emrys of the incident in the barn, and his threat that he would tell his father unless Waldo withdrew his opposition to his marriage to Catrin. 'I hate blackmail, if that is what it is, but it gave me the only way out.'

Emrys pondered a few seconds. 'I shouldn't worry.' He shrugged his shoulders. 'I hope it works.'

'Yes.' Adam was pensive for a moment. His mind, excited by the multitude of happenings during the day, had already changed its focus and he was living again the exquisite moments he had experienced on the hill. 'Oh, Emrys, how lovely it was to hold her in my arms, to put

15

them right round her, stretching from my shoulders to make them longer so that I could hold her more.'

Emrys smiled. 'I'm sure it was.'

'I got all excited.'

'Better watch yourself, boyo.'

'I could feel her breasts straining up against my body. Do you know, Emrys,' – he blushed, though he knew Emrys could not see his embarrassment in the gloom – 'I dared to touch them. She didn't seem to mind. I've never touched a girl's breasts before. At least not since I was fifteen.'

Adam told him of that occasion. It had been a Sunday. He had gone with his mother and brother to Pisgah Chapel in Coalway and had sat in their usual places on a long pew on the south side. The rays of the summer sun, now sloping low, were coming through the window and the only interest he could find was in the bees that were buzzing insistently against the glass. The pew could accommodate up to eight people, and the Turleys squeezed up as the Dobbs family who lived up the lane, mother, father and two daughters, joined them on it. Adam was at the end, and Rosie Dobbs, a big jolly girl two years older than he was, sat down next to him. She gave him a smile as she settled herself. He felt her body against his and her warmth reaching out to him through her dress and his trousers.

The service began. There was plenty of hymn singing. Mrs Phelps, the village midwife, accompanied on the harmonium.

The Rev Gwilliam began his sermon:

'The Covenant, as we have seen from the pages of eternal truth, was made before the world began – made from eternity. What a wide expanse for the mind to range in, but we need a guide, or else our minds will soon be lost in wandering mazes and dangerous speculations. This guide is the Bible...'

The Chapel was hot and dusty. Adam reached down to take his handkerchief from his trouser pocket, but found that his upper leg was firmly against Rosie. Having got hold of the handkerchief he could not bring his hand up again. He glanced sideways, but Rosie was absorbed in the preacher's words. So he left it there; he found the sensation a pleasant one.

'Where the line of revelation enters into unfathomable depths of eternal wisdom, there we must pause and wonder, and adore. We must not dare to tread within the veil, or curiously pry into those hidden mysteries which God has wisely concealed from mortal eyes...'

Adam moved his hand round and placed the palm between the pew seat and Rosie's lower back. She wriggled a trifle, but did not seem to object. Adam felt a twinge in his groin and marvelled at his reactions.

'Here is no ambiguity, no darkness, no mystery – it is a faithful mirror held up to all mankind. Happy indeed are they who, beholding as in a glass the glory of the Lord, are changed into the same image from glory to glory, even as by the spirit of the Lord...'

Pressure with his finger increased his pleasure, and apparently caused no reaction in Rosie except a greater interest in the sermon. Adam continued thus until they had to stand.

After the service Adam's mother invited the Dobbs family home for a bite of supper. 'It won't be ready for half an hour, like, so you children can go off for a walk.' The young people went off obediently, pleased to get away from the stuffy atmosphere and restrictions of the Chapel. They went into the woods on a path that ran behind the Chapel and were soon running and laughing. Rosie took Adam's hand and slowed their pace. The others raced ahead, and soon Rosie and Adam were alone. She led him off the path and invited him to sit next to her in some ferns. She lay back and stretched out, her arms above her head. 'I didn't want to go to Chapel tonight, Adam, but I'm glad I did, see.' She smiled up at him and he sat beside her. She drew his head down and kissed him. He responded. It was the first time he had kissed a girl.

'Don't push so hard, Adam. Let your lips go soft, like!'

Adam blushed. He had displayed innocence when he had wanted to appear experienced; but he did as he was bid. After a few minutes Rosie repositioned herself and nuzzled her large breasts up against him. Never before had he been so near such beautiful, mysterious breasts. He smelt their warmth and delicately touched one with a finger. Rosie with a gleam and a smile obligingly undid the top buttons of her dress and placed his hand inside. So this was what it was like, he thought. But he knew there should be more, greater delights. The men in the pit at break time had told him all about them. But he was not certain he wanted to find everything out this evening. Rosie, though, clearly had ideas on the next steps and began to lead him through them. She fondled him, but her hands were hard and clumsy, and though he felt exhiliarated, he was afraid and struggled away from her searching fingers. He stood up and buttoned up his trousers.

'We must go back,' he said and looked round helplessly. Would she think him a coward, less than a man?

Apparently she did. She shrugged her shoulders and without a word, stood up and rebuttoned her dress. Then with an affected sigh, she walked back to the path. 'You're too young, anyway, and don't know what to do. Fancy encouraging me to do things like that! I'm surprised at you.'

When Adam had finished his tale, Emrys smiled. 'I suppose it was an initiation of sorts.'

'Yes. Fortunately Rosie went into service in Cheltenham the following week and I've never seen her since. It was very embarrassing at the time, like, but I remember deciding on the spot that I must have a girl completely and utterly as soon as I could. I set my twenty-first birthday as the last date when this would have to be done.'

☙ ❧

The following Sunday came slowly. After his midday meal Adam prepared for his visit to the farm. With his face flannel-clean and bright from the rubbing, his best suit on, and boots shined to see his face in, he was off. He hurried up the street out of Erwgoch, leaving its smoke and filth behind. How soon would he be able to marry Catrin and say goodbye for ever to this repulsive place with its squalid cottages, their windows like blind eyes, their walls pock-marked by weather and age? Outside the town on the ridge the afternoon sun shone on his face and he felt cleansed. Sunday sun always seemed warmer, he decided. The wind blew steadily, and he raised his face to it and took a deep breath. The pure fresh air that never reached Erwgoch caressed his lungs.

The first person he met when he arrived at the farm was Waldo. He greeted him as usual and waited for his response. He was disappointed it was the usual grunt. At teatime Waldo sat at table without any attempt to join in the conversation. His only acceptance of Adam's presence was to glower at him across the pile of bread and butter. No sign here, thought Adam, of any change in his attitude, and he wondered what his next step should be. He could not go to Mr Evans and tell him what he had seen in the barn; that would be too cruel. And even if he did, he was not sure it would persuade Mr Evans to accept him as a son-in-law. Indeed, Mr Evans might decide that he did not want a man who told such tales about his son to marry his daughter. And what would Catrin think about his attempted blackmail when she heard about it? He decided to see what happened in the next week or so, hoping, in spite of his doubts, that Catrin would tell him that Waldo had withdrawn his opposition to the marriage.

18

At nine o'clock promptly Mr Evans pronounced as usual that it was time for bed. Adam rose, wished everyone goodnight and strolled with Catrin down the farm track to the road. The sun was setting after a warm day and the shadows were fingering up the hills, purple and slow. When they were clear of eyes from the house Adam put his arm round her and she put hers round his waist, under his coat. He could feel her thumb hooked on to his belt and thrilled at her touch through his shirt. He kept the sensation until he reached his lodgings.

'Da says you may come on Saturday next week and stop the night if you would like to.'

His spirits raised. 'Of course I'd like to. Mind, I work till four on Saturdays, but I can come about six.' He kissed her, and with a squeeze of her hand he was away up the hillside and disappearing into the darkness.

As he walked back to Erwgoch, Adam thought to discover why the invitation had been made. Did it reflect a change in Waldo's attitude to him? Surely it did. It must. There could be no other reason. He was now more cheerful about getting Mr Evans's consent to his marriage to his daughter. He ran up the stairs of his lodgings with the energy that comes only with joy and excitement, and burst into his room exulting in what he had decided was a change in his fortune. He found Emrys reading a trade union newspaper. A great one for the union was Emrys, and he was interesting Adam in it. But tonight Adam did not want to talk about the union. Tonight he wanted to tell Emrys the news that he had been invited to spend the night at the farm. He launched straight in, and his eyes gleamed as he spoke.

Emrys smiled and looked at him questioningly. 'It's a fine weekend I hope you have, then,' he said when Adam had finished. 'It is good when a collier gets his feet under the table of such respectable Welsh folk.'

The next weekend it was shaving on Saturday and not on Sunday. A good scrub with carbolic soap and he was out of the tin bath in the yard and up into his room to dress. A blade of his jack knife applied to his nails did not get all the dirt out, but it sufficed. He felt clean and shiny outside, and clean and shiny in his heart, too.

After tea Catrin cleared the table and went into the back kitchen to do the washing-up. Adam accompanied her and sat on the table and talked to her as she worked.

'Come here and pump some water,' she said; and he jumped off the table and cranked the handle until the water gushed into the deep sink

19

in uneven surges. He went behind her, put his arms round her waist and kissed her neck. She shook him off.

'It is the washing-up I've come here to do, Adam,' she said with mock severity. 'You go and sit on the table and talk to me.'

Adam sat on the table again and swung his legs. He looked down at them. He was proud of his firm and solid thighs, tight now against his trousers, and hoped Catrin had noticed them.

'Adam, you told Waldo you had come to Wales because you had no job in the Forest.'

'Yes, it was the slump and I got the sack. My father was dead, Grancher was too old to work and my brother George was the only other person in the family apart from me who could earn anything. I lost my job but George hung on to his, and he was willing to keep me until I could find work.'

'That's what families are for,' murmured Catrin. She began to wipe the dishes.

'But I hated having nothing to do. Money was tight – there was only George's pay coming in, and most weeks he could only get two or three shifts' work. So I decided to leave the Forest. "Be adventurous," the old men said. "There are good jobs in Wales. Go to the top towns; and come back here when there is work again." So I did. Aren't you glad?' He grinned.

She looked sad. 'But when there are jobs in the Forest again, Adam, you'll want to go back.'

'There are jobs there now. I had a letter from George last week. He wants me to go back and work with him. I'd love to go back and see my family and mates again, but I won't go until I can take my wife with me!'

She gave him a smile and hung the tea-towels in front of the fire.

'Now, if we're finished,' he said, 'I'll give you that kiss you didn't want earlier.' His lazy, relaxed eyes smiled at her.

'I didn't say I didn't want it.' She turned to see that the door was closed and put her arms round his neck. 'A shameless woman I am, is it?' She looked up at him and smiled.

'No, just as I likes you.' He smoothed down her fringe with the back of his forefinger.

'A few minutes only, now. Then we must go back or someone will come out to see what we are up to.'

She fingered a coal mark on his cheek. 'Tell me how you got this, Adam.'

'Oh, in the pit. I walked into somebody's shovel, like. All colliers have coal marks on them. I've got plenty on my body. Show you sometime.' He embraced her and hugged her tightly.

It was ten minutes before, at Catrin's insistence, they returned to the main room, Catrin blushing and Adam exhilarated. They sat on the settle, Adam between Catrin and her grandmother. Catrin was soft and yielding. Gran was hard and her knitting needles frequently poked him; but she soon went to bed. The others chatted. It was a pleasant evening.

Then out came Mr Evans's watch. 'It's nine o'clock and time it is for bed,' he said, once again as if enunciating some previously unknown fact. Adam made to rise, But Catrin squeezed his hand and he sat tight. They waited. It was several minutes before Mr Evans said 'A good night to you, Adam,' and withdrew with his wife.

Waldo remained. There was silence, a waiting silence. Then at last, feeling his sister's hostility, he rose. 'I hope you sleep well,' he said to Adam and went off.

'I expect he will,' said Catrin tartly to his back.

Adam watched Waldo disappear upstairs. He had humbled him in the barn and a pathetic and contemptible figure he now seemed. The blackmail seemed to have worked, for Waldo was much more polite to him now than he had been; but Adam could not be sure of the attitude he was urging his father to adopt should he ask him for Catrin's hand.

Catrin poked the fire and returned to the settle next to Adam. 'Lovely to be alone at last, it is.'

Adam put his arm around her and held her, and his hostility towards Waldo disappeared. He hunched his broad shoulders as he leaned over her. The sweet smell of her skin arose, and he felt her eyelashes against his cheek. 'I loves you, Catrin,' he whispered, using the only words he knew that even remotely conveyed his feelings. She put her hand behind his head and pressed it down close to hers. They kissed, not the gentle brushing of lips they had known before, but firm contact, with determination and eagerness. Adam felt his soul striving to give to her, and he held her firmly against him and savoured her body. After a few minutes she gently pushed him away and whispered, 'As Da said, it is time for bed.'

'So soon, Catrin?' he asked. He wanted to continue the physical contact that produced such a delicious glow in him, and he pulled her to him and held her closely again.

'Oh, yes, my dear,' and she disengaged herself and got up. Then he realised that, rather than experiencing a delicious glow, he was suffering from a physical discomfort that he knew could not be satisfied. Perhaps, he concluded, it would be better to yield to Catrin's wishes, stop his caresses, and go to bed.

She tidied the fire and blew out the candles. Then, taking his hand she led him in the gloom up the staircase and into her bedroom.

'Your father will kill me,' he whispered.

'No, no. You sleep with me tonight. Don't you want to, cariad?'

CHAPTER 3

Adam told Emrys all about it in the pub on Monday evening. They had taken their beer to a quiet corner. Emrys leaned back and looked at him with amusement.

'I thought you didn't understand, man,' he said with a grin. 'It's an old Welsh custom, you might say, at least in some parts of the country.'

'So Mr Evans must have known what would happen when he invited me to stay the night, and it wasn't only Catrin's idea I should sleep with her. But the hypocrisy of it, Emrys. Catrin won't let me even hold her hand if she thinks her father is watching. And then he lets me sleep with his daughter, almost invites me to!'

'Morality is a strange thing, Adam boy. What we condone is different from what we profess if we think there are good reasons for it. But don't think it was for your benefit, leastways not entirely.' He paused, wondering how best to express himself. 'Men don't want wives who are barren, see. It only leads to trouble later. So when parents see a suitable young man is after their daughter and they approve of him, they let him stay the night.'

Adam did not comment, just gazed at his friend. Emrys laughed. 'Better than in the fields, isn't it? Can be very draughty and uncomfortable under a hedge.'

'I don't know.'

'No, I can see you don't. You *are* an innocent. But you're a good fellow for all that.' He looked at Adam curiously. 'Very pure in the Forest, is it?'

'But if the girl gets a baby?'

'Well, she's proved she's fertile, and then you marry her.'

'Just like that?'

'Just like that. And you'd better not try and dodge it, man.'

They laughed.

'It was good, then, was it?' said Emrys. He gazed at Adam, pleased for him.

Adam felt the flash of friendship pass between them. Their affinity was deep and consisted of far more than sharing a pint in the evening after a gruelling day underground. Adam realised they were different in many ways. On the outside Emrys was tough, as all colliers had to be or pretend to be, and when it came to union matters he could be as hard as the iron from which his mattock was forged. Yet on the inside he was strangely sentimental and romantic. It must be the Celtic element, Adam concluded.

❦ ❧

Adam stayed at Dwrclyr Farm every weekend now. Little was said about marriage by either him or Catrin, though her love continued to give him much delight, and the weekends seemed as short as April showers. Adam realised that her father did not expect him to ask for Catrin's hand until she was pregnant. He now found himself in an intriguing situation. If he had not been given access to Catrin's bed, he would have married her as soon as formalities allowed. Now that his physical love for her was being satisfied, there seemed no hurry for marriage, at least from that point of view. But he wanted more than laughter and fun under the feather eiderdown in Catrin's enormous bed; he wanted to marry Catrin and settle down with her in the Forest.

Yet he accepted there was some sense in this strange Welsh custom, so contrary to Forest morality. He wanted to wed Catrin and live with her, but he wanted sons as well, lusty sons, who would take his name and whom he could watch grow up and be proud of. And daughters as well, of course. He visualised his children, the sons quick and intelligent and the daughters industrious, obedient and loving. And they would be generous and comforting towards him and care for him in his old age. This fantasy of sunshine and warmth often filled his mind – as he walked over to Dwrclyr Farm, as he lay in bed in his lodgings and as he hewed coal from the face. In short, he was blinded by love and dreams.

But what would happen if Catrin was barren? Would he want to marry her then? He would not face up to the question. Soon, he hoped, Catrin would tell him she was pregnant. But the weeks went on and there was no announcement. His lovemaking as he gained experience became more intense, and their weekly bout, though urged on by love, became more purposeful. He became almost desperate as he forced himself down into her and willed a son.

But still no announcement. He began to worry and talked to Emrys about it. But Emrys did not have much advice to give.

'Early days it is, I expect, Adam. But I don't know much about these things. Perhaps it takes some time if you don't get together more than once a week. Perhaps you have to have it at the right time, see?'

Then, four months after his first overnight stay, Catrin's body informed her that she was with child. She told Adam the next Saturday as they walked up the farm track. Her face was blooming. She pressed his arm and looked up into his face to get his reaction. He stopped, hardly believing her words after all the waiting. Then he hugged her, lifting her off her feet and twirling her round; and he sensed she knew all was well.

'Better go and ask my Da right away,' she said when they reached the farmhouse. 'He's round the back, I expect, admiring his pig.'

Adam did, indeed, find Mr Evans leaning on the pigsty wall. He approached him, casual like, hands deep in his trousers' pockets.

'Evening, Mr Evans.'

Mr Evans glanced round reluctantly. 'Evening, Adam,' he said. 'Now there's a lovely pig for you, is it? She will farrow in about a week. Blodwen, she's called, after my wife's maiden aunt from Gorseinon.'

Adam looked at the enormous animal, six foot long if it was an inch, its large ears covering its wicked little eyes, its sides quivering as it lurched forward to receive a caress from Mr Evans. Adam liked pigs but could raise no interest in this one or in its pregnancy – a word that should not be applied to both this revolting animal and his Catrin. But he agreed that it was a beautiful pig, and then came to the point.

'Mr Evans, I would like to marry your daughter.'

'Aye, I thought you might.'

A pause.

'Does she want to marry you, Adam?'

'Oh, yes.'

'Yes, I thought she did.'

Pause.

'Where will you live then,' asked Mr Evans. 'You can't live here,' he added hurriedly. 'When Waldo marries he'll bring his bride here. And the farm don't need no more men.'

He wants to make it clear there will be no job for me here, thought Adam. Not that I want to come. 'I thought we might live – '

'And I wouldn't want her to live in Erwgoch. Too dirty, from what I've seen of it.'

'I thought of taking her back to Coalway. There's work in the Forest again now, and we can live with my mother at first. It's a nice little cottage. Not as big as the farm, of course, but there's plenty of room.'

'Aye, perhaps so. Well, if she's agreeable, you can have her. A woman must follow her man.'

'Thank you, Mr Evans. It do mean a lot having your agreement.' He was relieved, though he knew he would have found a way to marry her if he had refused.

'We'd better arrange a wedding soon, then, from what I understand.' Mr Evans gave his pig a last look, and turned to Adam with a smile. The gleam of his teeth and the light in his eyes chased away his usual glumness and suspicion. He offered Adam his hand to shake.

Adam ran off to tell Catrin the news. They took the path to the top of the hill to share their glee privately like small children. They ran to the edge with joy and looked over the valley. The wind from the north was cold, but they needed no stimulation. Adam's thoughts turned to the future. 'I shall be working with George all day, you know. We're going to take out a stall. That's a working face in a pit.' He looked at her. Did she want to know about his working arrangements? He decided to tell her, anyway. 'We shall be butty men and butty men make a contract direct with the colliery owners, like, and employ their own daymen. The money should be good.'

'But you'll be working in a pit?'

'Yes. At the coal face, both of us. But we shall be in charge.'

'I'm looking forward to seeing the cottage,' she said.

He glanced sideways and read her thoughts. 'It's only for the time being, Catrin. We shall get ourselves a house of our own when we've settled down.'

'Da is going to give us fifty pounds for a wedding present. I'll give it to you as soon as he gives it to me.'

'That's generous. You can do a lot with fifty quid. I could build us a house for that.'

The day before the wedding Catrin showed Adam the wedding clothes she had made for herself, a white and red woollen skirt flaring from the waist that just cleared the ground, and a blouse of cambric, decorated round the neck with a thousand stitches. Over this she wore a flannel shawl, fringed and white, that fell generously to her waist. Adam was proud his wife-to-be was so handy with her needle, and pronounced it a sensible outfit that would serve her as best for many years to come.

They were married at Pen-y-garn Chapel. Relations of the Evanses came from Ffair Rhos and Fforest Fawr, Llandeilo and Llanelly. Aunt Blodwen was there from Gorseinon and endowed the whole cermony with a dignity it could not otherwise have achieved. It was too far for Adam's relations to come.

It was only a quarter of a mile over the hill to the Chapel, but Waldo, resplendent in his new bowler hat, drove Catrin and her father there in the trap, which he had repainted especially for the occasion. Though it was winter time, fluffy clouds like angels in flight hurried across the blue sky, and the sun smiled down on them. Emrys was best man, and he and Adam walked to the Chapel. Adam, striding ahead, was overjoyed that he was to be joined to Catrin at last. Emrys was quiet. As they came near to the Chapel and could see some villagers gathered outside to welcome them, Adam looked down at Emrys and noticed his eyes were moist. 'Why so sad, Emrys?' he said gently.

'True it's sad I am. It's the emotion, see.'

In a flash Adam realised what emotion Emrys was referring to. In the joy of his wedding day, he had forgotten this was probably the last time they would see one another. But Emrys had not forgotten. Adam recalled in a flash the confidences they had given each other unreservedly, knowing they would go no further; the good times they had shared when they had been boisterous and foolish and had gloried in their youth; the tranquil times they had sat together side by side, when there had been no need to speak; and the tough times they had had down the pit when, in moments of crisis, they had relied implicitly on each other's judgement and had come through danger together. How could Adam express all that, how to put into words all the warmth he felt towards him. All he said was, 'We've been good friends, Emrys, and I shall always remember you.'

'We shall probably never meet again.'

'Who knows? But we can write to one another.'

'Yes,' said Emrys, dubiously. Then he smiled. 'Well, that's the way it is, boyo.' He clapped Adam on the shoulder and led the way quickly into the Chapel.

The villagers and hill farmers and their families crowded the tiny place full. They opened their hearts as they sang the hymns, and their harmonies, pressing on the roof and whitewashed walls fit to burst them asunder, spread their joy to heaven.

At the reception back in the farmhouse there was a grand celebration. As the guests entered the living room, hungry from the cold walk from the Chapel, they gazed at the food laid out on side tables. Lying succulently before them on the best blue-and-white plates were legs of cold mutton, ready for the carving, cold pies from rabbits shot earlier in the week and from pigeons flying to the dovecot only the day before, whole hams covered with breadcrumbs, fat capons, cheeses. To help it all down were hunks of crusty bread made that morning inviting the lavish spread of creamy butter made on the farm. Hot food taken from the oven tantilized their nostrils, pork chops dripping with fat, sizzling bacon and grilled herrings bought last week from the visiting fair. To follow were trifles and apple pie, with cream made that morning, standing yellow and proud in its dish. Adam particularly admired the cake. It had been made by Jones the baker, and rose like a castle from the sea, all white from the waves.

Waldo and Adam passed glasses of rhubarb and sloe wine to the ladies; and for the men there was home-brewed beer. Adam contemplated his new brother-in-law as he acted as host. Catrin followed his gaze. 'Waldo has lost all his old antagonism towards you, Adam. I think he even likes you.'

'Yes, perhaps. In a way.' Adam felt a twinge of compassion for Waldo. He was not proud of his blackmail; but the prize had been worth the deed.

Emrys proposed the toast. 'To Adam and Catrin Turley. Dymunwn i chwi eich dau oes hîr ac hapus. We wish them long life and happiness. This is a marriage of old rural Wales and an English coal village. May it work out well.' The guests cheered.

Then there was singing and dancing to a fiddle. When the party was over, the villagers had gone home and Catrin's parents and the relations who were staying overnight had gone to bed, only Catrin and Adam remained. They sat for a few minutes before the dying fire, rose-coloured shadows flickering over their faces, with their backs to the untidy, exhausted, room with its tables littered with beer mugs, glasses, dirty plates and the unappetising stale remains of the feast.

Adam took Catrin's hand in his. Life was going to be good now, a thousand times better than before. With Catrin behind him his ambitions for getting on in the world would be achieved.

Catrin cut into his thoughts. 'Gran has knitted you a lovely jersey. She likes you, you know. You'd never think so, but she has a heart of gold.'

But it needs quarrying, he thought.

'She spun the wool from farm sheep and dyed it in cold tea. It's a lovely dark brown colour – she likes strong tea.' Then Catrin whispered in a low, almost frightened voice, 'May the little one be like you, Adam.'

CHAPTER 4

An unpleasant smell, the reek of sulphuric acid and stale grease, overwhelmed Catrin as she descended from the train at Park End. It cut through the clang of trucks, the trundle of carts, the whinnying of horses and the shouts from the workmen who surged round the station. Catrin shivered and pulled her shawl around her. The smell and the hubbub frightened her. This was not much of a welcome to the Forest of Dean, and Park End was not the pleasant place its name suggested. She drew near to Adam, and he put his arm round her; but she could see that his thoughts were elsewhere than on her; his face was shining with excitement at being back in the Forest.

'What's that smell, Adam?'

He looked down at her and smiled. 'It's only the tin-plate works,' and he pointed vaguely up the village. 'We have an ironworks here, too, you know,' and he indicated a higgledy-piggledy collection of ill-shaped, dirty grey buildings dominated by a tall chimney from which smoke, driven by the wind, plunged down almost to the ground, only to rise again and disappear into the surrounding hills. The ironworks buildings squatted close together on the very precinct of the station like a monster awaiting its prey. One of the furnaces was emitting sparks and flames and roaring frighteningly.

'The furnaces are in blast, see,' explained Adam.

The ironworks hooter cut through the frosty air, demanding action from everyone whether concerned with the ironworks or not. Catrin shrank back as men, arriving for the new shift with noses red from the cold peeping above their mufflers, pushed past her. Anxious not to be late, they swarmed round the entrance, confronting workers who had just finished work and were coming out.

Adam's brother George, who had just arrived, greeted Adam with a clap on the shoulder and Catrin with a kiss – just an impression of beer – and gave a bright smile to both. He was a bluff fellow, coarser and beefier than Adam, with a brashness that Catrin did not take to. He swung their trunk onto his shoulder and conducted them up the road to a horse and cart. The men helped Catrin climb up and seated her between them.

With a crack of the whip they were off, the cart's iron-ringed wheels grating on the road. Catrin looked at the people in the street as they passed. They were intent on going about their own business, pulled their coats more tightly around their bodies because of the cold and gave the cart and its occupants no more than a glance; in Pen-y-garn they would have looked up and greeted you, she thought, even if you did not know them.

George looked down and examined her with what was intended to be a cheery grin. She forced herself to smile back, but could think of nothing to say. He patted her hand, which did not please her.

'Bert Preece did lend me this horse and cart, Adam. Remember him?'

'Yes, of course. He's a friend of mine.'

'He be a good chap. Lend you anything. Even his wife.' He put his hand to his mouth in mock consternation, and looked to see if Catrin had noticed his indiscreet remark.

They began a gentle two-mile climb up the valley to Coalway. On both sides of the road were oak trees and beeches, their bare branches bowing in the wind. The grey clouds had cleared and the afternoon sun was piercing the cold air and brightening the dead leaves that lay under the trees. Catrin became more cheerful. Adam was right. The Forest was lovely, even on this wearisome day. The horse slowed as the hill became steeper, its nostrils breathing steam, its body throwing out its horsey smell. George let it choose its own pace.

'Tell me what you've got for us at the pit, George,' said Adam.

'Well, I saw Gunter about a stall last week. You know him, he's the manager now at the Park End Royal.'

'A good stall?'

'Could be worse. I went down yesterday with young Billy Dobbs, who I've took on as a day man.' He looked at Adam with a grin. He was glad he was back. 'We be going to do all right, you and me. You see if I'm not right.' He turned and beamed at Catrin. She smiled back shyly, not wishing to offend him by a frigid response. She must be friendly with Adam's relations if she was to be happy in the Forest, though if this was Adam's brother, what was his mother like?

At the top of the hill some cottages came into sight. They had reached Coalway. The cottages were small and grey and bore the stains of poverty. A few sheep, dirty and ragged, grazed on the rough ground that fronted the cottages, picking their way round brambles. The dejected air of the place reached out to Catrin. So this was what a Forest mining village looked like.

George drove the horse and cart up a lane and stopped outside a small cottage. This must be where the Turley family lived. Catrin noticed its sides bulged under a faded, flaking covering of paint, and the slates on its uneven roof were jagged and cracked. The dry-stone wall that surrounded the property was falling down in places. The cottage, Catrin decided, was much smaller than Adam had led her to believe.

George lifted aside the old bedstead that served as a gate, and they went round to the back door. The garden was given over entirely to growing vegetables; but at this time of the year it contained only a few tired cabbages and stumps. Halfway down the garden was a pigsty and at the end a privy. Beyond, the Forest loomed.

Adam opened the back door. Catrin, clutching his arm, peered inside. A middle-aged woman was busying herself at the grate. Her hair was thin and grey, parted in the middle and worn close to the head. She had heard the door open but was clearly in no hurry. She finished what she was doing, wiped her hands on her apron, and then turned. Her face, thin and lined, moved only to give a slight smile.

'Welcome to you both.' There was little emotion in her voice. She gave Adam a token embrace and looked at Catrin. She did not offer her her cheek, nor her hand. 'Sit you down. You must be tired coming all that way.'

Catrin eyed one of the wooden armchairs by the side of the fire, but decided on a bench behind the table. She felt she wanted something between her and Adam's mother, who, in her turn, seemed to want something to distance herself from Catrin. She decided to talk on a subject she knew Catrin would know nothing about. 'George, before I forgets, young Billy Dobbs from up the lane called to see you about the job.' She was, Catrin concluded, embarrassed by her arrival. Or perhaps she was determined to show that life must go on as usual in spite of it.

'I'll go round,' replied George.

Mrs Turley turned to Adam. 'You all right, then?'

'Yes, I be all right.'

Catrin noticed that Adam had slipped into his mother's unemotional, under-expressed way of speaking. How different he had been in Wales, where he had reflected her own quickness and liveliness. The room was hot and she took off her coat and looked round. Some years ago the kitchen walls had been whitewashed, but they were now grubby. There was a black stain on the yellow of the door where a dog had pushed its way in and out. The mouldy smell of damp pit clothes drying in front of the fire was overwhelming.

The dog, a sort of whippet, the one that had no doubt made the black mark on the door, left its basket by the side of the fire and stood before Catrin timid and quivering, ready to flee, eyes fixed on her pleadingly but unwilling to approach her.

'Him won't hurt you,' said George.

'It's George's dog,' explained Mrs Turley as she poured cups of tea. These were her first words to Catrin, and she shot a glance at her as she spoke. The woman was weighing her up, thought Catrin, just as she was weighing the woman up. There was a silence, a cold silence.

'Well, Adam,' said his mother to cover it, 'let me tell you what the arrangements are. George is going to carry on sleeping in the same room as Grancher, but they'll move to the little bedroom at the back. It'll be a bit tight in there, like, but we've managed to get the bed in. Then you and Catrin,' she hesitated slightly over the name, 'you can have the front bedroom.'

She sat down with her tea by the fire and continued her recital of the 'arrangements'. 'I'm moving down to the front room.' She indicated the room behind her. 'It was the parlour', she added, glancing at Catrin, 'but it's so small we only used it once in a blue moon.'

'But, Mam,' said Adam, 'we shall have the best bedroom. Anyway I thought George was going to lodge out.'

'No need to. There's room here.'

There was silence. Catrin realised Adam was questioning his mother's decision. However, Mrs Turley decided that further explanation was necessary. 'Mrs Worgan wanted two shillings a week for George just to share a bed with her Harry. I told her it were too much, but she wouldn't come down.' She paused. 'Well, there it is.'

There was silence again.

Mrs Turley noticed that her purse was on the table at which Catrin was sitting. She took it and put in on the mantelpiece between a cocoa tin and a mustard tin. Catrin, embarrassed, looked out of the window.

The door of the back room opened and Grancher emerged.

'Have you bin on my bed again?' said Mrs Turley.

Cornelius Turley ignored her. His was a grand name, suggesting poise and dignity, but his appearance belied it. He wavered uncertainly on his legs as he shuffled in, supporting with his hands his way from door to table and then from table to his chair by the fire. He wheezed as he sat down, and coughed and spat a black, shiny lump of mucus at the fire. It caught on the front of the grate and hung there sizzling. Catrin turned away in disgust. No-one else noticed.

Cornelius ground his toothless gums together. 'So you be back, Adam,' he quavered. 'You looks well.'

'Aye, I'm fine. This is Catrin.'

The old man examined her. 'Catrin, did 'ee say?'

Catrin leaned towards him; she realised he was deaf. 'It's a Welsh name – Catrin.'

'Never heard it before. 'Tain't Forest.'

'It's like Catharine.'

'Is it? Well, welcome, anyroad.' And he looked away.

'Are you going out to work?' Mrs Turley addressed Catrin. 'There's not much work for women round here, you know, 'cept on bank at the pits.' She paused. 'You might find something at the tin-plate works, though, I suppose.'

'I thought I would be staying at home and helping in the house.'

'No need for her to go out to work,' said Adam. ' I shall be getting good money. Anyroad the baby'll be here soon.'

'A baby,' said Mrs Turley. 'Already?' She clearly didn't know. 'When's that, then?'

'In August.'

Mrs Turley thought for a second, but made no comment.

'He'll be my great-grandson, won't he?' said Cornelius.

'If it's a boy,' said Mrs Turley, shortly.

'Oh, he'll be a boy, all right. Don't you worry 'bout that.'

Mrs Turley shrugged her shoulders. There was no point in arguing. 'Well, we haven't had a baby in the house for over 20 years.' She didn't seem displeased at the thought of having one around.

'Now,' she continued before they became sentimental about babies, 'George, you go and see young Billy; and Adam, you take your things up to your room.'

The stairway was boarded in with a door at the bottom. Adam opened it and guided Catrin up the narrow, steep stairs. She hesitated as the only light came from under the doors on the landing at the top. In the room that was to be theirs she looked round. In one corner was a double bed, high and broad, and made of iron with brass knobs. It bulged with a bolster and pillows and was covered with a blanket, worn, thought Catrin, and of no especial colour. Above the bed was a framed text, 'As ye sow, so shall ye reap.' By its side was a chest and on the opposite wall was a rickety wash-stand supporting a bowl decorated with red roses in which stood a jug with a broken spout. There was no other furniture. Indeed, Catrin decided, the room could barely take any more – but a cot would have to go in somewhere.

So this is the 'big' bedroom, she thought. The place was clean but did not sparkle as her own bedroom had in Wales. The curtains were not so crisp as hers; the carpet by the bed not as bright; the floor boards were rougher and unpolished.

While Adam went down to bring up their trunk, Catrin went to the window and looked out. It was beginning to get dark, but beyond the end of the lane she could see a field in which a horse was walking alone. It stopped, glanced around, continued its walk, and then stopped again. Sad it was, she thought, a pity, because it seemed a handsome animal. Then she smiled, for she realised she had never seen an ugly horse: however old and worn they were, horses were never ugly. She turned and looked at the room again. This was her bed now, these were her curtains, this was her floor, hers and Adam's.

'It's a lovely room,' she said when Adam returned with the trunk. 'Perhaps we can buy some new funiture. We've got my father's fifty pounds.'

Adam looked surprised. She realised he had sensed her reaction to the room. He was silent for a moment and then he took her into his arms. 'You'll soon settle in,' he whispered.

'Yes.'

He held her close and kissed the top of her head and she felt safe. 'They like you, I can see.'

'I'm sure it'll be all right, Adam, but you must give me time to settle in.' She tightened her arms round his trim, taut body.

George, having returned from seeing Billy, clattered up the stairs to tell them that the meal was ready. 'I hopes you're hungry, Catrin. It's special tonight because Adam's back. Did you know, in the Forest we always has our big meal at this time of the day?' He looked at her, waiting for a response. When he did not get one he tried again. 'The

35

men want it when they come home from the pit, see? Don't have nothing much before then; can't work on a full belly.'

'*Cook* we calls it,' added Adam.

The meal did not seem to Catrin to be a special one. It was a stew, with little meat but plenty of thick gravy, a lot of potatoes and some greens, all very filling stuff. Adam's mother, stooping by the range, plated up each person's portion from cast-iron saucepans, their sides black with soot, and handed it to George with the name of the person it was for. Cornelius was served first, then Adam, then Catrin, and finally George and herself. Cornelius paid no attention to anyone after he received his plate; he mashed his food with a fork and shovelled it into his mouth. Occasionally he picked up a piece with his fingers, dribbling and moaning quietly to himself. His whole soul was concentrated on consuming the contents of his plate.

Apple dumpling followed. Perhaps, thought Catrin, this was the special part of the meal; but she declined her plateful, to her mother-in-law's obvious annoyance.

When the meal was over, the men sat drinking tea while Mrs Turley brought in an enamel bowl and a tin tray. She put them on the table and filled the bowl with hot water from the kettle, and then began to wash the plates and pots and stack them on the tray. Cartrin offered to wipe them, and after a moment's hesitation her mother-in-law accepted.

The chores done, Catrin excused herself, took a candle and went up to their bedroom to unpack. She opened the lid of the clothes chest and was relieved to find the chest empty and, as far as she could judge, clean. It was lined at the bottom with fresh newspaper. Into the chest she put her clothes and Adam's, smoothing with her hand the brown jersey her grandmother had knitted him.

She was pleased to be alone. The meal had been an ordeal, and she had not eaten much. What a disgusting old man Cornelius was. She was going to find it hard to live in the same house as him. Adam's mother, she foresaw, was also going to be difficult to get on with. She was clearly hostile towards her. Why hadn't she offered her cheek or her hand to her when she had arrived? Plain rudeness? But perhaps it was not rudeness, perhaps she was just shy. Or perhaps it was not the custom in the Forest to shake hands with anyone. But make excuses though she might, it was going to be hard to live wih her mother-in-law. She clearly ran the house and told everyone what to do.

Her clothes tidied away, Catrin rose and turned to the window. In the distance was a red glow from the Park End furnace. She could not see the horse in the field, but she imagined it was still standing there, alone. She felt sorry for the animal for some reason she could not discover, desperately sorry. Then she realised why. Like her, it was alone. But, as she immediately told herself, she was not alone; she had Adam. She looked fascinated at the pulsating red glow of the furnace for a minute, and then turned away from the window. Overwrought she was, and tired. She must make an effort. This was a new world, a world in which she had not yet been assimilated. She would soon get to know it, she would soon adapt. Adam loved her and would be there when she faltered, to comfort her if she despaired.

It was only later that night when she was in bed in the security of Adam's arms that she began to relax. He was soon asleep, and as she lay against him his warmth pervaded her. His arms were protective; his chest, gently breathing, was her defence. With the unique smell of his flesh to comfort her she at last enjoyed a delicious feeling of bliss. It lasted but a few seconds before she slipped into a deep sleep.

CHAPTER 5

The next morning Adam and George rose late and dawdled over their breakfast. They were in no hurry. Arthur Gunter, the pit manager of the Parkend Royal, wanted to see them before they began work, but not before half past eight. Adam sat and watched his mother prepare their bait. She took a cottage loaf – dark brown, heavily crusted and unevenly textured – that she had baked the previous day, scooped wedges from it, buttered the holes and replaced the wedges. She wrapped up two lumps of cheese and two raw onions, and put the food into blue checked tommy bags. Into two enamel tea cans she poured cold tea, no sugar or milk, and set it all ready on a corner of the table.

'There you be,' she said, eyeing Catrin. Adam saw that this was going to be his wife's job from now on.

'It doesn't seem much for a man to work on all day,' said Catrin.

'They has a good cook when they gets home,' Mrs Turley retorted.

Adam and George took the short route to Park End through the woods. Adam contrasted this walk to work with the one through the slums and stench of Erwgoch. He ran and showed his delight by kicking a stone with an exaggerated swing of his leg. The days at Erwgoch were in the past; from now on he would be working in his own country and for himself. For he was a buttyman at last, and had enough experience to be a good one. He could size up a coal face and undercut coal and bring it down a treat. His prospects were good and he should be able to earn enough to give Catrin and the baby everything they wanted.

He glanced at George with affection. He liked him more now he was back than before he had left for Wales.

'If we're going to set up as buttymen proper like, we need more equipment, you know,' said George.

'Such as?'

'One or two new mattocks and shovels and a new hod. And some new harnesses for the boys. The ones I got cheap weren't worth the money I give for them.'

'Where did you get the money from?'

'Our Mam.'

'If I have a word with her do you think she'll give us some more?'

'Doubt it. There'll be an almighty row if she knows I was done over the stuff I got last time.'

Adam decided there was no point in criticising George for his mistakes or telling their mother about them and asking her for more money. 'How much would a new lot cost?'

'At least another five quid. Then there be the odds and ends, like candles. You got any money?'

'A bit.' Adam had the fifty pounds Catrin's father had given them, but he wasn't going to tell George.

'And we shall want something for the wages of young Billy and the boys on payday. And money for us until we begins to make a profit.'

Adam grunted. This partnership was going to be expensive. There wouldn't be much left of the fifty pounds at this rate. 'I've got fifteen pounds. See how far that goes.'

The Park End Royal Colliery offices were on the other side of the ironworks in a desolate, grey building with a large forecourt in front of it. Adam and George went up to Gunter's office on the first floor. He looked up as they entered, his eyes as hard as the coal he was paid to secure. He was a big, broad-shouldered man in his late thirties with a face of granite. Smoothing his hair down with oil and carefully combing his moustache did nothing to tone down his rough appearance. Adam recalled that some women called him manly and attractive, but that others thought him coarse and domineering. The men called him a bastard.

'You've come to sign the contract, then?' He reached behind him for a bundle of papers. 'You've inspected the stall,' he said to George, 'so this is only a formality. One or two things I must make clear, though. We pay three shillings and tuppence for each ton of coal you bring to bank provided it's got no stone or small coal or dust in it. Understand?'

'You told me three and fourpence, sir,' said George.

'No, it's three and tuppence.'

This was tightfisted and despicable, but Adam suspected that if they argued Gunter would tell them to go to some other pit.

'The law says you can't employ boys under twelve,' continued the pit manager. 'Mr Sully says I've got to tell every buttyman this, though who you employ is up to you.'

George nodded.

'Sign then,' said Gunter; and he pushed the document over the table to George, who signed his name painstakingly.

'And you.' Gunter lowered his eyebrows and let his eyes slide over Adam's face.

Adam signed. Insolent bugger. He looked Gunter in the eyes as he handed him back his pen.

'Well, get going.'

The colliery was on the edge of the woods, not far from the offices, and the brothers went up a muddy track to it. It was alive with noise, but the din of rumbling trams and clanging signals at the pit-head were no new sounds to Adam. He dodged out of the way of men and boys as they hurried hither and thither, carrying, pushing and shouting. A cage with trams of coal had just come up. Banksmen jumped the trams onto the rails outside the cage, and then attached them to horses, which pulled them to a train at the back of the colliery.

While they waited for an empty cage to take them down, Adam and George walked around the site and looked in the various buildings. In contrast to the noise outside, they found the stables, the smithy and the carpenters' shop quiet. But the engine house was alive with the clatter of rods and wheels and with safety valves hissing as they released clouds of white steam. The engine itself was humming quietly, and Adam was intrigued by the way its well-oiled cranks rose and fell without a sound, the shining steel piston going up and down, up and down, firmly and positively, in no hurry. Perfect in its masculine force, he thought, and beautiful in its grace and movement.

They climbed into one of the empty trams that had been shunted into a cage. The cables whirled on the large wheel above them, and the cage lifted warningly and then dropped into the depths like a stone in a well. It plunged them from day to immediate night, and snatched away from their ears the sounds of the machinery and the men working on bank. They dodged the showers of water spouting from the cracks in the pit side, and pressed their backs against the side of the tram to counter the feeling of their stomachs pressing upwards as the cage fell. As it hit the base above the sump they clung to the side to brace themselves. It shuddered to a halt, and they tumbled out.

They were in a cellar-like cave that had been partly carved out of rock. A large oil lamp, hung high on the wall, flaring unevenly. Adam felt again the closeness of the noise and bustle of the men as they manoeuvred the empty trams off the cage and the full trams on; and as usual was sickened by the overpowering stench of human sweat mingling with pit horses' excrement.

'Come on.' George beckoned him to follow. 'It be nigh on two miles to the stall.' Every now and then they had to jump aside, backs pressed against the dripping walls, to let the coal-trams, linked together and drawn by a shire horse, clank by on their rails. Adam held his breath as the sweating, stinking horses passed, and breathed as shallowly as he could as he moved through smoke from a recent blasting. The puny lights of flickering candles stuck in lanterns on the wall at intervals pierced the blackness of the roadway and led them on. Hell could well be like this, thought Adam. But not quite: there was no return from Hell.

He forced his mind from such thoughts. 'How many hodders have you got us, George?'

'Only one, Jack, young Billy Dobbs's brother. I be after his other brother, Tom. We must find out soon if we can have him.'

As they turned into a side road, groans as if the earth was in labour came from above. 'That's no earth settling,' said George. 'Hope it don't get worse. We don't want no pit roof collapse.' They waited a moment. Then the noise subsided, and they moved on. The road became narrower and its ceiling lower, and they had to bend their heads. Along the main roadway with its ventilating doors the air had been cold; now, away from it, it was warm and stuffy. George took off his coat and Adam did the same.

A rat scurried across their path and ran up the wall. Adam saw it turn and survey them with its evil, twinkling eyes before it disappeared into a crack. Adam looked down to see that his yorks were secure. 'Don't want any bloody rats up my trouser legs.'

'Did you hear of thic fellow from Cinderford who got a rat up his leg that bit his balls?' asked George. 'They swelled up as big as pumpkins, they did.'

'Better pumpkins than cannon balls.'

They reached the loading stage where the hodders tipped their hods of coal into the trams. George pointed out to Adam with satisfaction their mark, a pair of scissors, chalked onto the side of a tram. He then dropped to his knees and crawled into a tunnel, the hod road. Adam followed. It was lit by the occasional candle and was about three feet high. Water was running down it, smooth and black, and the air was hot and stuffy. After 30 yards they emerged at the coal face.

Young Billy was sitting in the light of a candle, resting, his knees apart, a mattock across his thighs. Behind him was the coal face, a firm, gleaming mass of black two foot high, wedged between two layers of sandstone rock. It ran in each direction into the gloom. Adam could hear muffled voices from adjacent stalls, so he knew other miners were not far off.

'You know Billy Dobbs,' George said to Adam.

Adam remembered him as a boy. This was a man. He was a compact little fellow, trim and tough, with straight black hair and a good profile. The upper part of his body, thin like most colliers but sturdy, was unclad and gleamed yellow in the candlelight. His dark eyes shone white in the gloom. Coal dust was clinging to his sweat.

Beside him his young brother Jack was sitting, his arms hugging his knees. Adam greeted him. Jack grinned and clutched his knees more tightly. His grin spread to a generous smile, but it was spoilt by his cracked and decaying teeth.

George had been relieving himself in a corner. On his return he looked at a heap of small coal and dust near the coal face.

'What's this, young Billy?'

'Well it sort of fell like that. I told Jack not to put it in the hod.'

'What you mean, fell like that? I leaves you in charge for a morning and look what do happen.'

'It came down all wrong. This ain't a good seam.'

'You mean you didn't undercut properly, and didn't bring the coal down clean, like.'

'Some come down all right.'

'Well, p'raps, but all we've got here is a heap of rubble and dust. It'll have to go on the gob.' George was angry. 'Adam and me will have to pay for that.'

George turned to Jack. 'And what do you think you be doing, sitting around? This ain't bait time.'

Jack ceased to grin and reached for his harness. He put it over his shoulders, passed the chain between his legs and attached it to a hod that he had just filled.

'I be off then,' he said, and crawled down the tunnel on his hands and knees, dragging the hod behind him.

'And don't stop talking to them other boys,' George shouted after him. Then he took off his waistcoat, shirt and vest, selected a mattock for himself from a heap of tools in the corner and threw one to Adam.

42

'Let's get cutting,' he said. He lay down on his side and began to chip into the bottom of the coal face.

৵ ৶

Catrin noticed that her mother-in-law had sniffed in disapproval when she had kissed Adam goodbye that morning. But she had no time to ponder on it for Mrs Turley asked her to clear the table and do the washing-up while she made George and Cornelius's bed. 'I gets all behind when they goes off late to work,' she grumbled as she went upstairs.

'You'll be able to help Emma a bit now, like,' said Cornelius from his chair by the fireside. 'She have plenty to do, what with Adam back again and she ain't getting no younger.'

'Yes, I want to help, of course,' said Catrin. She did indeed want to integrate with the family. But this wasn't what she had expected. Clearly she was going to be just an asistant to her mother-in-law, fitting into her autocratic way of running the house, doing her bidding at all times. But it wouldn't last for long. She would soon have her own place, one she would look after, keep clean, put flowers in a pot on the table, all for Adam and the baby.

Mrs Turley came downstairs.

'What shall I do with the dirty washing-up water?' Catrin asked. She wondered how she should address her. Mrs Turley was too formal; and she couldn't call her Emma; or Ma or Mam, like Adam. She decided to call her nothing.

Mrs Turley looked at her impatiently for not knowing. 'Throw it on the cabbages outside the back kitchen.'

Catrin disposed of the dirty water. 'What shall I do now?' she asked.

'You can get the water.' Mrs Turley rummaged in the back kitchen, found her two buckets and a yoke. 'The well's fifty yards up the lane,' she pointed vaguely. Catrin returned with two full buckets and wet feet.

'We shall need another six bucketfuls, you know,' said her mother-in-law, and Catrin found six more buckets and filled them. She wondered why they needed so much water.

When she had changed her shoes and stockings Emma asked her to go to Alf Baldwin's shop at the crossroads for some cheese and a bar of soap. You'll want a bit of money.' She searched in her purse but there was not enough there. She looked at Catrin and decided that she must explain her system. 'I might as well tell you now how I deals with the money,' she said.

'Yes, please do.'

She took down the cocoa tin from the mantelpiece. 'This one,' – she held it up – 'is the housekeeping money. And that one' – she pointed to the smaller mustard tin still on the mantelpiece – 'is for saving for a rainy day. I always tries to put a bit away when times is good, like, but don't always manage to.'

'Yes,' said Catrin.

'Maybe the cocoa tin seems a bit full at times, but the men are only paid once a month, and it has to last.'

'Do they give you all their money on pay day?'

'Yes, and I gives them something back for spending.'

Catrin felt timid and alone as she walked through the village to the shop. The street was deserted, but she felt the eyes of the village women on her, eyes from behind curtains, from alleyways and from doorways on the other side of the street. People were watching her, inspecting her, seeing what sort of woman Adam Turley had brought back with him from Wales. Later, when she had passed by, Catrin was sure, they would gather together and talk about her, conjecturing her background, discussing her clothes, dissecting her appearance.

As she entered Alf Baldwin's shop, a smell invaded her nostrils that she had never experienced before. It did not displease her; indeed, it was exciting and novel, a combination of the different odours that every item in the shop could give off. Sweet and sour, it was, gentle and harsh. Mostly, Catrin decided, it was the smell of soap, with – and a glance round confirmed her guess – a hint of leather and paraffin, of sugar and candles.

Baldwin came in and banged a tin of paraffin on the floor. Middle-aged and shifty, his eyes lingered over Catrin for a second. 'Wait till I washes me hands,' he said and disappeared again.

Catrin looked round to see what the village shop had to offer. If she was going to do the shopping she would need to know. On the floor were bundles of Welsh flannel shirts and miners' moleskin trousers. Catrin inspected them, but they were of too poor a quality for Adam. She searched for cheese and found it on the counter with a few dried bloaters and the remains of a quarter side of bacon. The soap she located on a shelf behind the counter jostling for position with packets of tea, mothballs, candles, boxes of matches and packets of tobacco.

Alf Baldwin returned.

'Two pounds of cheese, please.'

'We have Gloucester or local. Local be cheaper.'

Mrs Turley had not said. Catrin chose the local.

'Anything else, love?'

'A bar of soap, please.'

'Like this?' He reached behind him for a bar of yellow soap. Catrin decided it was the sort she should buy and said yes. She did not like the look of the man and resented being called 'love'. Yet, she realised, this was the first warm word that had been thrown at her since Adam had left that morning.

The midday meal was a snack – bread and cheese and cups of strong, sweet tea. Her meal was the same as Adam's, Catrin reflected, yet he was doing all the strenuous work and bringing in the money. When she had her own place she would see he had plenty to eat.

After the meal Grancher went up to bed for a nap and Emma went into her room 'to tidy up', as she put it. Catrin was now alone, and could relax. Through the steam of her second cup of tea she day-dreamed. She placed her hand over her belly, and hoped she was carrying a girl-child. Adam wanted a boy, but men always did. She wanted a girl, someone she could cherish and hug and dress neatly. Then she thought of Adam. Ah, dear Adam, so kind and considerate. After dinner that night they would be able to sit by the fire and talk about the day's happenings. She would ask him where he had eaten his bait and what cold tea tasted like and whether he wouldn't prefer hot tea.

Emma returned and glanced at the clock. 'Must get the water on.' She bustled briskly. 'They'll be home at six. Will you start on the cook?'

She hurried out to the back kitchen and poured into the copper some of the water Catrin had fetched earlier in the day. Then she lit the paper and wood she had placed under the copper that morning. Meanwhile Catrin put some coal on the kitchen fire, big lumps at the front, small ones at the back, for cooking the dinner.

Cornelius came down. 'What be the time, Catrin? What be for cook?'

'Stew it is, like yesterday.'

He grunted and helped the time along by patting George's dog. The dog liked it and settled down in front of the fire.

'Get away,' said Emma on her return, giving it a kick. The dog crawled into its basket.

The two women busied themselves getting the meal. When it was ready they put it in the oven to keep warm. Then Emma unhooked the tin bath from outside the back door and put it in front of the fire, forcing Cornelius to retreat into a corner. She poured some buckets of cold water into the bath, and placed two towels to warm before the fire.

'Nice and clean tonight,' she said, admiring her washing. 'They won't be tomorrow, you can be sure. But you can't wash towels every day.'

She heard the gate open and hurried to the back kitchen to draw the first bucket of hot water from the copper. 'Never keep them waiting,' she said.

The men came in.

'What be for eats?' said George, collapsing into a chair.

Adam came over to Catrin. As he did so she smelt the sweat from his body, an acrid, unattractive smell, distressingly male. It had been reheated several times during the day and was now being revived by the warmth of the room. She had smelt the odour rising from his body when he had put his arm around her during their courting, and had found it clean and sweet; but this was an objectionable, frightening smell.

She drew back and he no doubt thought it was his dirt that repelled her. 'Sorry, Catrin, I be all smot up with dirt. Wait till I've had me bath.' But he leaned forward and kissed her on the tip of her nose, leaving a black smudge. She looked in the mirror and they both laughed.

Meanwhile Emma had poured another bucket of boiling water into the bath and George was removing his clothes. Catrin looked away.

'Get me some clean clothes, love,' said Adam, and Catrin was pleased to go upstairs. She stayed until she judged that George was out of the bath and dressed.

'My turn in first tomorrow night, then,' Adam was saying when she returned. He was sitting in the bath, his hair washed, his face shining clean, his knees close to his chest. He was rubbing a bar of yellow soap on a flannel. 'Wash me back, love.'

Catrin approached timidly, rubbed the flannel over his back and then rinsed the grey scum off. She was appalled at the scabs of coal-dust embedded in his back, and wanted to kiss them, but did not dare in case the others saw her. Adam, unaware of her thoughts, got out of the bath and took the towel his mother handed him.

'When I was down the pit,' said Cornelius. 'I used to 'ave me dinner before I washed. We all did in them days. Nowadays you must be all clean 'afore you sits down.'

'Filthy lot you must have been, too,' said George.

'And when we did wash we never cleaned our backs. Made for weakness in the spine, that it did. Them as washed their backs couldn't work as well as them as didn't.'

Emma had been outside shaking coal-dust from the men's clothing. On her return she collected their underwear for the wash. Then she signalled to Catrin and together they lifted the heavy bath and edged with it to the door. The greasy, grey contents rose and fell up and down the sides as they went.

'Careful,' said Emma, and together the carried the bath outside and emptied its contents on the garden.

The men, their faces red and shining, sat down at the table. Cornelius followed them, and Emma took up her position by the range to serve up the meal. She loaded each plate and passed it to Catrin, steaming and sloppy, with the name of the recipient. There was silence while they ate. Then came suet pudding, heavy and solid, to top them up.

With the serving of a cup of orange-brown tea, conversation began again. Now the family relaxed, and Catrin felt the togetherness of the other four. Adam was her line to the family, and he tried to ease her in. They talked about what had happened during the day. George and Adam spoke briefly about the pit; Emma told them about a loose brick in the copper and asked Adam to cement it in again; and Catrin, determined to join in, told how she had had her first walk in the village to fetch cheese and soap and had wet her feet getting the water.

'She did pick the sprouts for the meal as well,' said Cornelius, kindly. 'and very tasty they was, too.'

∂ ∾

Later Billy Dobbs came round. George boomed a welcome. 'Come in young Billy.'

'I wish you wouldn't call me young Billy. I'm 18 and I gets fed up with being treated like a child.'

'All right, all right. What about Tom?'

'You'll have to see me dad.'

'And Jack? A shilling a shift?'

'Yes, to start with.'

'And yours? Three shillings a shift?'

'Not likely.' Billy looked indignant. 'I got three and eightpence from my last buttyman.'

'Three shillings. Can't manage no more. Leastways, not for the time being.'

'Come on, George.'

'Look, if you don't like it you'd better go off and be a buttyman yourself.'

'Ain't got no money to start up with, you know that. Come on, George.'

'No.'

'Three and four pence, then.'

'No, and I advises you to take what I be offering. You wouldn't make a buttyman, anyroad. You haven't the experience. Look at you today, bringing down all that coal in tiny pieces. You've got to learn to undercut proper, like.'

Billy glowered, but returned on a different tack. 'You buttymen wants to get better rates from the masters. They be doing well, getting good prices for the coal. But they don't put up your rates. That's why you won't improve ours.'

'That's your opinion.'

'I'm not the only one who says so. You ask the other day men. And some of the buttymen are fed up with the rates they get, too, and moan about it more than you.'

'I know, I know.'

'And the masters be fiddling on the weighing as well,' added Billy. 'You ask the others.'

'Never mind the others. Three shillings.'

'Oh, give him his three and fourpence, George,' said Adam.

George was silent.

'Give him three and fourpence,' Adam insisted.

'All right,' said George. 'Persistent bugger.'

Billy smiled. But as he rose to leave his face became serious. 'I tell you, George, the men are fed up. There's going to be trouble soon, mark my words.'

CHAPTER 6

Ever since Adam had brought his bride to Coalway he had looked forward to the luxury of a morning in bed, with nothing to hurry him, nothing to divert him, when he could just lie in Catrin's embrace. Five days after his return, an eternity, came Sunday. Barely had he awakened from his usual deep sleep than he found he was caressing her, feeling her softness, his hands running slowly and sensuously over her body. She responded as she awakened and her love came from her inner being to meet his. She passed her hand gently over his face, her finger tips smoothing his eybrows, and then she allowed her hands to wander gently over his body as if she wanted to examine every secret place to make sure he was there and was hers. He suddenly seized her and held her tight. Afterwards they lay half asleep in a world of warm contentment.

They were awakened by Emma. 'Aren't you two going to get up this morning?' They jumped apart. 'I be going to Chapel in half an hour and Catrin said she wanted to come with me. Are you coming as well, Adam?'

'No.' Adam had never got the uplift and satisfaction that his mother obtained from attending Chapel. Nor did he regard attendance there, as he was sure his mother did, as an insurance against everlasting misery in this world and damnation in the next.

'You ought to.'

'No.' Adam's refusal was firmer the second time. Since his return from Wales it had occurred to him more forcibly than before how his mother liked to tell everyone what to do. Emma withdrew without another word.

Adam lay back, his arms above his head, his shoulders and chest bare, oblivious to the cold of the room, and watched Catrin. She had jumped out of bed and gone to the window. It had snowed during the night, but the sun was shining and the snow reflected a strange rosy light into the room. A quick wash from the bowl with the red roses

49

painted on it and she began to dress, her movements quick but precise. She donned her best clothes, the ones she had worn for her wedding. And how sensible and thrifty she had been, thought Adam, to insist on having a wedding dress she could use later for best.

Emma bustled off to Pisgah Chapel with Catrin in tow. George waited for his mother to depart and then went down to the Albion for a drink. Adam, with an upsurge of energy, found a spade and cleared a path through the snow to the gate. Then he went into the back kitchen and, humming a tune, replaced a few hobnails that had come out of his working boots and greased them with fat from the goose George had killed last Michaelmas. That would keep the snow out a treat when he walked to the pit on Monday. It would be Catrin's job to grease his boots now, he supposed, but he would do it this once.

Still brimming over with energy, he went outside again, cleaned out the henhouse and put down new bedding for the pig. He tipped into the sty the contents of the bucket in which Emma had put the kitchen waste, and as he patted the Turley pig on its bristly flanks he remembered that Catrin's father liked pigs, too. But Adam never forgot the purpose in keeping a pig, and as he patted he envisaged the quantities of black pudding, brawn and faggots this one would make in due course. He could almost smell the bacon, the pork chops, sizzling hot, and the ham, firmly cool, that would supplement the family's food. Catrin loved pork, so he must nurture this pig. He threw it an apple and, urging it to get fat on it, went indoors.

 ❧ ❧

The afternoon was bright and fine, if still a little cold.

'Let's go for a walk,' whispered Adam to Catrin, and they put their coats on and left before anyone could try to join them. In the lane they threw snowballs at each other and the exercise brought colour to their cheeks.

'Good to get away from the rest for an hour or two.'

'Yes, just the two of us. Oh, Adam, this is a precious moment.'

They went to the stone quarry at the top of a hill where there was a rock so big that a hundred men couldn't lift it. 'It don't seem so high now as when we was young.' They climbed it and sat on top in the snow. Catrin drew her skirts round her ankles and put her arm through Adam's. He sat with his knees apart, proud to have her at his side.

Then they went down the valley. At the bottom was a pond. 'George and me used to swim here before I went to Wales.' They sat on a log by the bank, close to keep warm. The water, grey-blue flecked with white, shimmered coldly under the afternoon sun. Willows leaned over and touched the surface with their fingers. Catrin thought it a good opportunity to raise the question of their own house.

'Adam, you said you could build a cottage for us with the £50 my father gave us.'

He gave her a lazy smile. 'I'll build you a lovely cottage, my love. I'll use all my strength to build it. Especially for you.' And he put his arms round her and hugged her close. 'There, you see how strong I am?'

Catrin laughed and struggled away. 'Mind the baby, Adam.'

'But I must tell you, Catrin,' he said after a pause.' I've had to use a few pounds to buy things for the pit. Anyroad, I think 'twill be best to wait until the baby have come before we think about a place of our own.'

Catrin squeezed his hand in trust. But he could see his words had disappointed her.

☙ ❧

On the Friday night following, after doing the washing-up and putting away, Catrin sat before the fire knitting some socks for Adam. Emma was mending a pair of George's moleskin trousers, and Grancher was contemplating the flames in the grate. Adam and George were behind the table chatting. Suddenly the level of George's voice dropped and Catrin heard him whisper, 'Coming down to the pub tonight, Adam? You haven't been to the old Albion since you got back.'

She strained to hear Adam's reply but could not catch it.

'But you haven't seen Bert or any of the others since you come back,' pursued George. 'You can't stay in every night. Got to start as you mean to go on, you know.'

There was a pause. Catrin concentrated on her knitting. Then Adam said, 'Do you mind if I go out for an hour this evening, Catrin?'

Catrin looked up as if she had not heard the conversation. 'No, of course not.' But her heart had dropped. Having spent all day with Adam's mother and Grancher she must now spend the evening with them as well. Disappointed, she looked at Adam as he donned his coat. He was hers and he was going out. But, she told herself, she must not become possessive. He had to go out with his friends sometimes.

'Down to the pub, I suppose,' said Emma, with a sniff.

'Must see young Billy about another boy for the pit,' explained Adam. 'We won't be long.'

51

The thought that Adam had made up the excuse crossed Catrin's mind, but she thrust it aside. However, the idea nagged at her. If it was not the truth, this would be the first time he had not been open with her. Soon she put aside her knitting, pleaded tiredness and, taking a candle, went up to bed. She placed the candle at the side of the bed and stood looking out of the window. Over on the right she could see the glow of the Park End ironworks flecking the sky. Then she remembered the horse she had seen in the field on the day she arrived, her lonely horse; but it was too dark to see it. She shivered, undressed quickly and got into bed. The brick that earlier she had warmed in the oven and wrapped in flannel and put on her side of the bed comforted her. She put her hand out to where Adam would lie later, feeling the cold sheet. Then she held the child in her belly, and comforted herself by talking to it. She turned over, and told herself not to be silly. Adam would soon be back. He had said he would only be away an hour. She realised that she was only happpy when Adam was present. But things would improve, she would settle in. She would, she would. But in spite of herself tears sprang from her eyes.

George and Adam approached the Old Albion. The buzz of good comradeship and boozy laughter from inside bade them enter. Here the price of a pint of beer bought conviviality and freedom from yelling children and nagging wives. The place was crowded, for it was pay day. The Albion was only a beerhouse and did not pretend to be more. It stood on the edge of the woods, and many a collier trudging home at dusk had seen its lights beckoning through the trees and been tempted in to clear the dust from his throat with a pint of beer or cider.

This was a pub for the men. Coalmasters and ironmasters shunned beerhouses; they kept to the hotels and inns. Nor did the men want the masters and their cronies in their places of recreation. You could say what you wanted in a beerhouse without fear, for any stranger or employer's spy was easily identified and could be surrounded with silence and frozen out. The Old Albion was the most disreputable of the three public houses in Coalway, but it was the most popular.

Daniel Baglin, the proprietor, sat as usual in a corner of the public bar, his opaque eyes sightless, with his right hand in his pocket clinking coins. When on occasion he took money for beer, though he was blind he could withdraw the correct change from his pocket without effort or error. He was a stout man of about 60. His short dishevelled hair was greasy, his swarthy face peppered with stubble.

He was devious and you had to watch him; but he ran a good house and was not too fussy what went on in it.

'Evening, Dan,' said Adam. 'Remember me?'

Dan paused, but only for a second. 'It's Adam Turley. Good to see you again.'

'Beer or scrumpy?' asked George.

'Scrumpy, it be cheaper.'

Mary Jane, young Billy's sister, her bare shoulders glinting in the lamplight, served them. They took their cider and squeezed on to a bench by the fire. Though still early in the evening the air was thickening with tobacco smoke and faces were becoming red and shiny in the heat. Adam put his drink on the table before him and contemplated the logs of Forest oak piled high in the grate and burning brightly. Their light dimmed the oil lamps that hung from the beams. Adam was going to enjoy the evening, chatting with a pint in front of him. He looked round. Most of the men there were old friends or workmates.

Bert Preece hurried clumsily over as soon as he saw Adam. One of his legs was shorter than the other, the result of an accident in the pit when he was a lad. 'Hallo, old butt. I heard as how you was back.'

'Hallo, Bert.' Adam felt a surge of affection and gripped his arm. They were old friends and had started in the pit on the same day. Adam looked over his face, his straight dark hair parted in the middle, his big shining moustache and his eyes, which normally darted in all directions as he talked, but were now beaming at Adam.

'And brought a Welsh wife with you.'

'Aye.'

'They do say she's a stunner.'

'You keep your eyes off her,' said George.

'Oh, don't worry. I'm married myself now, you know.'

'Who to? asked Adam.

'Martha Kear.'

'Don't know her.'

'She's from Gloucester. Born in the Forest, though.'

'Where you working, then?'

'Park End Royal, like you.'

A drunken collier lurched up. 'Come on Bert, give us a song.' Bert grinned selfconsciously, but was pleased to get up. He had a good

53

strong voice, honed by years of hymn singing in the church choir, and as he sang the chatter abated.

'Beautiful girls, beautiful girls,
'Saucy, teasing, pouting girls,
'I love them all, both short and tall,
'Beautiful, wicked young girls.'

The tune was simple and the men soon joined in. As Bert warmed up, he gesticulated with his hands and his audience roared.

Adam joined in with gusto. 'When did he learn that one, George?'

'At the Alhambra in Gloucester, most likely. He goes there a lot on Saturday nights.'

'Must be earning good money to afford that.'

'Not specially, though he never seems short of a penny. The house do belong to his wife, so they've no rent, and she do go out to work, I think. No, it ain't the train fare to Gloucester or the ticket for the Alhambra that takes the money with Bert. It's what comes after, like.' And George winked.

Adam laughed, but did not comment.

'I don't reckon Bert and his wife get on all that well,' continued George. 'That be why he's always in Gloucester on a Saturday night.' George became expansive. He enjoyed a bit of gossip. 'They live over on t'other side of the village, and I've only seen her a couple of times. She don't mix much with the village wives. Bit snooty, they reckon.'

George's monologue ended when Bert, after acknowledging the applause for his song with an exaggerated bow, came and sat beside them again.

George looked round for young Billy and waved him over. His hair, blue-black like a crow's wing, was sleeked back with macassar oil. 'Now, Good-looking,' said George. 'What about Tom? Be he coming to work for us?'

'Yes. Dad says he can start tomorrow.'

'A shilling a shift, same as Jack?'

'Yes to start with.'

'How old is he?' asked Adam.

'Ten,' said George. 'I think.'

Adam thought he was younger and glanced at Billy, but Billy was looking the other way. 'Gunter told us we mustn't employ boys under twelve.'

'No, he didn't. He said the law says we mustn't. He said we can employ who we like.'

Adam did not want to start an argument on such a night as this, and got up. 'Let's have another drink,' he said, and went to the bar.

'Four pints of scrumpy, please.'

While Mary Jane drew the pints Adam admired her figure. Cider had enhanced her charms, and he blushed at his thoughts, him so recently married. When he returned with the cider George, Bert and Billy had their heads together, talking seriously.

'Look at the row there was when we collected our pay today,' Bert was saying. 'There must have been a dozen men complaining they'd been paid short. And all because that mean bugger Sully insists on weighing the trams at Lydney. Lydney, I asks you, four miles away. Why won't he weigh them at pit-head?'

'He says it's easier to do it there when he unloads the trams from the train,' said George.

Adam joined in. 'What we want is weighing at pit-head and a proper sheet every pay day showing every tramload we brings up.'

'And we wants paying every fortnight not every four or five weeks like now,' added Bert.

'We wants lots of things.' Billy flung up his arms. 'We wants more money. More and more lovely money. Then we could spend it all in the old Albion.'

'Be serious for a minute,' said Bert. 'The scrumpy's going to your head.'

Billy turned away. 'I've had enough talking about the pit. I want to sing. What about another song, Bert? What about the Jovial Foresters?'

'Right,' said Bert.

'For we are the Jovial Foresters,
'Our trade is getting coal;
'You never knew a Forester
'But was a hearty soul.

'Though black we are when at our work,
'You'd take us for some smoking Turk;
'When that is done we're ripe for fun,
'To laugh and chat with anyone.'

Men from the tap room heard the singing and crowded in like herrings in a barrel. Bert sang another verse, then a third. There were six in all, and the men waved their tankards and joined in the chorus. But hiccups and yawns soon interrupted the melody, and the beer and cider began to thicken the men's heads. Reluctantly they decided it was time to go home; they would be up at five in the morning with a long day at the coal face to follow. So they bade goodnight to Dan Baglin and staggered noisily off home through the silent village streets. Not a light peeped from the cottages but a full moon lit their way.

George and Adam supported each other and sang another of Bert's music hall songs.

'Oh, I must go home tonight, I must go home tonight.
'I don't care if it's snowing and blowing,
'I must go home tonight.
'I only got married this morning,
'It fills me with delight.
'I'll stay out as long as you like next week,
'But I must go home tonight.'

Adam undressed and slipped into bed beside Catrin without lighting a candle. He lay on his back, recalling the evening. She cuddled up to him. He murmured a few words, careful not to breathe beery breath over her, but she did not reply. Then she awoke and clung to him fiercely, and he was afraid for her. But he fell asleep so quickly that he did not know whether she fell asleep with him or remained awake.

CHAPTER 7

Adam knew he had upset Catrin by leaving her on her own when he had gone to the pub. He told George of his concern.

'What be you worried about? Every man must have a night out at the pub now and again.' George leaned over and put his arm round his shoulder. 'You mustn't get soft and ask Catrin's permission to go out every time you wants to, or you'll end up doing nothing without asking her.'

Cornelius pricked up his ears. 'Yer'll be greasing yer own boots next, Adam, if you're not careful. And don't you go and give up all yer pals, now you're married, like. I was so besotted by my wife when I got married that I never went out of an evening. That be the way to lose pals, you know.'

George nodded. 'Grancher's right.'

'Men should rule the roast,' continued Cornelius, 'and wives should do as they're told.'

Adam was well aware that many colliers in Coalway not only had full control over every aspect of their domestic lives, but bullied their wives as well. And the wives in most cases were content to do as they were told. But he ignored Cornelius's pronouncements. It was George he was annoyed with. He grabbed his arm. 'I'm not falling under Catrin's thumb. Anyway, what do you know about how husbands should deal with their wives? You're not married.'

'No, but I'm close enough to see what married life is like.' George turned away angrily.

Adam attempted reconciliation. 'George, we can't always be going out to the pub. We get up at a quarter to five, and late to bed means that next day we can't work proper.' George did not respond. 'We haven't got the money to go out every night anyway. When you goes out for a night with your pals you don't want to sit behind one pint all evening. It be better to go out less often and enjoy yourself when you do go out.' George's only response was to grunt.

Adam said nothing about the evening out to Catrin. However, he did not visit the Albion, or indeed any other pub in Coalway, for some weeks. Nor, in spite of the temptation, did he drop in at any of the pubs in Park End on his way home from work as many colliers did.

The conversation between the brothers made Adam think about the small sums their mother gave them for pocket money. This, in turn, made him consider the general state of their finances. 'We're not bringing in as much money as we thought we would when we started up,' he said to George a few days later. 'Other butties seem to take home more than we do.'

'We don't do so bad. In some families with half a dozen kids there is only one man working, and he's often a day man.'

'And look at the miserable lives they lead, with a dry crust of bread for bait. You've seen them.' Adam wondered at George's lack of sensibility. Or was it that he was just selfish or too unintelligent to appreciate such obvious facts? 'I've been wondering what we can do to earn a bit more money. Truth is we be fitter now than we'll ever be and should be able to earn more money now than we ever shall.'

'If you work at full stint all the time you'll be dead at forty. Anyway I'm knackered after twelve hours.' A thought struck George. 'We could cut Billy and the boys' wages, I suppose.'

'No. What we really need is more money from Sully for the coal we dig. But we could cut down on the breaks.'

George raised his voice. 'What, cut down on the twenty minutes we stop for bait?' Confronted by Adam's attempt to find a solution to their problems, he was uncertain and nervous. He glared angrily at Adam. 'Or are you suggesting we don't stop to have a drink to take the dust from our throats?'

'Don't be silly. And don't shout at me. Perhaps we could organise ourselves and the boys a bit better. I've seen them sitting and waiting because they've got no coal to load into the hods. Other times there's so much coal they can't clear it.'

George was upset. 'Well, if you don't like the way I be running things, you take it over.'

Adam had long ago decided that he would be better than George at organising the pit work, dealing with the pit manager, allocating the wages and buying the tools, the candles and the lamps. But he was not optimistic that he would be able to produce any more money to give their mother on pay day than they did at present. Nevertheless, he agreed. 'All right, I'll have a try.'

George reached up to the top of the dresser and took down a cardboard box in which he kept a pen, a bottle of ink and the exercise book he used for the accounts, and handed it to his brother. 'There you are. See if you can do better.'

The next pay day when they handed over their earnings to their mother Adam raised the question of the family's finances with her. He had to be careful because he did not want to suggest that she was not administering them competently.

To his relief she was quite willing to talk about them. 'We has enough for food and there's still meat most days. But I must say I don't put much away in the mustard tin nowadays, even though you boys be working full shifts. It be the extras that's the trouble, like buying new pit clothes and boots. You never has any worn clothes – Sunday best, like – for you to wear when your old pit clothes drop off your backs. We has to buy new. But there it is.'

His mother's remarks allowed Adam to lead into his next point. 'I was wondering whether me and George could have all our share and buy our own clothes and so on. And Catrin needs money for herself and she don't want to come every time to you and ask. It would be best if I give her what she needs from my money.'

Emma thought for a second. 'All right,' she said ungraciously. 'If that's what you want. The way I did things for your father was good enough, and you were satisfied until you come back from Wales.' She looked at Catrin, suspecting she was the cause of the request.

Catrin was pleased with the arrangements now reached. At the same time she wanted to support her mother-in-law on the cost of food. 'I buy most of the food nowadays, Adam, and true it is that prices are going up.' Adam's heart still purred with pleasure when he heard her Welsh accent. 'I paid five pence a pound for cheese today. Five pence. Four pence ha'penny it was last week.'

'And cider went up ha'penny a pint yesterday, as well,' added George flippantly. 'What a bloody life!'

Emma seemed to resent Catrin's contribution more than she deplored George's bad language. She decided to ignore both.

'We was poorer when I were a young man,' said Cornelius, 'But we didn't moan about it.'

'Not much, you didn't, I bet,' said George.

'We just accepted it. It were one o' them things you couldn't help – like an act of God.'

Adam turned and, surprising himself, spat out his reaction. 'If you believe that being poor is an act of God, you'll believe anything. If God had to live the life he do inflict on us, he'd change things.'

'Adam,' said Emma, shocked.

Adam's realisation that he had upset his mother did nothing to make him want to apologise to her. His outburst had released feelings he had been harbouring unexpressed for some time. 'I'm fed up with the paltry wages we brings home and the conditions we works under and the way we're treated by Sully. And there are lots of others who agree with me.' He looked at George. 'Young Billy and Bert were right the other night in the pub. We've got to change things.' But George was scared by these revolutionary thoughts and did not respond.

The tension was eased by a knock on the door. Bert limped in. He puffed a little as he had been hurrying. Ignoring the women he addressed Adam and George. 'Got some news. The Trafalgar men have come out on strike for tuppence on the rate. It's the first strike we've ever had in the Forest. And the miners at Cinderford are thinking of coming out as well.'

'This will affect our men,' said Adam immediately.

'Yes. Joseph Cowmeadow is organising a meeting at Cinderford tomorrow night to talk about the strike.

'Who's Joseph Cowmeadow?' asked George.

'My cousin,' said Bert. 'He works at Lightmoor pit for Crawshay. Does a lot for ordinary folk. Very religious. Teaches the kids at Sunday School.' He turned to Adam. 'What about coming to the meeting with me tomorrow? We might pick up a few ideas about how to deal with Sully.'

They took Bert's horse and cart and rode the six miles to Cinderford. A roar of cheering assailed them as they neared the Upper Bilson pub. It was a barn of a place, full to the brim. Adam blinked at the haze of cigarette and pipe smoke that confronted them like a wall.

'What a turnout,' said Bert. 'There must be two hundred men here, all from Cinderford pits.' The colliers sat, jam-packed on benches and stools, all within stretching distance of a table on which they could place their tankards. Bert went to the bar at the back and bought drinks while Adam found some seats.

On a platform at the end of the room a heavily-built man was making a speech. He was about 50 and had a large bushy beard, every hair of which sprang out from its root aggressively. Clearly he was a collier, yet his years in the pits had not weakened his physique as they had so many of his fellows. Hardship had spurred him on to tougher resolution and greater resilience. He bristled with energy. But it was not so much his size that intrigued Adam as his magnetism. He stood easily on the platform, rising occasionally to the balls of his feet. The words rolled off his tongue, fluently and compellingly, and he opened his arms to his audience as if to welcome them into his embrace.

He was in full spate. 'And the demands of the Trafalgar men are justified, I tell you. And so are those of you colliers from Cinderford. All the men are asking for is fair treatment. But there is no fairness in the way the coalmasters in Dean treat their men. They act quite arbitrarily. And I say this: nobody is fit to be trusted with arbitrary power but the Supreme Ruler of the universe.'

His audience clapped and cheered. Adam sat entranced. 'Who's that?' he asked Bert.

'That's Joseph Cowmeadow.'

The speaker held up his hands for silence. 'There are five thousand colliers in Dean, and we are a mighty force. If we stand by one another, if we openly defy the tyranny and injustice of our masters, we shall win.'

A voice came from the front of the hall. 'We want a strike, like the Trafalgar men.'

There were more cheers, more calls for a strike.

'No.' Joseph Cowmeadow stood easily, balancing his huge body first on one foot and then on the other, and pointed his finger at the man who had demanded a strike. 'No, we want no strikes, leastways, not if we can avoid them. Disputes can be settled peacefully. The men must send representatives to meet the masters and talk things over.'

'Talk to the buggers! That won't do no good,' said the voice from the front.

'Has it ever been tried in the Forest?' was the rejoinder. 'Have the masters ever met their men to discuss their complaints? No.' He moved to the very edge of the platform and lowered his voice. 'Now listen, friends. What we need is a trade union to speak for all the colliers in Dean, for the men in the pits at Cinderford, at Trafalgar, and at Park End, where there is also unrest, indeed at every colliery in the Forest. With God's help we shall succeed in our endeavours. And remember, we need God's will. For nothing can be done that benefits mankind in this world without God's help.' His eyes swept over his audience. 'But I must warn you, once you have formed a union, you must remain faithful to it. Only then will it support you and defend you in time of need. In hard times you must take it for better or for worse – same as you did with your wives.'

His eyes twinkled and they laughed.

'Let's make a start here tonight,' he continued, 'and form a lodge – lodges, that's what they are called – let's form a miners' lodge here in Cinderford. Give but six pence a week. It's only the price of four pints of your beer. Then we shall have some money behind us. If we organise ourselves we shall be so powerful that the masters will have to listen to us.'

'Yes,' shouted the men, 'we need a union. Organise one for us, Joe.'

Adam was swept along on the tide of elation that engulfed the hall. Joseph Cowmeadow had given his audience the vision of a better life. Shimmering dreams of improved conditions rose in their minds, more food for their children, better clothes for their wives. They had been kept low and bullied for too long by their employers. The nightmare of their existence, the dark, damp grinding despair of the pit, which they had accepted for so long, could and must be be transformed. And Joseph Cowmeadow would lead them. They pushed to the front to sign their names or make their marks on the paper he held out to them and to put their sixpences in the hat he had placed at the edge of the platform.

Adam remained seated, his mind in a whirl. He was overwhelmed by the man's sincerity and conviction. He had expressed so clearly what he himself had felt in recent weeks, but his thoughts had been so vague and unfocused that he had not been able to formulate them properly in his mind, let alone put them into words. Now he knew what he should have thought and said.

That evening, in a beer hall in Cinderford, Adam felt he had been present in history.

CHAPTER 8

Adam couldn't get to sleep that night. He was haunted by the vision of Joseph Cowmeadow at the Upper Bilson standing on the platform under the yellow oil lamps and surrounded by the murk of cigarette smoke. He heard his words again as they had thundered across the hall to him at the back. 'The coalmasters are acting arbitrarily... There is no fairness in the way they treat their men.' Yes, it was the unfairness that was borne in on him. All through his life he had tried to be fair in his dealings with people. Even as a little boy when some rich relations from Monmouth had visited his family he had demonstrated his wish for fairness. A big man with a black beard had given him half a dozen sweets, but had given George only four. When Adam remonstrated about this unfairness the man with the beard excused his action by saying, 'But you're younger than him.' Adam did not think the reason a good one and insisted on giving one of his sweets to George.

As he tossed from side to side in bed, Adam recalled how unfairly his mother had been treated after the death of his father. He had been ten at the time, but some years later he had read of the terrible circumstances of his father's death in a faded yellow newspaper cutting that had fallen out of his mother's bible when he had accidentally dropped it on the floor. Painfully tracing each word with his finger, he had read that his father, who had been a labourer in the Park End tin-plate works, had been pushing a tub of molten cinders from a furnace when it had accidentally tipped over into a pool of water and exploded. His father had taken the full force. His clothing had caught fire and he was a mass of flames. Adam remembered vividly the newpaper account, word for word: 'His right hand was burnt to flakes, and bits of flesh hung from his wrist.'

He had asked his mother about his father's death, but she had grabbed the newspaper cutting from him and would not say a word. So he had asked Grancher. 'You be old enough to know, I suppose,' he had said, pausing to recollect his thoughts. 'They said his screams could be heard t'other end of Park End. Women ran out of their houses when they heard him. And the men in the ironworks wondered what it was all about and stopped work and came out into the street.' Cornelius paused again as he thought about the way his son had died. 'Aye, it were horrible. They brought him home in a terrible state. Doctor came, but could do nothing for him. In agony he was. Died the next day, he did. He had his faults, but he didn't deserve a death like that. And Emma didn't get a penny from the tin-plate works.'

It was unfair, thought Adam, that his father should have to die like that, and unfair, too, that his mother had not received any recompense. But, as Adam realised, the world was not fair, and he had decided the day he learnt the details of his father's death that when he could he would do his utmost to make it better than it was.

      ॐ   ॐ

On their way to work two mornings later Adam and George were waiting their turn at the pit-head to go down when trouble erupted, with voices raised high, at the back of the area where the trams, full of coal, were being loaded onto the train for transportation to Lydney. A swirl of colliers anxious to find out what the trouble was about surged round the train. Adam and George ran up.

'That were my dram. It did have my mark on it.' Matthew Teague, who had just come off the night shift, jumped up and down with annoyance. 'I did put it on only half an hour ago, and I see you rub it off just now, like.'

'No you didn't,' retorted the overman. 'I be in charge here, and you didn't see me nor anyone else rub no mark off nothing.'

'I lost a dramful of coal last month and I reckon it were lost in just the same way. I be bloody fed up with this sort of thing.'

'There was no mark on thic tram.'

'Yes there was. Don't you think I don't know me own dram mark?'

'You'd best buy yerself some more chalk and chalk it on thicker.'

Matthew ran at the overman, his fist raised, and made to hit him.

'If you strike that man, it'll be the end of you in this pit and any other pit in Park End.' Gunter the pit manager pushed his way through the circle of men.

'Mr Gunter, Sir, that were my dram, I know. There were two hours of slogging at the coal face in it.'

'You've no proof, so forget it.'

Adam stepped forward. 'Who gets the value of the coal in drams with no marks when they gets to the other end?'

Gunter looked at him. His eyes swept him from head to foot and back again. 'Now I don't want any trouble from you.'

'Well who does?' shouted someone.

'Mr Sully does, of course.' Gunter was defiant.

A chorus of groans arose, frightening, menacing groans. But Gunter as he looked round could not see where they were coming from; the men were looking straight ahead, their faces dour but unmoving.

Gunter impatiently went over to the train driver and signalled to him to depart, and the train steamed out. 'Now you lot get to work, or get home, but get out of here. If there's any more trouble of this sort, you'll get the sack.'

All the morning Adam thought of the scene he had witnessed. Men had long suspected that trams marked with their own sign were not being recorded on their arrival at Lydney, and now an instance of how it could happen had been openly revealed. It was unsettling, and he decided something must be done.

He looked at the big candle fixed to the wall – it was twelve inches long and would last a shift – and decided it was time for bait. George and young Billy dropped their mattocks and the two boys threw their shovels aside. They shook the coal dust off their bait bags and squatted, backs to the wall, on one heel. 'Move over,' said Adam to the boys as he chose a place to sit. He deplored the fact that eating and drinking in the pit had to go on in the same place as pissing and shitting. They wiped their coal-grimed hands against their trousers and, careful to avoid getting the food dirty, levered with their pocket knives the bread and cheese into their mouths.

Bert limped in from a neighbouring stall, his dark eyes swivelling from one to the other.

'I've called a meeting of the men tonight.'

Adam looked up sharply. 'Be this the result of the row about Matthew's dram this morning?'

George drew back, unwilling to get involved, but young Billy inched nearer. He positioned a candle so that it lit Bert's face. The two boys paid no attention. They were arguing about who was responsible for a snowl of bread falling into the black dust.

'Yes. Someone had to. I've had a bellyful of this weighing business. So I've called a meeting. Then we can talk about it proper like, just like Joseph Cowmeadow said.'

'There are a lot of other things that need sorting out,' said Adam. 'I'll come.'

'And me,' said Billy.

Bert grinned with satisfaction, his eyes gleaming. 'But we has to be careful that Gunter don't hear nothing, or we'll all get the sack.' He turned to go. 'See you at the double oak tonight when it gets dark, then. Tell any others you see, but be careful. We got to keep it quiet.'

George drew Adam aside. 'He'll get us all bloody hung,' he whispered. 'Suppose Sully sends his spies and we all get caught?'

'If we sticks together we'll be all right. If you wants better conditions you've got to take chances.' But George shook his head.

On his way back to his own stall Bert spotted Tom. 'How be you getting on, then, young Tom?'

Tom, a smaller version of Jack but with a bigger grin, said in as deep a voice as he could muster, 'Fine.'

'And how long you bin working here?'

'Nigh on five months, I reckon.' Then his childish nature intervened. 'But me privates is all sore from the chain when I pulls the hods. Like raw beef.'

'You'll have to learn to keep your legs wider apart then, won't you.'

'And I still keeps scratching me back on the roof.'

'Well, you'll have to keep your back lower. You want a good remedy for backache?'

'Aye.'

Bert put his hand on Tom's shoulder and spoke confidentially. 'When you gets up in the morning, pee in the pot and soak a flannel in it. Right? Then wipe your back with the flannel. Best thing in the world for bad backs that be. Same with the other place.'

Tom laughed.

'And chilblains.'

Tom laughed again.

'I be serious, lad. You try it.'

'I will. But I don't reckon my piss be as strong as yours.'

'Cheeky bugger.'

There was no moon that evening. Adam had persuaded George to come, and they walked together to the double oak. Other colliers, in groups of two or three, were also leaving their cottages and going in the same direction. The occasional nervous glance backwards showed that they realised that what they were doing was unusual, something that their employer would frown upon, something that might perhaps even be against the law. They went in silence, and the only sound was their boots swishing through the grass and the occasional hoot of an owl.

After a mile they turned into an open space where little grew but brambles and bracken. In the middle was the double oak, a healthy but unusual specimen, fully 20 foot in circumference. Two oak trees had grown together and their trunks had become merged, their sap nourishing each other. But higher up the trunks had separated and each tree had soared up a hundred feet or more competing, in contrast to the co-operation lower down, to see which could reach higher. Adam gazed up at it. He had not seen it since he was a boy.

Near the oak some men had started a fire with timber that had been cut down by Office of Woods men the previous summer and left uncleared. The flames were jumping high. They lent colour to the nearby bracken and trees and bushes, but not sufficient to light up the higher branches of the double oak, which swished slowly in the wind. Stars trembled in the air above the fire.

About two hundred men were present. They stood around talking, joking and warming themselves before the fire, for the weather had chosen to be chilly that evening. But soon their mateyness began to wear off and they became impatient.

'When be we going to start, then?' shouted a voice.

Bert climbed onto the slope of a fallen tree; the men crowded round. He held up his hand for silence and cleared his throat. He was no public speaker, and he was nervous. But the men encouraged him with a cheer.

'I – er – have asked you to come here tonight because I know you – we – ain't satisfied with lots of things, things the masters do, that we – er – don't like.'

'Spit it out, Bert,' shouted young Billy.

'You know what I mean.' Bert paused, uncertain what to say next. The men became impatient again.

'We wants weighing at bank,' shouted Matthew Teague who had had the row with the overman that morning.

'And proper weighing, too,' shouted another. 'I didn't go to school, but I know there be twenty hunderdweight to a ton, and that we gives Sully twentyone.'

'Aye, Sully fiddles the weighing machines,' shouted a third.

'We wants tuppence extra on a ton o' coal,' came from the back. 'Sully can afford it out of his profits.'

'And if he don't want to cut his profits, he can put his prices up,' said another. 'It be simple.'

Amid the cheers Adam wished it were simple, but said nothing.

The crowd pressed forward. Faces gleamed. Excitement grew. Arguments came from all sides, some inadequately expressed, but all spoken from the heart. Complaints that had been accumulating for years were shouted, challenged, supported, agreed, disagreed. Bert held his hands up and began to speak again, but the buzz swelled and became a roar and he could not be heard.

Adam found his mind cutting like a knife through the mass of verbiage and mixed thinking. He felt the urge to reduce it to order. 'This is no way to run a meeting,' he said to George, who was enjoying the shouting and the excitement.

'Maybe not, but they're getting their complaints off their chests.'

'They should be doing more than letting off steam. We've got to take some decision, say exactly what we want and do something about it.'

Bert, disheartened, looked round. He had lost control. Adam decided that a wonderful opportunity was being wasted, and sprang up onto the tree trunk. 'Like me to take over, Bert?' he said. He raised both his arms for silence. The flickering of the fire played red and yellow on his face as he began to speak. He knew he had to speak loud to get his voice across, and he forced it. It sounded strange to him; but it was powerful enough to compel silence.

'Fellow Foresters,' he began. They gave him a cheer. 'Fellow colliers of the Park End pits. I agree with you. We need more pay. A wage of one pound a week is a disgrace.'

'We want shorter hours as well,' cried young Billy. The men roared agreement.

Adam held up his hands to contain them in case there should be disorder again. 'Yes, we want that as well, and a lot of other things, too. But it's no good just yelling our heads off and then going home.' They laughed. He had them. He raised his hands again. 'We have to do something if we want things put right.'

'Go on strike,' said a voice.

'Yes, yes, a strike.' they roared. All the frustration, the annoyance, the poverty, the nagging of their wives for more money, the weariness of their work, the dullness of their lives, their broken tolerance, all coalesced and burst out in a fever. The suppressed resentment of a generation rose up. 'A strike, a strike!'

'How do we go on strike?' asked one beleaguered soul, showing his naivety and ignorance as well as his honesty.

'Not go to work, you dolt,' said a big fellow with a face like a swede.

The men laughed, but he was not the only one who was uncertain where he was or where he was going.

Adam was inspired by the excitement of the moment. 'It be within our rights to go on strike, 'tisn't illegal.' Adam remembered Emrys had once told him this in Wales. 'And if we don't dig Sully's coal, he'll suffer as well as us.' He forgot Joseph Cowmeadow's advice to talk to the coalmasters before going on strike.

The colliers crowded close and listened. 'What we do is go to the office tomorrow – all together, mind, we must keep together – and tell Gunter to tell Sully that we want tuppence more a ton on coal, and we want the coal weighed at bank.'

'And we want paying every fortnight, as well,' yelled Matthew Teague.

'Yes, we'll tell him that, too.' Adam shook a fist. 'And we'll tell him we gives Sully a week to agree and if he don't agree we won't go back to work till we gets what we want.'

'Yes, Yes,' the crowd shouted.

Flamboyant words, frightening words. Adam had surprised himself as he had uttered them. But the men cheered him and shouted his name, and he was flattered at the reception they gave his words. 'All right, then,' he continued. 'all the buttymen outside the colliery offices tomorrow morning. And the daymen as well. And tell anyone who isn't here this evening to join us. If we stick together we will win.'

They cheered him again.

On the way home with George, walking through the pitchblack Forest, Adam was silent. He was a little frightened and wondered what he had started among the colliers of the Park End pits. At the same time he was pleased with the dominance he had been able to exert over them. He tried to envisage what might happen next, but his mind would not function clearly and logically; he could not cut through the haze and muddle that permeated it. Oh, if only he were more educated, had some experience in this sort of thing. Would Joseph Cowmeadow support him or would he castigate him for proposing to threaten Sully with a strike? Would threatening Sully succeed? Would he give in if they went on strike? Would the men who had not been at the double oak join in? Had he stressed sufficiently to the crowd the importance of involving everyone? He wished Emrys was here to help him.

Then he thought about what would happen the next morning outside the colliery offices. There must not be the same incoherent shouting, coupled with bad temper against Sully, that had occurred this evening. The men must keep calm or they would get nowhere. He would pass round words of warning.

When he arrived home he reached for the cardboard box on the dresser, tore a sheet of paper from the exercise book and, as neatly as he could, wrote down:

'Coal to be wieghed at bank

'Two pense more on a ton of coal

'Pay day every fortnight

'Hours on saterday down by 1½. Work til 4 not half past 5.'

That night the colliers who toiled in the Park End pits had found their leader.

CHAPTER 9

James Sully had an early breakfast and went into his study before his wife came down. There was a lot of work to do in the next two hours. His mail had been sent over as usual from the colliery offices and he stacked it neatly in front of his inkstand and selected the top letter. His cat, which had followed him into the room, jumped up onto his lap, and stood, tail in the air, frozen for a few seconds. It was black and white, long-haired and untidy, a stray that he had taken in a few months ago, much to Hermione's disgust. He stroked it and then lifted it gently to the floor, resignedly brushing off its hairs from his clothes. The cat settled at his feet.

A servant announced Arthur Gunter, one of his pit managers. Gunter stood, hat in hand, in front of the desk. He was polite, but confident. 'Something serious has arisen, Sir.'

Sully put down the letter he was reading, and leaned back in his chair. Gunter was a good man and he trusted him.

'Continue.'

'Well, Sir, when I arrived this morning the yard in front of the offices was filled with men, jam-packed full, buttymen, day men and boys. They had been waiting for me since six.'

'Yes?'

'They were all excited, and several of them started talking to me at once, demanding this and demanding that, better rates and shorter hours, that sort of thing. I told them to get to work.'

'Quite right.'

'A man called Turley pushed his way to the front. He gave me a list of demands and said the men were giving you a week's notice to meet them, and if you didn't give them what they wanted they were going on strike.'

'Indeed.'

'Turley seemed to me to be a bit nervous, but he was forthright. I must admit I wanted to give him a punch and send him and the rest packing.

In the end I told them I would tell you what they had said, and they went off to work grumbling and shouting.'

'Was there any violence?'

'No. I was jostled a bit, that's all.'

'Have you their list of demands?'

Gunter handed Sully the list Adam had written the previous evening. Sully read it carefully; then gazed at his inkstand and tapped the note with his thumb nervously. When he looked up he found Gunter was staring straight into his eyes. Trying to discover what his reaction to a strike would be, Sully supposed.

'What do you know of this man Turley?'

'He's one of our buttymen. A bit of a troublemaker, I think. I had a brush with him once at the pit-head about marking trams. Worked for a time in Wales, I believe. Then came back.'

'He seems to have brought some objectionable habits back with him.' Sully got up and went to the window. His house was on a slope overlooking Park End, and he could see the colliery offices only a few yards from the bottom of his front garden. 'How many men were there in this – this demonstration?'

'I don't rightly know, Sir. The yard was full. About 300 I should think.'

Sully returned to his desk. 'Very well. Thank you, Gunter.'

'What shall I say, Sir, if I am asked for your reply?'

'Tell them they'll get it when I'm ready.'

After Gunter had left Sully sat and thought. He had half expected trouble like this. Rumours of unrest had come through from some of his managers who had their ears to the ground. It was a nuisance when business was good and profits were rising. William Brain, he had learnt a few days before, had a strike on his hands at Trafalgar Colliery. Perhaps he should have gone over to see him and offer a bit of sympathy when he had heard. Brain was a Forester, of course, but he was a coalmaster first, and a Forest-born coalmaster could tighten the screws as neatly as a foreigner if he were so minded.

Sully smiled at the word foreigner. He was one. As he had said to his wife Hermione only the previous day, he sometimes felt a real foreigner in this strange part of England. Since their arrival eighteen months earlier they had found it difficult to make friends with local people of their own class. But the position might improve today. He and Hermione were dining that afternoon with Henry Crawshay, another Forest coalmaster, who had more and bigger pits than he had.

Sully went to the window again, and looked over Park End. He was not, he decided, going to give in to the strikers without a fight. He could weather a short strike, though a long one would be ruinous. If only he knew how long the men would stay out. Of course, if he refused to give in hunger would ultimately force them back. But did he really want to starve them back? He thought of the faces of the men he passed in the village, and their women and children. Their thin, pale faces always seemed to proclaim hunger; and because of this his fastidiousness made him hurry past them.

He shrugged off his thoughts. He was sentimental this morning. Working people were not like him and his family. They had different standards, wanted different things. They were used to hardship; poverty meant less to them. In any case he must run his business properly. If the strike came it would have to be dealt with.

Hermione threw open the door, and the room was filled with her presence. 'You must go and get dressed, James, or we shall be late.' She was a big vibrant creature, not yet 40 years of age, dressed expensively in bright colours. She glanced at her husband sitting at his desk. 'You look worried.'

'No, no,' he replied, and rose.

'Well, come on. Alice is ready.' She smiled briefly at him. He was surprised, and his heart flickered at the smile. Nowadays she was so harsh towards him. This morning, though, a smile had broken up the outlines of her face, softened them, warmed them, smoothed them to what they had been in earlier, happier days. He responded by leaning forward and giving her a gentle kiss on her cheek – gentle because he knew he must not disturb her hat or her veil.

She turned away. 'I am placing high hopes on today's visit to the Crawshays, James. We must make more social contacts like this, otherwise we shall never find a husband for Alice. Don't you agree?'

Sully did not comment on the problem of getting Alice married. This business of finding a husband for their daughter was becoming a mania with Hermione. He ignored her question. 'I'm interested in meeting Henry Crawshay, my dear. That is why I accepted his invitation. I want contact with people in the same business as myself.'

They set off in good time for Oaklands Park where the Crawshays lived. The carriage had been polished bright at Hermione's special order, and the horses were stepping high, their bearing reins cruelly tight. The sun shone and the breath of summer invaded the carriage.

Alice, a quiet girl of nearly twenty, sat opposite her parents and surveyed the villagers as they drove past. At the top of the hill Sully gazed at his Brook-All Ditches pit. It wasn't very profitable, and if he had any trouble with strikers there, he would close it down.

Hermione was engaged with her own thoughts. 'Will the Crawshay children be at the lunch?'

'Only their son Edwin, I believe.'

'Edwin's married, I'm told. Haven't they another son who is grown up?'

'I don't know.'

'I expect you to find out these things.'

'I know why you want to know, Hermione, but please don't keep on. Let's enjoy the journey.'

They drove on in silence.

'James, you're very quiet.'

'I'm thinking. There's likely to be a strike in the pits.'

'A strike?' She seemed uninterested.

'I shall have to tell Charles, I suppose.'

'Well, he is your brother, and he does own half the pits.' She smoothed with sensuous fingers the silk of the coat she had bought especially for this visit.

Sully desperately wanted to confide in someone about the strike. Without hope of a helpful reply he continued. 'I suppose whether I face up to the strikers or give in to them to save the markets, there's bound to be a loss in profits.'

Hermione suddenly showed interest. 'A loss in profits? You know I need an increase in my allowance, don't you?'

He did not answer and after a few seconds she looked ahead, absorbed in her own thoughts. He gazed at her profile. The lines on her dissatisfied face had become more pronounced. She was not interested in his problems. He suddenly felt very lonely.

At the top of the hill he could see the smoke rising from his New Fancy colliery, his most profitable pit, one of the biggest in Dean. There was enough coal here to last a hundred years. A strike at this pit would be a tragedy, but he would recover. As he constantly reminded himself, people always wanted coal for their fires; there would always be furnaces and factories demanding it.

Hermione was eyeing Alice. Satisfied that she was engrossed in admiring the scenery, she leaned over to her husband and whispered,

He could feel Edwin sizing him up. He did not want anything to do with Edwin, but since he was there, he must be pleasant to him. 'You have some pits of your own, I understand, Mr Crawshay,' he said.

'Yes, but my father and I work closely together.'

'Edwin has taken over a lot of the work relating to my pits now, as well as attending to the management of his own. But we always talk things over together.'

'You are fortunate, if I may say so, that you have such a competent son to assist you.'

'Yes, now I am getting on in years I want to spend more time at home with my wife and family. We still have Hubert living with us, and there are several girls still to marry off.'

'What sort of neighbours do you have, Mr Crawshay?'

'We are rather isolated here, but we know people from all over the Forest. They are mostly coalmasters and ironmasters and other industrialists.'

Henry Crawshay read Sully's thoughts. 'Of course, we're not accepted by the gentry round here. I doubt if coal and ironmasters ever will be. Not that there are many gentry in the area.'

'My experience has been much the same as yours.'

'But we are the new gentry in the Forest,' said Edwin. 'We are the ones with the money now, the ones with the intelligence, the ones with the industrial sinews. We are the new force in the Forest.'

'Yes, indeed.' Sully was surprised at Edwin's outburst.

'Industrialists are now the backbone not only of the Forest but of the nation.' Edwin leaned forward, excited. 'We industrialists are making Britain great. We are on the crest of a wave. Nothing can hold us back, not even the unions. They are gaining strength all over Britain, Mr Sully, and causing mischief, but we can deal with them.' He leaned back. 'Fortunately, we haven't any miners' unions in the Forest yet.'

'I have heard that one was formed in Cinderford a few days ago.' Sully was pleased to give the Crawshays news it seemed they did not know.

'Yes, so I'm told,' said Henry Crawshay, and Sully's face fell. Crawshay knew. 'One of my croppers, Joseph Cowmeadow, who works at my Lightmoor colliery, has formed it. A cropper's duties, as you will know, involve him in seeing that the men do not send up more than the stipulated percentage of small coal in their trams.' Crawshay grinned. 'How he will be able to do that efficiently on my behalf and at the same time represent the men, who are always trying to slip in as much small coal as they can, will be interesting to see. But he's an honest man.'

'But aren't you going to dismiss him?' asked Sully, shocked at Crawshay's easy attitude.

'Oh no, not as long as he continues to do his job properly.'

'But he's corrupting your men, and causing unrest.'

'I don't know about that. The men of Dean are not easily corrupted, and the causes of unrest are there whether they are concealed or not.'

Sully did not reply.

'I have seen this union business coming for some time,' continued Crawshay. 'and have come to the conclusion it will be best to accept the unions and deal with them the best we can.'

'And if we must accept them,' said Edwin, glancing at his father, 'neutralise them. But whatever our attitude, I'm sure we shall be able to handle them.'

Confident puppy, thought Sully. His elegant good looks and smooth manners only increased his dislike of him.

'And if we cannot, there are always Acts of Parliament we can ask our MPs to make to enable us to do so.'

'Come, Edwin,' said his father. 'I thought we objected to the state interfering in our business. In any case, I suppose the workers deserve a share of the profits. At least as long as we get the lion's share.'

Sully shook his head. 'I'm afraid I can't take such a tolerant view as you, Mr Crawshay. I believe trade unions to be dangerous. All over the country they are inflaming the men to extravagant demands. All these new ideas coming over from France and other places. And they've now reached the Forest. Brain has a strike on his hands, and I was told only this morning that if I don't make some concessions to my colliers I shall have one on mine, too.'

'Well, there's no talk about a strike at our pits as far as I know,' said Edwin.

'Nor should there be,' said his father, 'though I can't speak for other coalmasters. Trade is good for us, you know, and it must be similarly good for you.'

'Yes, so-so, but my men's demands are outrageous. They want an increase of 2d on a ton. That's 5%, no small increase. Further, they want reduced hours and are not satisfied with our system for weighing coal.

They want it weighed at the pit-head not at Lydney. And they want fortnightly pay.'

'Do they now?' Henry Crawshay smiled. 'What do you intend to do about it, Mr Sully?

'I am minded to reject their claims completely.'

'Do you not think it would be wise to compromise?'

The question spurred Sully to opposition. He forgot his earlier squeamishness about using hunger as a strike breaker. 'No, let them come out on strike, if they will. They'll soon find they are short of money and that a four or five week pay gap is better than no pay at all.'

'Yes, I can see you have a problem.' Edwin yawned. He had had enough of Sully and his difficulties.

'Don't forget that what I say to my men will influence your men's claims,' rejoined Sully. He had become annoyed with both the Crawshays.

'And what we do will affect your position,' said Henry Crawshay, with an edge to his voice. 'And Brain's and the others.'

Sully wondered whether this was a threat but, realising the conversation was becoming heated, said, mildly, 'That means that the coalmasters in the Forest should stick together, Mr Crawshay, does it not? Perhaps we need an employers' federation?'

'Perhaps.'

Sully persisted. 'Well, Mr Crawshay, until we get a federation, how will you respond when your men demand an extra 2d, as they surely will?'

Henry Crawshay glanced at Edwin. 'I think we should probably concede it. After a proper period of delay and a show of reluctance, of course. We can afford it with market prices as high as they are.'

'What about the weighing business?'

'We weigh at bank already. I don't think it matters much where one weighs. It is whether the employers are cheating the men that concerns them. We've never had weighing problems with our men, but I believe it is a source of friction in some pits.' Sully realised that Crawshay knew more about his collieries than he showed.

'I'm not so certain about fortnightly pay,' said Edwin, 'and we probably wouldn't agree to reduce hours. But we must wait and see. No point in rushing in. Let the men make the running, I say.'

Sully decided to let the matter drop. He smiled at his hosts. There was silence. Then Edwin yawned. 'Let's see what Charlotte and the others are doing.' He rose.

They went through a French window to the gardens. Sully was impressed by their grandeur. They walked along paths edged with low, neatly-clipped hedges. The lawns were broken with flower beds, square, rectangular and circular, which offered splashes of red and orange, yellow and indigo, with the brown earth, piled high in the beds, making its contribution to the colour. Sully decided that flowers were even more attractive when seen with the lawns behind them. He must introduce this idea into his own garden.

Surveying the gardens had taken his mind off the conversation he had just had, but his thoughts soon returned to it. He had sounded the Crawshays out and now had an idea of their attitude. Henry was on the soft side as far as the men were concerned – how he had made all his money with that approach Sully did not know – but Edwin, he concluded, was tougher, though he did not openly dispute with his father. He was playing a waiting game, perhaps, letting his father have his way until he inherited his pits. In the meantime Crawshay senior was not going to be very sympathetic to Sully's way of thinking; and he decided he must find out what the other coalmasters would do if their men submitted demands and threatened strikes. He did not think they would be like Henry Crawshay and give in for a quiet life. But he must find out how far they were prepared to go. Then he could decide on a campaign against his own men. He also pondered his idea of forming an employers' federation to combat the spread of trade unionism in the pits. Perhaps if he initiated it he could be the Chairman and prevent Crawshay or any other coalmaster controlling it.

Eliza waved to them from the park, and they walked towards her party. Sully could see that Hermione had enjoyed her tour of the estate. Later she would no doubt tell him about it at great length and in envious terms. 'We must go now, my dear,' he said. He had had his discussion with the Crawshays, found out what he had wanted to know and was ready to go home.

They wandered back to the house, the Sully coach was summoned and, with a chorus of thanks and you must come to lunch with us sometime, waves and bows, the Sullys departed.

❧ ❧

'I know what she came for,' said Eliza to her husband as they moved off.

'What, my dear?'

'Young Hubert.'

'What do you mean?'

82

'She wants our Hubert for that girl of hers.'

'What makes you say that?'

'The questions she was asking about him in the garden, man.'

Henry smiled and took her hand. 'You're a suspicious one.'

'Well, that's what she came for, I'm sure. But such a marriage would be hardly suitable. But what did he come for?'

'They both came because we invited them. I think they want to be neighbourly. Don't forget that they haven't been living in the Forest very long. We've been here nearly 30 years. He badly wants my support in some labour trouble he is having in his Park End pits, poor chap.'

'Well, watch out.'

CHAPTER 10

Catrin took off her sack apron, gave Cornelius his cup of tea and sat down before the fire with her own cup. Emma had gone to Park End to visit her sister. To save Catrin lifting now that she was near her time, she had filled the copper in the back kitchen with water for the men's baths before she left. Catrin had only to light the fire under it. But there was no hurry this evening. It was payday, and the men were always late home on payday.

Cornelius drank his tea with slow slurps. 'They'll be later than usual tonight, I 'spect. They have this strike business to settle.'

'What do you mean?'

'It be the last day of the notice they have given to Sully. They won't know what to do if he don't reply. Serves them right. Shouldn't have said they would go on strike in the first place.'

Catrin shrugged her shoulders and sipped her tea. 'I don't understand what it's all about.' She was tired. It was kitchen day. Blackleading the grate, it had been. Then floor rugs and furniture outside the back door, and down on her knees to give the paving stones a good scrub. She had laid sheets of newspaper to walk on until the stones dried, and now only scrubbing the table and polishing the furniture remained to be done. Then everything would be clean and sweet.

She stretched her feet out in front of the fire and folded her hands over her swollen belly. It was not an elegant posture, but it was comfortable and she did not feel self-conscious in front of Cornelius. Catrin had warmed to him in recent months. She was pleased he had stopped spitting on the fire and had abandoned some of his other more filthy habits. She was touched by the way he would do small services for her if they were within his capability. This was more than he would do for Emma. But then Emma tended to bully him and treat him as a nuisance. He got his own back on her by never doing anything for her and by expecting her to wait on him.

She thought about the baby. She was keeping well and the vigorous kicks by the new life inside her gave her shivers of wonder. 'Plenty of work and forget about it and it will be all right,' Emma had said; and that, Catrin accepted, was no doubt the best advice. She reckoned the baby would come in two or three weeks. Mrs Phelps, the village midwife, whose other jobs were playing the harmonium on Sundays at Pisgah Chapel and scrubbing the floors of the Albion during the week, thought it would come any time. Catrin imagined the look on Adam's face when she presented the baby to him. Most evenings nowadays they sat contented behind the kitchen table, his arm round her thickened waist, and whispered to one another their hopes and expectations for the child. Those evenings were precious to her and she would remember them forever.

Catrin poured them another cup of tea, and they sat quietly. Then Cornelius asked what time Emma would be back. He was always conscious of time; he had so much of it.

'Later this afternoon. In time to carry the water in for the baths, I hope.'

'No such thing as afternoons in the Forest. We 'as mornings and evenings and nights. But no afternoons.'

'Oh,' said Catrin.

Cornelius's thoughts were still on time. 'Reach me watch down, there's a good girl.' He indicated a drawer in the dresser. Catrin passed him a small cardboard box with broken edges. He took out the watch, a fine timepiece it was, heavy and thick, with a silver chain attached. Watch was too inadequate a word for it.

'I be going to give this to Adam. But he don't get it till I'm put under. I ain't told him, like, but Emma do know.' He leaned over to Catrin confidentially. 'He'll need a leather bootlace instead of the chain when he takes it down pit, you know.'

Catrin raised her hand to her mouth.

'What be the matter?'

'Heartburn. Just a little.'

'You know what you want to do? Suck a bit o' coal.'

'Suck coal?'

'Yes, just a tiny bit, like. Good for women who are carrying, any collier's wife will tell you that. I reckon that there Dolly Dobbs up the lane have sucked tons of coal in her time. She be heavy with twins, so they tell me.'

He rummaged in the coal bucket and selected a suitable piece. 'Here, stick this in your mouth.'

Catrin put it in her mouth cautiously.

'It'll be nice having a baby round the house again,' Cornelius contemplated. 'Nice, that is, if he don't holler too much. Young Adam used to holler, by God. George were all right, though.'

'The baby will be sleeping in our room. You shouldn't hear too much noise in yours.'

'No, I shouldn't reckon. You'll need more room when he grows up, mind. But I shall be dead by then.'

'I'm hoping we shall have a home of our own long before then, Grancher.'

'Home of your own?' He looked up in surprise.

'Adam says that if he can't find one for rent, he will build one.'

'There ain't no land round here for building houses on. That there Office of Woods sits on it all. Won't sell it, even if it be no use for growing trees on.'

Catrin looked doubtful.

'It be true, I tells you. And don't you think we be crowded here, my girl. Some houses smaller than this one have two families in it, with all the kids. And they has to take in lodgers sometimes to pay the rent. We haven't got no lodgers here because we gets enough money from our boys.'

Cornelius leaned forward in his chair and wagged a finger. 'There have been some terrible consequences of all this overcrowding, you'd never believe. Sisters have had children by their own brothers, and fathers have had connections with their own daughters. 'Tain't proper, but it goes on.'

Catrin was horrified. She had never heard of such happenings. What sort of a place was this Forest Adam had brought her to? But her thoughts soon seized on Cornelius's message: she should be satisfied with what she had and not expect a place of her own. Yet she could not be satisfied; and knowing that others were worse off did not comfort her. She had expected more from her marriage. The hope, the dream, that her baby would be born in her own home had been slowly eroded and was now practically gone. But surely there was hope that one day Adam would find them a house of their own. Otherwise they would have to stay here until George moved out, if he ever did, and Grancher and Emma were dead.

❧ ❧

George slapped Adam on the back. 'I'll get the drinks. Good thing we gets beer on credit on payday.'

Adam smiled cynically. 'Only because they can insist on getting their money as soon as we get our pay.'

The British Lion was perched on a hill midway between the colliery offices and the ironworks. The brothers, coming straight from the pit, had joined the other colliers there. Today was not an ordinary payday; the men sat quietly, subdued as if someone had threatened them, chatting in hushed tones to one another, waiting to hear what Sully would say about their claims. Concern was concealed beneath their quiet, like black water under ice.

George plonked a pint down in front of Adam. 'If we keeps our threat to strike we shall have to come out on strike tomorrow morning, won't us?'

Adam's only response was to say, 'Ned Screen be late today.'

'Always is. I reckons the pub do pay him to come late. The later he is the more beer we drink on tick.'

Ned Screen, the colliery clerk, and a cashier with two bags of money puffed up the hill and into the pub. A third man, hefty and with suspicious eyes, followed them and stood, arms across his chest, behind the other two as they prepared to pay the men.

'Park End Royal first,' said Screen.

The first buttyman in the queue was told the amount owing to him. He queried it. 'This be wrong. I've kept careful count and it should be much more.'

'That's what the book says.'

'Well it's not what I reckons. The book be wrong.'

'If you don't like it, go to the offices at nine tomorrow. Next.'

Adam was next. He signed for his money. 'Anything about the demands of the men?' he asked.

Screen looked up at him. The expression on his face showed he recognised Adam as the ringleader and his duty to his employer demanded that he must say nothing to him.

'Better go to the offices at nine tomorrow. Next.'

Adam suppressed his annoyance, and looked round the bar for Bert to consult. He couldn't see him, and decided in the meantime to pay Billy and the boys. He pushed empty mugs aside and wiped spilt beer off the top of the table with his sleeve. Then he produced his exercise book and did his calculations. He paid Billy and his two brothers.

'That leaves eight pounds three shillings for us, George. Not much for a month.'

George didn't comment; winning coal had been hard going the last few weeks because of stone in the seam, and he hadn't expected more. He turned to Billy and the boys. 'Come on then, let's have yer money for the drinks kitty.'

Billy spun a shilling from the pay he had so recently received over to George. George looked at Jack and Tom. 'Come on, you two. Four pence each.'

'We can't afford it, not on the money you pays us.'

'Come on. Boys have paid towards drinks on payday since your grandfather was knee high to a piss pot. You gets a pint out of it, don't you?'

The boys groaned and searched in their pockets.

'Oh, let'em off with tuppence each this week, George,' said Adam impatiently, frustrated because he had had no news from Gunter. The boys hastily handed George their tuppences.

Adam spotted Bert and went over to him. They talked for a few minutes and then went to seek out Gunter at the colliery offices; he was just leaving for home.

'Mr Gunter, Sir, has Mr Sully said anything about our claim?' asked Adam.

Gunter neither stopped nor slowed down. He ignored them, and they had to hurry to keep up with him. He looked at Bert. 'So you're another ringleader.'

Bert was nervous. 'It be all the men, not only us.'

'Mr Sully hasn't said anything to me, and I'm the person he would tell.'

Adam stood in Gunter's path so he could not go any further. 'You mean he's refusing all our demands?'

Gunter looked at him and gave a twisted smile. He did not deign to give a straight answer. 'Your demands? You'd better tell your supporters to turn up for work as usual tomorrow.' He pushed past Adam and continued on his way.

Bert looked at Adam. His eyes, which normally darted in all directions, were still and pleading like a dog's. 'Seems our gamble hasn't come off, Adam. Why did we think Sully would give in as easy as that?'

Adam ignored his remarks. He thought for a few seconds, and then grabbed Bert's arm and hurried him back to the British Lion. The men sitting waiting outside on the grass sensed Adam and Bert had news. They jumped to their feet and crowded round them. Someone shouted to those still in the pub to come out.

Adam climbed on a bench. 'Sully's refused our claims and Gunter tells us to go back to work as usual tomorrow.'

The men groaned and looked at one another. 'What about the strike, then?' ventured one.

'We'd be stupid to go on strike,' said another.

'Bloody silly idea from the beginning.'

Incensed by these remarks and fearing they might encourage a collapse of the men's determination, Adam yelled 'No.' The vehemence with which he shouted made them stare at him and stand still and silent. His hair fell across his forehead and he pushed it aside impatiently. 'No, we mustn't retreat at the first sign of opposition. And we must stick together.' He remembered all his exhortations at the double oak and the cheers they had given him. 'We must strike as we agreed we would.' He raised his voice. 'We go on strike!'

There was a pause while his words sank in. The silence seemed to Adam to last for ages. He droppped his hands to his sides and nervously tapped his legs with his fingers. Had they rejected him? Then those who had expressed their opposition were swept aside and Adam's words were snatched up. 'We go on strike. We go on strike.' Enthusiasm was borne aloft to the skies by cheers and shouts. Adam sobbed with relief; they were behind him; their resolve to strike was even greater now than it had been at the double oak.

'Three cheers for the strike,' said a collier, raising his mattock above his head.

'Stick together,' said another.

'Park End plays tomorrow!'

'We're coming out.'

'We'll stay out until we win.'

They swept cheering down the hill from the British Lion, their earlier lethargy replaced by the energy of excitement, their faces animated, their hair wild, their bait tins and tea bottles flying on their strings. At the bottom some decided to go back to the British Lion to chew over yet again their injustices and the hardships they had borne and to celebrate their decision to strike. The more prudent went home. The money saved would soon be worth more than a pint of beer.

On reaching home their euphoria evaporated temporarily. Collecting their money and waiting for news about the strike had taken a long time. Their bath water was cold, their meals were dry in the oven and their womenfolk were angry.

CHAPTER 11

Adam was up early on the first day of the strike. Many of the men, though, stayed in bed until the sun was high and shone through the window and picked out patterns on the bedroom wall. Their wives had a lie-in, too; they did not have to get up at four o'clock to light fires and prepare breakfast. It was like Sunday but different. The men felt guilty, not because they were deserting their employer, but because they were not doing something they had always done and always expected to do. They felt like children playing truant from school, though few had ever been to school. Their wives suggested jobs for them to do – digging the garden, mending the fence, cleaning out the pig sty, repairing the water butt, mending boots and shoes – but they refused to do them. Today was a holiday, and those were Sunday jobs, anyway. Nor were they going to do women's work like minding the childen. After a leisurely breakfast they congregated in the street. The young ones kicked stones and joked and chased one another; the older ones, conserving their energy, sat on garden walls, face to the sun, enjoying its rays.

After breakfast Catrin took Adam's hand and sat him behind the table. 'What's all this about you leading the strike?'

A little shaken by her forthright approach, he put his arm round her and explained. 'I suppose I am the leader. We had a meeting at the double oak, and no-one seemed able to organise the men's complaints but me. And before I knew what was happening, there I was telling the men what they should do. It just happened.'

'But why a strike?'

'We must fight for better conditions. It's only by banding together that we'll get more money. You could do with more couldn't you, with the baby coming and everything?' He could see Catrin was not convinced, and pulled her closer to him and gave her a kiss hoping that it would settle her. But it did not. He sighed and rose, and tried to edge past her. 'Come on let me out. I must go now.'

'Where are you going?

'To see Bert.' Then seeing her worried face, he became more conciliatory. 'It'll be all right, Catrin. We'll win this fight, not to worry.' He gave her another kiss and left the house.

As he walked along the village street he felt good. He winked at the young women and saluted the men. Here and there he stopped to chat, and felt a tremor of pride inside him as he realised that they treated him with a new respect. The young housewives were charmed by his lean athletic body and his clean-cut good looks and ready smile. As fine a fellow as ever lifted a hat to a lady or a boot to a blackguard, they reckoned.

But the older women were less attracted. 'Shame on you, Adam Turley,' said one, hurrying to her front gate to catch him. 'You been back from Wales no more than six months, and you be causing trouble bringing the men out on strike. They never done that before.' She shook her broom at him. 'Where be the money coming from to feed the kids at the end of the month? Did you think about that?'

He tried to calm her, to reason with her. There would be a lot of this, he thought, and for a moment fear spread through him. What was he doing leading all these good men into a strike? What did he know about such things? He prayed that the strike would be short.

Bert's cottage was up a lane on the far edge of the village. Roses on a shaggy bush over the front porch dropped their petals over the path. Adam knocked on the door.

'Come in,' said a voice. He entered. A young woman sat at the kitchen table with a large mirror propped up before her. She was piling her hair on the top of her head. She glanced in Adam's direction, but continued piling her hair. This must be Bert's wife.

'Mrs Preece? Be Bert in?'

'Yes, he's upstairs.' She spoke in a low voice. 'Let me finish my hair.' She patted it. It was gleaming, honey-coloured, and seemed to be the focus of everything in the room. Her face, broad-cheeked, narrowing to the chin, was smooth and the colour of a peach, with all its sunshine and smoothness. She was calm, indeed cool, Adam decided. She continued to pile up her hair, pinning it as she went. Occasionally she would move her head sideways to see the effect. Adam stood and looked at her. She was taking her time, but he was content to watch her.

He noticed how her bare arms, elegant and smooth, curved up over her head. Indeed, she was all curves, with not an angle to her body. Yet she was not fat. Just curves, soft curves, grand sweeps from the neck to the elbow, from the neck to the waist, tiny curves round her cheeks, bigger curves round her elbows.

She put down her comb, and looked straight at him. 'Do I know you?'

He looked away, embarrassed. 'I be Adam Turley.'

'Yes, I remember. Bert told me about you.' She spoke carefully in a low voice, with only a slight Forest accent. She rose and smoothed her dress. She was not tall. 'I'll get him.'

When she had gone Adam looked round the room. A typical cottage kitchen, perhaps, but better furnished than most in the village. The table was covered with a red chenille cloth edged with tassles and there was an aspidistra in the window. There was no sign of children.

She came down and began to put on her coat. She accepted Adam's help without a word. Bert followed her. 'I'm going to Baldwin's for some groceries,' she told him.

Adam watched her close the door. 'Haven't met your wife before.'

'No, she come to Coalway after you went to Wales.' He did not seem inclined to talk about her, and lit a cigarette. 'Now, this strike, Adam. We've started something here, you and me. How do you run one?'

'We'll learn,' replied Adam. He spoke more confidently than he felt. 'The first thing we've got to do is form a union and collect some money. We need a meeting for that.'

'Yes.'

'The main thing is to keep the men keen and see they don't start drifting back to work.'

'Yes.'

'Joseph Cowmeadow will help us. We'll get him to come and talk to the men.'

'Yes.' Bert was relieved that Adam had some firm proposals.

'Then we'll negotiate with Sully.'

'Let's go and see Joe this afternoon.'

She felt the first twinge as she was coming downstairs. It was a strange tightening of the muscles over her hips, and it caused reactions deep inside her. She accepted it less as pain than as a sign that the great experience that she had been both looking forward to and dreading had started. Determined not to tell Emma right away, she walked to the bottom of the garden and waited. The next pain came stronger and she leaned against the wall, looking down at the grass along the edge, until it passed. She wondered at the child inside her, signalling that it was ready to come. Soon it would signal again, and then again, more impatiently. And each time there would be pain, and then the final urgent moment. She would have to tell Emma soon, but not yet; it was still her secret. Mrs Phelps, the midwife, had told her that it might be many hours after the first onset before she would have to go to bed. She was pleased she had put the oldest sheets on the bed that morning, sheets that would take the blood and could be destroyed if necessary. Though she wanted a girl, for Adam's sake she hoped it would be a boy. 'I reckon you'll have a boy,' Mrs Phelps had said. 'You be carrying low.'

As she entered the house she felt another twinge. 'I think I've started,' she said to Emma.

Emma donned her coat and bonnet and sped off for the midwife. She returned with Mrs Phelps, important and businesslike, at her heels.

'Don't go to bed till you have to. They send 'em to bed too soon nowadays.' She looked at Catrin's bulge with an expert eye. 'Of course, you never know what's going to happen, but I reckon you have a bit of time yet. I'll look in later.'

When the pains became more frequent Emma advised her to go to bed. She visited her periodically, had a few words, nodded, and went down again to continue cooking the evening meal and heating the bath water for the men.

After he had bathed Adam came up to see her. He bent over and embraced her. 'How lovely it'll be when the baby have come.' But after a few minutes he had to return downstairs to have his meal. After eating it he came again and sat concerned as she had a contraction. After it she quietened down, but he was still unsettled. Catrin thought it was the mystery of childbirth that frightened him. He placed his hand on hers, and she pulled it to her face and kissed it, red and rough and engrained with coal though it was.

'My hand's dirty,' he said.

'No, it isn't.' Distraught, she seized it with both her small white hands, as if she was trying to envelop his flesh with her flesh. She wanted him to stay with her.

'I be sorry, Catrin, I must go now. To a meeting. I'll be back as soon as I can.'

Of all the people in the house he was the only person really close to her, the only one who was part of her. She wanted him to stay until her baby was born, but he had to go to a meeting. Or was he like other men and thought having a baby was a woman's job and wanted to keep clear? No, he would have stayed if he could. She realised she must not be unreasonable, so said nothing. The next contraction came, and she turned her face to the wall.

When it was getting dark Emma put an oil lamp on the side table. It lit up the sweat on Catrin's brow. She placed her hand on her swollen belly to see if she could feel movement. Then another pain gripped her inexorably. She shouted out just as Mrs Phelps bustled in. She examined her and drew back the bed clothes.

'Start pushing when you're ready, love.'

Catrin clung to the brass rail at the top of the bed and pushed.

'Cry out when you want to. It helps. You should have heard Dolly Dobbs up the lane pushing her twins out yesterday. Now it be your turn. Come on. Push!'

The shadows cast by the oil lamp leapt against the wall. Catrin pushed and cried out. The pain, the tension, the sweating, went on for hours, or so it seemed. She bore down again and again, and then just as she felt she could push no more, there came relief. Like the whimper of an animal came the thin, hesitant cry of a child. She listened as it grew louder and firmer. It was her child. She heard Emma say, 'It be a boy, Catrin, a lovely boy.'

She opened her eyes to see Mrs Phelps peering down at her. 'There, there my love. About six pounds, I should think. Now you just lie quietly for a bit while I tidies you up.' Mrs Phelps and Emma bustled about.

Catrin did not care for herself. She felt torn, ravaged and tired; but she had brought her child into the world. She asked for him and placed him on her breast. In the dim light she could just see his red face, beautiful in its ugliness. He had stopped crying and was whimpering, moving his head from side to side. Then he smelt Catrin, opened his tiny mouth and sought her nipple.

Later Emma wrapped him gently in part of an old flannel blanket and put him in a cot Adam had made from a wooden box, and covered him with the brown jersey that Catrin's grandmother had knitted for Adam.

Cornelius visited her on his way to bed. He touched the baby's cheek with a shaking finger. 'Lovely, my dear. I said it would be a boy, didn't I? He's going to be my boy, you see.'

George followed him, and stood at the bottom of the bed, embarrassed. Catrin gave him a smile. 'Not gone to the meeting, George?'

'No, thought I'd stay home in case we had to fetch the doctor.' He looked at the scrap in the cot, smiled at Catrin and then backed out of the room, pleased to go.

All she wanted to do now was sleep.

'Any more hot water?' asked Mrs Phelps.

'Yes, plenty,' said Emma. 'Up here?'

'No, downstairs. Let's have a nice cup of tea.'

❧ ❧

Adam had booked the big room at the British Lion for the meeting which Joseph Cowmeadow was to attend. The colliers arrived early, collected their pints and went upstairs. The room was full; the air hummed with a buzz of excited conversation, enlivened by an occasional guffaw.

Joseph Cowmeadow arrived in good time, and tethered his horse in the stable at the back of the pub. Adam knew he did not approve of drink and apologised for holding the meeting in a public house. 'But it was the only place big enough in Park End. I asked Mr Meek if we could use the Chapel, but he said unions was the instrument of the devil and the answer was No.' Adam had, in fact, been relieved that the Minister had turned him down. At the British Lion the men would get their beer. Beer always lubricated proceedings.

'I believe,' said Joseph grandly as he expanded his chest, 'that our movement is nearer to the church than to the devil. We, too, are following God's work in improving the lot of working people. But to the meeting.'

He made a rousing speech. He treated his audience to a catalogue of iniquities indulged in by the coalmasters, and then got down to the essentials. 'The first thing to do is form a lodge. Since one was formed in Cinderford last week we have set up others for the Trafalgar and Lightmoor men. Now we want one here in Park End. Later we'll set them up in Berry Hill and Whitecroft and Yorkley – everywhere in the Forest where there are collieries.'

He guided the men through the technicalities, and the union lodge for Park End was formed. Then they elected lodge officials and a committee. Adam was elected secretary; Bert was elected chairman.

'Now,' said Joseph Cowmeadow, 'the next step is to approach Mr Sully and arrange a meeting with him to discuss your grievances. I shall be happy to arrange that. And then we'll end the strike on our terms.' The men cheered.

'Remember,' Joseph said in conclusion, his eyes twinkling as he delved into his well-stocked memory of biblical quotations, 'the labourer is worthy of his hire.' The men stood and stamped and cheered again. Adam reckoned with satisfaction that the cheers could be heard by Sully in his drawing-room two hundred yards away.

Adam and Bert accompanied Joseph Cowmeadow to the stable. 'Things are going well,' he declared. 'We shall soon have enough lodges to form a proper Forest of Dean Branch of the Amalgamated Association of Miners.' He paused as he took the horse's reins. 'And I expect I shall become the branch agent.' He mounted his horse. 'You know,' he said once he was aloft, 'you shouldn't have brought them out on strike before they were in the union. Negotiations with Sully should have come first, and only if you got nowhere should you have called a strike.'

Adam had been a little put out that Joseph Cowmeadow had taken it on himself to arrange the meeting with Sully. This vexation was now compounded by his annoyance at being admonished for not enrolling the men in a union before calling the strike. 'You know, Joseph, I've the greatest admiration for you, but you weren't at the meeting at the double oak and you didn't get the strength of the men's feelings. They were bursting. The decision to strike was spontaneous.'

'I know, I know. But I would have done it differently. However, you'll learn to handle things in time.'

'Wonderful chap,' said Bert when Cowmeadow had gone.

'Yes. But I hope he isn't going to interfere too much in our lodge.'

Adam arrived home flushed with the excitement of the evening. George had gone to bed. Emma was sitting at the side of Catrin's bed, knitting by the dim light of the lamp. 'Adam, at last,' she said, rising. 'Come and sit with Catrin and admire your son.' She went downstairs to her room. As Adam took her seat, he noticed the smell of childbirth and of blood. Catrin held out her hand to him and he grasped it. He pulled his chair closer and leaned over and kissed her. The baby, his son, was asleep in his box. Adam looked down at him, his creation and hers. Tears came into his eyes. He had always wanted a son and now he had one. So small he was, so helpless.

'How are you, Catrin? You've had a rough time.'

'Very tired I am. Mrs Phelps said it wasn't an easy birth, but the baby's here now.'

He kissed her again, and then undressed and climbed gently into bed beside her and put his arms round her shoulders. She caressed his chest with her cheek a few times as if trying to get to the heart of him.

He contemplated the day. It had been one of the most eventful of his life. A son, which he had always wanted, had been born, a healthy, lively child that now lay sleeping in the cot beside the bed; and thankfully Catrin had survived.

But the day had also released in him a feeling of pride and achievement in a different direction. His yearning to make something of his life, to do something more than be a collier grinding away day after day at the coal face for a pittance, so confused and vague a yearning, had suddenly been clarified and had borne its first fruit. He had brought about a lodge that would be a step towards forming a colliers' trade union in the Forest, and he knew that this was where his future was. Contemplating his achievements, he forgot that in both creations he had not been alone.

Then, as he lay there, he was suddenly shocked to find himself wondering which was the more stimulating, the arrival of his son or his election as secretary of the Park End Lodge.

CHAPTER 12

'Adam, carrying a baby downstairs be nothing to be frightened about,' snapped his mother. Abandoning the washing-up, she went upstairs, brought the baby down and dumped it in his lap. 'Now give it a cuddle.'

Adam did as he was bid, avoiding George's look of disdain, because he knew his views on men nursing babies. But this was a special baby, and he nursed it willingly; this was his new son and he was fond of him.

Catrin had also come down, for the first time since her confinement. 'So boring it is just to lie up there,' she said, settling before the fire, 'and me feeling so much better.'

'You and Adam made up your mind what you be going to call him, then, Catrin?' said George.

'Yes. Leonard, after my father.'

'In the Forest we never call boys that,' said Cornelius. He was about to elaborate when there was a knock on the door, and Bert entered.

'Hallo, me old butties,' he greeted everyone, his eyes darting round the room. He admired the baby briefly and then sat with Adam away from the fire at the table and talked union business with him. The others pretended not to listen.

'You know you have to write some letters, being secretary, like.'

'Yes.' Adam realised this was a problem. He could read and write, but slowly. 'Will have to do me best, I suppose.'

'I could ask Martha to write them. You could tell her what we wanted.' He looked at Adam. 'She be educated, you know. I'll ask her tonight.'

He rose to go, and Adam rose also.

'You going out, Adam?' asked his mother.

'Just seeing Bert up the road.'

'I know what that means.'

Adam was aware his mother did not like him going out drinking. 'No, I'm not going to the pub.'

'You don't have to go yet, do you, Mr Preece?' said Emma. 'Stay and have a cup of tea.' She lifted the kettle and shook it to see if there was enough water, put it back on the fire and reached for the teapot and the caddy. Bert willingly drew his chair up and joined the circle before the fire.

'Don't agree with this 'ere strike,' said Cornelius.

'Don't start again, Grancher,' said George.

'Well I don't. Don't do no good. You ends up with no money and nothing to eat.'

'You haven't gone without anything to eat yet,' said Emma as she poured water into the teapot. 'Nor have any of the others.'

Cornelius ignored her. 'Next pay day there won't be no money, you know. That's when you'll feel it.'

'Must see how we go,' said Emma. 'We may have to cut down, but we've got a way to go yet.'

Adam suspected she had more in her mustard tin than she let them believe. 'The strike won't last long,' he said.

'I hope not, indeed,' said Catrin. 'I don't know what you want to go on strike for.'

Adam was irritated. He had explained it all to her already. But she pretended she did not understand. 'We be on strike for more money,' he said patiently.

'You see,' Cornelius continued, 'you spends all your savings, and have to let the shopkeeper take the pig to pay your bills. Then you sends your children to bed wi' empty bellies, and you all end up starving.'

'Leave it, Grancher,' said George.

'We had all this when I were a young man,' persisted Cornelius. 'We was starving then. We had no work and no money. And we had riots as a result. The hotheads pulled down all the enclosure walls in the Forest. Caused a lot of damage, but it did no good. We was made to build them up again. And some went to gaol. The leader of them riots was sent to Australia. Transportation, they called it. Good riddance, too, I say. He never come back.' He fell silent, remembering the exciting events of his youth.

'Yes, Mr Turley,' said Bert, 'but things was different when you was a young man.'

'Aye,' said Cornelius. 'Things was different. We was all Foresters then. Nowadays you get foreigners here from England and Wales, from all over the place. Why there be one at Cinderford from somewhere called Poland. They call him a Pole. Now whoever heard of that?'

'Till recently it used to be Foresters against foreigners,' said Bert. 'Nowadays we splits the other way. It be workers against bosses.'

Catrin, was impelled to join in. 'Why can't people stop arguing? Foreigners, unions, strikes, workers, bosses. I don't like all this arguing. Like a war, it is.'

'It is a war,' Adam said, abruptly. 'That's why we be on strike.'

'Adam, stop it,' said Emma. 'Drink your tea.'

Adam shrugged his shoulders and got up. Catrin had annoyed him and he was sorry his emotions had been so high that he had snapped at her. If he stayed in the room he feared he would come out with something else he might regret. 'Come on Bert,' he said and they left the cottage.

☙ ❧

The next evening Adam went round to Bert's house with some union letters for Martha Preece to write for him. He knocked on the door and went in. Martha was reading a book by the fire.

'Hallo, Mrs Preece. Where be Bert?'

'He's gone to see his mother. He won't be back till late.'

'Don't matter.' He smiled tentatively. Though she was about his own age he was, he had to admit, a little frightened of her. Something about her overwhelmed him. Was it the straight look her eyes gave him? He would not want to tell her a lie. Bert had said she was educated, and perhaps that was the reason for his feeling distant from her. She was a strange woman, seemed detached from the world. No wonder the other women in the village didn't get on with her.

'Bert said you would write some letters for the union.'

'Did he? Yes, I'd be pleased to.'

He produced a sheet of paper from his accounts book. On it in his bold but uneven hand he had written the names and addresses of people he wanted to write to. She invited him to sit down, and he told her what he wanted said. She listened, asked a few questions and made notes. She seemed so confident.

'You find writing easy, don't you?'

'I used to be a clerk at the ironworks.'

Adam was losing his uneasiness in her company. His mission now accomplished, he supposed he should get up and go, but he decided to stay until she hinted she had had enough of him. He was pleased when she asked him about his work in Wales and what life was like there. Then she asked how he had met and married Catrin and brought her back to the Forest.

She made some tea, and they sat before the fire drinking it.

'How's the strike going?' she asked.

'We hope Joseph Cowmeadow will be seeing Sully about the men's claims shortly, and I'll be going with him.'

They talked about establishing more lodges and forming them into a Forest union. Adam was surprised at her grasp of the problems that confronted them.

'Have you read much about trade unions?' she asked.

'No, not much. Not anything, really. It be new to me, all the detail, like. I had a friend called Emrys in Wales who was always reading trade union books and newspapers. He used to talk to me about union matters. I wish I'd listened more to him now.'

He rambled on. She said little, letting him do the talking. Suddenly something he had wanted for some time to tell a sympathetic listener burst out. 'I've always felt us colliers should have something a bit better than a long day in the pit and a bed to sleep in at night and should have more money to buy things with. But it was only when I got back to the Forest that I realised we should do something about it.'

'Yes.'

She uttered but that one word, but he felt she was storing away in her mind all he was saying. 'I learnt a lot from that meeting I went to at Cinderford with Bert. Joseph Cowmeadow really inspired me. He made it all so clear what we should be doing. But I'm not sure – ' He stopped abruptly; he had never spoken out like that to anyone before in his life.

'Go on. Not sure about what?'

'I want to be a miners' leader like Joseph Cowmeadow, but I don't know if I can. When I talk to the men as I did at the double oak I feel I could do it. But afterwards I wonder if my mind is clever enough to argue with people like Sully.'

She said nothing and drank her tea. He wondered whether she thought he was talking rubbish, and glanced over at her. She had been gazing into the fire, but looked up at him at the same instant. He looked away quickly and she directed her gaze into the fire again, and he felt cut off from her. What did she think of him? He searched for a new topic of conversation. If he did not find one he would have to go. Yet he wanted to stay. 'You say you used to work in the ironworks,' he said at last.

'Yes, in the office.'

'I've heard of girls working in the ironworks pushing trucks around, like, but never of them working in the office.'

'They were desperate for a clerk and I knew the manager. He got the job for me.' She looked at him with a smile. 'It's only rich women who don't work when they get the chance, you know.'

'What about the men in the office?'

'They didn't like it. People always assume a man can do a job better than a woman, and I didn't think I would keep the job for long.'

'You didn't lose it, though?'

'No, I kept it – at least until I had a row with the boss.' She stood up and went to the mantelpiece and looked down at him. 'I kept it because I was better than they were. And the boss knew it. But he paid me less than the male clerks. It's amazing how people's scruples are overcome when cash is involved.'

'Did you find the work easy, like?' asked Adam. He, too, would have thought a man better at office work than a woman, though office work was not particularly manly. His experience of office workers was that they did little work and thought no end of themselves with their tidy suits and clean hands. And they earned more than colliers.

'Yes, it was easy enough. It was the only job I've ever had.' She turned round impatiently with a quick movement that sent her skirt swirling. Her face became animated. 'I'd like a real job, one that I could get my teeth into.'

Adam looked up at her. For a moment he visualised a tiger seizing a lump of meat. But she was calm again immediately. She went over to a cupboard, took down a tobacco pouch and some cigarette papers and sat at the table.

'Do you smoke?' she asked.

'No – er – I don't.'

She began to make a cigarette, her neat fingers manipulating deftly. Adam had never seen a woman smoke.

'I do occasionally. This is Bert's spare set.'

She took down a spill from the mantelpiece and lit it at the fire. He looked at her profile, her face rosy in the glow, as she leaned forward. She lit the cigarette and threw the spill into the fire, where it flared yellow. Then she sat down and crossed one leg over the other so that her skirt revealed her ankles. As she puffed smoke into the air she looked at Adam and smiled, amused at the impression she had caused.

'Only Bert has ever seen me smoke,' she said. 'And you.'

She thinks she has shocked me, thought Adam. Perhaps she has, he admitted to himself. 'Where did you learn to do office work, then?'

'I didn't. But I had a good education when I lived in Gloucester.'

'I thought you come from the Forest.'

'I do. I left when I was six. My mother was ill and had so many kids she did not know which way to turn. So her elder sister offered to take me. She had gone to Gloucester as a servant when she was twelve. Board and lodging and five pounds a year in exchange for ninety hours slavery a week. She was the only servant in the house and had to do everything. But when she was eighteen she married the only son.'

'She what!'

'Yes, it's probably the first such case in history. She was with child, of course, but he insisted on marrying her. A very loving marriage it was, too. The baby died, and my aunt couldn't have any more. Then some years later he died – smallpox I think it was – but he left her quite comfortably off. So when she heard my mother was going under with illness and children, she took me over and brought me up. Gave me a good education, too. I've always been grateful to her.'

'Why did you come back to the Forest?'

'My father died, my brothers and sisters had married and gone off, and not one of them wanted mother to live with them. Can you believe it? The sods.'

Adam winced. He had never heard a woman use the word. But he was experiencing a lot of new things today. Though she could be calm outside, she was clearly capable of feeling strongly inside.

'So I came to this house where my parents had moved to, and I lived with her. At first she was well enough for me to work at the ironworks. Then I married Bert and he came to live with us here. Then I lost my job and a few weeks ago she died.'

Adam looked at her. She was an amazing woman, aggressive and frightening, attractive and feminine, by turns. Why was she telling him all this?

She cut through his thoughts. 'You said you thought you could lead men like Joseph Cowmeadow does and argue with Sully. Well, why

104

don't you join in when you go to the meeting with Sully? You can but try, though from what I hear of Joseph Cowmeadow he never stops talking.'

She stood at the mantelpiece, with one hand on her hip, puffing at her cigarette and, with a faint smile on her face, coolly surveying him with her green eyes.

CHAPTER 13

Hermione Sully was returning from a trip to Lydney where she had paid a social call. Her carriage had entered Park End and was going up the hill towards the gates of her house when it was forced to halt. She sensed trouble. A crowd of colliers with apparently nothing to do were standing in the road ahead. As she saw them they turned their heads in her direction, ugly ragged men, she noted, no doubt employees of her husband out on strike. They began to make a passage for her vehicle when one of them ran up to the carriage and peered inside. She felt his hot breath on her face, and drew back in horror. Having surveyed her, he turned triumphantly to his mates and shouted, 'It be Mrs Sully!' Immediately the crowd surrounded the carriage and cried, 'Mrs Sully, Mrs Sully.'

'Drive on, Edmunds,' shouted Hermione to the driver. 'Use your whip. Drive right through them.' But the horse's harness had been seized and the whip snatched from the driver's grasp.

'Drive right through us, would you?' leered the man who had forced his head into her carriage. 'You be just like your old man. But you won't succeed in driving right through us. Nor will he.'

Hermione seized her umbrella, the only weapon she had to defend herself with and glared at him, She was stricken with fright but was determined not to show it. 'Come on Mrs Sully,' another cried. 'Tell us when your husband be going to give us what we want!'

'Aye, aye,' shouted the mob.

The men, their faces now red with excitement, surrounded the carriage, gesticulating and shouting, and began to rock it. The horse, eyes white and ears back in terror, reared up and tried to free its head from the grasp of the man who had seized it. Hermione gasped as she was rocked against the sides of the carriage. The men looked in and grinned at her.

'One, two. One two,' the colliers chanted in rhythm as they rocked.

The carriage was near to rolling over when a voice rang out over the chant of the colliers. 'Stop you fools. Stop!' Hermione saw a young man pushing his way through the crowd. He tore at their clothes in his determination to make a path for himself and, reaching the carriage, grabbed at the men rocking it. 'Stop. What the hell do you think you're doing?' he panted with fury. He looked into the carriage. Hermione stared at him, her face white and her eyes large with terror. Having confirmed who the occupant was, Adam turned and faced the men. 'This isn't the way to end the strike, mates. Mrs Sully's not the enemy. Don't you understand that?'

The men drew back and when he saw that he had them under his control he looked again into the carriage.'It's all right, Mrs Sully. They won't hurt you. They're on strike and their families are hungry.' He looked down at her well-nourished body, and Hermione could read his thoughts. 'They're angry because your husband won't see us and discuss our grievances.' The crowd, though backing, continued to shout abuse. 'You might remind him we're waiting,' he added gruffly to Hermione, and turning away he addressed the men. 'Now stand back and let the carriage through.'

They stood back obediently if sullenly, and the carriage drove on and through the Sully gateway.

❧ ❧

Sully looked up from his desk as Hermione flounced into his study with long strides and pouting lips. He did not like to see her upset. For one thing she unloaded her anger on him; but more than that, he wanted her to be happy because, in spite of all her ill humour and her demands, he was fond of her.

'James, you must do something about this wretched strike. I had an intolerable experience when I came back in the carriage just now. There was a crowd of your colliers in the road outside the house. They surrounded the carriage, and rocked it and jeered at me. I thought it was going to be upturned and they would assault me. I was extremely frightened.'

Sully was concerned. Things were turning nasty. He came from behind his desk and took her hand.

'I shouldn't be here now if a young man hadn't come along and rescued me.'

'Who was he?'

107

'I don't know. He had brown hair and was quite young and good-looking. But he was one of the mob. They paid attention to him so he must have been a leader of some sort.'

'Oh, my dear,' Sully could understand her distress, especially as she normally saw his workmen standing respectfully aside raising their caps. He pressed her hand and wanted to take her into his arms.

She shook him off impatiently. 'James, if all this is the result of the introduction of a trade union among your men, I must say I cannot approve of it.'

'I don't approve of it either, Hermione, and it's shocking that you can't drive freely through the streets. But fortunately you suffered no harm.'

'I don't know I want to stay in this wretched village if this sort of thing is going to continue. You must end this strike as soon as you can.'

'Yes dear, I will.' He led his wife into the drawing-room and suggested she should rest before the fire. She subsided into an armchair and relaxed; she loved the luxury of a fire. Sully noted that his concern had mollified her and he rang for a maid to bring some tea. When it arrived she was well recovered, and presided over the teapot with an elegance that only she possessed.

'How did your visiting go?' he enquired.

'I left our cards with that newly arrived woman in Lydney. I didn't call, of course, but I will do so next time.' She offered him a sandwich.

Sully sensed that, apart from the incident, the afternoon's excursion had been satisfactory.

'Lady Campbell thinks it is worth cultivating her.' She always referred to Lady Campbell with awe, for she was the wife of a knight, and the highest person in the social scale Hermione knew. 'Lady Campbell thinks she has an unmarried nephew in his twenties coming to stay with her.'

'Good,' said Sully, though he was not clear whether the nephew was Lady Campbell's or the woman in Lydney's. But it didn't matter. Hermione was never happier than when she was husband hunting for Alice. Yet afterwards it seemed to bring her so much anguish.

'I don't think you take Alice's problems seriously, James.'

'She wouldn't call them problems, my dear.'

'We shall never get her suitably married if she never meets any men.'

'She's only twenty, Hermione. There's plenty of time yet.'

'She gets no fun. A girl of her age should be out visiting every day and dancing every night.'

'You took her to a dance at Coleford Town Hall once.'

'And a most unsuccessful outing it was, I must say. It was patronised by rough, red-faced tradesmen, as I recall, who trod on her feet and ruined her shoes. They preferred the gallops and couldn't dance the waltzes. Not the sort of men we could possibly invite here.'

She sipped her tea, her mind continuing to concentrate on pursuing her prey, a man for Alice. 'James, nothing has come from that visit to the Crawshays and we know there is an eligible unmarried son there. We must return their invitation to dinner soon, and make sure the son – what's his name? Hubert? – comes as well.'

'Yes, if you wish.'

'We could invite the Campbells at the same time.'

If they came, thought Sully, it would raise our status in the eyes of the Crawshays. But the Campbells tried to keep their distance from Hermione.

'Yes, my dear. We'll invite the Crawshays when I have less to worry about.' It would have pleased him if she had asked what he was worrying about. But she didn't; she was selecting another sandwich.

He went back to his study and looked out of the window. It was a dull, windy day. Smoke from the furnaces was sweeping down over the station and sheets of old newspapers were blowing against the railings. Six hundred of his men were now on strike. The pits had an unreal, desolate appearance. They were silent; and noise meant money. All the profits that he had piled up in the last two years were being eaten into, like a bag of oats savaged by an army of rats.

He had never had a strike on his hands before. Perhaps he had been lucky. Unrest among the workers he had experienced, scowls and whispered remarks, yes, though he had always pretended not to notice them. But not a strike. He was, of course, in a strong position to beat them. The Brook-All Ditches colliers, he had been told – and he hoped his spy service was reliable – were agitating to go back to work and it was only pressure from the New Fancy and Park End men that kept them out. He was not surprised that they wanted to return. They probably knew he was considering closing the pit. He'd also been told that the men might be prepared to give up their claim for a five per cent increase if he agreed to weigh their coal on bank. On the other hand, rumour had it that the Crawshays were prepared to yield the five per cent to their workers, and Brain at Trafalgar had reached some sort of agreement on weighing. Such actions by these other coalmasters would make it hard for him to resist the claims of his own men.

It was becoming dark and he called for a lamp to be brought in. He tried to set aside his thoughts about the strike. He had a theory that in the end problems solved themselves. If so, the solution to his present problem would come in time, and when it came it would show itself to be the obvious and only one. But he could not forget the strike.

He pulled the lamp nearer, for he liked plenty of light, and began to write to his brother Charles in Somerset about it. When it was over, he said, he was certain trade would improve. The demands for fuel for the ironworks, to say nothing of the coal scuttles in the sitting-rooms of Gloucester and Cheltenham, would mend their fortunes. He went on to ask Charles's advice on how much he should yield to the strikers. After all, even if he was in control, half the Park End pits belonged to Charles, and he didn't want to take sole responsibility in case things went wrong. His pen scratched across the pages as they filled with his small, neat handwriting.

❧ ❧

Catrin loved young Lennie so much that she was always picking him up just to feel him in her arms. Every time she nuzzled his head to her face his baby smell drifted to her nostrils and enchanted her afresh. Emma said she was spoiling him, but this was her hard exterior talking. When Emma nursed him there was a gentleness in her eyes that Catrin had never seen before, and when she thought no-one was looking she would coo at him and tickle him and smile at him as he lay gurgling. Emma never complained about the dirty nappies that had to be washed, and she supported Catrin against Cornelius when he suggested that nappies that were only wet should not be washed but dried in front of the fire.

But though Catrin was enchanted by her baby, life was not all bliss. She was disappointed that Adam did not spend more of his time with her and the baby now he was not at work all day. Until the strike had begun she had at least seen him occasionally in the evenings, but nowadays with the strike she did not even get that. She felt so alone when he was out. Emma and Cornelius's company was no substitute. She had reached an accommodation with Emma, a kind of truce with both sides watchful and suspicious, and old Cornelius was friendly enough; but it was more of Adam's company she wanted.

Today she stood behind him as he sat at the table writing. As she put her hands on his shoulders and kissed his neck and smelt his thick

110

unruly brown hair, she realised she would do anything for him. She would even write the union letters Bert had suggested his own wife should write, letters she had been disappointed Adam had not asked her to write. She was educated enough and would have done it for love of him, even though she had no wish to help the lodge or union or whatever it was called.

'Come with me to Baldwin's while I do some shopping,' she said. 'We can push Lennie in his pram.' She looked at the second-hand pram that Mrs Phelps had procured for her. It had cost only three shillings but, as Mrs Phelps had warned, it had needed a good scrub.

'Catrin, my love, men don't like being seen out with babies in prams. Anyway I'm afraid I'm too busy with the union today. I must be off in a few minutes to a meeting.' He gave her a smile and pulled her towards him.

She pushed him away. Another wretched meeting. 'You're obsessed with this union thing you've got yourself involved in.' Immediately she wished she had not spoken; she could see her unaccustomed fire had unsettled him.

But he ignored her aggression and responded quietly. 'I love what I'm doing, Catrin. This is me, you must understand. I told you before we were married I wanted to be more than an ordinary collier. That sort of life would be too dull for me.'

He took up his cap. 'I didn't know then what I wanted to do with my life but I know now I want to do something to improve the lot of Forest colliers. And I know that this strike is important and I'm going to work for it.'

Catrin was taken aback by his sincerity. She also realised the firmness of his reply. She had not seen this side of his character since the trouble with Waldo back in Wales. She was not convinced by what he had said but she knew he would beat her in any argument because his logic and intelligence were greater than hers. She decided not to pursue the matter for the time being. 'Well,' she replied weakly, 'I suppose I must be pleased to see you occupied during the strike, not like the other men, lolling around getting in the way of their wives.'

The following evening Catrin could see Adam was tired and depressed. The family had a quiet meal together, while Lennie slept in the corner in his cot. When the baby woke up and cried Catrin fed him; but he would not settle and began crying again. Cries became screams and they resounded from wall to wall relentlessly. Adam glared at the baby. The

111

two women discussed the cause of Lennie's distress at length while he sobbed away in Catrin's arms.

'You used to holler like that, Adam, when you was his age,' said Grancher. 'Sent us all mad, you did.'

'That's not helpful, Grancher,' said Emma. 'If you can't make a suggestion to stop the poor mite crying, you'd best shut up.'

Suddenly and perversely Lennie stopped in mid-screech and fell asleep. But it was too late for Adam. He got up. 'I'm going out.'

'There is no moon tonight,' said Catrin. 'It's pitch-dark. Covered in mud you'll be when you get back. Why not stay in?'

'No.' He went to fetch his cap and muffler from behind the door. Catrin got up and followed him.

'Adam, what is it, cariad,' she said quietly, placing a hand on his arm. 'Is it the crying? Have I done something to annoy you? If so, tell me.'

'It's not only the crying.' He kissed her on the forehead. 'I be on edge tonight. I feel stifled. I must get some fresh air.'

'You go out for an hour, then.' As she returned to her seat, she felt her shoulders droop in absolute weariness. First Lennie would not stop crying, and then Adam had walked out.

'Let him go,' said Emma as the door closed. 'He's probably going to the pub.'

'It's the drinking I don't like,' said Catrin.

'He don't drink much,' said Cornelius. 'Can't afford to with the strike. He'll sit all evening over half a pint, you'll see.'

'I don't suppose any of them drink much now,' said Emma. 'But in normal times some do drink a lot. And then it be the wives and children that do suffer, with the kids hurried off to bed before their father come home in case he belts them, and an overcooked dinner in the oven. And then he won't eat it, throws it on the floor and beats up the wife. Or forces her up to bed. I've seen it.'

'The ones that gets beaten most are the ones that nag most, I reckons,' said Cornelius.

'Don't talk rubbish,' said Emma, wearily. 'Well, I be going to bed.' And she went into her room.

'Emma knows all about drunken husbands, you know,' said Cornelius when she had gone. 'She had one herself. Because of that she won't brew beer like the other housewives round here. I've told her more than once it be cheaper to brew our own. It be better than what you gets in the pubs and it do keep the menfolk at home. I'd get a drop now and then, too, if she made some. But she don't take no notice of what I says.'

Cornelius was entering one of his expansive moods. 'Now Adam's new pal, Joseph Cowmeadow, he be a temperance man, they tells me, always waving the banner. And he be very religious, too, they do say.' He paused and thought, then continued. 'Being religious is all right, I suppose, but you can overdo it. Get a bit too enthusiastic, like. Anyway, I be surprised that Adam haven't let that there Joseph Cowmeadow make him a teetotaller, he thinks so much of him. But Emma's right. There be a lot of drinking in the Forest.'

'A lot in Coalway, to judge by all the noise and brawling in the streets at night,' said Catrin.

'In Coalway the battle lines between pub and chapel have long been drawn, you know. I reckon we be lucky that in this house we be on neither one side nor the other. Or be we on both?' He chuckled at his joke. 'But I reckons the pub men have won in Coalway. Otherwise there would be three chapels and one pub in the village, not t'other way round.'

He laughed, then became serious. 'Bill, her husband, drank a lot, you know. He were my son, but I must speak as I find. He weren't good to her. I remembers once the men were on short time, like, and Emma hadn't much saved up and there were two small children. He wanted some money for beer. "Just give me a bob, old dear," he said. "You can't expect me to stay in all evening." But she wouldn't give him any and he grabbed thic cocoa tin up there where she keeps her housekeeping money. She grabbed it back and put it behind her. Over there, she was,' he indicated with his hand, 'before the fire. "No, Bill," she said, "You can't have it. When it be in this tin it's as good as spent." But he forced the tin from her hand, emptied it and stormed out.'

Cornelius looked severely at Catrin. 'He'd do anything to get money for his beer, would Bill. Emma found a sovereign in his boot one night. Payday, it were, and she reckoned he did hide it in his boot from his wages before he come home and forgot he put it there.'

The two were silent. Catrin was distressed at the thought of any woman with a sot for a husband, even Emma; and for the first time she felt warm towards her.

∂ ∂

Adam was concerned he had slammed out of the kitchen so precipitately. Yet at that moment he had felt that the narrowness, the ordinariness of the house and the restrictions it imposed on him would send him mad. He peered into the night. Catrin was right. There was no moon and it was dark. But when his eyes had adjusted he could see the faint outlines of the walls and hedges. No-one who had experienced the intense blackness of the pit when the candle had gone out would call this pitch-dark. But he realised his annoyance for Catrin's calling it this was petty.

Where should he go now? What should he do? Certainly not go to the Albion. The place would be dull with lack of customers because of the strike, and he didn't fancy that sort of company anyway. He would walk round the village and think.

Catrin did not seem to grasp what, in his enthusiasm, he had told her about the strike, about his desire to do something useful for his fellows and not be just one of the crowd, taking whatever came. She did not want to know why he was prepared to involve himself in union matters so selflessly, how he could draw sustenance from these ideas. It seemed there was no point of contact between them on this matter. She did not understand what made him tick. 'Why devote yourself and all your energy to other people when you have a family who want you so badly?' she would have asked.

He raised his face to the black heavens and clenched his fists in despair. Then he relaxed. It would have been wonderful if she had supported him, but she had not, and he must accept it and be patient with her. But at the moment all he wanted to do was to heal this pain of conscience he had inside him. He turned and went home, ready to apologise.

CHAPTER 14

When Sully had received a letter from Joseph Cowmeadow asking if he could meet him to discuss the colliers' grievances, he had cursed the man and condemned his impertinence. How dare he ask for a meeting at which he intended to tell him how he should run his business! In his annoyance he had tossed the letter aside; but now, a week later, he sought it out and read it again.

The strike had become worse. As far as he could judge, it had resulted from a spontaneous outburst of rage; and emotions that had risen so quickly could as easily subside. But in this case they hadn't. After the men had come out they had formed themselves into something they called a lodge, which, along with lodges formed at Trafalgar and Cinderford and other coalmining areas, had become a union. By uniting, their strength had increased. *Unitate Fortior* had been Sully's school motto. He now realised its full meaning. Yes indeed, strength did lie in unity. Gunter had told him about a mass meeting of strikers at the Speech House only a few days before. Two thousand men had attended and this agitator Joseph Cowmeadow had urged them, amid great applause, to continue their various strikes until they had attained their aims.

He summoned Gunter to his study. 'Any news on the strike front?' Sully was surprised to hear himself talking as if he were engaged in a military operation.

'I hear, Sir, that Joseph Cowmeadow wants every miner still at work to give one day's wages to a fund he is setting up, so that every striking miner can have 8/- a week strike pay.'

Sully considered. Strike pay would prolong the strike, but he doubted if they would collect enough money for that; the colliers wouldn't want to give away so much of their wages. However, it was a sign that they were not ready to give in.

He sat back in his chair and closed his eyes to think. His head sank on his chest, his body slackened in his chair. Gunter kept silent. After a few minutes he sat up, his mind made up. He would have to yield, just a little. 'Arrange for a letter to be prepared for Cowmeadow saying I will meet him and some of his striking fellows to discuss the Park End men's grievances. Fix an early date.'

     ∾ ∿

When Sully walked over to the colliery offices a few days later he sensed for the first time the discomfort that defeat might bring. He had expected to hear his brother's views on how he should handle the strike by now, but no letter had arrived. So he decided he would give away no more than tactics demanded. At the moment he was not inclined to give away anything.

Waiting for him in the big room on the first floor were Gunter, two other pit managers and a clerk to take notes. Sully and his team sat on one side of a long table with their backs to the wall. Behind them were the windows; a pale autumn sun, already low in the sky, was shining through them. Just right, thought Sully. The sun will shine into their eyes. My face will be in shadow.

The men's delegation entered. Sully was surprised to find it consisted of only three men. They stood in front of the table and Sully scrutinised them. He did not invite them to sit down indeed he had had extra chairs removed and two of them stood awkwardly. The third he guessed was Joseph Cowmeadow. He stood tall and impressive, his greying beard jutting from his plump face. The others he did not know until Gunter passed him a note to say that the man on Cowmeadow's right was his employee Adam Turley who had brought the men out on strike in the first place, and the other was Albert Preece. Sully eyed them up and down, Turley especially. He could not discharge Cowmeadow because he worked for Crawshay, but he could sack this Turley fellow and his mate, and would do so when the strike was over; if he did so now other colliers would only take their places, and there was no point in upsetting the men more by sacking them now. Sully remembered that Crawshay had said he would not discharge an employee because he was involved in a union. Perhaps he was wiser than he appeared.

But Sully had no time to think about such things now. 'Well, Cowmeadow, I see you have brought with you two of the men who appear to have grievances against me.'

'I have,' replied Joseph Cowmeadow.

'You don't work for me, and there is no reason why you should be present here, but I am told you are against strikes in general and presumably against this one in particular.'

'That is true, Sir. I am against strikes. I believe the way to solve difficulties between masters and men is to get around a table and talk about them.' Joseph Cowmeadow stared impassively down at Sully, and the coalmaster regretted that he had not offered him a seat on the other side of the table.

Sully searched the other's face for knowledge of the man. He feared he was going to be a doughty opponent; and he decided he did not like him. He had thought that with his reputation for being against strikes Cowmeadow would be easy to deal with. But it seemed he was wrong, and he now wished he had not agreed to accept him as a member of the delegation.

Joseph Cowmeadow began with the men's case for a five per cent increase in rates. He kept his eyes on Sully, only occasionally allowing them to flicker over Sully's team. He spoke slowly and compellingly and, ready as he was to despise him, Sully was surprised at the grasp he had of the intricacies of the case he was making and could not but marvel at the flow of words that came so readily from him.

But Sully was unused to being talked at, and he soon interrupted. 'I am not to be lectured on the economics of the coal trade. You appear to have no idea of the cost of running a colliery and the enormous risks of investing money in one. The simple truth is that if I granted the increase you are asking for I would have to put up coal prices. If I did this, I would lose my share of the already diminishing autumn trade.'

His words, as they left his lips, inflamed his growing anger, though his cold exterior remained calm. 'Now tell me what you have to say on the other matters you are concerned about.' He referred to some notes. 'The weighing of coal at bank, the reduction of hours on Saturdays and the payment of wages fortnightly.'

He listened impatiently to what Joseph Cowmeadow said about them, and argued on each point; but a feeling of unease spread gradually over him as his opponent calmly dealt with each reply he made. On some occasions he realised his arguments were unsound as he uttered them, and this annoyed him more. But he reminded himself that the initiative was always with him.

When he decided he had had enough, he rose. 'I have given good, solid reasons why it is impossible to meet your demands, and I advise the men to return to work before they become even more impoverished than they are at present. The meeting is over.'

After the delegation had left the room he sat down again and thought. That might do the trick. He had received three of the men's representatives to discuss matters and allowed Cowmeadow to let off steam. The others seemed to be nonentities; they hadn't uttered a word. Perhaps his show of determination would convince them he was not going to yield an inch. Then they would give in and advise the men to go back to work.

He went to the window, which overlooked the yard. The light was going now, but he could see the yard was filled with colliers. As Joseph Cowmeadow emerged from the building there was a buzz. He pushed through the crowd, jumped on a low wall by the gate and began to address them. Sully could hear his voice though not his words; but there was no doubt of the colliers' response. They turned and looked up at the window where he was standing. He drew back. He heard the boos and shouts of rage. Then there was a shout, 'The strike goes on!' and with a cheer they surged out of the yard and down the road.

So he had been unsuccessful. Sully turned from the window and sat at the table in the empty room. It seemed bigger now everyone had gone; all humanity had been drained from it. He reflected again on the afternoon's events and then, realising how tired he was, rose and slowly left the room. The staircase and hall were deserted; everyone had gone home. He suddenly felt alone, terribly alone. As he walked home he could still hear the men shouting and cheering as they went through the village – hungry and shabby though they were, they were not alone.

❧ ☙

After the meeting with Sully, Adam invited Bert and Joseph Cowmeadow to the British Lion to discuss the meeting with Sully over a drink. Joseph Cowmeadow refused, his whiskers bristling at the thought of taking liquor. 'Alcohol is the drink of the devil. It causes more problems than it's intended to solve. But I'll sit outside with you and talk about this afternoon's events while you have your drinks. I'll have water.'

So Adam and Bert sat down at a bench outside the pub with scrumpy before them – half a pint each was all they could afford – and Joseph Cowmeadow had a glass of water.

'You made a first-class case, Joseph,' said Bert.

Adam agreed. 'I wish I could put the facts as well as you did. But we didn't get anywhere.'

Joseph Cowmeadow grunted. He had made a rousing speech to the men in the colliery yard after the meeting to keep their spirits up, but his true feelings now came out. 'Sully didn't yield to any of our claims. There was no sign of compromise. I think we had better admit defeat.'

Adam was aghast. 'We can't give in like that. P'raps you overwhelmed him a bit. That's why he wouldn't carry on talking.'

Joseph Cowmeadow shot him a hostile look. Adam could see he had upset him. 'I made my points as well as I could. No, I think we must concede.'

But Adam was not to be suppressed by a few haughty words. 'Perhaps you should have handled him differently. All we can do is persuade and show we accept he is boss but it be in his own interests to give us what we want.'

'When you've my experience, young man, you'll think differently.'

Adam was now ruffled in turn. 'I think the only way I can.' He attempted a more tactful approach. 'Look, Joseph, there are different ways of dealing with Sully. We must try again. I want to get something for the men out of this strike. In the end it may not be everything we want, but it must be something.'

Bert, who had been watching the argument with apprehension, his eyes darting from one to the other, stroked his moustache nervously. 'What happens now, then?'

'I'll write to Sully,' said Joseph Cowmeadow 'and ask for another meeting. At it we'll settle the strike, and if we can salvage anything so much the better.'

'We'll fight,' said Adam. 'We must fight. And next time I should like to say a few words, if you don't mind, Joseph. After all, Park End is my pitch. Perhaps I could put the case for weighing on bank. I feel specially strongly about that. I think it be the key to our wages problem.'

'We'll see.' And with that Joseph Cowmeadow rose and departed.

There was a silence. 'Come on, old butt, cheer up,' said Bert. 'Come inside and have another drink. It's too early to go home yet.'

'Can't afford it.'

'I know we pays for our own in these hard times, but have one on me.' They went inside the pub. Bert bought the drinks and pushed his way through the throng of workers from the Park End Ironworks and Tin-plate Works – there were no colliers – to Adam who had found places on a bench in a corner by the fire. They sat side by side in silence, a companionable silence that contrasted with the abrasive discussion with Joseph Cowmeadow earlier. Since Adam's return from Wales the ties of friendship between him and Bert had pulled them closer than they had been before.

'I came round to see you on Saturday,' said Adam at last, 'but you wasn't there.'

'No. Went to Gloucester.'

Adam was silent. He guessed from gossip what that meant. Then, feeling the pause must be filled, he said, 'Go to the Alhambra, then?'

Bert moved closer to him. 'Want to know?'

'No, no.'

'Well, I'll tell you. I'd like to, but don't say a word to the others.'

'All right.' The warmth of Bert's friendship stole across to Adam and he sensed Bert's need for someone to confide in.

'Well I, er, see someone there, like.'

'Where? At the Alhambra?'

'Yes, she works there. In the pit bar. I noticed her the first week I went there. I only went because I'd had a row with Martha and wanted a bit of life and fun away from Coalway, like. I had a drink at the bar, and I thought she was a nice girl. Rather tarted up, you know, barmaids always are, but a nice girl. She looked you in the face when she gave you your beer, not like the others who thump it down and look over your shoulder while they wait for the money.'

Bert was now in full spate and grateful for a willing listener. 'I began to go most Saturday nights, and after a few weeks we got quite friendly and I asked her – her name's Molly – if I could take her home after she finished. She said yes, so I did, but she didn't ask me in. I didn't expect it, really. Same thing happened the next few times. I wanted to take her somewhere, but there's nowhere to go after the theatre is over except to some pub or other. Then one night when we got to her house she asked me if I would like to come in and have a cup of tea. She said her mother wouldn't mind. So I said yes, and met her mother. Nice woman. Didn't like her daughter working in the bar at a music hall, but she had to do something. She seemed pleased Molly had picked up with a decent man!'

Bert grinned. 'That was me,' he said and nudged Adam, who laughed. 'I was soon going home with her every night I went to Gloucester. The first thing she did when we got to her home was to take off all the muck on her face. Underneath it all she was lovely. Her mother usually went to bed when we got in and we spent the rest of the evening just talking, and I would catch the last train home, the mail train it was.'

So far, thought Adam, this did not sound like the unsavoury rumours about Bert's visits to Gloucester he had heard. But he was curious now. 'Was that all?'

Bert considered, and then he grinned. 'No, it wasn't. We got more and more friendly, really close. And then it happened. It was lovely. Never had anything so exciting, I can tell you. To put it crudely, me boy, I got right in, belly to belly. Never had it like that with Martha.'

'How long did it go on for?'

Bert looked surprised. 'About half an hour, I suppose.'

'No, the affair.'

'Oh, I still see her.' He took a drink of his cider. 'You know, somehow I don't think Martha ever really fancied me. I was always begging her for it.' His eyes swivelled round to look at Adam. 'You don't approve of all this, do you?'

Adam smiled sadly. He sensed that Bert was harbouring a feeling of guilt for his relationship with Molly and wanted to dispel it with Adam's approval. 'I wouldn't judge you, Bert. We're all of us different.'

'One time I stayed all night,' Bert continued. 'Got home first thing Sunday morning. Told Martha I missed the last train and had to spend the night at the station. I don't reckon she believed me.'

As they got up to leave, Bert grinned. 'Oh, what the hell. We've got to enjoy ourselves while we can. We never know when we're going to have an accident in the pit or get typhoid or be hit by lightning – anything can happen.'

CHAPTER 15

Adam realised he had to ask Martha Preece to write him another union letter. The necessity of walking to the other side of the village to do this in no way irked him. On the contrary, he set off with a lift to his heels.

Then he remembered what Bert had told him the previous evening. The revelation explained a coolness he had sensed existed between the two. But Bert's relationship with Molly and their drift into bed was none of his business, and he wished Bert had kept quiet about the affair. Bert was an amiable, easygoing fellow and a good friend of his, and he was sorry his marriage was not as happy as it might have been. But then, whose was?

In any case Adam could not see his knowledge of the rift would have any effect on his relationship with Martha. This, he realized, so slight at present, was developing, and he wanted to encourage its development. She was an interesting person and good company; and she understood his thoughts and attitudes and aspirations. And he believed she wanted their relationship to thrive.

He was about to tap on the cottage door when he heard a strange sound. It was a violin, a sad mournful sound that hung in the air. He listened for a few minutes, unwilling to cause the player any disturbance. When the music stopped, he knocked.

'Come in,' Martha called. She returned the violin to its case.

'That was lovely, Mrs Preece.'

'Not really.' Her reply was matter-of-fact, not apologetic.

Adam knew nothing about violins or indeed about music generally; but he knew a good piece of work when he saw one, and he examined the music stand, a solid contraption of oak decorated with brass that shone as if it were alive. Then he looked at Martha's music.

'I've never seen music up close before. Each of these black spots means a note you play, does it?'

'Yes.' She took up her violin again and demonstrated. He looked at her fingers, long, delicate and smooth, with the nails clean and manicured.

'Have a try.' She offered him the violin with a wrinkle of encouragement in the corners of her eyes.

'Oh, no.' He drew back. He did not wish to do any damage. 'Where did you learn?'

'When I lived in Gloucester.'

'Do you practise much?'

'Yes, when Bert is not about. He doesn't like it.'

'Where is he?'

'Out somewhere. He shouldn't be long.'

'I've come to ask you to do another letter for me.'

'Of course.'

He explained what he wanted.

'I shan't be able to do it until the day after tomorrow. I'm going to Gloucester tomorrow. I must see my aunt and do some shopping.'

'I've got to go to Gloucester meself sometime,' he said, 'to get some printing done for the union. Some membership cards, with the name printed on them, all proper like. Joseph Cowmeadow's given me an address.' He paused. 'I haven't ever been to Gloucester.'

She smiled. 'It's easy enough to get there. By train from Park End. Why not come with me?'

He was hoping she would say that. 'That be a good idea.'

'I'm catching the eleven-twenty. We could meet at Lydney junction where we change trains.'

Adam took her point immediately: it was best that no-one saw them leaving Park End on the train together. 'Yes, let's do that.'

Bert came in. For a reason he could not immediately explain Adam was flustered. 'Mrs Preece said she'd do another letter for me,' Adam told him, and was immediately annoyed for being so hasty in explaining his presence.

'Oh, aye, she'll do it.' Bert was casual and seemed more interested in finding his tobacco pouch and rolling a cigarette.

Adam did not mention to Bert that he was going to Gloucester the following day for the printing. There seemed no need to do so. Later he remembered that this was his first deception.

Adam almost missed the eleven-twenty the next morning. He had spent too much time combing his hair and dressing. He retrieved, from the moth balls and lavender at the bottom of the chest, his best suit bought specially for his wedding. This was the first time he had put it on since that day. Then there was finding a collar and a tie to go with it, no muffler today.

Grancher agreed to lend him his watch. 'You puts the bar at the end of the chain in the special hole on your waistcoat,' he instructed. Adam spent a few seconds practising taking the watch out of his pocket, looking at the time and returning it neatly. As he explained to Catrin, one had to be smart to go to a big city.

'You seem pleased with yourself this morning,' commented his mother.

'Never been to Gloucester before. Going on union business.'

'Good thing you be on strike or you wouldn't have the time,' said Grancher. 'Who be paying the fare?'

'Don't worry, Grancher, You're not. It be the Union.'

Adam saw Martha on the platform at Park End station but did not approach her. At Lydney where they had to change trains he followed her up the platform. Neat she was, well dressed and confident. She was wearing a brown suit with a flounced bustle. It did not conceal the curves of her body, the everflowing curves that swayed in sympathy with her graceful movements. Her hat was alive with ostrich feathers. Adam felt proud that he was to accompany such an elegant woman to town. The immense bulk of the Gloucester train came in, clouds of black smoke billowing from its chimney and steam hissing from its pistons.

He followed her into a compartment. She greeted him with a slight but cool smile. They sat opposite each other and looked out of the window for a time. Then they discussed the weather. The easy conversation they had had the previous day was not there now. He was nervous and she seemed taciturn.

By the time the train reached Gloucester, however, they were chatting freely. He helped her down, her hand resting lightly on his arm. He was surprised at the bustle and noise outside the station. A line of hackney carriages stood waiting for customers on the concourse. Some of the horses were tossing their heads and were anxious to be off; others stood quietly, content to stay where they were.

Martha dismissed with a wave of her glove a hackney carriage man who wanted their trade and, grasping Adam's elbow, shepherded him across the cobbled forecourt. 'I think we had better have something to eat before we do anything else, don't you think?'

Adam had not thought about dinner, though now he considered it, he found he was hungry. But where to go, and how much would it cost?

He would have to pay for both of them. 'Yes, but I haven't brought much money.'

'Colliers on strike can't be expected to have money to spare. Come as my guest.'

But women didn't take men out to lunch and pay for them. This expedition was getting quite bewildering.

'We can have a good meal here,' she said, and steered him into the Wellington on the edge of the forecourt.

They sat in the dining-room upstairs by a window overlooking the street. The waiter brought the menu and they consulted it, Martha making suggestions. She ordered steak and kidney pie followed by a sorbet for herself. Adam decided to have the same.

He looked round the room. The other diners were mostly men. At the the next table were three businessmen, talking volubly about their concerns and pausing only to take another mouthful of food or drink another gulp of beer. They were hard-faced and coarse and their confidence and obvious wealth did not conceal it. Did they, wondered Adam, deny their workers a decent wage like the coalmasters? Further away two friends were talking in a slow, smiling manner while they waited for the next course. Adam was fascinated by their easy manners, their sparkling white shirts and well-cut suits. What were they talking about? Did elegant people like this talk about the same things as colliers – money and betting, women and making love to them? Adam glanced at a middle-aged couple at the fireplace, looking ahead, passive and dull, as they slowly munched their food. They spoke not a word to each other the whole time they were there. Adam hoped he and Catrin would never become like them. But he knew they wouldn't; there was always too much to talk about.

My, this was a different world, at the same time intriguing and frightening. Yet it did not attract him. He didn't envy the lives of any of the other eaters in the restaurant – middle-class he supposed they would be called. Life in the Forest with his fellows suited him if only it were more tolerable. He thought briefly about the strike, and then glanced back at Martha and smiled at her.

He had now recovered from his initial embarrassment at being taken for a meal, and began to talk freely. 'I'm glad we come together. I shouldn't have known where to go or what to do.'

'I like it, too.'

Adam wondered if she really meant it. 'Doesn't Bert ever come with you to see your aunt?'

'No.'

Adam realised he was on dangerous ground. He finished his steak and kidney pudding and left his knife and fork at an angle over the edge of the plate. Then he noticed that Martha had placed hers neatly together. He repositioned his own.

'When are you seeing Sully about the strike?' she asked.

'We have done once, but got nowhere. We're seeing him again in a few days time, we hope.' He looked at her with a smile. He wanted to make a confidence. 'You know, I'd love to lead this time instead of Joseph Cowmeadow. Though I suppose I'd be scared and might muck it up.' He became lost in a daydream.

Martha brought him back. 'While you are seeing to your union cards, Adam, I shall go to my aunt's. She lives at Wootton, and I'll be about an hour.'

It was the first time she had called him by his Christian name. Presumably he could now call her Martha. 'Is an hour long enough for you – Martha? I'm in no hurry.'

'It will be today. I don't usually stay long, anyway. I sometimes have lunch when I go –'

Adam felt it was his fault she was not lunching with her aunt.

'– but not always. And this is one day when I don't.'

At the end of the meal she pushed half a sovereign over to him and said quietly. 'Ask the waiter for the bill. And give him a threepenny tip.'

Adam did as he was bid. He knew now how it was done. He could quite confidently bring Catrin here if they ever came to Gloucester together.

'You must let me pay next time,' he whispered as he handed her the change. And then he realised what he had said. She did not comment, but put the change in her purse, snapped the catch and rose.

They walked down to the centre of Gloucester, Adam marvelling at the size of the place. He stopped to watch a coal merchant emptying his coal through the manhole in front of a house – Park End coal, perhaps; gazed through the shop windows at the shop girls, so neatly dressed and polished; marvelled at the whole sides of beef hanging outside a butcher's shop, not one or two, but seven or eight; and avoided being wetted by an apprentice slopping water down the marble slab outside a fish shop.

'Now, this is the Cross,' said Martha. 'Meet me here at 3 o'clock. That will give me time to visit my aunt and you plenty of time to order your

126

printing. And you can have a look round the town as well.' She told him where the printers were. 'And don't get lost!'

The printer's shop was down a twisted back street, close and intimate, older than anything in Coalway. When he had finished his business he ventured further along the street and turned down an alley. Suddenly, the Cathedral revealed itself. Rapt in wonder at its beauty, he compared its size, height and intricacy of design with Park End Church, the only church he had ever known. Was there time to go inside? He looked at Grancher's watch, and decided there wasn't; he must find his way back to the Cross.

He was there early. Martha was on time. She took his elbow and piloted him across the road, dodging the carts and carriages and the horse dung on the cobblestones. 'I'd like to go into the bookshop at the Cross before we catch the train back. Do you mind?'

In the bookshop Martha examined a selection of newly arrived novels. 'I spend all my spare money on books.' She picked up one and began to read at random. Then she looked at the price and handed the book to the shopkeeper. 'I'll take this one, please.'

Adam could not but marvel at her calmness and confidence. He picked up *Flashes of Light* from a nearby display, but could not understand what it was all about. Then he saw *The New Socialism*. It looked interesting.

'If you like it, why not have it?'

'I will, next time I come to Gloucester.'

Martha took the book. 'Wrap this one as well, please. Separately.' She paid for both.

At the station they had twenty minutes to wait before the train came in. Adam bought cups of tea in the waiting room. He suggested that they should have some cakes from under a glass cover on the counter, but Martha declined.

'Tuppence,' said the tired middle-aged woman behind the counter, bored by the discussion about the cakes.

As they sat at the table in the waiting room Adam did not want the train to arrive.

127

CHAPTER 16

Sully fingered Joseph Cowmeadow's letter asking for a second meeting. At their first encounter he had rejected the men's arguments completely. Looking back, he decided his refusal to compromise had, perhaps, been unwise. It had been heavy-handed and it hadn't worked: the men had stayed out on strike. Since then Brain had settled at Trafalgar and he had heard yesterday that Goold was settling at Bilson and Crump Meadow. No doubt there had been other settlements in the Forest as well. These coalmasters would now grab his markets.

His brother Charles had at last written to him from Somerset. His letter was brief and castigatory:

'To allow this damaging strike to continue in the hope of winning outright in the end will, in the present economic climate, have a greater effect on our dividends than reaching a compromise with the strikers now. Once our markets have been lost to our rivals it will be difficult if not impossible to regain them. You must settle at once. It goes against the grain, I know, but it must be done. Do not think about the trade you have lost so far; that's in the past. We'll make it up in time. In settling, concede as little as you must, but give the men all that is necessary to get them back to work.'

Charles had always hectored him even as a child, and his tone grated on him now. But he was right; he usually was. He sent Joseph Cowmeadow a letter agreeing to meet him and his team in two days time.

The first thing Adam did when he rose on the day of the meeting was to look out of the window. It was the dullest day of the autumn so far. Drizzle formed a film of grey round the trees, and moisture dropped from the leaves; everything was in soft focus. He saw the boy from the Park End post office come up the garden path and knock on the front door, and hurried downstairs. It was a telegram! He had never before received the benefit of such a modern wonder as the telegram; nor, as far as he knew, had anyone else in Coalway.

It was from Joseph Cowmeadow. 'Cannot come to meeting today. Ill and unable to move from bed. Cancel meeting.'

The family examined the telegram one by one.

'That have torn it,' said George.

'Well, that be that,' said Emma.

Adam felt as lost as if he were in a coalpit without a light. Then his mind brightened. It seemed liberated. This was the opportunity he had wanted. 'If Joseph Cowmeadow can't come, I shall lead the deputation.'

The others looked dubious.

'I must. The men be this minute assembling outside Park End Church. I arranged it yesterday so we could march down to the colliery offices behind Joseph Cowmeadow. Now it will be me. I can't call it off now.'

On his way to Park End Adam talked to George about the problems that would arise now he was taking on Joseph Cowmeadow's mantle. 'I'll put all the arguments Joseph Cowmeadow put, plus my own.' He gained confdence as he spoke. 'I aim to encourage Sully to believe that it's in his own intersts to yield to us. My proposals, I'll tell him, will make the pits more efficient and the men more contented, and all this will lead to more coal being produced and more profits for Sully.' When George looked doubtful, he said, 'Well, I'll try such arguments.'

They reached Park End. The Church was on the edge of the village. It had an open space in front of its churchyard, ideal for a public meeting, and several hundreds of striking colliers had gathered there. Rain was now falling heavily, sweeping in gusts from the Forest waste. It was washing the Church to a shiny cleanliness, gushing from the gargoyles and splattering on the flat-topped tombs below. On the ground it made pock marks which were instantly washed away; and it soaked the men in their thin coats and woolly hats.

Adam climbed on to a tree stump and addressed them. 'Fellow colliers, in spite of the rain you have come to demonstrate, and demonstrate you shall. Unfortunately Joseph Cowmeadow is ill in bed and can't be with us, so I will lead the deputation. I promise to do my best, I can't do more.' As the wind gusted his words to them, he sensed the men sighed inwardly because Joseph Cowmeadow would not be there. But they gave him a cheer. Heartened by their support, he led them down the path beneath the oak trees to the road and then into the colliery offices yard. He selected half a dozen men, including Bert, to accompany him. With a final wave, but with his heart apprehensive, he led his team up the office steps and through the doorway.

❧ ❦

Outside the men waited.

They waited five hours. Then the front door opened and Sully came out, looking stern and forbidding. He stood at the top of the steps. Behind him was Gunter and other members of Sully's staff, still clean in their suits and collars and ties, with their hair neatly combed. Behind them were Adam and his team, their clothes tattered and ruffled, though the rain on them had now dried off. Adam's face was composed; passive, but not dismayed. Indeed, there was an encouraging light in his eyes.

The crowd pressed forward.

Sully spoke. 'I have just concluded a long discussion with your representatives and make the following offer to end this crippling dispute. These are my final concessions. Take all or none.'

The men were silent.

'I can offer no shortening of the monthly pay period. But I'm prepared to authorise advances when there are five weeks between paydays.'

There were groans.

'Nor can I reduce the hours worked on Saturday.'

'What are you giving us, then?' shouted a collier.

Sully looked up with distaste. 'I am prepared to erect a weighbridge at the colliery and I will provide a checkweighman of your approval to see that the coal is fairly weighed before it leaves the colliery.'

The crowd stirred. That was good.

'I am also prepared to give you the five per cent increase you ask for.'

The men cheered.

'I will now withdraw so that you can discuss the matter. But I advise you to accept.' He was about to go when Bert spoke to him. Sully turned. 'I have also agreed that no man shall be discharged for taking part in this dispute.'

When he had gone, the men shouted acceptance of the settlement. Fortnightly pay could wait, so could a reduction in hours. They had got what they wanted on weighing and had obtained their five per cent. Gunter, who had remained, was asked to tell Sully of the men's decision.

Then they surged forward and hoisted Adam onto their shoulders, and with cheers and shouts marched with him out of the yard and through the village. Down past the ironworks they carried him. The furnacemen in the yard, guessing what the commotion was about, came out in their leather aprons, wiping the sweat off their brows, and waved the tools they had just been using and shouted congratulations. At the tin-plate works some girls rushed out; this was excitement indeed, though any happening would relieve the monotony of their twelve-hour shift. Even the supervisor, who came to see what all the noise was about, looked and waved before he herded the girls back to their work. And so on to the stoneworks and back past the station. Never had Park End known such a demonstration.

~ ~

It was return to work tomorrow, but tonight there would be celebrations. On the meadow in front of the post office two sheep bought with the remainder of the strike fund were killed, gutted and roasted in preparation for a feast. The proprietors of the British Lion, the Bear, the Fountain and the New Inn hastened to the site with barrels of beer and scrumpy to be sold on tick. The colliers arrived with their children and womenfolk; old men who hadn't walked so far in years hurried up with sticks a-flying. The smell of roast mutton rose on high and late-comers to the feast walking down from Coalway stopped and sniffed the air before hurrying on. The mutton was sliced and, clamped between bread bought from the fund from every village shop in the neighbourhood, was passed around until everyone had a helping. They hadn't enjoyed such a good meal in weeks.

Adam was sorry Joseph Cowmeadow was unable to be present, and that Catrin did not come to celebrate his triumph because she had to stay and look after Lennie; but Emma came and took back some mutton for her and Cornelius. Mrs Phelps, the midwife was there, touring the field, greeting the pregnant women and chucking her successes under the chin. Martha joined Bert, and nodded distantly to Adam with just the faint suspicion of a smile of congratulation. Young Billy was there with his girl friend Bessie Tingle and bought her a lemonade to drink with her mutton sandwich.

When the sheep had been reduced to skeletons and the villagers were replete, they stood around the bonfire, the flames flickering shadows over their faces. With tankards of scrumpy in their hands, they congratulated Adam and themselves on a successful end to the strike and joked and laughed until their thin bodies began to protest. Bert sang some of his songs and the villagers joined in. Then the fire burnt low and it was time for bed.

~ ~

131

That night when Adam snuggled down with Catrin in his arms a glow of contentment and satisfaction enveloped him. As they had carried him on his triumphal journey round Park End, his throat had been full and his eyes brimming; but he had smiled, and hoped nobody had noticed his emotion. He was thankful to the men. They were the salt of the earth, these patient, hardworking, comrades of his, and he had been able to do something for them. In Joseph Cowmeadow's absence he, Adam Turley, had taken over and secured a satisfactory settlement. He had argued with Sully, the great Sully, and had won concessions. He had not known his ability.

Yet he felt something stirring within him. He realised that it was ambition. At present it was like that cloud in the bible, no bigger than a man's hand. But it was there, he knew it was there, vague but with the potential to grow and assume immense proportions.

CHAPTER 17

Adam did not see Joseph again until the first meeting of the union executive committee at Cinderford Town Hall, its sole prestigious building. Joseph Cowmeadow was puffing up the steps when Adam came running along the street, skidding in the snow, his face rosy, his eyes bright. He was curious to know what Joseph Cowmeadow thought of his success in ending the strike, but when they met Adam asked him about the illness that had prevented him from leading the delegation.

'It was a severe bout of – er – diarrhoea.'

This was not a dignified illness worthy of the great man, thought Adam, but he expressed his hope he was now better.

'Prevented me from taking the Service at Chapel on Sunday. It was no doubt due to the insanitary conditions in the town, which I have long railed against but which I shall be able to do something about now that I am a member of the Health Board.'

Trust Joseph to turn his indisposition into a public matter that he would put right, thought Adam. 'Well, I be glad the trouble was not more serious.'

Joseph Cowmeadow nodded agreement. As they went in he looked sideways at Adam. 'I gather you handled the meeting at Park End successfully and I congratulate you.' There was no warmth or enthusiasm in his words, but Adam thanked him. At bottom he's disappointed I pulled it off, he thought. He did not know whether he was pleased or sorry at his conclusion.

They walked in silence to their committee room, one of the smaller rooms at the back of the building. It was freezing cold, for though the building was newly built its heating system was not of the best and only lukewarm water reached the pipes in the rooms at the back. But when all the delegates had assembled, the heat engendered by the enthusiasm for the new ideas they formulated soon warmed them up.

Joseph Cowmeadow chose a seat at the head of the table and, without any prompting, Adam noted, began to chair the meeting. 'We can't stop here, fellow delegates,' he said, addressing the other members of the committee as if he were talking to a hallful of colliers. 'Half a dozen lodges is not enough. We must set up one everywhere in the Forest where men are working in pits. I am willing to carry out this task, but I shall need some assistance.'

Adam hastened to volunteer to help him, but suggested they should put first things first. 'We must have a full time secretary – agent, I think they call him.' He knew this was the plum job and he would have liked it. But he realised Joseph Cowmeadow would also want it and he could not challenge him. So he got in first. 'I think Joseph Cowmeadow's the man.'

'If he's full-time he'll need paying,' said the delegate from Trafalgar.

'At the rate we're recruiting members, we can afford it.'

The Trafalgar delegate was cautious. 'If we pays him, I don't reckon he should get more than a collier.' He turned to Joseph Cowmeadow. 'You be a cropper and earns more than most. If you takes this job, you'll lose a bit, you know.'

'Of course,' responded Joseph Cowmeadow with dignity, and formally accepted the job.

Throughout the winter that followed that meeting Adam and Joseph Cowmeadow worked side by side to bring the gospel of trade unionism to the colliers. Together they toiled over difficult roads with snow pressing round their ankles and mud splattering their knees; they addressed meetings in village halls and pubs and formed more and more lodges. Enthusiasm for forming a colliers' trade union swept round Dean like a forest fire.

Joseph Cowmeadow always took the lead at these meetings and allowed Adam only to make a few brief remarks. However, the news of Adam's achievements in the Park End strike had spread through Dean, and Adam felt that, in spite of the inferior role Joseph Cowmeadow had allocated him, by his obvious keenness and sincerity he was eclipsing him in the esteem of many of the men. These were in the main the younger colliers. The older ones were more attracted to Joseph Cowmeadow who, by his spine-tingling oratory, combined religious fervour with appeals to their conservative instincts in his promise of a better life.

But Adam, though now accepted by the committee as Joseph's second in command, was not satisfied with being an appendage to him. He put it tactfully. 'Joseph, we can't carry on going round all the villages together like we do. It's taking too long.' Joseph Cowmeadow glanced at him suspiciously. 'Let's split the load. You do the big meetings, I'll do the others.'

Joseph combed his beard with his fingers and considered. Adam saw he resented his suggestion; he probably did not trust him to do the job as he wanted. 'I suppose it makes sense,' he at last grudgingly admitted; and from then on they campaigned in the villages separately.

Soon Joseph, with Adam in support, was knocking on the doors of all the Forest coalmasters and asking if the union could come and talk about money, hours and weighing machines. More, they asked for the provision of doctors and safety measures in the pits.

Many of the coalmasters slammed the door shut without a word, but some were willing to talk, for the coal trade was now booming and the coalmasters were gathering in greater profits than ever before. With them they could afford to buy off the union and still have ample profits for themselves. The Crawshays embellished the embellishments at Oaklands Park; William Brain invested more money in the experiments he was carrying out to introduce electricity into his pit at Trafalgar; the two Goolds moved into new luxurious residences; and even Sully, though his profits were lower than they would have been had he not obstinately prolonged the Park End strike, could afford to buy Hermione a diamond bracelet for Christmas.

And Adam was learning all the time, not only how to address meetings, but also how to marshal his thoughts, read fluently and write better. He stretched his mind back to his days at the dame school he had attended and tried to recall all he had ever learnt there. It had been a poor education and had ended at the age of ten when his father had died and he had had to go to work in the pit. But it was a foundation on which he could build. His abilities and his confidence grew; and he knew it.

He had realised for some time that he did not support all Joseph Cowmeadow's ideas about the union, but he did not openly oppose him over the committee table on major matters, There were occasional clashes on minor ones but he was careful not to push opposition too far. However, he could see, from an occasional nod of encouragement or a smile at veiled remarks he had ventured opposing Joseph Cowmeadow that he was gaining support among some members of the committee.

'Don't let all this success go to yer head, young lad,' murmured an old collier to Adam as they left after a meeting at which Adam had been praised for making a particularly good contribution to the debate. Adam responded with a smile, though he realised later he had scarcely absorbed the message.

❧ ❦

Catrin's heart rose when Adam came into the kitchen the following Sunday afternoon so much earlier than she expected. She put down her knitting and smiled her greeting to him. She knew that the lift to her emotions she experienced every time she saw him confirmed she still loved him dearly. But all she said was, 'Your Da's here, Lennie.'

Lennie was squatting and patting George's dog which, Emma being out, had taken the opportunity of warming itself in front of the fire. On seeing Adam, Lennie straightened his legs slowly and walked unsteadily over to him, his legs apart, and his arms upstretched. Adam picked him up and sat him on his lap. Lennie was never demonstrative, and Catrin knew that he was honouring Adam by choosing him to be sat on. Adam put his lips on the soft black hair on top of his head, and whispered, 'Hallo, old butt, how bist?' Adam's Forest accent was never thicker than when he spoke to his son.

Lennie did not reply but turned and inspected Adam's face seriously with his large dark eyes. Adam touched his cheek with a finger and pulled him closer. The lad snuggled into his jersey, the brown one old Mrs Evans had knitted.

'Now I didn't see thy vust step, did I? But thy Mam told me all about it. She says thou bist the best baby in the Vorest, and thee only eleven months old, like.'

'Lovely it is to see you talking to Lennie,' said Catrin. 'You so seldom do it.'

Adam sensed criticism but smiled. 'I've so little time.'

Yes, thought Catrin, he has so little time because of this union. He had tried to explain it all to her, but she did not understand what it was all about, mainly, she had to admit, because she did not want to. She certainly could not understand its fascination for him. When the strike had ended she thought he would spend more time with her and Lennie, but no. It was still the union. She hated it for snatching even half an hour from her. Nowadays they no longer sat by the fire of an evening and talked; nor did they go out for walks together at the weekends. Adam's routine most nights on his return from the pit was bath, evening meal and out on union business. When he stayed in it was to receive a visit from Bert, or to clear the table and do some union work.

136

So this afternoon, when he was back early from wherever he had been, was a special treat for her. They could have a happy family hour or two until tea time.

But, no. He put Lennie down on the floor, took down his pen, ink and paper from the dresser and drew a chair up to the table. 'I can get some work in before Mam returns.' He was soon immersed in his work and a contented smile came over his face.

Words rose in Catrin's throat to speak, but she swallowed them. She must not interrupt him. So instead she let her mind wander. She thought about the early months of their marriage when the baby was growing within her, when Adam's eyes sparkled when they met, when she could ruffle his hair in fun, touch his hand, catch his sideways glance as they walked or sense the glow that surrounded him when he held her close. Folly, perhaps, to have thought those days could continue for ever. Any married woman would tell you that life was not like that.

'Where be my *British Miner*, Catrin?' For some weeks he had bought the newspaper to learn how other unions striving to improve their members' conditions were faring. Without waiting for a reply he searched and found it and began to turn the pages. At first when reading it he had run his forefinger under each line, but now he dispensed with this aid. 'This be shocking,' he murmured aloud.

'What is, cariad?'

He read out an account of a strike in Durham, but she could not grasp the point he was making. He started to explain, but let his voice trail away as he read on. In situations like this she could have offered some comment if she could only understand what it was all about. But she did not, and that was that.

She resumed her knitting, glancing from time to time at his face, no longer relaxed and happy, but tautened and worried about what he was reading, and went back to her day-dream. She thought about their first time in her enormous bed on the farm. He had been so timid, so gentle, so anxious not to hurt her, so willing to do what she wanted him to do. He was the first man she had had, indeed the only man she had ever made love to. Timid virgins they had been, finding their way. And as the weeks went by and experience increased, her bed at the farm had become a haven of warmth and leisure, with an expectancy that was always fulfilled.

She wondered sometimes whether he still loved her, but when once she had asked him while they lay in bed at night he assured her he did.

Indeed, he still made love to her, even though Lennie shared their bed, being now too big for the cot Adam had made for him. But he was often tired. There was no sparkle or fun, and afterwards he rolled over and was asleep within seconds. The thought crossed her mind that nowadays he did it more to please her than himself.

Adam finished reading the paper and without a glance at her took down from the dresser his book *The New Socialism.*

She wanted to talk to him. 'Where did you get that book, Adam?'

'In Gloucester when I went to order the union membership cards,' he replied and stuck his head in the book.

Catrin remained silent. Once she had picked up the book to see what it was all about but she could not make head or tail of it. It seemed mostly to be about socialism, whatever that was. However, she hoped he was getting something out of it.

His reading was interrupted by Lennie crying, and he put his book back on the dresser. 'Oh, well,' he sighed contentedly. 'I've had a good read.'

Catrin put her knitting aside and picked Lennie up. 'Time it is for your tea, my pet. Your Gran will be back any minute and we must wake Grancher and get him out of her room or there'll be a row, yes?'

CHAPTER 18

One evening when Adam arrived home there was a letter waiting for him on the mantelpiece. The address was written in an unschooled hand:

> Mr. A. Turley,
>
> Coalway,
>
> Forrest of Dean.

It had a Welsh postmark. Full marks to the postman, thought Adam. He did not wait to have his bath before he read it.

'Dear Adam, I hope this letter arrives safely. It's all the address I can remember. I hope you are well and Catrin, too. I write to ask if there is any jobs in the pits in the Forrest as I have lost my job here. After the last big strike they would not take me back, me being on the blacklist of all the pits round here, see, for what I did in the strike as a strike leader. The coalmasters are getting their own back. They weren't satisfied with winning the strike. They won't know me in the Forrest. Write to me, Adam, in remembrance of our old friendship – Emrys.'

So Emrys was suffering for his union activities, and anger arose in Adam's heart for him. He felt tenderness for his pain and wanted to be beside him, even though he knew that in his tough, leathery way he would repel sympathy and want to confront his troubles alone.

When he showed Catrin the letter she was pleased that Emrys might be coming to Coalway. 'Another Welsh voice would be welcome,' she said. 'But will he get a job here easily?'

'Yes. There be plenty of work.'

'But where will he lodge?' Catrin was fearful now. 'He can't stay here, Adam.'

'He could sleep with George and Grancher.'

Cornelius perked up. He did not take to this idea. 'He can sleep down here in the kitchen.'

'There's no bed,' said Emma.

'Don't need no bed. Sleep under the table.'

'Oh, no!' said Catrin.

'I used to sleep on the floor when I were a young man. Eldest sons always do when pressure upstairs gets too much.'

'Watch it, Grancher,' said George.

'Better in the kitchen sometimes, with no kids in the same bed kicking yer ribs. You ask young Billy Dobbs up the lane. He do sleep in the kitchen under the table for sure, with all them kids they do have in that house.' He pulled his beard and ruminated. 'In the winter it be nice and warm from the fire, too.'

Catrin turned to Adam. 'Adam, it's so crowded here already.'

'It's not crowded, Catrin. You be used to all that space you had in Wales.' But he relieved her fear. 'No, he won't stay here, he's not family. We'll find him somewhere else.'

Later Adam told Bert about Emrys. 'He told me a lot about trade unions when I was in Wales, though I must admit I was more interested in courting Catrin at the time. He knows a lot about them.'

'He'll be useful then. But I hopes he ain't too radical, pushing strikes too much. Joseph don't like that.'

'The problem is where can he lodge.'

'He can stay with us,' said Bert. 'With just the two of us we be rattling around in our house. And we has a spare room, like, now Martha's mother's gone, so he won't have to share. Not very big, but big enough for a single bed. We could do with the money, too, now Martha ain't working.'

'Hadn't you better ask your wife?' said Emma.

'She'll say yes. Have to. Anyway, give her something to do now she be home all day, and the old woman's dead.'

Emrys came to Coalway ten days later. He arrived at Park End station just as Adam and George were leaving the pit, so they met him without losing any work time. Adam was surprised to see how small and crushed he had become, how lean and pale his face was. Emrys refused at first to let Adam carry his bag, saying it was light. Indeed it was, for it contained little; but Adam insisted on carrying it. Even so, Emrys was glad to sit down when they reached the Turley cottage. The family welcomed him, especially Catrin. After Adam and George had bathed, they ate. Emma cast her eye over Emrys's thin body and served him first, even before Grancher, and with the largest helping. After the meal they sat around the fire, and talked about Wales.

Cornelius had been peering suspiciously at Emrys since his arrival. Then he broke his silence. 'Ain't never seen a Welshman before.'

'What about Catrin,' said George. 'She's Welsh.'

'She be a woman. I'm talking about men. Not very big, be 'em?'

'Don't be rude, Grancher,' said Emma.

'Ah, but good they are,' said Emrys gallantly. He grinned, but Adam could see how nervous and anxious he was to be accepted.

Later Adam took Emrys round to Bert's. As they walked Adam looked sideways at him. His thin frame seemed to shake in the wind. God, he has been brought low, thought Adam, wondering what hardship he had undergone in recent months. He took Emrys's hand, put half a crown in it and forced it closed. 'Just to see you through the next few days.'

Emrys looked down at the money, and swallowed. 'Thank you, Adam. I'll pay you back, you know that.'

Adam put his arm round his shoulder, and a spark went between them, an urgency of friendship, an ineffable brotherliness. They walked on in silence.

'You say I can find a job here?' asked Emrys after a few minutes. This was clearly worrying him, and Adam realised how cruel it would have been to encourage him to come to the Forest and then not to find him work.

'There be many a buttyman wanting a day man. The coal trade here is good just now. They must be eating the stuff somewhere.'

'That's good news.'

'Bert says Enoch Tingle wants a day man. Me and George don't want to take on another, leastways, not at present, but happen we may later. And then we'll see how you be fixed.'

Emrys was relieved, and smiled nervously at Adam.

'Cheer up, Emrys. You'll be all right here. We earns good money nowadays compared with a year or two back, thanks to the union.'

'You must tell me about the union sometime.'

Adam introduced him to Bert and Martha. Bert welcomed him with a grin. Martha looked at him straight and gave him a faint smile, reserving her opinion. Then in her businesslike way she invited him to look at his room. He followed her upstairs, clutching his bag of possessions.

'He do seem all right,' said Bert. 'But he's a bit skinny, like. Enoch be a fussy fellow, you know, and he may not want to take him on when he sees him.'

'He'll be fine when he's had a few good meals.'

'Well, I'll take him round to Enoch when he comes down, and settle it one way or t'other.'

'Good.'

'Sooner he starts, sooner he'll have some money. But we shan't want no rent till payday.'

When Emrys came downstairs, Bert said he would take him to meet Enoch.

'No need for me to come,' said Adam, 'so I'll be off.' But he did not go when they had departed. He sat down in Bert's chair by the fire while Martha went upstairs for a handkerchief. As he saw the hem of her skirt disappear up the stairs he realised that nowadays in his spare time his thoughts were no longer devoted exclusively to the union, but included a sprinkling of pleasant thoughts about Martha. His fear of her had gone now, and he could talk to her in a way he could not talk to Catrin, not only about his hopes for the union and his dreams for it, but also about less important things. But, satisfactory as it was in its way, it was all impersonal talk, and not enough. He wanted to know more about her; he wanted to tell her more about himself. But he dared not initiate personal revelations; nor did she offer any of her own.

Martha returned and sat opposite him. 'When are you going to Gloucester for the union again, Adam?'

His remembrance of their last trip there was ever bright, and he was eager with his answer. 'I can go next week.'

'You'll lose a day's work, won't you?'

'George don't like me taking too much time off because while I'm away I'm not digging coal. But I always draws less pay when I don't do as much work as him.'

'That's fair.'

Adam laughed. 'But then both our wages go to Ma, so it don't make no difference, really. But I don't take as much pocket money as he do.'

'What are you going to Gloucester for this time?' She gave her half smile.

He guessed the implication behind the question and smiled back. 'Oh, I have a reason. The other night the union committee agreed we should have a miners' gala, just as they do in Durham and other places.

142

It was my idea but they all liked it and we've set up a committee with me as chairman to organise it.'

'When will it be?'

'Not till July, but we're getting on well with it. Each lodge will march to the Speech House; we've booked the big field there. It will hold thousands.'

'Just for the men, is it?'

'Oh, no. All the wives and children can come. It's to be a grand occasion.' His enthusiasm had been unleashed, and his words fell over one another. 'Families will come from all over the Forest. It'll be a right old get-together – back slapping and smiles and chatting to friends and discovering relations you haven't seen for years.' Then his enthusiasm embarrassed him, and he became silent. 'I'm so pleased,' he ended simply.

'Wonderful news, and all your own work.'

'Oh, no, the others are doing a lot. But I've got to go to Gloucester about one or two things soon.'

She smiled and turned to the fireplace. He looked at her as she sat in the firelight. The sight of her shoulders, barely visible through her clean crisp blouse, made him forget the gala. He wanted to touch her. He recalled what Bert had said about her in the pub; but he could not imagine her cold in bed.

Perhaps she caught his thoughts, for she looked at him strangely. It seemed some magic passed between them. But all she said was, 'Well, I think it's about time I visited my aunt again.'

They fixed a convenient day to go. 'And it's my turn to buy dinner this time,' said Adam.

'If you want to, but I'm not short of a few pennies, you know. My aunt always pays my fare and gives me a bit of money when I visit her. I don't want to take it, but she insists and it pleases her.'

'I'd like to pay, please. I can afford it.'

Martha started to talk about the gala, but Adam became uneasy. He could happily stay and talk all evening, but he dared not. 'I must go now. I told Bert I was going. He'll be back soon.'

'Go if you must.' She seemed indifferent to him now, and it hurt him. But it would be imprudent to stay. He bade her farewell, put on his muffler and cap and left; but he went reluctantly. As he walked up the path he asked himself why he felt guilty about staying after Bert had left. However, after a few paces along the village street with the winter breeze whipping round his face, the feeling disappeared and he began to run, not because he was cold, but because of exhilaration as the blood rushed through his veins at the thought of accompanying Martha to Gloucester again.

ॐ ॐ

Adam could not see her on Lydney platform, and he had to run to get on the train before it left. At Gloucester station he hurried to the exit and waited for her there. But it seemed she had not been on the train. He waited several minutes, just in case she had gone into the ladies' convenience, but no-one came out and the platform was now deserted.

What had happened? Had she had an accident? He suddenly felt lost. He had looked forward to this outing so much, and was now stuck in Gloucester by himself. He walked despondently out of the station and over to Eastgate street. They should have been ordering their meal at the Wellington by now.

He carried out his trade union business – it took only half an hour – and then decided to go straight home. The crowds he passed in the streets on his way back to the station were much the same as the last time when he had walked among them with Martha, but now they seemed drab and uninteresting. The colours of the women's clothes were duller; the men had worried faces; the errand boys hunched their shoulders and plodded.

Then the idea occurred to him to visit the bookshop at the Cross. He had read *The New Socialism* and wanted to learn more about politics and see the connection it had with trade unions. When he had been in Wales Emrys had explained something of the economics of the capitalist system. *The New Socialism* had told him what socialism was. Now he wanted to know more about it.

'Have you any books on politics, please?'

The shop assistant looked at him severely, as if a working man should not interest himself in such a subject. 'Over there,' he indicated briefly.

Adam examined the books on display. There were several he would like to buy, but felt he could afford only one. He chose *Radicalism and Socialism* because it had a chapter on trade unions and the new order. Savouring the pleasure he would get from reading it, he left the shop clutching it to his breast.

He felt in better humour as he continued his way to the station and glanced in the shop windows as he walked along. At first he looked aimlessly; then he thought he would buy a present for Martha. He wouldn't have been able to do that if she had been with him. But what should he get her? He looked more purposefully and stopped before a jewellers, in whose window he saw a brooch with a bright green stone. Was it an emerald? He did not know, but it attracted him. The ticket had slipped and he could not see the price. It was probably too expensive for him, but he decided to go in and ask. This was the first time he had ever done anything like this and he hesitated before he pushed open the door and entered. The shop was dark but over the counter flickered a yellow gas light. The assistant inclined his head towards him.

'How much be the emerald brooch in the window, please?'

'Actually, it's not an emerald, but it's a very good imitation. The assistant took the brooch from the window and handed it to Adam.

'How much is it?'

'Three shillings and sixpence. The catch is an especially strong one, so the brooch won't fall off.'

Adam considered. He felt he had to make up his mind quickly and not keep the man waiting. He held the green stone up to the gas light and examined it. It was a fine piece of work, and he could imagine it at Martha's breast; its green would reflect the green of her eyes. Unfortunately it was dearer than he thought, and he had already spent a shilling on his book. But he had the rest of the money he had brought with him to pay for the dinner and it would be enough. He smiled at the assistant. 'I'll take it, please.'

The assistant found a black box lined with silk to put it in, and Adam placed it carefully in the inside pocket of his coat.

Feeling in a better mood, he decided he would have something to eat after all. He had only a few pence left, so he went into a working men's eating house that specialised in shellfish. He would have some whelks; he had always fancied trying whelks. It was a pity Martha wasn't with him to share the experience, though he would not have wanted to bring her to this place, where the smell of stale fish, strong vinegar and human sweat was overwhelming. He ordered a plate of whelks and a slice of bread at the counter.

'Tuppence, mate,' said the man.

Adam doused his whelks with vinegar from a bottle standing on the counter as he had seen other customers do, and sat down on a bench at a table covered with brown paper stained with grease. Not much like the Wellington, he thought. Loudmouthed labourers pushed past him on their way out. Cheer up, he comforted himself; you have always wanted to try whelks. But these made him feel sick and he pushed the plate aside and left.

When he returned home he went straight away to the bedroom to change his clothes. Catrin was there, tidying, and he wondered where to put the brooch. Wait till she went down and then hide it in the drawer where his socks and shirts were kept? No, Catrin was always going to it. Better leave it in the pocket of his coat in the chest where their best clothes were laid. It would only be there for a day or so before he gave it to Martha.

Then the full import of his action in buying something for Martha was borne in on him. He had not bought a present for Catrin, his wife, indeed had had no thought of doing so. Perhaps, on reflection, he should give the brooch to her and not to Martha. But he had no wish to do so. It had been Martha he had bought it for, and he decided to go ahead and give it to her as he had intended. Catrin would never know.

                                                        ❧ ❧

The next day as Catrin did the ironing she looked at Lennie sitting on Grancher's knee and realised the affection that had grown up between the two. Lennie, now eighteen months old, had climbed laboriously on to his lap, stroked his beard (which Catrin noticed was washed most carefully nowadays), looked into his face with his big dark eyes and pointed to George's dog. From the day Lennie had been born Grancher had never tired of attending and comforting his great-grandson, rocking his cradle when he was a baby, rescuing him from awkward corners when he was crawling, shutting the door to the stairs to avoid accidents when he began to walk and feeding him the last spoonful in the bowl when he rejected it from herself, his own mother. And now he talked to him constantly. He had spare time which Catrin had not, and used it unstintingly in caring for the child.

She put her cooled iron down before the fire and took up its companion. She spat on its face and, when the drops of spittle ran spurting down, knew it was the right temperature. As she ironed she listened to Grancher telling Lennie about George's dog and its fleas, and then about the fanciful shapes and shadows made by the fire in the grate and about the coal in the bucket and where it came from. The lad did not, of course, understand everything, but Catrin recalled what her mother had told her about the way babies learnt to speak, and was sure that Grancher's words, their sounds and cadences, penetrated his mind and lay dormant there. Later they would come out in childish sounds that probably only Grancher would understand; and then they would be formulated painfully into precise and clear words. Catrin expected them to be Grancher's words and expression, words sometimes that the younger generations no longer used, for she had not heard Adam or George use them, and she certainly could not understand them.

When she had finished the ironing she took the basket of clothes upstairs. As she entered her room she remembered that Adam had come back from Gloucester the previous day and put his best suit away hurriedly in the chest where they kept their best clothes without brushing it. She took it out, waving aside the overpowering smell of mothballs, and started to brush it. She felt a box in the inside pocket. Curious, she opened it, and discovered a magnificent brooch. Dear Adam, she thought, he must have bought it for her birthday next week. All her old love for him flooded back as she took it over to the window to look at it in the light. It glinted and reflected the sun's rays as she examined it. But he must not know she had found it and, kissing it, she replaced it in the suit. Her heart was overflowing as she went downstairs again.

CHAPTER 19

Alice Sully knew she had the ability to stand back from herself and analyse her attributes and feelings. She was, she admitted, no beauty, but she was reasonably bright, though she feared her potential would never be realised. Her father had given her a good education – good for a girl, that is – and while they had lived in Somerset he had engaged for her a private tutor whom she shared with two cousins. The tutor, Miss Harrison, was well grounded in common sense and, in her occasional comments on society and its habits, had tried to sow in her charges' minds a few ideas about women's independence, such as votes for women.

'I must warn you, though,' she said, 'that if you form any ideas about women's independence you must be very circumspect on how you voice them.'

Alice's first reaction to some of Miss Harrison's exciting new ideas was that they were heretical. She had never heard her mother utter them, but when she thought about them she came to the conclusion they held much sense. But she was careful not to tell her father or mother about them. Miss Harrison had been employed to give her lessons in more orthodox subjects. These included water-colour painting and embroidery, for neither of which Alice could raise any enthusiasm, and English, French and arithmetic. Alice enjoyed English but found French difficult and decided arithmetic would do no more than enable her to check the grocer's bill. But she also had piano lessons from a wild-eyed man who demonstrated his musicality by wearing a large floppy black tie. She enjoyed playing the piano and was rather good at it.

Outside the classroom her loves were walking and reading, both fiction and non-fiction. In recent years she had sated herself with books on architecture, the Wars of the Roses and the Renaissance, and was at present delving into Ancient Greece. However, she found that these subjects, though interesting, lacked the human element. For this she turned to contemporary novels, where she learned more than her parents – or even Miss Harrison – had been able to teach her about morality, friendship and the pitfalls of love.

Since the family had moved to the Forest life had been dull. The only young lady of her class in the village was Lizzie Prendergast, the vicar's daughter. Lizzie was a pretty girl, the eldest of six children and about Alice's age. Though Alice realised she was not over-bright, they got along tolerably well. Lizzie found her mother as overbearing as Alice did hers, so they had a lot in common. Lizzie was also unfortunate in having a bad-tempered and unsympathetic father. As Lizzie in one of her brighter moments said, 'His milk of human kindness does not fall on me as generously as it does on his congregation.'

Like most young girls of her age Lizzie spent much of her time thinking and talking of romance. 'I shall never attract a man,' she once bewailed. 'My complexion's too pale and I'm short.'

'But so was Jane Eyre,' responded Alice, 'and *she* nourished great romantic thoughts in her bosom just like you, and these thoughts led to marriage.'

Alice was prepared to talk to Lizzie about young men, even about romantic attachments; but she was not interested in marriage. At least not yet. Romance was one thing, marriage quite another. And because of her opposition to practically everything her mother favoured (and one thing she was always stressing was the need for her to get married as soon as possible) she had almost convinced herself that she did not want to be married. However, she listened with interest to Lizzie's accounts of the Adonises she had met while away visiting relations and friends, and her surmises of what it would be like to have their company at dances – indeed, what it would be like to be wooed by them. Alice had little to contribute to such discussions, since she seldom left Park End, and there were no young men of their class in the village. She did, however, tell Lizzie about her visit to the Crawshays and what she thought of young Hubert, which wasn't much.

Recently Alice had accompanied her mother on her monthly shopping visit to Gloucester. They had visited the bookshop at the Cross.

'Now Alice, choose some books to buy with your allowance if you wish, but let me see them before you pay for them.'

Hermione always authorized Alice's purchase of non-fiction books with no more than a glance, though she could not imagine why Alice wanted to muddle her head with such subjects as Ancient Greece; but her choice of fiction was subject to greater scrutiny.

'Yes, another novel by Anthony Trollope. I must say you have excellent taste in fiction. Trollope's novels always look improving and he must be a good author because he had written so many.'

When they returned home Hermione removed her hatpins, placed her hat carefully on a chair in the hall and sailed into the sitting room. Alice went up to her room with her books, congratulating herself on having had a pleasant day out with her mother. But when she went downstairs again she found her remonstrating with her father on the old subject. 'How can we ever hope to get Alice married if she never meets any unattached young men? I don't believe you have invited the Crawshays over for dinner, and it must be quite a time since I suggested you should.'

'Yes, Hermione. I'll invite them over today.'

Oh dear, thought Alice. All day her mother had succeeded in suppressing her ever-present thoughts about getting her married; but they had now exploded. She shrugged her shoulders. A visit from the Crawshays might perhaps be more interesting than no visit from them, except that it would provide an opportunity for her mother to push her into the company of that uninteresting young son of theirs.

At his first opportunity Adam went with some union papers under his arm to see why Martha had not gone to Gloucester. In his pocket he carried the brooch he had bought her. He hoped Bert would not be there and cursed that he had to go to his cottage every time he wanted to see her. But Bert was there, and he had to conduct union business with him. From time to time he looked across at Martha, who was sitting by the fire, and watched how the flickerings from the burning coals caressed her cheek and burnished her hair. She did not look in his direction, but stared ahead, blank, bored. She's lost interest in me, that's what it is, thought Adam. That's why she didn't go to Gloucester. He felt bitter and the present burned in his pocket. Again he felt guilty he had not also bought something for Catrin while he had been in Gloucester.

Then Bert went upstairs to search for some papers and Adam forgot his guilt. He seized the opportunity Bert's absence offered. 'Why didn't you come?' All his annoyance, kept below the surface since he had returned from Gloucester, boiled over. 'There's me wondering if you'd had an accident.'

'Keep your voice down and don't be stupid,' she hissed. 'I couldn't come. Bert's mother was ill, and he insisted I should go and look after her.'

150

Immediately Adam was remorseful. 'I'm sorry. I was worried about you.' His eyes screwed up in pain, showing his distress.

'We'll have other opportunities to meet,' she said more conciliatorily. Then she gave a smile, the smile that puckered her cheeks under her cheekbones, and Adam knew that everything was all right. He produced the brooch and gave it to her. With a cry of interest she examined it carefully. Then she went up to him and looked him in the face. 'Thank you, Adam. It's very kind of you. I appreciate it.' She gave him a kiss on the cheek.

Bert could be heard coming down and opening the door at the bottom of the stairs. She put the brooch in her pocket and turned abruptly away and began to make a pot of tea.

The combination of the kiss and the danger that Bert might have seen it embarrassed Adam. He turned away, but Bert seemed not to have noticed anything. Adam was glad when the front door opened and Emrys came in.

'Tea is it then, Martha?' said Emrys. 'Good idea.'

'Sorry we haven't no beer,' said Bert. 'She won't make it.' He grinned and paused, waiting for Martha to comment. It was a strained grin and Adam felt the discord between them.

'Never learnt to make it,' said Martha.

There was an awkward pause. Emrys covered it by asking Adam for news of the gala.

'We've invited all the ironminers in the Forest to come and any other workers who want to, as well,' Adam replied, his poise recovered.

'To demonstrate the solidarity of the workers, is it?' said Emrys. 'Marvellous.'

'It will be an enormous rally. Each lodge will march to the Speech House separately, with its own flag at the front of the column and led by the village band if there is one. It'll be wonderful.'

'And there'll be lots of speeches and resolutions, I suppose,' said Bert, dubiously.

'Yes, but there'll be stalls and entertainments and jollifications as well. And there'll be food and beer and cider.'

Bert cheered up. 'That'll lubricate the proceedings. I'm looking after the Park End banner,' he went on. 'The main thing to decide is what the motto on it should be, and who should sew it on. Needs someone good with a needle.'

151

'No good looking at me,' said Martha. 'I can't sew.'

'I know you can't.'

'What about "Workers Unite"?' said Emrys.

'Don't mean much,' said Bert. 'We need something classy, something dignified.' He thought. 'What about, "May our union blossom like the rose and may peace and prosperity reign triumphant throughout the Forest of Dean." Something like that.'

'A bit long,' said Adam. 'But I leave it to you. Nothing too religious, mind. Leave the religion to Joseph Cowmeadow's lodge.'

CHAPTER 20

The coalmasters closed the pits on the day of the miners' gala. They knew that, whether they did or not, the men would not turn up for work even though they would forfeit a day's pay. But loss of a day's pay didn't prevent the men and their families from looking forward to the gala. They had been saving up for it for weeks and they were determined to enjoy it.

As the old men had forecast, it was a fine day. A few white clouds were chasing across the sky, and a thin haze, golden in the sun, stretched over the gardens and woods.

Adam and George were up and out of the house by half past eight. George brought his dog with him, for there were to be dog trials. A crowd of colliers, wives and children had already gathered outside the ironworks when they arrived at Park End. No downtrodden labourers and their families these. The men had taken their suits out of mothballs and their bowlers from the box under the bed and put on collars and ties, though these already promised to be uncomfortable before the end of the day. The women had donned their black bombazine skirts which fell straight as a tube to the ground and their Sunday-best blouses, and they stood smoothing selfconsciously their puffed-out leg-of-mutton sleeves with pride. For most of them this would be the only day in the year when they had a holiday, and they were going to make it one on which they could cast aside their everyday worries.

Adam picked out Bert and Martha talking to young Billy and his brothers, Jack and Tom, and went up to them. He noticed with pleasure, but with some apprehension, that she was wearing his brooch.

'Where be Catrin?' asked Bert.

'Lennie's got a bad cough, so she's not coming,' said Adam. 'Anyway, someone has to stay and look after Grancher. But Mother's coming in the timber cart.' A waggon had been laid on at Coalway for those who could not walk the three miles to the Speech house.

153

'Here be the banner.' Bert unfurled it with a flourish. It was glorious and substantial. At the top it was inscribed 'Park End Lodge'. Below was embroidered a collier in the pit with a lighted candle in his cap. At the bottom was the motto in golden letters emblazoned on a red background:

'We'll have shorter hours and more pay. Success to the union.'

'Fine,' said Adam. 'Very much to the point.'

He began to organise the march. 'Banner first,' he shouted, clapping his hands, 'with the chairman of the lodge in front of it. Then the band, then lodge members. Then ironworkers and tin-plate workers with women and children at the back. And commmittee members on the outside to keep order.'

They formed ranks obediently, the boys, including Jack and Tom, proudly lining up with the men. Then Adam gave the signal to start. The bandmaster, moustache bristling, raised his arms as high as he could and brought them down with force. The big drum gave four unaccompanied beats – boom, boom, boom, boom – and with a twirl of his stick the bandmaster encouraged the band to start a sprightly march from a Donizetti opera.

The procession moved off. At the last minute Bessie Tingle and her friend Mary Jane ran up, gorgeous in their finery. They took up position one each side of the banner and danced along, lifting their skirts and showing their petticoats, to the delight of the young men. Bert, the chairman of the lodge, decided to ignore such frivolity and turned to acknowledge the thin cheers of the old folk who had hobbled to their gates to watch. The men marched easily and proudly, the women trod gently as they chatted, looking out for stones so as not to damage their best shoes. The children excited and still fresh, skipped at their mothers' sides, singing and shouting. Out of the village and into the Forest they marched, under the railway bridge, past Wet Wood where the bluebells grew in the spring, along the valley skirting the ponds that supplied the water to the Park End Ironworks, and on towards the Speech House. The sun shone down on them.

As they marched Emrys touched Adam's sleeve. 'Is it true the union are thinking of putting forward a working man as parliamentary candidate at the next general election?'

'Well, not exactly. Union headquarters are thinking of backing a collier for parliament and have asked us if we could nominate someone for the Forest constituency.'

'Time it is that working people returned one of their own class to parliament and not support the master's man.'

'Yes, we've had the aristocratic Berkeleys and Beauforts representing us for too long.'

'There was a fellow called George Odger – funny name – who stood for somewhere in London a year or two back. He was only a shoemaker but he got nominated.'

'Did he get in?'

'No, but there will be working class MPs in parliament soon, you see, man.'

'And one of the first could be from the Forest,' added Adam.

'Who is the union likely to put up?'

'The committee haven't decided yet. Could be Joseph Cowmeadow.'

Emrys was aghast. 'No, not Joseph, man. We want someone better than him. Someone with a broader outlook.'

'Who, then?'

'What about you?'

'Me!'

'You've got the right approach, man, and the drive.'

Adam laughed. 'No, Emrys, not me.'

'You think about it, boy.'

Adam thought about it as they marched on. He had sat through an hour-long discussion on the subject at the last union committee meeting at Cinderford and had not once thought of himself as a candidate. He had ideas of going higher in the union, of taking over Joseph Cowmeadow's job of agent, even to working at union headquarters in Birmingham, but becoming an MP was different.

However, the flame of ambition had once again been lit and was flickering inside him. Why not? Was he too modest in not recognising his own potential? Member of Parliament for the West Gloucestershire Division! That would sound good. More importantly, if he was elected, he would be able to do something really effective for working people, for all working people, not only Foresters. But this was moonshine, he told himself. You a Member of Parliament! The idea's ridiculous; your ambition knows no limits. And he laughed. No, if Joseph Cowmeadow stood he must support him not contest him.

The Park End lodge contingent were the first to arrive at the Speech House, and union officials were waiting to guide them through the gateway into the field behind. Superintendent Chip of the Cinderford police, standing at the gate, his moustache to attention, gave them a salute. As they broke ranks they looked round at the pleasures awaiting them. For the children there were roundabouts, a helter-skelter, coconut shies, and a Punch and Judy show. For the men there was donkey racing and a rifle range, and a wrestling booth where the champion of all Gloucestershire was ready to take anyone on. For everyone there were raffles and guess the weight of the pig, and stalls whose goods were mostly brought from Cinderford in wheelbarrows: pet rabbits which, when the children lost interest, could go in the pot; young puppies just taken from their mothers; racing pigeons in cages waiting philosophically to be released; hens slung from poles by their feet, clucking away upside down, their eyes glaring furiously. And there were, of course, bran tubs and stalls of sweets, coughdrops, toffee apples, pop corn, tiger nuts, cakes, lemonade and sarsparilla. And there was beer and cider, gallons of it. A dozen barrels had been stacked in the shade outside the inn, and a bathful had been placed by the back door. 'And there must be more inside,' said George as he went off to enter his dog in the competition.

Meanwhile other Lodge contingents were arriving, all headed by their village bands. Adam, Bert, Martha and Emrys sat on the grass inside the gate and watched them arrive. From all parts of the Forest they came; from Berry Hill and Yorkley, from Trafalgar and Foxes Bridge, from Coleford and Mitcheldean, from Ruardean and Lightmoor. Adam felt he could be proud of the part he had taken in building up this healthy and massive organisation. Last, fittingly enough, came the biggest contingent of all, Cinderford. Their band was the largest, its noise the loudest, the uniforms of the bandsmen the smartest and their banner, with gold letters on a blue background, the biggest.

'Fear God,' it said. 'Masters, give unto your servants that which is just and equal, knowing that ye also have a Master in Heaven.'

'Good old Joseph,' said Adam.

'Don't be sarcastic,' said Martha. 'In church you only hear "Servants obey your masters".'

Behind the banner came the Cinderford colliers, heads up and smiling as they swung through the gate into the field. At the end of the procession came Joseph Cowmeadow. No anticlimax he, but the parade's highlight. He was borne in a carriage drawn by two black horses. With him were distinguished guests who had been invited to speak during the afternoon. But no-one paid any attention to them. It was Joseph Cowmeadow the crowd applauded. He stood in his carriage beaming at them, his cheeks rosy, his thick white beard glistening soft and clean in the morning sun. He held out his arms to them as they cheered him.

'He's certainly the Forest hero today,' said Bert, and he hurried over to help him descend from his carriage.

Adam turned away. 'The showman.'

'What is it, Adam?' asked Martha.

'He's a showman. Look at him standing there blessing the crowd like a bishop.'

'He seems very popular.'

The dam of Adam's feelings had been breached and he could not contain the flood. 'He mesmerises the men and plays on their emotions with his charm and smooth talk, like he's doing now. They don't see his other side.'

'What do you mean?'

'Under his amiable smile he's quite ruthless, you know. They don't see him throwing his weight about at committee meetings and always insisting he's right when he isn't.' Adam realised he had shocked her by his outburst, but he went on. 'He's not popular with a lot of the committee. They don't trust him and reckon he'll let the union down if we don't watch out.'

Martha was inclined to ask more questions, but Emrys intervened. 'Come on, Adam,' he said, tugging his arm. 'Let's have a look round the field.' And he dragged him away. 'Eight thousand people there must be here,' he said to distract him. 'Two bonnets to every hat. All in their Sunday best and excited and happy. No cares today.' He put his arm round Adam's shoulder. 'Lovely to see people so happy, is it, Adam?'

But Adam was still upset, loathing himself because of his uncontrolled outburst against Joseph Cowmeadow. 'Come on, man,' continued Emrys. 'You've got a busy day today. You're speaking on the same platform as Joseph Cowmeadow this afternoon, and you've got to give a better speech than him, isn't it?' Adam could not resist Emrys's blandishments and smiled. He recovered his usual good humour; but he resolved never to lose control of himself like that again.

They undertook a tour of the field, stopping first to listen to an organ grinder churning out a creaky melody. His monkey, in velvet jacket and trousers, was sitting on his shoulder holding out a bag for coins.

'Look at the grief in the monkey's eyes,' said Adam.

'Aye,' Emrys responded.' We all have our griefs, some are more hidden than others.'

Next to the organ grinder was a man writhing in the grass, bound in chains, his muscles bulging with effort as he struggled to free himself.

'Symbolic of the militant worker, is it?' said Emrys.

As the man threw off the last links the crowd cheered, and then, when his wife, as small and pale as he was big and brown, tried to collect a few farthings in a hat, they hastily dispersed.

'I hope they're not symbolic of the other workers,' said Adam, with a laugh.

They came upon George and Emma, sitting under a tree with Enoch Tingle and his wife Nelly, a large woman, soft and motherly. George was explaining to his mother how his dog had won a prize at the dog trials.

'The judges must have made a mistake if they gave any sort of prize to that animal,' said Emma tartly.

'Time to eat,' said Adam, breaking it up. 'What will you have, Mam? There be ham with pickles, eel pies and roast pigeon, trifles and cakes, beer, tea and fizzy lemonade.'

'Have a pint, Mam,' said George, still smarting under his mother's reference to his dog. 'It'll cheer you up a bit.'

After the meal they lay on the grass, happy to relax, greeting their friends as they passed and waving to their acquaintances. Bert and Martha came up. 'Come on, Adam,' said Bert. 'It be nearly two o'clock. You ready with your speech?'

At the platform which had been set up in the far corner of the field away from the noise of the bands, the colliers were gathering for the serious part of the day's proceedings, the speeches. Joseph Cowmeadow was in the chair. He welcomed his audience and the guests behind him, and read a telegram from the local Member of Parliament apologising for being unavoidably detained. Can't believe I would let myself be stopped from coming if I was the MP, thought Adam. Then Joseph Cowmeadow asked Adam, 'my young colleague, who has done so much to help build up the colliers' union in the Forest,' to say a few words.

Adam spoke without notes. He had bored George with practising his speech on the way home from the pit, and had rehearsed it a hundred times to himself, at the coal face, digging the garden and in bed at night.

Now all his hard work was to be put to the test. His power of language and ability to speak at public meetings had improved recently, and his belief in what he was about to proclaim must, he thought, lend sincerity to his utterances; and while perhaps he was not so good a speaker as Joseph Cowmeadow, he could, he knew, speak compellingly.

Now, as he threw his voice to reach the back of his audience he could hear the words tripping off his tongue. As he stood on the platform edge, erect and relaxed, leaning forward and raising his arm to make a point, he swept his glance along the front rows of his audience. They were listening, unblinking and attentive, laughing at his jokes, moved by his pathos. The speech was going exactly as he had planned. His eyes returned time and again to Martha. Her eyes were unswervingly focused on him, encouraging him, urging him on.

Then the speech was over. It had lasted half an hour, but the time had passed in a flash. The audience clapped hard, willing him with their eyes to accept their appreciation. His own piece over, Adam was disinclined, selfishly as he acknowledged, to sit and listen to any more speeches. He wanted to talk to Martha. But he stayed for an hour while Joseph Cowmeadow went on inexhaustibly. When he had finished, Adam slipped from the platform and joined Martha.

'Where's Bert?' he asked.

'He's tired. Had enough of speeches, I think. And enough beer as well, I shouldn't wonder. He's gone to find a quiet spot for a sleep.'

Couldn't be better, thought Adam. 'Let's go for a walk.'

'We mustn't let anyone see us together.'

'You go out through the gate and I'll slip over the fence here. A little way up the road there's a milestone with a path to the left. I'll meet you a few yards along it.' As he went to climb over the fence he saw young Billy and Bessie Tingle disappear into the bracken that bordered the road. He smiled.

Martha joined him near the milestone and they walked down towards the bottom of the valley. Martha praised his speech and referred to Joseph Cowmeadow's. 'A bit long,' she said.

'Yes. And as I expected he introduced a lot of religion into it.'

'You must keep quiet about Joseph Cowmeadow's religion. He believes in it and he knows most of his audience are the same.'

'I can't stand the smarmy side. Emrys doesn't like it either.'

'Most people aren't like you and Emrys.'

'God don't play much part in our lives.'

159

'But He does in most people's,' she said. 'And you must have noticed that most trade union leaders are full of religion. Methodists and Baptists have always been the fighters for working people.'

'Religion and trade unionism both offer the promised land. But only one delivers.'

Martha did not reply but squeezed his hand.

They stopped to listen to a skylark and strained to see it, but couldn't and moved on. The warmth of a sundrenched afternoon rose up. After all the strains and irritations of the day Adam was at last content.

'Pleased to see you are wearing my brooch.'

She smiled and fingered it. 'I told Bert my aunt gave it to me.'

They were now on a narrow path surrounded by bracken, strong and healthy and striving upwards, five, six, seven foot tall. It held the warmth of summer and the hum of bees.

A secret excitement rose inside Adam. 'Let's sit down. In here.' He indicated a small opening in the sea of bracken, and beyond, a haven, quiet and secret. He placed his coat on the ground for her to sit on, and rolled up his shirt sleeves. She threw down her large straw hat, and stood waiting.

As he marvelled afterwards, he did the most obvious thing in the world. He placed his arms loosely round her waist and kissed her gently on the lips. A shiver went through him. She was as soft and delectable as he had imagined.

She looked up into his face, her faint smile breaking. 'Don't treat me like Dresden china.'

Adam did not know what Dresden china was. In reply he pulled her close and kissed her again. He felt her soft belly against him and then, as he held her more tightly, her gentle thighs pushing against his. A stronger feeling of urgency and need for relief that had been suppressed for too long overcame him. He hugged her fiercely as if this was the only thing he wanted to do if he should die immediately, and with a sob, he pulled her to the ground.

☙ ❧

Afterwards, they returned to the field separately, as they had come. He did not see her again that day after they parted. He walked emptily around the stalls and sideshows and felt alone. He greeted George, saluted Joseph Cowmeadow and chatted with Billy and Bessie Tingle who, rather unwillingly, was pushing a pram containing her youngest brother. But the boy reminded him of Lennie, and Lennie reminded him of Catrin. His mind became agitated. If Catrin had come today all this would not have happened. Was he glad she had not come? He went to the bar with George and had a pint of ale strengthened with gin. His emotions subsided and he felt better.

It was getting dark. The glorious day, glorious in more ways than one, was ending. The sun was relinquishing its hold on the sky, reluctantly fading behind the puffy yellow clouds on the horizon. Some of the women with their children, full of lemonade and sticky cakes, had set off for home. The brakes were departing each to its own village. The Coalway timber waggon was the last to leave.

But the festivities were not yet over. In one corner of the field couples were cavorting on the grass to tunes played by the Cinderford band, their arms pumping up and down, the men's bowler hats perched on the backs of their heads, the women's skirts swirling round their ankles. In another corner Bert, refreshed by his afternoon sleep, was leading the singing of 'The Jovial Foresters'. Adam turned away. The thought that he had just made love to his wife embarrassed him.

As darkness fell the hot chestnut man's brazier glowed more brightly, and the flames from the naphtha lamps over the stalls fluttered and hissed. The bonfire was lit, and the firework display began. But exciting as it might prove to be, Adam did not want to see it. He wanted to be alone, and he decided to go home.

He slipped away from the field and walked down the Speech House Road. As he did so, he took out the treasure that he had stored up in his memory that afternoon and began to examine it, to glory in it, to remember the exquisite ecstasy. Then the thought hit him like a bomb. He was in love with Martha. He remembered how the bonfire had been lit. One match and the whole edifice was ablaze. A bonfire had been laid inside him months ago, and today Martha had applied the match.

But was he really in love with her? All this excitement because he had laid a woman in the bracken? Young Billy had had a tumble with Bessie Tingle that afternoon, he had no doubt, but Billy would make light of it. He would have enjoyed it and forgotten it.

But this was different. He was in love with Martha. Why hadn't he realized it before? Or had he realized it and refused to admit it? He had not thought about their relationship. That was his trouble, he did not think things through. He did not analyse. But it was plain now, plain as a piece of coal. He had been in love with Martha since that trip to Gloucester.

And what about Catrin? If he had not met Martha would he have remained contentedly married to her? All this time, he had told himself, he was reasonably happily married. But had he been? There had been something gnawing quietly and insidiously in him for months, but things were clear now. He had to stop and shout it out to the oaks and elms that lined his path. He was in love with Martha! She was life to him. She raised him to ecstatic heights. She inspired him to feats of mental activity he had never known before and stimulated him to draw on hitherto untapped sources of energy.

But what was this love of his? Was it wholesome? Or was it an infection? And if so, would it heal? Did he want to be cured? Would it last for ever? Even if it didn't, would he be grateful for what he had had? Did he want it to last for ever? Yes. No. Perhaps he would not be able to stand it. Even in his moment of revelation, he could see the bitter humour in his thoughts.

He reached Broadwell, and started on the last lap home. The sky was dark now and the full moon was turning the hedgerows to silver. Suddenly, a great fear came over him. He must not do anything he might regret. His mind raced ahead, seeking out difficulties but not providing solutions. Should he give up seeing Martha? Knowing that she was so near and yet unapproachable would be agonising. What had happened so easily and unexpectedly that afternoon might happen again. Indeed it would happen again if the choice was his. He wanted to repeat that ecstasy, that fleeting moment that he had wished would stay for ever.

He must carry on seeing Martha, love her more. But that would mean being unfaithful to Catrin. He considered the word 'unfaithful'. It had an old-fashioned ring about it. Adultery, a word flung so often from the pulpit, was the correct word, for it implied guilt and cruelty. Oh, how he was tormenting himself now! Yet he must face up to it: he was proposing an adulterous relationship with Martha. Indeed he had begun one.

But faithlessness – he decided to use the other word – was not uncommon. Many men did it on the side, as the saying went. Several he knew did it occasionally, one or two regularly – look at Bert. Often they were justified, or so they said. But everyone kept quiet about it, though in the pub, behind the cigarette and pipe smoke, the men would sometimes discuss their pals' transgressions and snigger. But they kept them quiet, especially from the womenfolk. Even if they did not approve, the men stood together.

Adam asked himself if he was joining this band of adulterers. But surely his love for Martha was pure and his relationship not in the same category as theirs. One thing was certain, though: honesty was impossible. Another certainty was that society was hard on so-called sinners if they were publicly exposed. But unfaithfulness could be concealed if you were careful. Then you could remain respectable in the eyes of the world; and respectability, Adam realised, was especially important to him if he were to maintain his position in the union. He loved the union and the work he was doing for it, and his prestige was increasing daily. Things were going his way; his popularity was increasing. But his world would collapse if he lost the love and support of the men. He feared that if an affair with Martha became known, there would be many – the first being Joseph Cowmeadow – who would point a finger at him and hound him out of his union job.

He arrived home apprehensive, unable to think clearly, unable to clear his mind of the inconsistencies that floated in it; and he was tired. Catrin was in bed asleep, with Lennie between her and the wall. He threw his clothes on to the floor, his best clothes that should have been carefully hung up, and sank down on the bed at Catrin's side. She sleepily snuggled up to him. Sensing his tenseness, his turmoil, she half roused herself to comfort him.

'What is it cariad?' she asked. 'Tell me.'

CHAPTER 21

Alice Sully was tired of practising on the piano and had finished her Trollope novel. The problem now was how to fill in the hour until tea time. She decided to visit Lizzie. Normally she went to the vicarage by the gate in her back garden. Her mother said she must always go that way: it was a short cut. But her real reason, Alice suspected, was that it stopped her encountering workmen going along the road in front of the house to and from the colliery offices and the pits.

But Lizzie was not good company for her today, and she soon left. For variety's sake and to spite her mother she decided to return home the road way. As she went round the corner to her house, she stumbled on the uneven road and went sprawling. A gang of colliers were walking up from the pit, having just finished their shift. One hurried over and helped her to her feet.

'It's nothing,' she said. 'I'm most grateful to you.' He was about her own age, and she noticed what bright, kind eyes he had.

'Sorry me hands is dirty, Miss. Shall I see you home?'

So he had recognised who she was. They went the few yards to the iron gates leading to the drive of her house and he opened them for her.

His companions were standing waiting for him on the other side of the road and watching them. 'Come on, young Billy,' said one.

The young collier glanced at them without responding; then, turning again to Alice, he smiled and touched his cap and went off to join his mates.

Her coat was soiled with dirt from the road and coal-dust from her helper's hands, but she did not mind. So his name was Billy. In spite of his rough, torn clothes and coal-besmirched face, he was good-looking and kind. And masculine, too, frighteningly so. She would like to meet him again.

Having reached her room and tidied up, she shook herself for mooning about an encounter with a young collier. No friendship could come of it because of their different positions in society. What would they have in common? He probably couldn't even read. Being helped to her feet after a fall by a labourer should not have been exciting. That, she suspected, was the trouble with her existence. If there were more young men in the area she could meet, she would not have found this one so fascinating.

Many times afterwards on her return from Lizzie's she went home the long way, hoping to see young Billy again so that he could smile at her and touch his cap with that combination of deference and swagger that had been so intriguing. But she didn't see him again.

ও ৯

Catrin was thinking about the lovely brooch she had found in Adam's pocket and had assumed he was going to give her for her birthday. But her birthday had come and gone, and there had been no brooch. Perhaps he was saving it for Christmas.

Her thoughts were interrupted by Lennie wriggling on her lap. 'Why don't you talk to Dadda?' she said, and put him on the floor.

Lennie ran unsteadily to his father, his arms held out, his face beaming with innocence and excitement, his eyes bright with overflowing love. 'Dadda,' he piped.

'I be sorry, old butty, but Dadda have to go out,' said Adam.

'Just give him five minutes,' said Catrin. 'It's Sunday after all.'

'Sorry, I have some union business.'

Lennie stopped and, falling backwards, sat down. His face became blank and he began to whimper quietly to himself. It was not a child's ordinary cry of annoyance or physical pain, thought Catrin. It was a cry of rejection from deep within, a cry of hurt that would linger, perhaps for ever. She pulled the lad onto her lap. 'Dadda's busy, dear,' she said quietly. When they had been courting Adam had told her many a time how much he looked forward to having children and playing with them. Why had he changed? Why did he not want to find time to devote to his son?

As Adam closed the door George glanced at Catrin; then he spoke to Lennie. 'I'll take you down to see Mr Phelps's ducks, Lennie. And I do believe that Mr Beddis do have some baby goats. Shall us go and see?'

Lennie's eyes lit up.

'You come as well, Catrin. A walk'll do you good.'

Catrin was surprised to receive the invitation. She was more friendly with George these days than she had been when she first arrived in Coalway. Initially he had seemed coarse and ill-mannered. She had

165

disliked the way he belched, the way he ate his food, the way he left his shirt unbuttoned revealing the hair on his chest; gross he was, and she had avoided him when she could. But he had never shown her any ill-will, and she had accepted him as part of the household and made his bed and got his meals and did his washing because it was expected that she should. After a time his roughness and uncouthness seemed less important – perhaps she was getting used to them – and she began to warm towards him, at the same time feeling guilty for her earlier coldness; and today she saw him in a new light. He had appreciated Adam's insensitiveness towards Lennie and was doing something to console him. And at the same time he had, in his simple, indirect way, offered a hand of friendship to her. She thanked him for the invitation and put on her bonnet.

The three walked up the lane and viewed Mr Phelps's ducks through the fence. George discussed with Lennie their size, their colour, why their feet were webbed and why Lennie's were not.

'I didn't know you were such an expert on ducks, George,' said Catrin. She saw he appreciated her remark.

Then they went round the corner to see Mr Beddis's two snow-white baby goats. They came to the fence and allowed George to stroke their noses. He showed Lennie where, in spite of their youth, they had tiny horns breaking through their heads.

'You stroke them, Lennie,' he said, but Lennie shook his head.

'Where be their dadda?' he asked.

'I expect he's inside the shed having a rest, don't you?'

'Yes.'

'Let's go for a walk round the village.' George lifted Lennie onto his shoulders. 'Hold on to me hair.' Then he said to Catrin, 'He don't seem to think much about Lennie these days. Or about you, for that matter.'

Catrin was silent. He was inviting her to criticise Adam, but she had never said a word against him to anyone, ever. She wanted to confide in someone. But not now. And not to George.

She was pleased George did not pursue the matter. They walked on through the straggly village to parts where Catrin had never been before. George, trying to make the walk interesting, pointed out the smithy, where Lennie watched a horse being shod, and told Catrin where various people lived, for in spite of the two years she had been in Coalway she knew few of the villagers or where they lived. 'That be Enoch Tingle's place, and up there be Bert Preece's cottage.'

↾ ↽

It was to Bert's cottage that Adam's union business took him after he left Catrin and Lennie. He knocked on the door and went in. No-one was there, but he could see Martha in the back garden, so he waited and inspected the aspidistra in the middle of the table. The door clicked and she came in. His blood rose in his body excitedly as he saw her, but he looked at her cautiously, uncertain of his reception.

Martha closed the door. 'Hallo, I thought you were never coming.'

'It's only a few days since the gala. I couldn't get here before, anyroad.'

Martha shrugged her shoulders. 'Well, you're here now.'

'Martha – ' He wanted to say that he had not come earlier because he had wanted to be certain of his feelings towards her. Now he was sure, he wanted to say that he loved her, that he only came to life when he was with her, and that he had never felt like this before in his life towards anyone; and so on. But he paused. If he said that she would probably dismiss it as the stuff of novels. Perhaps, indeed, it was a womanish way of declaring his feelings.

Instead he said, 'Have you any regrets about what happened at the gala, Martha?'

She turned to him, smiled a little and said, 'Have you?'

'No, no.' Then it came out, uninvited. 'Martha, I love you.' He took her hands in his and raised them to his lips and kissed the tips of her fingers.

'Yes, I know.'

Adam was relieved. It was all right, then. She placed her hands on his shoulders and raised her face, waiting, lips expectant, for him to lean down and kiss them. He did so, gently.

'Where's Bert?' he asked. He had been avoiding him since the gala. He could not face him. Indeed, for a few seconds at the gala he had hated him, or so he told himself. But he did not hate him now; he felt defiance and shame, a strange combination, perhaps. His defiance resulted from wanting his own way; his shame because Bert was a good chap, jovial and generous, and a good union man. But he was Martha's husband. Could he maintain good relations with him if the affair continued? He must, for the sake of the union if for no other reason. And if he and Martha were careful there was no need for Bert to suspect his relationship with his wife.

'He's working, on second shift, and won't be back till after midnight.'

Adam knew. He knew also that Emrys was safe in the Albion yarning behind a pint. He had seen him going there with a mate.

'What do we do, then?' asked Adam.

'What do you mean?'

'Us. Me and Catrin. You and Bert.'

'Nothing. There's no reason why we can't carry on seeing each other, is there? No need to tell either of them.'

'I don't want to hurt Catrin.'

'She'll find out sooner or later, I suppose.' She sounded brusque. 'Women know such things.'

'And Bert?'

'If he finds out there will probably be an unholy row, but I'm not worried whether it hurts him or not. I'll tell him about a few of his own indiscretions.'

The forthrightness of her reply and the intensity of her tone of voice surprised him, though it also heartened him. He decided to ask a question he had wanted to ask for some time. Surely it was not too intimate a question. 'Do you sleep with him?'

She hesitated a second. 'Haven't for some time. I won't have him.' I don't think he's all that keen on me, anyway.'

'How long have things been bad between you?'

'Some time. Ever since he started seeing that woman in Gloucester.'

This was the first time Martha had told him anything about her relationship with her husband. It gave him confidence, for he was still feeling his way. But the barriers seemed to be down now, though he could never be sure that she wasn't holding something back. There was always a mist surrounding her which he could not penetrate.

She sat down in her chair beside the fire, banked low, because the evening was mild. Adam sat opposite her. Where were he and Martha going, he wondered. They could not return to the platonic situation they enjoyed before the escapade in the bracken. He would not be able to see her now without wanting her. But where could they go? Certainly not in this house, or anyone else's that he could think of. In the Forest in some unfrequented spot? In the rain and cold? It would soon be autumn and then winter.

'What are we going to do?' he asked again. 'Do you think we can carry on?'

'I don't see why not. Why shouldn't we get what pleasure we can?'

He closed his eyes. Yes, get what pleasure we can. That was it. He sighed.

She turned towards him, her face tender and smiling, and went up to him as he sat in his chair and stood between his knees. He put his arms round her hips and felt her softness under her dress. He waited, uncertain what to say or do, and placed his cheek against her soft belly. She ruffled his hair.

Then she took his hand and drew him towards the staircase door. Holding him with one hand she opened the door latch with the other and began to mount the stairs.

'Close the door after you,' she said.

CHAPTER 22

Catrin was looking at Lennie's feet in the bedroom. They were sore and showed signs of malformation.

'Your boots are too small, my pet,' she said.

Lennie looked at her seriously with his large dark eyes.

She examined the boots. The soles were wafer thin, and yielded as she pressed. They could perhaps be repaired, but she doubted if the uppers could stand it. Anyway they were too small. Normally they would be put away for use by the next child, or handed on to another family as they had been handed on to her. But not these; they had had their day.

'Snuggle down then, dear, and I'll tell Grancher you're ready for your story, yes?'

'Yes.'

Adam entered the room, searching for his cap. Catrin indicated where it was. So he was going out again.

'We must find some money to buy Lennie new boots.'

'Sorry, I haven't none to spare. Have you asked Mam?'

'No. You should pay for such things out of the money she gives you on payday.' She pushed the boots into Adam's hands. 'Look! He can't wear these.'

Adam glanced at them. 'If they wants mending, I'll mend them; or George will if you ask him.'

'They are too old to be mended. It's been raining for days and Lennie's chest is bad enough without being made worse by wet feet.'

Adam grunted and tried to edge round Catrin to get to the door. 'Sorry, Catrin, I'm in a hurry.'

She refused to move. 'I don't like the way money is handled in this house'.

'Suggest something better then.'

'What's your hurry to get away?' She felt emotion rising and feared an outburst. 'You earn good money for a collier and Lennie and I should see more of it. I haven't spent a penny on myself for ages.' Then she saw Lennie, wide eyed and fearful at his parents' raised voices. 'Adam, let's not argue up here.'

'We can't argue downstairs with everyone joining in.'

That was true, thought Catrin. But if Adam had got them their own cottage – and she bitterly dredged up her sense of humour from the depths where it had lain for ages – they could have quarrelled to their hearts' content and raised the roof without anyone knowing what it was all about.

Frustrated, she decided to leave the question of new boots for the time being. 'Where are you off to, then?'

'I don't have to explain to you where I be going every time I go out.' He left the room and slammed the door.

Catrin sat on the bed and tucked the bedclothes round Lennie's neck. Adam had been so unfeeling, indeed rude. And this was happening more and more often these days. It was hurtful. But why did he want to hurt her? She had shaped herself round him; reached out and adapted herself to him; always given in to him; yielded to his judgement. Had he, perhaps, resented her compliance? Would it have been better to have stood up to him? Did he want her to resist him? She did not know. And could not ask.

'Why is Dadda cross?' Lennie broke into her thoughts.

'Very busy with his union, he is. He has lots of grown-up things to do. But we'll get some new boots for you, my lovely.' She bent down and held him close and kissed him. 'There. I'll tell Grancher you're ready for your story now.'

❧ ❧

After leaving the house Adam set off for the Albion. As he walked through the village his mind chewed over the scene he had just had with Catrin. How it had blown up from nothing he could not recall, but he realised he had been wrong not to acknowledge that Lennie needed new boots. He did not grudge him them, and the money could be found somewhere.

When Adam arrived at the Albion he realised he did not now feel like company, and walked past it and into the woods. He wanted to think. How the argument had started did not matter. The point was it had happened. He had to admit that nowadays he did not feel the same towards Catrin as he once had. Sometimes he found her company boring and occasionally she annoyed him in trivial ways – how she spoke, in her small actions, even in her movements. Yet he had no complaints about the way she looked after him. She performed all the duties one expected of a wife, she brushed the coal-dust off his clothes, did his washing, cleaned his boots, heated his bath water on time and prepared his meals. She was always busy making him vests, knitting him socks. Yet in his heart, while he wanted to be looked after, wanted to have things like that done for him, he did not want to be beholden to her.

And he had changed since they had married. Now he was busy with his union and studying trade unionism and politics, and he wanted a partner to share his new ideas. But Catrin did not share his enthusiasm for such things, as Martha did. He cried out in despair. Was he expecting too much of Catrin? Did this mean he did not love her any more? If so, it must be because he now loved Martha. It seemed his love for Catrin had flown out of the window when Martha had come in at the door. In his agony he clutched himself tightly round the waist as he walked, and rocked from side to side.

But could not a man love two women at the same time, each with her own attractions? It seemed not. Yet he must not be unkind to Catrin. After all, he had a responsibility. He had given her a child and had brought her to Coalway, away from her own people, and placed her among strangers. His stomach went taut as he remembered their old love. But what to do when love runs cold? He felt the weight of his unhappiness and stopped, looked up to the sky and in desperation kicked a stone.

After an hour of walking up and down, to and fro, his mind racing over the same thoughts, the same reasons, the same excuses, luxuriating in his misery, he decided to return home. He would try to live reasonably with Catrin. After all, why couldn't he maintain a civilised relationship with her and at the same time enjoy Martha's company? He must try.

Catrin was sitting alone before the fire when he came in, knitting him some socks it seemed. The others had gone to bed. He greeted her briefly and sat down at the table and pretended to read the newspaper. That he did not go straight up to bed was a sign that he wished to be conciliatory.

Catrin said nothing. After a time she rose from her seat, came behind his chair, put her hands on his shoulders and, leaning over, kissed his

172

head. She remained there unmoving for several seconds. He suffered her to stay. Neither spoke.

Then, 'Let's go to bed, cariad,' she said.

He sensed pleading in her voice. 'Yes, why shouldn't we?' he replied, knowing her meaning; and, even though he had no desire for her, he went up with her.

    ⇛ ⇚

Adam walked up and down the road just outside Coalway, waiting. When he had complained to Martha at their last meeting that he always came round to her cottage to see her and then had to take pot-luck whether Bert was there or not, she had suggested they should meet one evening by the milestone on the Park End road. 'Meet me at seven. We can go up the lane on the right. Nobody ever goes there.'

And here he was. He saw a couple coming down from the village and dodged into the shadows. It was young Billy and Bessie Tingle. They, too, had nowhere to go for a bit of privacy, and went up the very lane on the right that Martha had indicated.

When she arrived he steered her along the road, watching for anyone who might see them. 'I don't like meeting like this, always scared we'll be seen together.'

'Oh, I think it's exciting.'

She is implying I am a coward, thought Adam. 'If anyone sees us they'll spread the news all round the village. Then where shall we be?'

She brushed his fears aside. 'We must take things as they come. Look, Bert is on second shift all next week. Come round any evening. If Emrys is in, you can make out you've come round for a chat with him.'

Adam had already wondered whether he should tell Emrys of his affair and ask for his help in meeting Martha. He had decided not to; Emrys was too decent a fellow to be involved in such a business.

'But we can't repeat last time. I've been ashamed that we used your bed, like. Bert's bed, I mean. The enormity of it. Bert is supposed to be my friend.'

'Well, if he is and you don't like doing it, you'd better stop.'

'But it's a dirty trick, isn't it?'

'It's what we're doing not where we're doing it that Bert would object to, I imagine. But we've got to use what opportunities we have. Even so,' she conceded, 'perhaps home is too dangerous. You never know when Emrys or Bert might come in, even if you think they're safely out of the

173

way. Even on a Saturday night, when Bert tells me he's going out with the boys and I know he's going to see his tart in Gloucester.'

They went into the woods. Bert was soon forgotten. It had been a warm day, and the soft smell of moist earth rose up. They wandered off the path into the bracken. An owl swooped silently on a rabbit which screamed as it was carried off. Then there was quiet. Peace lapped round them.

He put his arm round her and held her close. Her body smiled. 'I love you, Martha. But what can we do?'

'Nothing. Just enjoy things as we can.'

'I don't want it to end. I can't conceive it ending.'

'I don't want it to end, either. But you've got to face the possibility. Meanwhile, as you say, we have to be as careful as we can. And that takes some doing in a village like this one.'

The talk slowed down and then stopped of its own accord. Their minds were stilled. They found a log sheltered from the wind and sat on it silently, content to be close to one another. Then the proximity of their bodies had its effect, and they slipped off the log to the ground and made love. Delicious love it was, on the soft turf of the Forest under the stars, with the sweet smell of evening enveloping them. An hour later they strolled back towards the village, hand in hand, relaxed.

'Have you finished that book on radicalism and socialism you bought in Gloucester yet?' asked Martha.

'Not quite. It's rather hard going, but I'm ploughing on. I want to talk to you about it sometime.'

'Yes.'

'Since I've known you, Martha, my mind have expanded, like. I can understand much more of what I read. And I want to learn more and more, about trade unionism and politics and how the country is run and why working people can't have a better deal. I want to help them get it, to do something about it myself.'

She pressed his hand. 'Yes, I know.'

They walked on in silence, happy to be in each other's company.

'You know, Martha, the union are thinking about putting up a collier for parliament at the next general election.'

'Yes. Emrys told me.'

'We need some working class MPs. Our present ones have no idea what sort of lives working people live. Emrys thinks I should stand as candidate if I get the chance. But I'm not so sure.'

She was silent, thinking. 'Well,' she said at last, 'you've no experience in being an MP.'

'Nor had any of the others when they started.'

'Do you know what you'd have to do if you were elected?'

She is doubtful whether I could do the job, he thought. 'I've been reading the parliamentary reports in the paper lately. I don't understand a lot of what goes on, but I do understand the bits about conditions of work for working men and wages and such like. Especially the bits about colliers. And I could learn more.'

'You could learn as quickly as anyone else.' Then she stopped and gripped him by the arms. 'You have a go. You'd be hardworking and sincere, and you have youth and will-power, as well. I'd be behind you.'

His gratitude for her proffered support surged through him. He put his arm round her waist, pulled her towards him and kissed her.

They strolled on. 'Emrys tells me that Joseph Cowmeadow is likely to be nominated,' she said. 'If he is, you'll have to fight him, and you'll have to start preparing now. Is he as popular with the men as they say? I can't judge; I don't go to meetings.'

'A lot of the men like him, but a lot of the committee don't and they're the ones who will do the deciding, although they will be consulting their lodges.' He stopped walking and faced her. 'But the committee like me. And the men like me, too. You should have heard them clapping and cheering for me at the meeting in Coleford last night. And last Wednesday at Berry Hill. The men really believe in me and trust me. I can tell from what they say at meetings and afterwards. I think they would follow me anywhere.' His eyes had became bright with excitement, his face red with enthusiasm and his tongue smooth with eloquence. 'I can hold an audience in the cup of my hand.'

Martha was silent. He realised he had been boasting and had shown her a side of him she had never seen before. Then he regretted his words. 'But I'm not sure I really am better than Joseph Cowmeadow,' he added lamely.

'Surely it's a question whether you get the nomination. And then whether you get enough votes at the polls.'

'A lot more working class men got the vote a few years back with that Franchise Act, and they said at the last committee meeting that nearly a quarter of the electorate in the Forest is now colliers.' He was proud of the easy way the unusual words slipped off his tongue. 'They would support me I suppose, but would that be enough?'

'You'd get the vote of practically all the working people, I'm sure – the iron workers, the stone men, the quarrymen, the agricultural workers at the other end of the constituency. They'd all rather vote for a working man than a middle-class Liberal or an aristocratic Tory.'

'True.'

'So, all you've got to do is get the union nomination.' She hugged his arm as they walked. 'But you'll have to go about it the right way.'

'What do you mean?'

'You'll have to let it be known that you want to stand. Take people aside, buy them a pint and talk to them. Joseph Cowmeadow's not down to earth like you. He can't talk about everyday things over a pint in the pub. You can.'

Such wise words. She believed in him and would support him. He held her tight and kissed her. He was more bound to her than ever.

The next day Adam had to see Joseph Cowmeadow about some disaffection among the colliers at Trafalgar. On his way he considered afresh his chances of securing the nomination as parliamentary candidate. In spite of the encouragement Martha had given him he still had doubts about standing. But did his doubts spring from a feeling that Joseph would be a better candidate, a worthier man, or from fear that he might be defeated? There was no doubt that Joseph would fight, would appeal to the men and to the committee for support, pointing out what he had done to bring about the creation of the branch and the work he had carried out for it since. He could be a tough fighter, as the coalmasters knew.

But Adam could fight too, and he knew he stood a chance. He went through the names of the men on the committee and clocked up supporters on the fingers of his hands. Then he took his decision. He would stand.

He was still thinking about his candidature when he sat down opposite Joseph to discuss the Trafalgar problem. 'Joseph, I think we ought to threaten Brain with a strike if he don't come forward with some compromise.'

'No, no. It's too early to talk about a strike.'

'You're always against strikes these days.'

'Strikes are to the social world what wars are to the political. They're crimes unless they are absolutely necessary.'

'Threats of a strike can do wonders. I brought the Park End men out on strike before they even joined the union and we got nearly all we wanted.' Adam's decision to stand against Joseph as parliamentary candidate gave him confidence and the encouragement to push his ideas firmly.

'You flatter yourself if you think it was your leadership and ability that achieved what the men wanted at Park End.'

Adam became tense with irritation. 'I do, do I? Don't forget that you tackled Sully first and got nowhere. It was only the second time when I went by myself that I got what we wanted from him.'

Joseph Cowmeadow shrugged his shoulders as if he couldn't be bothered to argue. 'Sully would have yielded if you had pressed for consultation at the beginning, I'm sure. All you succeeded in doing was lose the men a month's pay.'

'They didn't see it that way.' Adam got up, exasperated.

'Well, it's different at Trafalgar. Markets are contracting now. When you took the Park End men out there was a boom. If we call a strike, we'll cause the men untold suffering, and they'll be driven back to work like dogs.'

'You're not reflecting the views of the men.'

'The men are all behind me. You saw that at the last meeting we had at the colliery gates, didn't you?'

'Yes, you raised their spirits with your fiery talk and threats against the masters. Now you talk about negotiations, more negotiations. You say one thing at meetings, but when it comes to the point you want to do something different.'

'I may use my oratory at meetings with the men but it's always been my policy to be reasonable and persuasive with the coalmasters. You can learn a lot from what I do and say, young fellow.'

Adam fumed inside himself. He seldom became as annoyed as he was now. Why did this man have the knack of upsetting him? He knew what he was trying to do; he was trying to impose his experience and superior rank in the union on him to keep him subordinate. And his tactics to achieve this were to provoke him while keeping calm himself. So Adam relaxed, looked Joseph in the face with the faintest suggestion of a smile, and said nothing. After a minute's silence he decided to attack him on another front. 'It seems, in spite of all your wisdom, things aren't going too well in your little patch at Lightmoor. There be trouble there and the men won't swallow what you're trying to force down their throats.'

'You leave Lightmoor to me.'

'They say you're in Crawshay's pocket, that you accept his views because you're on good terms with him. Do you know that?'

'Crawshay is courteous because he respects my views and is prepared to negotiate with me.'

Adam deemed it wise not to pursue his point. Indeed, he scented danger in this method of attacking his rival.

Joseph Cowmeadow looked at him quietly. 'One thing I should like to say, Adam. Whatever our differences over Trafalgar, we must conceal them from the men. If all this wrangling becomes known it won't do the union any good.'

'I agree, Joseph.' Adam's good humour had returned. 'No-one will know as far as I'm concerned. It won't be in the history books.' He laughed. 'I don't think either of us will be in them. And I agree we should give negotiation one more chance at Trafalgar.'

Thus was the breach covered by a thin skin of reconciliation, but Adam knew that the slightest prick could cause it to open up again. As he left Joseph he reminded himself that, though he had given in over Trafalgar, he would still fight him for the parliamentary candidature. As he walked home he wondered whether he had been right in saying neither of them would be in the history books.

CHAPTER 23

'Good,' said Hermione as she opened a letter at the breakfast table. 'The Crawshays are coming to dinner next Wednesday. And they are bringing Hubert.'

Alice was sure her mother wanted young Hubert as a son-in-law. She had seen him at the Crawshay dinner party last summer and had satisfied herself he passed all her criteria: he was educated, presentable to friends and relations, came from a respectable family and had or would in time have a good income.

Alice smiled to herself, and then grew angry. Were her own views on whom she might marry of no importance? She was not attracted to Hubert; she did not even want him as a friend. She had not been impressed with him at the dinner with the Crawshays. He had sat, determined, it seemed, not to make any response that was not demanded of him. Perhaps he was just shy. More likely he was dull. Perhaps he was also unintelligent. Physically, he seemed a bit weedy – and Alice's mind went back to her encounter with young Billy who had rescued her when she had fallen down in the road; *his* masculinity had bowled her over. But mind was more important than physique, and she finally decided that, after all her lamentations that she never met any young people, she would give Hubert another chance. She sighed. There seemed nothing other than being courted for marriage and having a friendly relationship with a member of the opposite sex. Not being hostile to him would also stave off her mother's wrath.

There was, of course, another factor. Did Hubert accept that Alice was the woman for him? If he did not, clearly Hermione would have to exercise considerable ingenuity.

The Crawshays arrived on time. Henry Crawshay greeted the Sullys affably and Eliza beamed at everyone, her eyelids wrinkling with benevolence. Hubert hung back until his father drew him into the circle.

Hermione had expended much energy and money to make it a memorable dinner. Alice suspected her mother had two aims during the visit; the first was to watch how she behaved towards Hubert, and the second to curry favour with Eliza Crawshay because, though she thought her vulgar and disliked her because she was Welsh, she was an influential person in the Forest and could lead to introductions to other well-placed families.

Hermione had seated Hubert between herself and Alice at table, and whenever she caught her eye she gave a determined smile to encourage her in her dealings with Hubert. The conversation hummed – polite chatter mostly from Hermione. Superficial comment with no content, thought Alice. Her father also became bored and began to discuss his pits with Henry.

'James, no talk about coal, if you please,' said Hermione.

To relieve the ensuing tension and at the same time to bring her son into the conversation, Eliza said, 'Hubert, tell us about your visit to Mr Brain at Trafalgar last week.'

'Yes, Mamma, but that was mostly about coal as well.'

Everything seems to centre on coal in this part of the world, thought Alice.

'Well,' began Hubert diffidently, 'I'm interested in the development of the commercial use of electricity, and Mr Brain is experimenting with its use for shot-firing. He says it will revolutionise the extraction of coal from the pits.'

'Most interesting,' murmured Hermione.

'Do you know much about electricity, Miss Sully?' asked Hubert, to deflect the attention of the table from himself more than to involve her in the discussion.

Alice smiled her ignorance and got on with her meal.

'I suppose we shall all be lighting our pits with electricity some day,' Henry Crawshay joined in. 'Brain already lights his pits with gas, you know.'

'But would not a flame cause an explosion underground?' asked Alice.

'Oh, no, Miss Sully,' said Hubert. 'There is no fire damp in Forest pits.'

Alice was silent. Her attempt to join in the conversation had not been a success. She decided to keep quiet.

'The men seem to be against gas lighting,' said Hubert.

'Probably because they have to pay for the gas out of their wages,' said Henry.

'Colliers are quite illogical people,' said Sully. 'Lack of education, I suppose.'

180

Meanwhile Alice was appraising Hubert. He was dull, there was no doubt about it, and he could only talk about dull subjects.

Hermione decided to change the subject. 'Do you know this part of the Forest well, Mr Crawshay?' she said, smiling at Hubert.

Hubert blushed. 'No, but we had a very pleasant ride through the woods on our way over, and Park End seems an interesting village, if I may say so.' Hubert looked at Alice and allowed his face to break into a smile. 'Perhaps it may be possible to look round it before we return?'

Now that shows a bit of enterprise, thought Alice, even though she would have preferred a walk in the countryside. However, to suggest such a walk to a man she had met only twice would be improper.

They went into the sitting-room for coffee. Henry Crawshay looked out of the window. 'I see you have a flourishing ironworks here.'

'Would you like to go round it this afternoon?' asked Sully.

'I have one of my own at Cinderford,' said Henry modestly, 'but I am sure Hubert would like to, wouldn't you Hubert?'

Hubert thought he would, and Sully sent a servant to Gunter at the colliery offices to ask him to give Mr James of the ironworks his compliments and ask if a small party might pay a visit. 'Then tell Mr Gunter to come here and conduct this young gentleman and anyone else who wants to go with him on the tour.'

'Would, perhaps, Miss Sully care to accompany me?' said Hubert, and very daringly gave Alice a smile.

'What a good idea,' said Hermione.

Gunter arrived and was introduced. 'Now you young people go off with Gunter, and I will talk business with Mr Crawshay. Then when you return it will be tea time.'

'Get your coat, Alice, and don't keep Mr Crawshay waiting.' Hermione paused, and then added, 'I think I will come, too.'

It was but a hundred yards from the Sully's house to the ironworks. Alice decided that she would be reasonably friendly with Hubert. 'This is my first visit to these ironworks,' she told him, 'even though we've lived on top of them since we arrived in Dean.' Hubert smiled appreciatively.

As they entered the gates they could see the intense activity, the brawn that went into making iron. Men and boys were loading iron bars onto trucks and manipulating horses into shafts to pull them. The horses whinnied to the soothing cries of 'Whoa!' as their hooves clattered on the cobbles. Hubert seized Alice's arm and drew her back as three youths pushed past them with a tram laden with smouldering slag, hot, red, sulphurous and menacing, its wisps of smoke stretching out for the lungs of passers-by.

Hermione coughed and turned to talk to Gunter. Alice could see that, from the whiff of sulphur that her mother had inhaled, she was wondering whether she had been wise to come. But she would have insisted on coming if only to chaperone her, since it was not proper for a young girl to go to a place like the ironworks with only Hubert and Gunter, and the works were bound to be filled with common working men.

Mr James, the owner of the ironworks, came forward to meet them. He was an old bent man, well into his seventies, who had worked in iron so long that it had entered his soul. He told them what ironmaking had been like in Dean in the old days, how he had recently built a third furnace with all the up-to-date devices, how good his relations were with Mr Sully who supplied him with his coal and how unfortunate it was that today the wind was blowing in the wrong direction.

Alice found the stares of the workmen embarrassing and listening to Mr James above the noise fatiguing. Her mother, she could see, found the whole excursion tedious. But Herbert listened attentively, asked questions about technicalities and nodded when given the answers.

'You are particularly lucky this afternoon,' Mr James said. 'We are just about to tap a furnace.'

He ushered the party into a shed in front of one of the furnaces. Its time had come, and it was rumbling fearfully. It had digested the iron-ore, coke and limestone that had been poured into its maw, and was ready to give birth to its iron.

The rodder was there, swigging water from a bottle. His shirt was off, his body already glistening with sweat. The smell of his body drifted over towards them. Alice was embarrassed to look at him, but she noticed her mother was admiring his physique. His labourers stood around, waiting his bidding. Workers from other parts of the works had crowded in to watch, for tapping a furnace was a thrilling experience for everyone connected with the works and the climax of all their efforts.

'Stand back,' warned the rodder. He approached the side of the furnace, crouching and half turning because of the heat, his eyes screwed up as if fearing an attack from the monster before him. He positioned his iron rod in the tap hole at the base of the furnace, and with a sledgehammer drove it through the clay bung. With a hiss the molten iron began to emerge from its confinement, slowly for a second as if feeling its way and then rushing out. The rodder jumped back to avoid being splashed as the liquid metal, almost as fluid as water, spurted out in all directions. A most beautiful yellow it was, with a shot of violet, but so bright that Alice put her hands before her eyes.

Out the molten iron gushed, aggressive and insolent, bringing with it heat that rushed to the four corners of the shed. Into the troughs of sand in the pig-bed in front of the furnace it gushed, spitting and splashing in its haste and causing white sparks like fiery spiders to leap up wherever it met wet sand. Then it slowed a little, its anger cooling, and ran into the side channels that came from the troughs.

'You can see why we call the big channels sows and the little ones pigs,' said Mr James. 'They are just like piglets feeding from their mothers.' Mr James was proud of his analogy, but Hermione, fearing for Alice's sensitivity, looked reprovingly at him.

Alice went over to one of the pigs to inspect the molten metal. The heat from it reached up to her face and she was about to return to the party when there was an explosion and a lump of red hot iron hit her and set fire to her skirt. Where the lump had come from no-one knew. In her retreat she fanned the flame in her blazing skirt and smoke and yellow flame rose before her face. A vision of the old men injured in the ironworks, their faces pock-marked, their eyes raised-up and empty, whom she had seen in the village, rose before her. Mr James was nearest and turned to help her, but he was old and rheumaticky and it was Hubert who reached her first. He pulled her to the ground, threw his coat over her and put out the flames.

The workers, fearful at the enormity of the accident, cringed back in case any of them should somehow be accused of causing it. Perhaps it was the fault of one of the men at the tap-hole, perhaps it was the wind blowing down the furnace chimney.

Alice lay on the ground semi-conscious, moaning quietly. Inside a voice was telling her not to play the helpless female, but the pain was too great and she fainted.

'My poor lamb,' wailed Hermione. 'She's dead.'

'No, she's not,' said Hubert with decision. 'We must take her back to the house and send for a doctor.' And he picked her up in his arms and carefully carried her out of the ironworks.

Dr Batten, the pit doctor who also acted as the Sullys' private physician, was summoned. 'Her burns are severe,' he said as he eased pieces of charred clothing from the raw wounds, 'but they're mostly on her arms and legs. Fortunately the shock to her system is not so great as it would have been if her face or body had been burned. There will be some scarring, but it should not be too noticeable.' He applied temporary dressings and gave her a sedative. 'Now she must rest. I'll come back tomorrow.'

Hermione tucked her up in bed and hovered round her, while her father gave a bulletin to the guests in the drawing-room below.

ॐ ॐ

Hubert Crawshay rode over to Park End House the day after the accident to enquire how Alice was faring, but as she was still in bed he did not see her.

'He sent,' said Hermione, 'his heart-felt sympathy – and these flowers.'

Alice glanced at the flowers and put them aside.

'I must say he seems extremely concerned about you. I expect he will come every day with flowers,' added Hermione hopefully.

Hermione was right; flowers did come every day. Alice had to remain in bed, her legs and arms on fire, but she decided she must write to Hubert as soon as she could to thank him for his prompt action in putting out the flames, and for the many bouquets of flowers he had sent and his wishes for her recovery. As she eased herself up to write she vaguely recalled the comfort she had felt from his arms as he had carried her home – he was not as weedy as she had thought – and the concern he had shown when they got back to the house.

'I've invited him to dinner on Sunday,' said Hermione when Alice was able to get up and walk round the house.

In the afternoon after dinner Alice wanted to go for a walk, but was prevailed upon to accept that she was not fit enough.

'Why don't you two go into the drawing-room and have a cosy little chat?' suggested Hermione.

Alice swallowed hard at her mother's gushing and the obvious display of her aim, and led Hubert into the drawing-room. They chatted, but it was not a cosy chat and was little only in the sense that the subjects they discussed were trivial. When they ran out of conversation Alice offered to play the piano. 'Though I must warn you, Mr Crawshay, I am out of practice.' She asked him if he had a favourite composer, but it soon became clear he did not know the difference between Bach and Brahms. Nonetheless, he tapped his foot and moved his head from side to side in time with the music.

'You play divinely, Miss Sully.'

'Thank you, Mr Crawshay. You are too kind. Unfortunately, my piano teacher does not think so.'

They talked about Alice's piano teacher, according to her a grumpy old man, 'But mother thinks he's excellent, so I have to put up with him.'

Alice looked at Hubert, not knowing what to say next, and he sensed it was time to go. 'But I tire you, Miss Sully, so remiss of me. May I please call again?'

'Yes, indeed,' sighed Alice as she got up. Her reply, vague though it was, seemed to give him encouragement, for he began to call every week.

Soon she was recovered sufficiently to go walking with him in the Forest with Hermione as chaperone. Then he asked if she would care to come riding with him. Alice had a pony, a present from her father to make her life in Park End more interesting, but she had conceived no liking for it and consequently had achieved no great expertise. But now Hubert wanted her to ride with him and she was not averse to the idea. She looked at her mother for her agreement, for she knew she would not want her to forfeit such an opportunity. Hermione seemed uncertain. Of course, she ought not to go off alone with Hubert. But her mother could not chaperone her – she could not ride and had no horse anyway – and there was no-one else who could perform that office. As they waited for Hermione's reply Hubert glanced at Alice with a faint smile, and for the first time a link of friendship, a link of conspiracy, was formed between them. The answer came as Alice expected.

'What a good idea.'

So Hermione waved them goodbye for a couple of hours, after having told Alice that, for propriety's sake, she must not dismount. They rode to the Speech House; and Alice in flagrant disobedience got off her horse and they had refreshments.

This was the first of many rides in the Forest with him. She preferred it to sitting in the house, and while she was riding, she told herself, she did not have to listen to his limited conversation. Soon, however, she found she was looking forward to their rides together. More, the fresh air and exercise stimulated her and her pale complexion began to assume a glow. She was pleased when she first noticed it in her looking-glass. Jane Eyre, as far as she could remember, never went riding and had remained pale all through the novel.

Hermione, pressing the relationship, invited him to dinner occasionally on Sunday. Soon it was every Sunday, and he seemed to need no persuading to come. Alice thought he must be aware of her mother's motives, and was prepared to be embarrassed; but if he was aware of them, it did not seem to worry him. She herself was determined that however much Hubert was becoming more acceptable to her as a companion she would not be pushed into an engagement she did not want. However, she decided he was a pleasant if on occasion a dull companion, and she did not wish to spurn him. He was certainly better than no companion at all.

CHAPTER 24

Adam was mystified. As they had filed out of the Town Hall after a union committee meeting Joseph Cowmeadow had buttonholed him. 'If you're not busy tomorrow evening would you come to my place for a chat?' Perhaps he was not so much mystified as wary. Joseph had never invited him to his cottage before, and he was certain he did not intend it to be a social visit at which he could try to mend relations between them. Adam found Joseph's cottage at Bilson and knocked on the door. Mrs Cowmeadow ushered him into the parlour, which Joseph obviously used as an office. Joseph turned stiffly in his chair and greeted him. Adam decided that the beam of welcome was more artificial and calculated than usual and was placed on his guard.

'Sit down, Adam. You know the committee are considering selecting someone as parliamentary candidate. There's bound to be a general election in the next nine months.'

So that was it. Joseph Cowmeadow wanted his support for the nomination. 'Yes,' said Adam cautiously. 'We've talked about it enough times at meetings, but nobody has said he wants to stand.'

'Precisely. Well, I'm thinking of standing and I'm asking for your support.'

Adam was not yet prepared to declare his own interest. 'Be anyone else putting his name forward, then?'

'Not so far as I know.'

Then why does he need my support? thought Adam. If there is no rival he will get the nomination. 'You've got to be keen and strong to take on a job like that, Joseph. And have strong political views.'

Mrs Cowmeadow brought in two cups of tea.

'Would you be lining up with the Liberals or taking the same line as people like George Odger?'

'Never heard of him. Is he one of those socialists?'

Adam was about to give a few facts about Odger but decided not to be sidetracked. 'Presumably you would support the Liberals, then?'

'I am a member of the Liberal Party, which I gather you are not. Liberal MPs elected by working people will bring improvements to the lives of ordinary folk.'

Adam sipped his tea, prepared to listen.

'Such Liberal MPs will support the unions, especially financially, so they can provide really good benefits like sick pay and disablement pay and funeral expenses for their members.'

'A trade union should not be a benefit society, Joseph, all that paying in and taking out. Other organisations can do that. Your trouble is you aim at respectability, fob-watch respectability, and hobnobbing with the coalmasters, like. You accept society as it is, and want to soften the edges and cadge just that little bit more from the employers.' Adam was clearly upsetting Joseph but he pressed on. 'Working class MPs should set their sights higher than that. They should advocate a change in the economic system of the country. That's what I want: a complete recast of society.'

'Socialism?'

'Yes, if you want to call it that.'

'If you feel so strongly what a working class MP should be,' retorted Joseph sarcastically, 'why don't you put your name forward as a candidate?'

'I intend to.'

Joseph Cowmeadow stared at him. How stupid, Adam said to himself, that he never thought I was a possible rival.

Joseph got up and went to the window, and absentmindedly combed his beard with his fingers. Then he turned, shut his jaw with a snap and glared at Adam. 'To be an MP would be the climax of my career as a union man. Well, I'm standing, whether you stand or not. I have plenty of support in the union.'

Adam's reply was equally uncompromising. 'It's my ambition as well, Joseph. I've thought about it for a long time, and I reckons I could do the job.'

'Better than me, with all my years of experience?'

'Better than you, perhaps, because of my wider outlook.'

Joseph turned to him, his eyes white with fear and hate. 'I shall fight you, Adam, don't think I won't. I won't give in.'

Adam suddenly felt sorry for him. He realised he was not the strong opponent he had always thought him, but a vulnerable and uncertain man. But there was nothing more to say on the subject, and he rose.

'Let's leave it to the union committee to decide, Joseph. Please thank your wife for the tea.' And putting on his cap he left.

❧ ❦

While Adam was making his way back from Cinderford, Catrin, Grancher and George were at home, chatting round the fire. Too tired to chase the tail-end of the day, they were content to sit down with it until it forced them to bed. Emma had already retired.

Grancher poked the fire, and a sparkle of tiny stars fell on the hearth.

'That's right, Grancher, you have a good old poke,' said George.

'Never fear, I shall if I has mind to.'

'Why don't you go to bed?' said Catrin. 'Tired it is you are after looking after Lennie all afternoon.'

Grancher did not reply, but sat gazing into the fire, a flicker of red reflecting in his beard.

'Thinking of old times?' said George. 'When you was a young man chasing the wenches?'

Grancher looked up. 'Aye, them were the days. But I wasn't thinking about that. I was thinking about Lennie and how we played this afternoon. He kept climbing on me lap and pulling me beard and stroking it, like. I always knew he would be a lovely lad right from the day he were born.'

He paused and put a finger to his eyes. 'My blood may be watery and slow nowadays, you know, but I be proud that some of it do flow in his veins, and that his flesh be part of mine.' He looked round to see if the others were listening. 'They talks about immortality, but when I've been taken to the graveyard, I shall live on in him, even into the next century. Aye, that I will. That be the sort of immortality I wants.'

When he had gone off to bed, Catrin said, 'He loves to play with Lennie, but he suffers afterwards. I've seen him collapse in his chair tired out of an evening, but he always insists on going up to tell him his story in bed.' She continued with her knitting. Then she held it up, a vest. 'There. Done at last, it is.'

'Very nice,' said George.

'Here, you have it.' She threw it over to him.

'Like an old married couple we be night after night,' said George.

Catrin did not reply. She did not like the comparison, though it was true George stayed in most nights nowadays and Adam was out.

George caught her thoughts. 'Aye, Adam's not home much of an evening.' He got up and pulled his chair nearer to Catrin's. 'I know things is not going right between you and Adam,' he said. 'It's a shame. You started off all right, and now it be like this. P'raps the baby come too soon.'

'Yes, perhaps. But that's the way it is.' George was again trying to get her to criticise Adam. But she did not want to discuss him with George or anyone else; she still loved him so much. However, in spite of her resolve the words rushed out: 'If only he would give up the union work or even cut it down and give more time to me and Lennie things would come right, I'm sure.'

'I wonder.'

'What do you mean?'

'Nothing.'

'What do you mean, George?' What was he trying to tell her? It was revealed to her all at once. She formulated the idea and uttered it at the same time. 'George, do you think he is interested in someone else?'

He was silent.

'George, answer me.'

'No, Catrin.' He patted her hand. 'I know nothing about that.'

Catrin snatched her hand away. She was not reassured, but did not know how to pursue her question. And there was no-one else to ask, no-one in the village she was friendly with to whom she could confess her fears and seek advice. She rose, fearful and uncertain, and went to the dresser and straightened the ornaments with anxious fingers. The rosy calm of the evening had been shattered.

George made to approach her, but, embarrassed, changed his mind. 'I think I'll go to bed,' he said. 'I 'spect you'll wait up for Adam.'

'Yes.' Also embarrassed, and for want of something to do until George had left the room, she took the brush and tidied the hearth.

The next morning Emma came in from the back kitchen. 'What be that you have there?' she demanded.

Catrin was examining the label on a bottle of patent medicine. 'Something I've bought for Lennie.'

Emma seized the bottle. 'Where did you get this?'

'In Coleford when I went yesterday,' said Catrin defiantly.

'"Dr Joseph Holmes's Special Remedy for Stomach Cramp, Indigestion and Loss of Appetite",' read Emma. She sighed and shot her eyes towards Heaven.

'It's for Lennie.'

'Where did you get the money from?'

'From the mustard tin. Lennie's not eating, and he's getting so thin. I had to do something to encourage his appetite.'

'You ask me before you takes any more money from that mustard tin, do you hear?'

'You needn't be so mean about something for Lennie, poor mite.'

'I reckon he don't eat because of all that cow's milk you gives him. You fill him up with that and he don't want any real food.'

'The milk doesn't fill him. Anyway I've stopped giving it to him. Thin, it is, almost blue. I believe they put water in it.' She remembered the creamy milk they drew from the cows in Wales.

'Adam was fat enough at his age. And I didn't need to give him no cow's milk, nor any fancy expensive stuff from bottles.'

'Well he's my son, and I must do what I think is best for him.'

'And he be my grandson.' Emma looked at her, glowering.

But Catrin, pale and tight-lipped, would not look up or reply. The silence beat down on her head. Then, unable to restrain tears, she took Lennie and the medicine upstairs to the bedroom.

⇛ ⇚

That evening as she climbed into bed she told Adam. He listened as he undressed, then said, 'Ma knows a lot about feeding children, even though she only had two.'

'You're not much support for me. You don't seem to be interested in Lennie.'

'Of course I be interested in him. He's my son, isn't he? And I know he's not well. I can see it and I'm concerned.'

'Well, show it.'

'I've so much on my mind.'

Catrin turned away in exasperation and started on another tack. 'I have a right to some money to spend as I want to. I've told you before that you ought to have more money of your own. Look at the row we had before you would give me something to buy Lennie some new shoes.'

Adam sat on the edge of the bed heavily and rolled Catrin towards the middle. He took his boots off and threw them in the corner. 'Don't get me involved in your rows with my mother. I'm not interfering. They say two women in one kitchen always disagree. You must make the best of it.' He stood up, took his trousers off, scratched his belly and yawned. Catrin regarded him distastefully. Then he climbed into bed alongside her.

'Move over. I be tired.' And in a few minutes he was asleep.

CHAPTER 25

When Adam's attention was not concentrated on something specific he thought of Martha. He thought of her when he was walking in the woods to work; he thought of her when he was at the coal face plying his mattock; he thought of her when he awoke in the middle of the night and felt Catrin's body close to him and wished it was Martha's. He wanted to be with her, to relish her company and be charmed by her physical closeness, not occasionally, but always.

He was morose when they next met. At his suggestion they went to a hut deep in the Forest owned by a collier who ran sheep on the waste. They edged in and Adam lit a match. A broken-down table and a bench by the wall, a heap of rags and some hay in the corner flickered softly into view. They sat on the bench as the match went out, Martha snuggling beside him with her arm through his. It was a cosy haven, warm in the shelter of the trees and smelling stale but sweet.

'I wish we could meet openly and not have to scheme for every little minute we has together,' said Adam.

'Relax, my dear.' She fingered the hair on his forearm.

He grasped her hand and turned to her, trying to make out her features in the gloom. The ideas that had bombarded him with growing intensity in recent months came tumbling out.

'You give me something Catrin can't and won't ever be able to. Suppose I left her and we went off together, you and me?'

'My God. Have you thought of the consequences?'

'Yes, I have, a lot.'

'Presumably you think I'm prepared to leave Bert.'

'You say you hate the sight of him.'

'Perhaps I do, but it doesn't mean I'm prepared to go off with you.'

'Martha! How could you be so unkind?'

'If we went off together, what would happen to Catrin and Lennie?'

A noise outside made him start. He wondered who it was. Someone who had followed them, perhaps? Some peeping Tom who was looking

192

for details of their illicit meeting to whisper throughout the village? He disengaged his arm. 'Wait here.' He went to the door, quietly opened it and peered round. There was silence. He waited a few minutes, ready to pounce if he saw a shadow escaping. All he could hear was sheep cropping at the side of the hut. He clapped his hands and shooed them away. He went back.

'Sheep, that's all.'

'You're getting nervous. I said what would happen to Catrin and Lennie if we went off together?' She seemed determined to make him face reality.

'I suppose my family would look after them,' he said slowly, 'just as they would if I was killed down pit.'

'Deserting your wife and child is not the same as being killed in the pit. And it would not be fair on George. He'd have to find for four as well as himself. He'd never be able to get married and have children with that load on his back.'

Adam was silent.

'And what would it do to Catrin?'

The full horror of his proposal now bore down on him. He visualised Catrin's reaction when she learnt he was abandoning her, how she would curl up like a sick animal, pushing the pain deeper into her heart. His face convulsed at the thought and he shook his head to reject the vision. 'No, that's not the way.'

She took him in her arms. 'My dear, you are in trouble. Can't you just accept our relationship as it is, enjoy it for what it is?'

'Oh, Martha, we're in a mess. Have we done wrong?'

'Of course we have, but when you don't do wrong in this life, it's often because you haven't the chance to do otherwise.'

'I don't understand.'

She did not explain. 'Adam, we can't dodge our responsibilities, much as we might want to, either of us. You know that in your heart, don't you, dearest?'

'You don't understand what I be going through.'

'I'm not rejecting you, just being practical. You can see that, surely?'

He turned away. This was not what he wanted to hear.

'You are so sensible in other ways. Look how you deal with union matters. You set out the problems and the objectives and work out a solution.'

'That's different.'

'You must adopt the same approach here, love, don't you see? Separate the emotions from the practicalities. Logic, patience, perseverance, they have all helped you to the top of the union.'

He felt she had sidetracked him from love to ambition. Yes, his abilities had taken him to the top, or nearly to the top of the Forest union. If he could out-manoeuvre Joseph Cowmeadow, he would be its leader. More, he reckoned he would get the nomination for the parliamentary candidature. And if he didn't get into parliament, he could climb the union ladder further and get to Federation headquarters in Birmingham.

But now he was sidetracking himself. His mind returned to Martha's arguments against leaving Catrin, about accepting their situation, and they overwhelmed him; but he was determined not to give in without more thought. He would think again when he was not so tired.

'Yes,' he said to stave off any further arguments from Martha, 'perhaps you are right.'

'Of course, I'm right. And I think you know it.'

To soften her words, she put her hand at the back of his head and brought his lips down to hers. Then she rose and drew him to the pile of hay in the corner of the hut. They sat down. Soft and enveloping it was, and she held him close. The smell of the hay soothed him, and the warmth from it and from her body was comforting.

'Like babes in the woods we are,' she said. 'Bewildered and lost.' She laughed. 'But we have each other.'

Adam did not answer. As he lay in her arms and she began to calm him with her caresses he began to relax. Then his heart welled up and told him she had not consoled him. Remaining deep down, immovable as a rock at the coal face, was this awful dilemma that was consuming him, this terrible uncertainty that enveloped him. What could he do? If things went wrong in ordinary everyday life, you dealt with them. If your mattock handle broke, you mended it. If your hodder did not turn up for work you cursed and did the work yourself.

But this situation was altogether different. He could not cope with it. He blamed not himself for his plight, but fate. For how could he have acted differently once he had met Martha? He had been sucked along in the tide of events, with no chance of escape.

But there was no point in tilling old ground again. He thought of prayer. He wanted to pray but realised he had no God to go to for help, no powerful agent who could miraculously put things right for him. Until the present crisis he had always been able to manage on his own. He must do so now: there was no alternative. Anyway, he wondered, did people who prayed to God get the help they sought?

He nuzzled his face in her lap for comfort and continued his silence. But he realised he was silent, not because his problem no longer gnawed at his heart, nor because he did not want to discuss his grief and its solution any more, but because he was emotionally exhausted. Like a wounded animal pursued by its enemies all he now wanted was shelter and comfort. For the time being he had both. The miner's hut was a refuge from the world. The comfort, ironically, came from the person who had not found him a solution.

☙ ❧

Enoch Tingle stopped as he came up the road. He backed a few steps and peered over the brussel sprouts at the end of Bert Preece's garden. There was no moon but the night was clear and by the starlight he could make out a couple up against the wall of Bert's pigsty. He gave a shrug and was about to move on when it occurred to him that the form of the girl seemed familiar. He looked again, trying to make out the shape of her head, the shape of her body. Surely, it wasn't his Bessie making love so brazenly? Uncertain, he shook his head and walked on.

Back in his kitchen he picked up the newspaper. A few minutes later he heard the click of the garden gate and Bessie entered.

'You be late,' he challenged. 'Where you bin?' Bessie, he thought, looked disconcerted.

'Over at Mary Jane's.'

'You sure?'

'Ask her if you don't believe me.'

'Don't talk to your father like that.'

Bessie edged away.

'Didn't I see you round the back of Bert Preece's pigsty a few minutes ago?'

'No.'

'I've told you if I ever catches you doing anything like that I'll tan the arse off you.'

'It weren't me, I tell you. I saw them as well. Doing a right gig they was, too.'

'Don't be disgusting. If it weren't you, who was it, then?'

195

'Dad, I don't know.' She looked indignantly at her father. Then she said, 'I reckon it were Martha Preece.'

'Who was she with?'

'I don't know. I think it was Emrys, the Preece's lodger.'

Enoch turned to his newspaper again. So they were doing the dirty on Bert. Bert himself was no angel, if all he heard was true. But for your wife to do it with the lodger! It was a strange animal that messed on its own doorstep.

∾ ∾

Alice's relationship with Hubert had settled down to a routine that was predictable and dull. She could see it continuing for ages, plodding along the same path and getting more humdrum as the years went by. She supposed that Hubert, in his stolid way, had marriage in mind. Now a routine had been established, he probably called the present relationship a courtship and, when he thought there was a chance of her accepting, would make a proposal of marriage. She did not want her acquiescence in their companionship now to trap her into a loveless marriage later, and decided that she must make her position clear to him sometime. Whether that time had now been reached she was not certain, but until she was sure it had been she was content to allow the situation to continue. The alternative was to initiate a stormy confrontation with her mother for ending the relationship and a return to her previous loneliness with no one but Lizzie Prendergast to talk to.

Alice was contemplating her predicament one morning when her mother entered her room. 'Your piano teacher has come, but it's not Mr Redding, it's his son. I gather Mr Redding is ill.'

'I'm sorry,' said Alice automatically.

'I don't know that I approve of the substitute, but now he's here you'd better have a lesson from him.'

Alice did not like old Mr Redding. As she went downstairs to the drawing-room she speculated on the son, a younger edition of the father, no doubt, podgy with glasses.

He looked at her shyly as she entered the room. He was not podgy, nor did he wear glasses. He was tall and slim, his face serious, his eyes gentle and sad, and he had soft fair hair. A smile broke over his face when he saw her, crumbling away the shyness and leaving him, she thought, vulnerable; but vulnerable to what, she did not know.

'Perhaps you would like to play me something you have been practising, Miss Sully?' he said.

Without a word she found the music of a Chopin valse and began to play. It was her favourite.

He listened to the end without comment. Being nervous she had not played well, but she did not apologise.

'I can see you like Chopin. So do I.'

This was encouraging. His voice was gentle.

'That was good,' he continued. 'But I suggest that you forget you are striking the notes with your fingers. Imagine you are singing them. And may I suggest a little less sustaining pedal? When he was a young man my father heard Chopin play at a concert in London, and he said he used the sustaining pedal very sparingly.'

'Your father actually saw and heard Chopin?' Alice felt tears come to her eyes, she knew not why. His words had given her a link with the composer, a sense of contact, even of intimacy with him. His personality, his charm, his greatness had been borne in on her. And this young man had been the agent.

'Yes, and if that is how the great man played, why should we play his works differently?'

They laughed. The ice was broken.

Alice learnt a lot about piano playing from young Mr Redding that morning. Suggestions poured from him, and she assimilated them, though she retained her nervousness all through the lesson. But it was soon over. He suggested some studies she should practise for next time and, precisely on the hour, terminated the lesson. He said he would probably come in place of his father the following week.

She closed the front door after him, and stood with her back to it. What a likeable young man. So clean, so fresh, so eager, so attractive. So unlike Hubert. She did not know his Christian name, but she would find out. Somehow she did not think she would tell Lizzie about him yet. The new music teacher was not someone to share lightly.

Emrys, who had been reading by the oil lamp, put his book aside and gave a yawn and a stretch. Martha was upstairs in bed and Bert was at the Albion. As he bent down to rake out the fire, he pondered what he had been reading about socialism and a fellow called Karl Marx. He heard the gate click and then Bert hurrying up the garden path.

The front door was thrown open with such vehemence that it splintered the chair behind it. Bert lurched in, his bad leg causing him

197

more difficulty than usual. With a beery shout he grabbed Emrys by the jacket and punched him in the face.

'You bastard,' he shouted. 'You bastard, I'll teach you.'

Emrys staggered back and fell against the sideboard, knocking off a vase which broke on the floor. With the back of his hand he wiped the blood that was running from his lip.

Beer and his unsteady leg caused Bert to stagger, but he launched another blow at Emrys's face and knocked him to the ground.

'You bin fucking my wife, eh?'

Emrys got up. 'Listen, man,' he said.

'You get out of this house right away,' He shouted in fury. 'Now!'

Small though he was, Emrys was now wiry and fit and could have returned Bert's punches with more powerful blows more accurately aimed. But he had realised the cause of Bert's rage, and decided not to fight. He knew this would be seen as acceptance of guilt or cowardice, but he could see wider implications that mere retaliation would not solve.

Martha, hearing the noise, came downstairs. She looked at the broken vase on the floor and the blood on Emrys's face. 'What on earth is all this about?' she demanded.

'I'll talk to you in a minute,' snapped Bert, and turned to Emrys. 'You get out.' He advanced towards him, his fist raised to the side of his head threateningly.

'Let's sort this out,' said Martha. 'I'll not have a fight in this house.'

'Let him get out then.'

Martha, still mystified, looked at Emrys. 'Just go until I pacify him, the drunken lout.'

Emrys backed through the door into the garden. Outside he could hear their voices, charged with venom, coming muffled through the door and windows and straining the very confines of the house as they hurled invective at each other.

'As for you, you bitch, I've suspected it for a long time. Now I know.'

'Suspected what?'

'That you've bin going with another man. Now I know who it is.'

'It's not true. And even if it was, what's your worry?'

There was a short silence. Then Bert spoke, more in disbelief than anger. 'The shame of it, my wife, going with the lodger!'

'I haven't been with him.' She went on the offensive. 'And what about *my* shame, *my* feelings when I found out you were going with that woman in Gloucester?'

'That be different.'

'Yes, I thought it would be. You know something? I despise you.'

Emrys did not wait any longer. Standing one against the other, they were set for a confrontation that he did not wish to know about. He walked up the street in his shirt sleeves, for he had not brought his coat with him, trying to piece together the reason Bert had got it wrong, wondering what to do, where to go. He found himself at the other end of the village and it occurred to him to see if Adam was still up. There was a candle shining through the window, so he knocked. Adam was about to go upstairs; the others were all abed. He looked with astonishment at Emrys's distraught appearance and his bleeding lip and swollen cheek.

Emrys told him what had happened. 'It's all right, Adam. I didn't deny it.'

'Deny what?'

'I didn't say it was you and not me.'

Adam looked at him sharply. 'How did you know it was me?'

'I guessed. You couldn't live in the house without suspecting something. There's been some tittle-tattle about Martha in the village as well, but I don't think anyone has any idea it's you – except me. Bert guessed, of course, but he guessed wrong!' Emrys smiled for the first time. But he saw that a fearful thought had crossed Adam's mind.

'It hasn't been you as well, has it?' Adam stared into Emrys's eyes, penetrating for the truth.

Emrys looked steadily back. He felt for words; he had to establish with Adam that it hadn't been him as well. 'No, of course not. I've never had thoughts in that direction – for that sort of thing.' He stumbled. 'I mean – with a girl. In a way I only wish I had. But I haven't. I can't.'

He turned away. He hoped Adam understood, even if by his confession he had cast away any chance of retaining Adam's friendship. It had been agony to go so far and he did not want to have to explain more. In trying to establish his innocence with Martha – and, as he realised, Martha's innocence with him – he had confessed something he had concealed and smothered all his life. He looked round to see if Adam's face gave any clue that he understood. But there was no sign. Adam was thinking, his face set, his eyes unblinking. He indicated a chair to Emrys and took one himself.

Emrys sat down apprehensively as Adam began to speak. To Emrys's relief his reaction was not disgust at his revelation.

'You've taken the blame for me,' he said slowly, 'if you can call it that. Thank you. Why you should, I don't know. But I can't let you, I must tell Bert it wasn't you.'

'No, no, man. If you do that he'll know it's you. That will be the end, won't it? Do you want that?'

'The end?'

'The end between you and Martha, the end of your friendship with Bert and all the good you're doing with him in the union. More it will be the complete end of you in the union and of your chance of ever becoming an MP. If Bert ever learns it was you who went with Martha he'll destroy you. I've seen his anger, Adam, I know. Be sensible, man.'

Emrys could see Adam's eyes searching his face for a solution, could see that in his mind there was a conflict between his love for Martha and his prospects in the union and his desire to do the thing his conscience told him to do. Why, Adam was asking himself, did he want to take the blame? Why did he want to sacrifice himself? Why was there any doubt that he should do the honest thing and free Emrys from blame?

Adam rose and went over to the fireplace, and gazed into the embers. Finally he said, 'We'll see.'

Emrys hoped that by uttering these words Adam had yielded the argument and decided to hang on to Martha and his position in the union, though how long he would be able to do that was another matter. No doubt he would strive to the end to extract the last drops of tarnished joy from his doomed relationship with Martha.

Then Adam turned and put his hand on his shoulder; and immediately withdrew it. It was as if, Emrys thought, he were something unclean; and he flinched. Then Adam consciously replaced his hand, and by this action, this positive physical contact, Emrys knew he wished to continue his friendship with him.

'You'd better sleep in the kitchen tonight. I'll get you a blanket.'

With the blanket and the cushion from Cornelius's chair for a pillow, Emrys settled down on the hearth rug. The cold from the paved floor struck through and he slept badly, but he would have done so anyway.

200

CHAPTER 26

Adam's mind was in a whirl. What an extraordinary mess he had got himself into. Fortunately he would be seeing Martha the following evening. She had begun to use meetings at their cottage between her husband and Adam to slip him notes giving the place and time of an assignation outside the house, and had dropped him one of these only the day before Enoch Tingle had seen the couple behind Bert's pigsty.

'Thought you weren't going to turn up with all the to-do Bert caused last night,' she said when they met.

'Why shouldn't I?' He embraced her.

She disengaged herself. 'I thought you might think it was getting too hot and it was time we split up.'

She's testing me, thought Adam. 'But Martha, I love you more than ever.'

She seemed mollified. 'Adam, we must talk about this. Bert thinks it's Emrys not you, and he's furious. Wouldn't speak to me at all this morning. Sat there glowering over his breakfast and got his own. Not that I care. I shouted after him again as he slammed through the door that he was all wrong and it wasn't me and Emrys behind the pigsty. But he didn't believe me. He will in time, I suspect, if I keep on denying it. But what about Emrys? Won't he split and say it's you not him?'

'Emrys, bless him, is ready to say nothing, not a word, about anything. Tongues be already wagging in the village, and people think it was him and you, and he's prepared to let them carry on thinking it.'

'All right for you, you're not involved if this is what people think. Not much comfort for me, though.'

'No, and that's bad, but it's the way it be, Martha. In this mess we can't get it all right.'

'But why on earth is Emrys prepared to take the blame for you?'

'I suppose it's because he wants to help me. He be prepared to do it because of the trouble I'd be in if he split. There's you, the union and my relationship with Bert all at stake. I don't like it a bit, but I 'spect it'll soon blow over, like, if Emrys keeps out of Bert's way.'

'And you are prepared to let him take the blame like that?'

'Yes – for you.' He put his arms round her, and she did not push him away this time but returned his caresses.

'I think you really do love me.' They walked along the road, hand in hand. 'You know it's surprising that Bert didn't smell a rat before, but he is a bit thick at times.' She laughed.

On his way back from his tryst with Martha Adam thought about Emrys. He shrank from the idea of talking to him about Martha because, though Emrys was already heavily involved and was clearly sympathetic, he did not want to involve him further in what he no doubt thought a sordid business. And there was no other man he could approach – not even his brother George – who would give him the sympathy and support he wanted. He felt isolated. He brushed aside the thought that he didn't want to talk to Emrys because he was ashamed.

He was surprised that it had never occurred to him that Emrys never went out with girls. He recalled Waldo, Catrin's jeering, contemptible brother. His reaction on discovering him in the stable with a farmhand had been one of revulsion; but his discovery had given him the opportunity to blackmail him into supporting his efforts to marry Catrin; and he wondered in passing whether, if he had been unable to convince old Mr Evans with Waldo's help that he was a suitable husband for Catrin, he would have married someone else with happier results. But Emrys was not like Waldo. He was all that Waldo was not. And confused though Adam was, he hung on to the thought that Emrys had been his friend and had sacrificed himself when he had been in sore trouble. Adam wanted him to remain his friend; and he would keep his secret.

He insisted that Emrys should lodge with the family, for the time being at least. Even if Emrys had tried to find alternative lodgings, the Coalway housewives, fearful for their daughters, would have refused to have him inside their front door. They were not sure exactly what had gone on in Bert Preece's cottage, but there was no doubt that there must have been some hanky-panky. So they were prepared to think the worst.

The news of Emrys's ejection from the Preece house soon got round the village. 'Adulterer!' the housewives muttered over the fence, for they had often heard the word from the pulpit. 'Fornicator!' said others, and it was a more satisfactory word to get your tongue round even if you were not certain of its precise meaning. As for Martha, they had never really liked her, and were not averse now to showing it openly.

Their husbands were unwilling to discuss the matter with them. On the whole, they felt that Emrys had let his fellow men down in allowing himself to be thrown out by Bert with such lack of dignity. Even so, they would continue to drink a pint with him at the pub, for he was a good fellow really. Disappointingly, he was not prepared to give any details about either the affair or his ejection. The only information they could glean was that Enoch Tingle had seen a couple behind the pigsty and Bessie Tingle had thought, even though there had not been a moon that night, that it was Martha and Emrys – not very strong evidence. Those who were wise in such matters pointed out that Bessie's views might have been intended to throw her father off the scent of her own amorous activities, and they awarded her ten marks out of ten for ingenuity.

⇝ ⇞

'Shall we play some duos, Miss Sully?' Maurice Redding asked. 'I have brought some Schubert pieces.'

They sat at the piano on the double stool, close enough for their clothes to touch. He counted four, and gave his head a slight nod to indicate that they should start.

Alice liked his quiet authority, his seriousness and his gentleness. As the beauty of Schubert's music enveloped her, her nervousness disappeared and gave way to a sensuous dream of enjoyment. Then she stumbled over a note. They stopped and he showed her a better fingering. In doing so, he put his hand over hers and she felt the warmth of his fingers penetrating her own and their strength subduing hers. They reached the end of the piece and sat silently, both with their own thoughts.

'I like duos,' said Alice. Having uttered the words, she realised there was a message in them; and she hoped that he had interpreted them correctly.

⇝ ⇞

Catrin was sitting at the table teaching Lennie his numbers with small stones when there was a knock on the door. She opened it to find a woman she had seen about the village but had never spoken to. Clean and neat, she was, better dressed than other village women. She held a bundle of clothing in one hand and a bundle of books and newspapers tied together with string in the other.

'Does Mr Turley live here, please?'

'We have three Mr Turleys. Which one do you want?'

'I don't want any of them, really. I am Mrs Preece, Bert Preece's wife. Emrys used to lodge with us. I think he's staying here now. I've brought his things along.'

This, thought Catrin, must be Martha, who had had some sort of an affair with Emrys. At least that was what Emma had told her and her ears heard everything that was whispered in the village. Catrin hadn't believed the story and had been careful not to say anything about it to Emrys. But much as she disliked this sort of tittle-tattle, now Martha had presented herself on the doorstep she was intrigued.

'Come in, please. He doesn't live here, you know, only staying until he gets fresh lodgings.' Martha sat down and looked round. Then she looked at Catrin. For a second Catrin found her eyes piercing her as if trying to get at her innermost thoughts. She looked back defiantly. What did this woman want?

Martha looked away from Catrin and down at Lennie. 'So this is young Lennie?'

The lad stopped examining Martha and put his head in the folds of his mother's skirt.

'How did you know his name?' asked Catrin.

'Adam told me. He comes to our house occasionally, you know, to talk union business with my husband.

'He is often out on union business.'

'Yes, I imagine he is.'

'Though I don't know where he goes.'

'No.'

There was a pause. With her sack apron on and her hair uncombed, Catrin felt a slut. Martha was well-dressed, had on her best clothes, no doubt. No need for that just to bring Emrys's things round. But perhaps she was going on to visit some friends somewhere.

Then Catrin noticed that Martha was wearing on the lapel of her coat a small brooch with a green stone in it. She recognised it as the one she had discovered in Adam's coat pocket when she had taken his suit out to brush it. She had assumed he was going to give it to her as a present. Now she saw it adorning Martha Preece, and she knew in a flash that her suspicion that Adam was interested in another woman was true.

So this was the woman! How dare she flaunt the emblem of her possession of Adam before his very wife? A hard, self-assured, brazen woman! But as Catrin looked at her she realised she would be a frightening adversary.

'Lennie, why don't you go up the lane and play with the twins for an hour?' said his mother. Lennie thought this was a good idea, nodded his agreement and put his coat on.

Martha opened her bag, withdrew her purse and extracted a penny. She leaned forward and offered it to Lennie. 'Would you like to buy some sweeties?'

Lennie took the coin automatically, his big black eyes staring at Martha. 'Thank 'oo.'

Catrin opened the door and ushered Lennie out. She wanted to snatch the penny from Lennie and throw it in her face, but she did not want to upset him. She was unnerved by her discovery that this was Adam's woman and felt sick and frightened. Her thoughts tumbled over themselves – how long had this business been going on? Had they slept together? Did he really love her or was she just someone to sleep with? This woman had used the excuse of bringing Emrys's things round so that she could have a good look at her, to glory in her ability to take Adam away from her.

Martha had realised that she recognised her, and taking up her bag and muff from the table rose to leave. But Catrin, though she knew it was against her nature to be aggressive, was not going to let her go. Fury welled up inside her. All the agony she had endured during recent months because of Adam's indifference and coldness to her multiplied a thousandfold and changed to hatred, blind primeval hatred. She strode across the room. 'How dare you come here and flaunt yourself before me. Slut that you are.' She flung open the door. 'Get out of this house before I kill you.' She made a grab at the brooch but Martha turned aside and she could not reach it. Instead she snatched at the veil of Martha's hat and pulled it off her head.

'I only brought Emrys's things round.'

'That wasn't why you came. You wanted to see me. Well you've seen me now.'

Martha began a spirited defence. 'Yes I wanted to see what sort of a woman could make a fine man like Adam so miserable. Now I have and I know.'

Catrin seized her by the shoulders and shook her, and made another attempt to grab the brooch. Once more she missed but clutched Martha's blouse and ripped it to the waist.

'You bitch!' yelled Martha, but before she could respond Catrin turned her round and pushed her out of the house. She fell onto the

205

path. Catrin jumped astride of her, tore at her carefully combed honey-coloured hair and scratched her face.

'You're mad.' Martha pushed her off and getting to her feet began to run for the garden gate. Lennie had left it open so there was nothing to stop her from escaping into the lane. But Catrin was behind her and gave her an almighty shove into a pool of soft thick brown glutinous Forest mud on the other side of the lane.

Breathing heavily, her eyes staring, Catrin pushed back wisps of her hair from her face and returned to the cottage. She brushed the dirt and dust off her clothes as she went, glad only that she had not been wearing decent clothes. Inside she sat exhausted at the table. She put her head in her arms and burst into tears. Then she raised her face to the ceiling and allowed her sobs full vent. She was like an animal in distress.

❧ ❦

Catrin said nothing to Adam about the fight with Martha. She told him she had found Emrys's things on the back step when she had returned from shopping. Now that she was certain of the reason for Adam's coolness towards her she somehow felt more confident. Previously everything had been nebulous; now she had something firm to confront him with when she was ready. While he did not know she knew of the affair there was no hurry to confront him. Until she was certain what to say and when to say it she would keep quiet.

Emrys soon settled in. He stacked his few possessions in a corner of their bedroom and slept under the kitchen table. This was what Cornelius had suggested when he had first come from Wales. Catrin had objected to the proposal then on the grounds of the overcrowding it would cause, but she was now prepared to put up with overcrowding in her sympathy for Emrys. She had no doubt that he was not the man who had had an affair with Bert Preece's wife; so she retained her affection for him. As well as being Welsh – and his accent always brought her the sweet cool breath of the Welsh hills – he was a cheery fellow, and had been a good friend to both herself and Adam.

Especially had he been a good friend to Adam, for he had taken the blame for him and, as a result, everyone in the village believed he had been Mrs Preece's lover. Contempt for her husband rose in her breast; she could hardly believe that the honest and open-hearted lad who had wooed her should have descended to letting Emrys take his blame to protect his relationship with that woman.

CHAPTER 27

The carriage drove across the forecourt of Oaklands Park and nosed its way onto the road to Lydney. Henry Crawshay settled back and smiled at his wife. 'We're off!'

'Glad I am that we are seeing Willie and his wife for dinner.' Eliza patted her husband's hand generously and beamed at Edwin and his wife Charlotte who were sitting opposite them. 'It's good to know he's safely married. Only three more to go now, eh Henry?'

'Don't be enigmatic, dear. Three more what?'

'Marriages, of course. Eva will be married soon, and that leaves only Rosie and Hubert.'

'Hubert won't be long if he carries on mooning about that Sully girl.' Edwin looked bored as he mentioned his younger brother.

'Yes, I wish he had the same sense as you and Willie and only gone after nice girls, is it? I can't say I liked her much when she came over last summer, and then she had to go and get mixed up with molten iron or something at the ironworks and make Hubert fall in love with her. Now he's always at Park End, dancing attendance. He's ridden over there this morning.'

'Seems to have a good head on her,' commented her husband. 'We must invite the Sullys over to dinner again sometime. We'll have to keep in contact if they're going to marry into the family, though I can't say I care much for him.'

'Or her,' said Eliza. 'You could see she was hunting a husband for that girl when she came over last summer.'

'Brain saw them having tea at the Speech House last week. He told me yesterday when he came over.'

'What did he want to see you about, Father?' Edwin crossed one elegant leg over the other.

'He's touting to get support for Sully's plan to lower the colliers' rates. I didn't commit ourselves.'

'They'll be discussing this at Sully's meeting. When is it?'

'Today,' said Henry.

'Today! You mean – '

'Yes, I sent Sully a note that I couldn't come – going to Willie's.'

'We should have discussed this, Father. I think we should have gone.'

Henry knew he should have consulted his son. But he had not wanted to go to Sully's meeting. He had no patience with him or his business principles. But now he had upset Edwin, and he saw Charlotte put her hand on his and press it gently to console him.

'Edwin, I'm sorry. We should have discussed the matter. But we need no reductions in rates in our pits. Trade is still good, wholesale prices are high, and the men are working well. While there is peace in the pits let it remain. There's no point in stirring up trouble. Anyway, I am against screwing the men too low, as you well know.'

Edwin was silent.

'Edwin, winter will soon be here, and that always brings a shilling or two increase in prices. Let's wait and see, shall we?'

Edwin still did not reply.

'Edwin, listen to your father. Don't sulk,' said Eliza.

'I told Brain we would join him and Sully in a reduction if coal prices came down substantially. If we can show the men it is necessary for them to drop their rates, they will co-operate.'

'Who tells you they will? That fellow Cowmeadow? He influences you too much.'

Henry smiled to himself. Edwin had not yet learnt the art of dealing with the men. He doubted if he ever would. 'Cowmeadow's a persuasive talker, I admit, but he's fair.'

Eliza interrupted. 'Now you two, stop talking about your dirty old pieces of coal, is it? I want to enjoy the day.'

'Dirty old pieces of coal turn into clean new pieces of gold,' said Henry good-humouredly. 'Don't forget that.'

At Lydney their carriage was forced to stop. Outside the Feathers Inn a horse had collapsed in spite of the application of the whip to keep it upright. It lay motionless on the ground.

'Oh dear,' said Charlotte. 'The poor horse.'

'That's where the meeting is being held, Edwin,' said Henry, indicating the inn with his cane. 'Going on this minute, I expect.' He spotted Robert Mushet, a fellow coal and iron master, sitting at an

208

upstairs window, idly gazing down at the horse. 'I don't know why old Mushet has bothered to attend, though. I thought he'd retired. They won't take any notice of anything he says.'

᷆ ᷄

The private room on the first floor of the Feathers Inn was a good place for a gathering of Forest of Dean coalmasters. It was well-appointed, and served good coffee and excellent sherry; and there would be a substantial roast beef dinner after the meeting. With their drinks before them they felt as well disposed towards their fellow coalmasters as they would ever be. They were rivals for one another's markets, yet they had come here today, summoned by James Sully, with the vague feeling that they must show some sense of unity in the face of a common enemy.

Sully, waiting to begin the meeting, chatted to Sydney Trotter who smiled his fixed smile which, even when his face was relaxed, never disappeared.

'I hear that old man Goold has sold Bilson and Crump Meadow collieries to some London fellow for £130,0000,' Trotter was saying.

As much as that, thought Sully. 'Indeed,' he said, showing unconcern.

'Of course, he made £38,000 profit from them last year.'

'If that is so, I should have thought he would have got more than £130,000,' said Sully shortly. He did not like Sydney Trotter.

'But I doubt if they'll make as much next year,' pursued Trotter.

'No, that's why we are meeting here today.'

Sully was satisfied with the response from the Forest coalmasters to his invitation to meet together, even though the Crawshays had not come. He was glad Brain was there. Good man, Brain, even if he produced more coal at his one Trafalgar pit than Sully did in all his Park End pits put together. Yet he was always having trouble with his men. Joseph Cowmeadow apparently claimed he visited Trafalgar to sort out labour troubles more than he went to any other pit in the Forest. But Brain's toughness in dealing with his men would be an asset in Sully's plans. He would prove to be a good ally.

Sully looked round the room. By the fireplace Brain was drinking coffee and talking to Alfred Goold – Captain Goold as he liked to be called. He was the son of old Goold, and also a substantial coalmaster.

'The union invited me to speak at their miners' gala,' Goold was saying, his bright eyes darting right and left to ensure that he missed nothing. 'Invited me, just fancy! I told them I was too busy. Anyway, I

209

said, it was a colliers' meeting and they didn't want me there any more than I would want them to be at one of my shareholders' meetings. Or at this meeting here, for that matter.' He laughed.

'Stupid.' Brain pursed his thick lips. He wanted to talk to Mushet on the other side of the room, to see if he was interested in selling any of his pits. But it looked as if Sully was about to start. He would see him afterwards.

Sully tapped the table. 'Gentlemen, I have asked you here today to raise with you a matter that you are all aware of and presumably want to do something about. I refer to the need to cut wage rates in our pits to ensure, and I put the matter quite bluntly, that our profits are maintained next year at a respectable level. The boom is over. Sales, I think you will agree, have already gone down a little in the last quarter, and it would be prudent to cut the rates paid to the colliers now to make us more competitive in the market.'

'About time wages were cut, anyway,' old Goold broke in. He was a gnome-like man with sad eyes, who perversely preferred to burn wood in his fires at home rather than coal from his pits – even though, as he often remarked, coal was as cheap as colliers' sweat. He raised a gnarled hand to drain his sherry glass. 'Don't know why we gave in so easily when the union was formed a few years back. Those concessions on higher rates and all that. We let ourselves be frightened by the union. I think we ought to clobber it before it gets too powerful.' He looked round to see if he had any support.

'I quite agree,' said Sydney Trotter, but old Goold did not respond. He did not like him any more than Sully did. Crafty he was. Could bite the bottom off a frying pan without smutting his nose.

'It's all this compulsory education the government are foisting on the country,' continued Trotter, 'that's the cause of the trouble. Bad for the workers. Makes them argue with their betters, what?'

'The trouble is they've been spoiled by the prosperity of the last few years,' said Captain Goold. 'They don't need all the money they are getting. They only spend it on beer.'

'Do you know,' Trotter went on, 'at one of my pits last Monday only 84 men turned up out of 150 for the night shift. And those that did turn up were idling and drinking instead of working.'

Old Goold grunted. He agreed with Trotter's assessment of the laziness of the workers, but could not bring himself to say so. Brain, however, agreed. 'And when you run night shifts you get all the expenses of the door boys, the jockey boys and the weighmen. Then there is the cost of the extra horses. Can't overwork the day horses.'

Sully was anxious to get the meeting back on the rails. He raised his voice. 'The question is whether we can reduce rates. I think we can if we all act together. But we must be quite certain where we are going and what our aim is.'

'There'll be trouble with the union,' spoke up Mushet from his window seat. 'They won't be impressed if you tell them you must reduce the men's pay because the boom is over.'

'I'd like to smash the union,' said Brain, 'once and for all.'

'Hear, hear,' agreed Captain Goold. 'I'd like to institute a non-union colliery. You know, one which employs only non-unionists and anti-unionists. That would make the union conduct itself with fair and honourable principles in the others.'

'You mean make it agree to a reduction,' interpreted Mushet, wearily.

'There's no need for a union,' said Trotter. 'The men should be free to get the best price they can for their labour, just as we get the best price we can on the market for our coal.'

Sully was pleased at the way the meeting was going; the reaction was what he wanted. 'I think we all find the union irksome and growing in power and we must combat it.'

'Where are the Crawshays?' Trotter suddenly asked.

'Just gone past in their carriage, the pair of them.' yawned Mushet. 'On a jaunt with their wives by the look of it.'

'They were invited, but they said they couldn't come.' Sully bit his lip. To refuse to attend and then drive past the very meeting place he considered an insult, though he was glad at least that young Edwin hadn't come: he found his elegance, his good looks and his smooth behaviour odious.

'We can't agree on a reduction without their agreement,' said Captain Goold.

'Why not?' asked Brain. 'They'll follow if we show the way. They'll have to. Now, how much should the cut be? Twenty five per cent?'

'That's a lot,' said Sydney Trotter.

'Well, what about ten per cent now and ten per cent in six months' time?' suggested Sully.

'And a further five per cent a year later,' said Brain. 'Must take it gently, I suppose.'

Mushet thought there would be a strike, and a long one.

'Sooner we have a strike the better,' replied Brain.

Captain Goold looked round. 'Why?'

'Because the union is building up its reserves of money, that's why. They have set up a provident fund. The longer we wait, the longer they will be able to last out in a strike. And the bigger their reserves become because we are too timid to confront them, the more it will cost us in the long run.'

'Something in that,' said old Goold.

'But we'll win,' continued Brain. 'I've been building up my reserves as well, my reserves of coal. I expect everybody has. We'll win if we stick together. And our success will be complete if in the process of reducing rates we smash the union.'

There they go, thought Mushet, planning to increase their already swollen incomes, to decorate their wives with more expensive costumes and more costly jewels and to load their well-appointed homes with thicker carpets, heavier brocades and more ornate furniture. And they plan to smash the miners' union, as well. But I support them. I am, after all, one of them.

Sully called for order. 'Let us take a vote.' He summarised the views of the meeting. 'All those in favour of the first ten per cent cut in rates raise their hands. The reduction to take place from the first of next month with notices posted at all pits on Friday of this week. No mention yet of any subsequent cuts.'

All hands went up.

'Good,' said Sully.

CHAPTER 28

The day after the meeting of coalmasters at the Feathers, Sully wrote to Henry Crawshay giving him a full account of their decision to lower the rates by ten per cent right away. He explained that their plan should remain secret and, to have the greatest impact on the men, the announcement should be made at every pit-head in the Forest at the same time on Friday at the end of the afternoon shift.

As Sully sat down to his breakfast on that Friday morning he smiled, pleased that mainly because of his insistence the coalmasters had at last taken action. He took pleasure at the concern and turmoil that would be caused among the colliers all over Dean when they heard the news. So pleased he was that he felt generous and, when he thought Hermione was not looking, he slipped his cat a sliver of bacon. He turned to the *Western Mail*. There would, of course, be nothing in it yet about the intention to reduce rates. Then he saw a letter in the correspondence columns from Henry Crawshay. Sully folded back the paper to read it and lifted his coffee cup to his lips. Then he put it down again. Crawshay had written to the *Mail* opposing the cut in rates. Not only did he make public the details of the meeting at the Feathers which Sully had given him, but he told the world that he had no intention of reducing rates at his own pits. He backed up his case by quoting facts and figures.

Sully looked over to his wife and began to tell her, but she was absorbed in her correspondence and did not respond. He cursed, and once again reminded himself that he must never expect her to be interested in the affairs of his pits provided he gave her enough money from them.

Thoughts of another cup of coffee had now vanished and he rose, his lips compressed. 'I'm going over to see Crawshay this instant.'

'Well, whatever you say, don't upset him. Remember his son is courting Alice and we don't want that to fall through.' And she opened another letter.

He arrived at Oaklands Park within the hour. Crawshay received him courteously and offered him refreshment. He listened to Sully's remonstrances patiently, and then when he had exhausted his complaints and arguments and had run down to silence, he said, 'You know, Mr Sully, Edwin and I are not bound by decisions taken by other coalmasters. Everyone must run his business as he thinks best. While coal prices are high and there is peace in the pits I see no reason to stir up trouble.'

'But all the others agreed this was the best way to maintain our profits. And we must stick together. I've spent a lot of time cultivating them, listening to their complaints and smoothing them over – and a fractious lot I must say privately to you they are – and at last I've succeeded in forming this employers' association, for that is what it is in all but name. Now you break the unity.' He tapped contemptuously with the back of his hand the newspaper which he had brought with him. 'Why didn't you come to the meeting and put your views?'

Crawshay ignored the question with supreme confidence, and launched into a smooth speech in which he elaborated his point of view. He silenced Sully when he tried to interrupt with a lift of his hand, and when he had finished, he settled back in his armchair with a faint smile and waited.

My God, thought Sully, he has the temerity to smile at me. Then like a clap to the head, Sully realised how he had misjudged the man. His quiet, friendly exterior was backed by a will of steel. On his last visit to see Crawshay he had wondered how he had built up and maintained a flourishing coal and iron empire. Now he knew.

Crawshay stood up to end the interview and Sully found himself edging uncertainly towards the door. He suppressed the rage, indeed the fear, that was in his heart and managed to control his voice as he uttered a final warning, 'You will regret your action in going against your fellow coalmasters, Mr Crawshay. And I venture to suggest, Sir, that you will come in line with us sooner or later.'

డ్ ⚘

The bite of raw autumn was in the air that afternoon when an office clerk pinned up a notice outside the Park End Royal pit-head and ran off before he could be questioned about it. The men coming up from the pit pulled their coats around their shoulders against the wind as they stood in groups discussing it. Dismayed and bewildered at first, their reactions soon crystallised into anger. When Adam read the notice he

214

was silent for a few seconds, his face impassive. He looked on the ground, as if he were searching for something there; then he looked up. As he did so his face came to life. His eyes were blazing and his lips were compressed and red against the black dust that covered his face. 'This is outrageous.' There was emotion in his throat. 'Rates reduced by ten per cent.' He threw his mattock on the ground in rage. 'We'll fight this. We'll fight it with all our strength.'

Later in the day the men met to consider the position. The owner of the British Lion willingly agreed that the big room should he used for the meeting. Meetings meant men, and men drank beer. And the more heated the discussion, the more beer they drank.

A lot of beer was drunk that night, for the British Lion was crowded and the meeting was long. Adam rose amid cheers and raised his hand for silence. 'Men, we must oppose this monstrous proposal to cut our wages. I believe we can force Sully to abandon it if we remain united in our resolve.'

'Good old Adam,' shouted someone from the back, and it was echoed from all sides. The interruption cheered Adam's heart. He pushed his hair from his forehead and continued, his finger stabbing the air. 'We must come out on strike. And once out we must stay out until Sully yields. We must let every pit engine stand still. We must let every stall be silent. We must let the waters rise up and run over the tops of the pits if need be.' They cheered. 'Let us as men stick to what we know is right, and openly defy tyranny and injustice.'

Adam had captured them with his rhetoric. They cheered again, their faces rosy with excitement. They stamped on the floor and jumped onto the benches; they shook the slates on the roof with their noise, and the barmaid below had to rush to prevent glasses tumbling off her shelves.

Adam spoke at other lodges and persuaded them also to refuse to accept the lower rates. 'We won't go back till the coalmasters give in,' was the cry. In the Crawshay lodges, where there would be no reductions, there was support and encouragement, though as cynics remarked these were cheap and easy to give.

In private as well as on the platform Adam was convinced that with firm leadership victory could be theirs. He fired the laggards on the Executive, even Joseph Cowmeadow, to enthusiasm, and they agreed to approach the coalmasters in Sully's new association for a meeting at which they could advocate rescinding the cuts. The coalmasters, however, refused to meet them; they could, they said, see no point in any discussion, and the reduction in rates would come into force on the due date.

So the union had to accept that the coalmasters were set on confrontation. On the Thursday before the notices were due to expire Adam and Joseph Cowmeadow sat in a tiny room in the back of Cinderford Town Hall. Relations between them had improved since Joseph had learnt that Adam was going to oppose him as a rival candidate for the parliamentary seat, but they were still frosty.

'I wonder whether the Executive were right to try to get the masters to rescind their decision,' said Joseph. 'Perhaps a compromise of a five per cent reduction –'

'No, Joseph, we must have no cut. We owe the men nothing less. We've failed to get a meeting with the coalmasters, so all we can do now is tell the men we've had a complete rejection and that they must strike on Monday.'

Joseph was glum, but Adam had the gleam of battle in his eyes as they dipped their pens in the ink and wrote to lodge secretaries urging them to bring their men out on strike on the Monday.

On the last payday before the strike began Emma had given less pocket money to George and Adam than usual.

'Hey, Mam,' said George, examining his few pennies. 'All our wages going in the old mustard tin, then, be it?'

'Yes.'

'How much have we got there, then?'

'Never you mind.'

Adam realised the Turleys were lucky to have a mustard tin. Most housewives didn't. For many, with one wage-earner and a grannie and half a dozen children to clothe and feed, there was never any money left over at the end of the month, and any choice lay only between one necessity and another. Even so, in most homes the wives supported their husbands in not giving in. They did not understand the ins and outs of the strike, and their men didn't try to explain it to them; but life had taught them that if you let someone stamp on your foot and you don't protest, they will stamp again even harder.

On the Monday gloom settled over Dean. At Park End, as in the rest of the Forest, the pit-heads were silent; the steel cables no longer whined as they spun at the tops of the head frames. The only noise underground was the soothing voices of the stable boys who came to feed the horses, for Sully, expecting the men to toe the line and return to work soon, had decided not to bring the horses up. When the boys departed the silence was punctuated only by the sound of the horses, bewildered by the lack of noise and activity but enjoying their rest, champing their jaws and shaking their heads in the inky blackness.

Adam, too, for other reasons, believed the men would not be out long. Most of them were not averse to a rest for a week or two but, unlike the last time when they had been on strike, they weren't able to sit around in the sun; for winter was nearly come, and everything was cold and wet. But they had some coal in the coal shed and there was always wood for collecting in the Forest waste, so their houses were dry and warm.

ª   º

'Adam, just a minute.'

'I'm in a hurry, Mam.'

'I want to talk to you. How long is Emrys staying with us?' Her peremptory tone suggested something serious.

'Until he gets some lodgings.'

'When will that be?'

'Don't know. You didn't seem to mind when he first came here.'

'I wasn't asked.'

That wouldn't have stopped you objecting if you had wanted to, thought Adam. 'Do you mind him staying with us?'

'No, he be a nice lad. Considerate, neat and tidy, doesn't ask much, hands over his money every payday prompt, like.'

'What be your objection to him, then, Mam?'

Emma looked at him squarely. 'There be all this talk about him and Mrs Preece. Do you think it be true? You should know, you're his friend.'

'Everyone in the village thinks so.' But he could see she was not satisfied with this answer.

'Do you, Adam?'

'Don't know. Bert and his wife don't get on well together. Every one knows that.'

'Seems they're not the only ones. You and Catrin don't get on as well as you used to. All that lovey stuff have gone.'

Adam was on his guard. He put on his muffler and moved to get his cap. 'Well, that don't last for ever, do it?'

'No, but –'

217

'We gets on all right.'

'Don't seem so to me. You don't talk to one another these days. She hardly throws a word at you, or you at her.'

'I'm busy with the union all the time.'

'Listen, Adam. She be a good girl, looks after Lennie well, and you're not being fair to her.' Emma put a hand on his arm. Her concern showed on her face as she looked at him. 'What be the matter, son?'

'Nothing.'

'There be something. Why no more babies? Most couples of your age have a baby every year or two.'

'Don't think she gets a baby easy, like. She took four months before she began Lennie.'

'Well, that side is nothing to do with me, but it don't seem right. And I can't live in a house where people are glowering at one another all the time.'

Adam was silent.

'Have you got another woman somewhere?'

The dreaded question has been asked at last. What to say?

'No,' he lied, and looked away.

'If you have you'll regret it, my lad. You'll come back to Catrin with your tail between your legs. As my old grandmother used to say, if you burn your backside, you have to sit on the blisters.'

But his only reply was, 'I must go now,' and grabbing his cap, he escaped through the door and ran up the road to meet Martha.

He had been disturbed by his mother's close questioning. Did she suspect? She had switched her questioning from a possible liaison between Emrys and Martha to himself very quickly. And he did not believe she had been convinced by his denial. He wished he was a better liar, but he had always been the same. Too honest, that was his problem.

His run slowed down to a sharp walk. He thought about Bert. He had noticed that he had nodded curtly to Emrys the other day at the pit-head and Adam had hoped this meant he had accepted that Martha had told him the truth when she had said she did not have a lover. Perhaps he now regretted having attacked Emrys. Perhaps he realised that his judgement that night had been induced by a wild piece of gossip and influenced by the heady effects of rage and alcohol.

Adam tried to avoid him when he could, but he continued to go to his cottage on occasion, not so much to consult him on union matters as to preserve normality and to meet Martha and receive her assignation notes. Martha had told him she had not changed her attitude towards her husband since the Emrys scandal broke. She was still cold and formal to him but, as she told Adam, to be warmer now might suggest that there had been some truth in the idea that she had been unfaithful.

Nor did her friendliness with Adam change. In their moments alone she assured him she was more devoted to him than ever.

They met in the Forest. 'Is Bert still going to Gloucester on Saturday nights?' asked Adam.

'Yes, but I wonder how long he'll be able to,' said Martha.

'If he be anything like me, he'll be skint soon.'

'He doesn't go down to the pub much nowadays. So he's saving money there.' She put her arm through his and they walked on.

The contact cheered him, but only for a moment. 'What's the latest about the Forest having a collier for its MP?' asked Martha

'Off.'

'Because of the strike?'

'Yes.'

'What's happening then?'

'We're going to support some middle-class candidate.'

'What!'

'He'll be a Liberal, and it won't be as good as having a working man.'

'Are you disappointed, Adam?'

'Yes, I am. But I've got other things to worry about.'

There was silence. Then he burst out,'Oh, Martha, everything seems to be crushing down on me these days. I try not to let it show, and when I'm on union business or making speeches to the men I feel as confident and happy as ever. But when I'm alone I wonder if it's all worthwhile. Me mam was on at me earlier today. I think she suspects that it wasn't Emrys who was going with you, but me. She didn't say as much, she wouldn't, but I'm sure she suspects me.'

'What about Catrin?'

'She barely speaks to me, but I don't think she knows.'

Martha grunted. 'And George?'

'He's too thick to take that sort of thing in. He don't feel currents.'

They walked on. These assignations with Martha were dear to him, for his soul could curl up and shelter in her love. Since the bombshell of the Emrys business it was a more mature love, tinged with a little sadness on occasion, but he still found it compelling and he was more under her spell than ever. She was perfection, not only in her person and in her demonstration of her love for him, but in all ways in the world.

Yet all the time his conscience reminded him of Catrin, Catrin who had invited him into her home and bed in those uncomplicated days when he had lived in Wales, Catrin whom he had loved so much. But she was also the Catrin who had not moved on with him, who refused to recognise his ambitions and his desire to improve the lot of working people and who frustrated him at every step. He could no longer get satisfaction from Catrin's company, so why not turn to Martha?

In fact Martha and Emrys sustained him these days, Martha actively with words of love and encouragement, Emrys with silent comradeship and a sad smile that showed without logic or discussion that he was a true friend. Since their initial talk about his love for Martha on the night Emrys was ejected from Bert's house, Adam had never mentioned the matter to him, though he wanted to pour his heart out to him for comfort; and Emrys never raised the matter with him, either, though Adam suspected he would be willing to discuss it if he wished.

Together Martha and Emrys supported him, not only in his private worries, but also in his public concerns. They encouraged him to retain his views on the strike, his conviction that the union had right on its side, and that the men would win. But as the weeks wore on, the employers still refused to discuss the cut and it seemed the men would be driven back to work. But Adam contrived to keep them in good heart as he continued with his daily grind of rallies and meetings, feeding them the latest news, and giving them sympathy for their hardships, which were daily growing more severe, and promising them success.

And afterwards he would relax in Emrys's quiet company or in Martha's arms.

CHAPTER 29

Alice realised that her liking for Maurice had increased to affection and was now changing to love. Where was the dividing line, she wondered; but the answer did not matter. Merely listening to Maurice's voice excited her. 'Bend your fingers so, and hold your wrists like this,' he had said at her last lesson, and had shown her with his own fingers, his own wrists; and when she failed to copy correctly he had placed his hands on hers. His touch thrilled her. She felt guilty at enjoying such pleasure, but said nothing.

The amount of instruction that Maurice gave her had, she realised, been diminishing as the weeks had passed. But their relationship had become sweeter. Murmured words about playing the piano were extended to conversation about music generally, to discussion of the concerts Maurice went to in Gloucester and Cheltenham, to books they had both read, and to themselves. They talked quietly and quickly, falling over one another's tongues, completing one another's sentences, like twin souls.

She was living from one music lesson to the next, and now found it difficult to show any interest in Hubert. Indeed she wanted to avoid him, but dared not do so. Poor Hubert, he was trying to please her in his honest, dull way, trying so hard. Maurice did not try, he did not have to. She felt sorry for Hubert, and suspected he was feeling for her what she felt for Maurice.

She wondered how Maurice felt. She noted increased friendliness, but little more. Because of this she was now finding the weekly lessons in the music room, sweet though they were, more and more frustrating. Then came his first clear intimation that he was interested in more than teaching her to play the piano.

'Why can't we meet outside this house sometimes?' he asked. She rose, her heart excited, but at the same time her common sense replied for her, 'No, no, it's impossible.' She turned and went to the window. The garden with its bare, colourless trees and desolate grey sky – no clouds, just greyness – did not encourage optimism. Behind her he began to play. She knew the music, but could not at first identify it. Then she realised it was a Grieg song. The words of it came to her.

'I'll love thee, dear, I'll love thee, dear,

'I'll love thee, dear, through all eternity.'

He was sending her a message. If he were not, why should he play this piece? She had not studied it with him. At first she was annoyed that he should use this roundabout way of communicating with her on such a subject. Was he so timid that he could not say his feelings direct? But she must not be harsh. He was shy, and was feeling his way, leaving himself a path of retreat if she did not respond. He stopped playing and she turned and looked at him. He had said it at last. His face was taut, but his eyes were soft and moist. He rose and stood squarely before her. Ah, she thought, he was not so timid after all. Then she was conscious of an aura engulfing her, as if his rough, chestnut-coloured coat was putting out warmth. But it was not the coat, it was him, his essence reaching out. He looked down at her and put his arms around her. This was the first time a man other than her father had done this. She realised that he was trembling, but she felt calm and protective towards him.

'What's the trouble, Maurice?' she asked, but she knew.

'I love you, but haven't ever dared tell you before.'

'I love you, too.' The words came naturally and, unlike his, with no embarrassment. He held her close, yet she sensed that in spite of her response he was not happy. She realised the time had come. 'Maurice, I have something I must tell you.'

'Is there anyone else?'

'I will tell you. Please play something; otherwise mother will be suspicious and come in.'

She went again to the window. The clouds had cleared a little and the sun was trying to break through the trees at the bottom of the garden. She told him about Hubert Crawshay and the pressure she was under from her mother to marry him, and asked him to believe that she did not love Hubert. He made no response and she looked round to see the effect of what she had told him. He had stopped playing and was looking at his fingers. His shoulders had slumped.

'Oh, Maurice.' She ran to him and clasped him to her, his head on her breast. The combination of their declarations of love, her account of Hubert Crawshay's courtship and her mother's pressure had squeezed her emotions until the natural relief of tears took over.

He did not seem to notice her crying. 'It's all laid out for you, then?'

'No, no.' She wiped her tears away. Why was he so easily discouraged? 'We'll find a way, Maurice. In the meantime, we still have our hour each week.' She gripped him on both arms, looked him determinedly in the face and smiled.

                                                   ‿

Hermione was reading the local newspaper. 'I see Mr Crawshay's youngest daughter, Eva, has married.'

Back on her old subject, thought Alice, and continued to read her book. Sully looked up but made no comment and returned to a report from Gunter about the effects of the strike on the state of his pits.

But Hermione needed no reply. 'Married at Awre Church on Sunday,' she continued. 'Eight bridesmaids. Rather an excessive number, I should think. The groom's a captain in the 2nd Staffordshire militia and a grandson of the Earl of Shrewsbury.' Her voice, grudging so far, had now become envious. 'Did you hear that, James?'

'Yes, my dear.'

'There's a very detailed account here of the ceremony, two columns of it. I must say that seems rather a lot. Mrs Crawshay,' she read out, 'was attired in pale blue with a profusion of rich Irish point lace and ostrich feathers, the train being extremely long and elegant. How vulgar,' she murmured.

Sully grunted and adjusted his spectacles.

'There were 130 guests afterwards at Oaklands Park, and for their honeymoon they are going on the Continent.' Her own honeymoon had been at Sidmouth. 'And, James, they didn't invite us to the wedding.'

'No reason why they should, my dear,' said Sully. 'Crawshay and I are only business acquaintances. And not very close ones at the moment.'

'But we have dined with them at their place, and they have visited us here.'

Sully drew the tablelamp nearer, and tried to concentrate on his report. Hermione glared at him. He was no company. She looked at Alice.

'I'm hoping we shall be having a wedding in our family shortly, Alice.'

'Yes.'

'There is no need to be curt with me, Alice.'

Sully put his report aside, realising he must try to allay the row that was about to erupt between his wife and daughter. 'How are the piano lessons going, Alice?'

Alice sensed danger. 'All right, Papa, though I can't say I like Mr Redding junior as much as his father.' She felt traitorous, but Maurice would understand. 'He is a good teacher, though.'

'You may not like him but your playing has improved considerably under him. Hubert was saying so only the other day. He likes to hear you play, you know.'

Alice did not respond.

'I think you should be more pleasant to him, encourage him a little more. Not in any improper way, of course, just be a little nicer to him. You have a pleasant side, you know, though we don't often see it.'

'Mama, I wish you would not keep on about him.'

'You want to get married, don't you? If you are not nicer to him he won't propose to you.'

'I don't want him to.'

Sully's attempt to keep the peace was not proving successful. 'Perhaps we can introduce her to some other young man, Hermione. This acquaintanceship doesn't seem to be coming to anything. What happened to that woman in Lydney whose young nephew was coming to live with her?'

'He's not coming now,' snapped Hermione. 'But we have no need to search further. Hubert is a perfectly suitable candidate, and I simply cannot understand why Alice is so indifferent to him. I thought originally she liked him.' Hermione was wound up now. 'You know, Alice, you are not getting any younger.'

'I cannot fail to know, Mother. You are constantly telling me.'

Hermione went red and was about to retort when Sully intervened. 'Don't be rude to your mother, Alice. She has only your interests at heart.'

Alice was nearly in tears. 'You've been hunting for a husband for me ever since we arrived in Park End. That was the only reason you persuaded Papa to get us invited to the Crawshays shortly after we arrived here. You'd heard they had an unmarried son.'

'That's not true,' protested Hermione. She tried to be calm, though her breast was heaving. She decided to leave the matter for the time being and, with a shake of her newspaper, resumed reading.

ॐ ॐ

The hour each week that Alice and Maurice spent together in the music room was, of course, too short for all they wanted to say to each other. Yet they could find nowhere else to meet. Hiring a trap and going off in the countryside or meeting in Gloucester were considered and rejected;

Alice might be missed at home or someone might see them together and tell her mother. So they carried on cramming their endearments into the hour of the lesson. They lost track of time during that glorious hour, and one morning Hermione entered the music room and enquired why the lesson was running half an hour longer than it should.

Maurice blushed. 'I'm sorry, Mrs Sully. I have been explaining a way of playing this rather complicated piece of music.'

Hermione shot a suspicious glance at him. She's guessed, thought Alice, and turned away. The air was heavy with unspoken thoughts.

Maurice collected his things. 'Goodbye Madam, goodbye Miss Sully,' he said, 'I will come as usual next week.'

But there was no lesson next week. Two days later Hermione told Alice that she had written to Mr Redding terminating the lessons. 'I have paid him until Christmas, so he need not feel hard done by. Your father has agreed.'

'But why?'

'I've had doubts about that young man ever since he took over your lessons from his father. I don't know what your relations have been with him, but they are ended now.'

Alice did not reply. Hermione regarded her for a moment.

'I ought to have realised that there was something going on between you two. Such duplicity! And you as good as engaged to Hubert. You need not worry, I shall not tell him about this incident.' She moved to the door.

'I am not engaged to him, and I don't want to be,' shouted Alice.

Hermione snorted with annoyance. 'I am not prepared to talk further,' she said, and left the room.

Alice, in dismay, resolved to write to Maurice. Fortunately, from something he had said, she recollected his address in Gloucester, for she had no access to her mother's papers where she could have found it. She wrote the same afternoon, and slipped down to the post office when she knew her mother was engaged. In her letter she reiterated her love and begged him to write to her. But after a few days she wondered if she had remembered his address correctly, for she received no reply. She wrote again. If her letters were not reaching him, how would he know how she felt?

But perhaps he had replied and her mother had confiscated his letter. All letters for Park End House were taken up to her father's study on arrival, and Hermione went there to collect those addressed to the rest of the family and the servants.

On the other hand perhaps he hadn't written. Never had Alice felt so miserable and isolated and in need of someone to confide in. She wondered whether to go to her father; but he would, she was certain, only offer sympathy and advise her to do what her mother wanted. She thought of choosing her time and going to Gloucester and seeking Maurice at what she thought was his address. But if he had decided to give her up, such a visit would be embarrassing. She could not throw herself at him. She had done what she could by writing to him. It was for him, surely, to approach her now.

As the days went by and she did not hear from him, she closed in on herself. She reacted woodenly and submissively to all approaches from her parents. She received Hubert coldly and pleaded ill-health when he suggested rides in the Forest. Indeed headaches and retirement to her room occurred frequently on the days she expected him to call.

CHAPTER 30

Young Billy called at the Tingles to court Bessie. He frowned when he saw his sister Mary Jane, Bessie's friend, already there.

'How long be this strike going on for, young Billy?' asked Mary Jane.

'Don't call me young Billy, I've told you before.'

'Well, how long? I've lost me job at the Albion and Mr Baglin says I can't have it back till the strike be over and the men have some money in their pockets.'

'Don't know when it'll be over.' Billy turned and beamed at Bessie, squeezing her waist with the arm he had put round her, hoping no-one would notice. Sitting on the settee courting in the Tingles' house was a pleasant way of spending the evening if you avoided the spring sticking up in the middle: and a lovely couple they made, too. Everyone thought so.

'Mary Jane,' Billy continued, 'you don't want to come round here if you be going to talk all the time. Mr and Mrs Tingle don't like it.'

Mr and Mrs Tingle hastened to say they didn't mind.

'I come to see my friend Bessie, and have a chat with her. But there be a fat chance of talking to her with you here spooning with her.'

'Oh, Mary Jane, we can still chat,' said Bessie. 'I thought we was chatting anyway.'

'Well, it's not the sort of chat I want.'

'Not much to talk about, anyroad,' said Mrs Tingle, 'except the strike. I see old Baldwin have stopped giving credit. Won't do him no good, though. If he upsets them, folks won't want to go back to him after the strike is over.'

'He won't get his money back anyroad,' said Enoch.

Mrs Tingle rose, poked the fire and put a shovelful of coal on. 'That be the lot, Enoch,' she said. 'You'll have to get some more from the tumps.'

'Sully's men be patrolling, you know,' said Billy.

'Aye, that they are,' said Enoch.

Billy remembered something. 'Do you know, Mr Tingle, there be a truck full o' coal up in the woods behind Park Royal?'

'No, they took all them trucks down to Lydney when the trouble began.'

'No they didn't. I saw the truck this morning. All hidden by the trees, it were. You ask George Turley, he were with me. Mr Tingle, what about going along tonight with some sacks and see what we can get? We'll take George.'

'We'll have to be careful,' said Enoch. 'There are extra police about. I've heard tell they've got some new ones here from Gloucester.'

They crept along the side of the pit office. The cold sprang up from the ground and penetrated their boots. Even the mice in the office refused to go out in it. Then they slipped over to the shelter of the loading bay wall. The frozen grass crunched beneath their boots; otherwise all was as silent as death. They paused and listened. Then they looked over the wall. Billy had been right. There, under the trees at the end of the line, was the truck, loaded to the brim and higher with coal. It had been shunted into the woods and not taken to Lydney with the others. All that coal, dug by the very colliers whose families were now freezing because of the strike, was lying there forgotten. The moon's rays reflected from its blackness, hard and bright.

The three men glanced around cautiously and ran from the shadow of the wall to the coal truck. Up on to the buffers they climbed, then scrambled up the side of the truck and on to the top of the coal. Hands that would never lose their greyness but had grown soft during the six weeks of the strike were reintroduced to coal and experienced afresh its weight and texture. But the men had no time to caress it. They hastened to load the smaller pieces into their sacks, ignoring the scratches and cuts it dealt their flabby hands. Must take as much coal as possible, but still be able to run.

Enoch Tingle, older than the others and prudent by nature, only half-filled his sack. He jumped down and looked up at Billy and George still filling theirs.

'Come on,' he whispered, and moved into the Forest. It absorbed him in a second, only a low branch moving in the moonlight showing where he had passed. The others threw down their sacks and, with a crunch, landed on the gravel track.

Then from both ends of the track came the sounds of pounding boots and panting breath.

'Christ,' said Billy.

'Police,' said George; and police it was. Four of them.

'You there,' shouted one. He stopped cunningly as he neared George. He held wide his hands as if he were about to catch a bird, and then slowly advanced. George flung his sack of coal at him and escaped into the woods.

Billy decided to hang on to his coal sack and made a similar dash. But another policeman flung himself at his legs and brought him face down on the icy gravel. Billy wriggled and kicked and cursed, but the policeman was burly and well fed, and Billy was weak from lack of food.

The other police chased into the woods in search of the men who had got away, leaving Billy to the one who had brought him down. He sat, legs astride, on Billy's back. Tightening his grip on his hair, he pushed his face into the gravel and slowly moved it round and round.

'We'll teach you bloody colliers,' he said. 'Give in? Had enough?' He turned Billy over and sat on his chest, his knees on his shoulders. Billy, his shoulders aching to break, looked up at him through bloodied eyelids. He looked past his serge blue thighs up to his gross, heavy face. He smelt his warm breath as he leaned over and leered. Billy turned his head aside, his shoulders hard on the ground aching to kill, and spat out a piece of gravel.

'You bastard, you.'

'Yes, you've hurt your face, haven't you? Must have done it when you fell over.'

'You're not Forest,' said Billy.

'Forest police are no good at catching you lot.'

He took him to Park End police station and put him in the tiny cell which formed part of PC Marvell's dwelling house, and sat outside guarding him, for he did not trust the local police constable. The next morning Mrs Marvell tiptoed round the policeman who was asleep on the floor outside the cell, and handed Billy a cup of tea with a shush and a finger to her lips.

Later that morning Billy went before the magistrates and was given seven days for attempting to steal property belonging to James Sully, Esquire, coalmaster. Billy was taken with his hands handcuffed behind his back to Littledean Gaol. The horse dragged the cart slowly up the hill that fronted the gaol. As they approached Billy looked up at the high smooth walls that surrounded it. They were impossible to scale, though he had no intention of trying to escape. Under the portcullis and through the heavy oak doors they went, into the prison yard. The doors were slammed with a thud. Billy was inside. He descended from the cart and a gaoler unlocked his handcuffs.

'You've got to be fumigated first,' said the gaoler, and he pushed Billy through a stone-rimmed doorway on the right of the entrance.

Billy had heard terrible stories about what happened to prisoners in prison. He was, he had to admit, afraid. Littledean Gaol was a place apart; it was not of the Forest but of that world that was all hardship and cruelty. It was bereft of hope, every stone cemented in place with tears. Billy hated the gloom and the confinement it imposed. The restrictions of the cell were quite unlike those of the coalpit, and the thin grey light that struggled through the cell bars compared unfavourably with the yellow reflection of a candle on the coal face. The routine – chapel, breakfast, treadmill, dinner, treadmill, supper, bed – was remorseless.

The hours he spent on the treadmill were exhausting and empty, as they were intended to be. He found he had to concentrate on treading at just the right speed. Too fast and you rose too high. Too slow and you hit the platform. But once you had gauged the speed correctly, you could daydream. Billy thought about his mother, how she would shake her head at the news of his capture, and how she would enfold him with her arms and hug him to her breast when he returned. He thought about the twins and how they would miss him, and how he would play gaols with them under the kitchen table when he returned home, and about his Bessie and how he would hold her close and kiss her dimples.

He had so much time to spend thinking. He thought about the warmth that his body generated while on the treadmill and the cold he experienced at night with his knees bent up to his chest and his thin blanket clutched round his neck. He thought of the warmth his workmates at the pit showed him, and the hard coldness of Sully, who had more coal than he could ever need to heat that great house of his, yet who deprived him and his comrades of a sackful of coal to keep their families warm in this bitter winter.

Adam was waiting for him when he was released on the Wednesday morning. The gaolers slammed the door behind him and he stood in the pit clothes he had worn when he had gone in, empty handed, a slight and vulnerable figure, not knowing which way to turn. Adam ran over to him and grasped him to his breast. Gone was the relationship that had existed at the coal face, where Billy carried out Adam's bidding. In place was the warmth for a friend who had suffered for a cause that was dear. For Billy had shot up in Adam's esteem, as he had in all the other colliers'. Billy had, one could almost say, suffered imprisonment on behalf of them all.

'But your face!' said Adam.

'It ain't nothing. It be getting better.'

'What happened?'

Billy told him.

'We'll get our own back, Billy, never fear.'

'Aye. How be Mam?'

'Fine.'

'And the others, the twins?'

'Fine, fine. I told them I was meeting you. They'll be waiting at home. But there won't be no feast for the returning warrior!'

Billy smiled. 'How be the strike going?' he asked. 'Didn't hear nothing about it in there.' He laughed. Then he became serious. 'But I did a lot of thinking and I want to take a bigger part in fighting Sully.'

A shaft of sunlight pierced the clouds and lit up the snow on the branches of the trees, and he laughed again. His spirits were improving every minute.

But Adam thought he looked worn and considerably thinner. Underneath the tiredness he could see he had matured. His eyes still gleamed, his smile was still sunny, but his face had squared and the lines under his eyes were lines not of tiredness but of maturity. He was no longer 'young' Billy. 'No, the strike's not over yet. The men are in good heart and we've had no blacklegs yet. We've got a meeting with Sully tomorrow.'

'Good.'

'The strike committee want a compromise, a sliding scale. I don't like the idea, but I've had to accept. I'll fight for the best we can get.'

'Course you will.' They walked on in silence.

'Billy,' said Adam. 'Would you like to join us at tomorrow's meeting?'

'Me come with you to see Sully?'

'The committee think that now you've been to gaol for the cause you'd be a good man to come along.'

'More like they want to show me off as a martyr!'

'Well, maybe there be a bit o' that. But it would be good for the morale of the men. Will you?'

'Yes,' said Billy.

❧ ❧

Sully looked sourly across the table at the strike leaders. He knew the spokesman; his name was Adam Turley, and he was one of his butty men, a bright fellow, who knew his facts and could speak well though he was a bit wild with his statements. And he was one of those new-fangled socialists, or so Gunter had told him. Other members of the delegation from the strikers were ranged behind him. He knew many by sight, but only one or two by name. He was glad he wouldn't have to listen to that fellow Cowmeadow at meetings any more now that he had established that he would negotiate only with men employed in his own pits. Cowmeadow's eyes, penetrating and unblinking, made him feel uncomfortable; and he spoke at him as if he were addressing a mass meeting of his union.

On one side of him Sully had a clerk taking notes. On the other sat Gunter. He was glad Gunter was there. He was beginning to rely on him more and more these days, though he had been suspicious of him earlier, for he had seemed cold and calculating. But he was always polite and helpful, did what he was told and since the strike had begun had told him what was in the men's minds. Who his informants were, Sully did not know or care.

Sully began by lecturing the union delegates about the risks colliery owners took in their businesses. 'I myself have invested thousands of pounds in my Park End pits since I bought them, all my spare capital. It has gone in installing new equipment and extending the roadways underground. As you know, the present economic climate is hard and pits are closing down all over the country. I want a reorganisation of wages in my pits because without one I can't carry on.' He glared at Adam, waiting for his reaction.

But Adam was not impressed and stared back at him with no comment. Then when he was sure Sully had finished, he picked up his notes and began advocating as a compromise the introduction of a sliding scale of wage payments: when coal prices went up wages should also go up. When prices went down, so should wages.

Sully could not accept this and was irritated. He wanted an agreement, but there seemed little chance of one today. 'I don't think the time has come for a sliding scale,' he said stiffly.

Then a man at the back stood up and began to speak. 'Mr Sully, Sir, we've been hearing a lot about percentages and sliding scales this afternoon. But that don't mean much to people like me.'

Sully did not know who he was. He was thin and ill clad, like the other colliers present, but he had a vibrancy and a fire within him that reached out as he spoke. Sully noticed that his face was cut in a hundred places.

'I be a day man,' the young collier continued. 'I works for the buttyman that you contract with. I has to get what wages I can from him, and if he don't get much from you, how can I get enough to live on from him? You, Mr Sully, don't know what it be like to live on three shillings and six pence a day, which is what many day men get, and we only gets that when we works a full day. We gets less when we are on short time, and nothing when we don't work at all because you don't want no coal cut. Three and six a day divided between a family of six be less than what's given to paupers in the workhouse.'

Sully had folded his arms in front of him and was staring at the speaker. Not a muscle of his face moved.

'Have you ever bin down one of your pits, Sir? None of my mates have ever told me you bin down and seen what it be like there. And if by chance you have, I bet you never worked at the coal face, and come up tired and aching and all smot up with coal dirt.

'There be more in life than percentages and profits, Mr Sully. I don't deny you your profits. But enough is enough, ain't it? Think of your fellow men, Mr Sully, because that's what we are. I don't know what you usually has for dinner, but many of your colliers only has a piece of dry bread for theirs. Have you ever been hungry, Mr Sully? Real hungry? And your wife and daughter? Real hungry? Your colliers and their families have, and they are starving now. They are crying out for bread. They want bread, Mr Sully, bread.'

The speaker looked round uncertainly. Then not knowing what to say next, he sat down.

Sully did not speak, and the room was silent. He had been firm in his refusal to accept a sliding scale and did not intend to say any more. He could see Adam was put out by the way his colleague had taken over the meeting with all that emotional stuff, and he sat and looked at him.

Suddenly Adam rose, presumably realising that no progress could be made. 'Thank you, Mr Sully. We remain out until you either restore the cuts or negotiate a sliding scale.' He picked up his papers and left the room, followed by his delegation.

The colliery staff left, too. Sully returned home and went straight to his study. He did not want to see Hermione; she only pestered him with her petty complaints these days. He ordered a pot of tea to be brought to him. His cat came in with the servant, and stood rigid as it always did for a time by his leg and then jumped onto his lap. He adjusted his legs to settle it and placed his hand on its back. The cat stretched its front legs with exquisite pleasure and purred. Stroking the cat always calmed him and enabled him to think; and he stroked it now.

His mind wandered over the afternoon's events. He regretted he had not been able to conclude an agreement. Had he been too inflexible? Would he have to yield more? He thought not; the men would give in soon. But his losses were running into thousands of pounds and he was losing markets he would find difficult to regain. He must consult with Brain and the others and see how they were progressing with their men. If only he had someone at home to talk to, to lay his thoughts before, to help him shuffle them, evaluate them and put them in a new order. But he hadn't. Hermione was a woman and was not interested, anyway. Gunter served the purpose to a limited extent but Sully was too proud to expose his innermost thoughts to an employee.

He kept thinking about the young man at the back of the meeting who had addressed him. He seemed an earnest fellow, a likeable chap, really, in spite of the familiar way in which he had scolded him. He wondered how his face had become so scratched. As so often when he met a young man, he wondered what it would be like if he were his own son. He had applied this test to Edwin Crawshay when he and Hermione had gone over to lunch with the Crawshays, and had concluded that he would not have wanted him for a son. This young collier would have been the same age as the son Hermione had borne him who had died. He tried to imagine the young collier educated and better dressed.

And what about the content of his speech? He hadn't liked that. It was pure rhetoric. Of course he had never worked in a pit. He had not been born to be a labourer. Middle-class folk were different from working people. But were they? When you pricked them, didn't they bleed? Weren't they warmed and cooled by the same sun? He had heard or read that somewhere. And didn't it go on: if you injure them, do they not seek revenge?

Sully pushed these thoughts from him. He gave generously to charity, and that was enough. He was a businessman. He was going to hang on to his money and would make more by running the pits he and his brother owned as cheaply and efficiently as he could. Instead of thinking about what an illiterate collier had said, he ought to be writing to his brother and telling him of the latest developments and deciding on the next phase of his battle with his workmen.

He remembered some documents he had left in his room at the colliery offices, and went to get them. The place was deserted except for a cleaner going round with her son who was holding an oil lamp for her to work by. On his way back he saw behind one of the pillars of the office gates a couple against the wall. He stopped. It was a young girl in the arms of a man. The girl was gazing at him with love, smiling up at him. He pulled her tightly towards him, and pressed his lips heavily on hers, and they stood silent and unmoving. Then, slowly and gently, he pushed her back against the wall.

Sully continued to look. Disgusting it was, in a public place. Can't they go somewhere else to do that sort of thing? But the expression of love on the girl's face and the enfolding arms and gentle and caring approach of the man somehow stopped it from being disgusting.

Then the girl looked up and saw him. She whispered to her partner, who turned his head. Sully, embarrassed at being seen, walked on. But he had recognised the young man; he was the one who had lectured him at that afternoon's meeting, who had talked about starvation, about bread. The men wanted bread, he had said. Bread, bread, he had repeated. They did not demand love and affection. They had that without thinking. They did not realise that to be deprived of them was a hardship. He had bread – and meat and venison and cream and champagne. But no love.

He continued up the road.

CHAPTER 31

Lennie was walking aimlessly in the garden, pulling off brussel sprouts as he passed, when he heard the twins running down the lane shouting his name. 'Get a mug, Lennie,' they shouted. 'It be the soup kitchen.'

'What's a soup kitchen?'

'Soup, silly. Food.'

Lennie did not understand.

'Get a mug, quick,' said one of the twins, and followed his brother.

Lennie decided he must do the same and went indoors. Cornelius was there and he asked him for a mug. 'For the soup kitchen, Grancher.'

Grancher didn't seem to understand, either, but he took the largest mug off a hook on the dresser and handed it to him. Holding it with both hands so as not to drop it Lennie hurried out and trotted off after the twins. Down the lane they went to the Pisgah Chapel.

Here in the road the Revd Gwilliam and his wife had set up a table on which were an urn of soup and chunks of bread. Mrs Gwilliam was urging a crowd of children to queue up. Lennie, holding his mug to his chest, stood at the end of the noisy, impatient queue, not understanding what was happening but smelling soup and seeing bread.

The Revd Gwilliam was arguing with a boy.

'I'm sorry, but this is for children. Boys who work and who are on strike are not children.'

'I be only just ten, and 'tain't my fault we're on strike. And I be so hungry.' He burst into tears.

'Oh, give the lad some,' said Mrs Gwilliam, and her husband complied.

They worked their way through the queue. At last it was Lennie's turn. He held his mug up, his big dark eyes unblinking in his pale face. The Revd Gwilliam had to scrape the bottom of the urn to fill Lennie's mug. He handed it down to him and Lennie took it carefully in both hands.

'Thank you,' he whispered shyly.

'I'll put your bread in your pocket, dear,' said Mrs Gwilliam.

'Judged it nicely,' said the Reverend as they carried the empty urn and table back into the Chapel.

Lennie went over to the railings that surrounded the Chapel. He walked slowly so as not to spill the soup, and sat on the low parapet. He took his bread from his pocket and placed it beside him on the stonework, and began to drink the soup. It was warm and thick and he drank it slowly, savouring every drop. After a few sips he stopped to look inside the mug and identified pieces of swede and potato. It tasted good and Lennie could feel his inside welcoming it as it went down. But the mug was soon empty. Then he picked up the bread and began to munch it.

He looked round for the twins, but they had gone. So had all the other children. He had not noticed them going. For a few minutes he stood thinking; then, feeling the cold, he picked up his mug and walked home.

He must tell Grancher all about it.

        🔊   🔈

Alice left by the back door to go to the vicarage to see Lizzie Prendergast. She was desperate for someone to confide in and, inadequate as Lizzie would be to give good advice, she was the only person Alice knew to whom she could disclose her story. Lizzie had been told of Hubert's attentions and could not understand why she had become so lukewarm towards him recently. Now Alice would tell her the reason. She knew the revelation about Maurice would arouse great excitement in her, and hated the interest she would show and the intrigue she would conjure up. Nevertheless, in her desperation Alice decided she must tell her the full story. (Lizzie would not object to the greatest detail.) Maybe in doing so she would clarify her own thoughts and feelings and see a way forward.

Nowadays Hermione never permitted her to leave the house without knowing where she was going and without stipulating a time she must return. Alice had told her mother that she wanted to visit Lizzie to give her her Christmas present, and she was allowed to go for an hour.

It was a miserable day. Moisture dripped from the bare branches of the oak trees that skirted the path to the vicarage. As Alice walked along it, Lizzie's present dangling on its string in her hand, a figure emerged from behind a tree. It was him. It was Maurice. She ran up to him and he received her in his arms. She looked round to make sure no-one else was about.

'How did you know I was coming up here this afternoon?'

'I've been here several times this week hoping to see you. I didn't dare to knock on your front door. But I knew you had a friend at the vicarage and was sure I should see you if I came often enough.'

She squeezed his hand.

'Where can we talk?' he said.

Alice hurried him past the church, past the vicarage standing back in its sombre garden and along a Forest path that led deep into a plantation.

'Did you receive my letters?' she asked.

'Yes, yes, and replied to them.'

'They didn't reach me. My mother must have destroyed them. After reading them, I'm sure.'

Maurice placed his arm around her waist. 'My dear, what can we do? If only we could marry.' This was the first time he had mentioned marriage, and he looked at her apprehensively.

'Well, why can't we? I'm twenty-one.'

'Believe me, I have thought about it a thousand times.'

But he had not answered her question. She looked at him and could see his frustration. 'We must marry at once,' she said decisively. 'Then they can't keep us apart.'

'It seems fate is against us, Alice.'

"Don't give in, Maurice. Love is stronger than fate.'

'Alice, I've no money, except what I earn from five or six lessons a week. My father is too ill to earn anything himself now, and my mother is at home and I have to keep them. All my spare money goes in buying smart clothes that I can ill afford, but without them I can't hope to teach people like you.'

Alice was stung by this last remark, but accepted its truth. He pulled her closer towards him as they walked. 'I doubt it would work if we got married. Our house is small. You aren't used to the life you'd have to lead, cleaning and scrubbing and doing the washing and preparing meals.'

'My life is awful at the moment, Maurice. It couldn't be worse. I have nothing to do, I've no real friends, no-one to talk to. Oh, Maurice, I'm so lonely, and I want you.' But her head told her that there would be problems. 'My parents would try to get me back, of course. And we couldn't expect any financial help from them.' She knew immediately she shouldn't have mentioned money.

'I wouldn't accept it even if it were offered. No, it's not fair to ask you to marry me, Alice. And I don't ask you.'

Alice felt rejected and was silent. She realised that if he had made a proposal to her a few minutes earlier he had now withdrawn it.

'So you are jilting me now to use the common expression?' she tried pitifully to be humorous.

He ignored her attempted joke. 'Alice, I think the chances of our living happily together are remote. We must face facts. You have the chance of making a good marriage with your parents' approval to a man of your own class. He can ensure that life will continue for you just as it is at present, all the little luxuries, the pocket money to buy books and music and all that.'

She started to protest but he interrupted her. 'Don't reject all these things as unimportant, dearest.'

She turned on him. 'What sort of a man are you? Are you frightened to fight for me, to fight with me?'

Maurice did not reply; and she could see she had inserted a thin blade of truth into his armour. He was not prepared to fight. For a moment she despised him. Was it that he did not love her enough? No, it wasn't that. Perhaps he was right. Perhaps they wouldn't win through. Logic and commonsense were better guides than passion. What was certain, he was not wholly behind her, and she could not fight alone.

They went over all the same ground again, and then fell silent and walked on apart, untouching, unable to talk, unable to find a solution. They stopped and in the shelter of a tree he took her in his arms and she smelt his maleness. Whatever the weakness of his resolve, she thought, he had a strong body. She felt the warmth from it spread into her, its magic momentarily taking her over. But it was no substitute, and she moved away. Her annoyance at him, which she realised was really annoyance at her situation, annoyance that she could not get what she wanted, disintegrated into despair and she burst into tears.

He drew her to him again, wiped her tears – his touch was so gentle – and they stayed close, in silence. The mist separated into drops of rain. The grey afternoon began to darken.

'We mustn't give up hope,' she said at last. 'There must be an answer.'

'Yes,' he said. Then, 'I wonder if it would be any good if you told your father, to see what he says.'

It was the only suggestion he had made, thought Alice. But then she had nothing to suggest either.

'Perhaps I will, but he's under my mother's thumb.'

He released her, and with a kiss and a murmur he guided her back through the plantation and past the vicarage and church to where he had met her. Here they would have to separate, he to go to the station, she to return to hostility at Park End House. They kissed, and she walked on. She looked back and gave a wave.

Feeling weary and dead inside, she entered the house. She was glad he had made an effort to see her, but sad that his resolve had so easily given out. But she still wanted him. She didn't want a life of luxury with Hubert; she wanted him. But he was not prepared to fight for her. As she entered the house she knew she would never see him again.

As she took off her gloves her mind was snatched back to reality. Lizzie's present, with its string entwined tightly round her fingers, was still with her. She must send a maid with it right away before her mother discovered she had not delivered it.

❧   ❧

On Christmas morning Lennie came into the kitchen and climbed on to Cornelius's lap and looked up into his face. Cornelius put his arm round his thin body with its protruding shoulder blades. He held him tight, hoping that some of his own warmth and energy, little though they were, could be transferred to him.

'And what does my little boy want, then?'

'Help me do my jigsaw, Grancher.'

'Your jigsaw?'

Lennie produced a paper bag. 'Father Christmas brought it for me.' He emptied the bag onto the table. 'It's mine,' he said proudly.

Some twenty scraps of coloured cardboard fell out. Catrin had cut a coloured picture to form a jigsaw.

'Let's do it then,' said Cornelius. 'Edges first.'

'Edges first,' repeated Lennie.

They sorted out the pieces and connected them up. Lennie soon got the idea.

'Now the middle.'

'Now the middle.'

In ten minutes the puzzle was completed. They both clapped hands.

'What a lovely picture that be,' said Cornelius.

They admired it, a gawdy picture of a Christmas tree standing in a middle-class sitting-room. Its branches were weighed down with mock snow and decorations and sparkled with tinsel. The candles flickered yellow. On top was a fairy queen waving her wand. Stacked around the bottom were presents wrapped in festive paper, some square, some irregular in shape, some big, some small, but all intriguing.

'Look,' said Cornelius. 'They got a tree from the Forest and have decorated it, just like us.'

'Yes,' said Lennie. He looked at the picture, but hardly comprehended it. The comfortable, warm sitting-room it portrayed was unlike their own drab kitchen. The Christmas tree was different from their tree which George had cut in the woods and squeezed between dresser and fireplace and Catrin had decorated with scraps of ribbon.

He soon lost interest in the picture, and snuggled into his great-grandfather. 'Grancher,' he whispered. 'I be hungry.'

Cornelius gave him a squeeze. 'Let's see what we can find.' He put his hand in his pocket, and gave him a crust saved from breakfast. 'Now chew it slowly. The more you chews it before swallowing, the more good it does you.'

ʘ ʘ

Sully stood in his drawing-room in front of the fire and surveyed his Christmas tree. It was a handsome specimen, no doubt about it, and its appearance was enhanced by ribbons, tinsel and glitter. Around the base of the tree, reflecting the firelight, were the presents, presents from Hermione and Alice to him and from him to them, presents brought by his brother Charles and his family, who had joined them at Park End for Christmas, and presents from the Sullys to them. Piled high, they were, under the tree, waiting until after dinner when the family would sit round the fire and open them.

Sully tied two small packets to branches of the tree. They were so small that he feared that if he put them on the pile they might be lost. One contained a bracelet for Alice and the other a ring for Hermione. He hoped she liked it. It was a plain gold band with a sapphire set in it, a ring fit for a cardinal. He had paid far more for it than he had intended, for these were hard times, but the purchase would be worthwhile if she liked it. He was sure she would, for she was fond of jewellery. It was the one thing she welcomed from him, the one thing nowadays that produced a smile from her.

He sat before the fire, pleased to be alone for a moment. His cat jumped onto his lap and he stroked it while he thought about the

241

wretched strike he had on his hands. There seemed no sign of it coming to an end. The Chief Constable in Cheltenham had already augmented the Forest police force and had promised to send down some mounted police to Park End after Christmas in case bad came to worse and the men turned violent. He would arrange for the men and their horses to stay down the road at the Fountain.

But he must put his cares aside and think about Christmas. Hermione and Alice with his brother and family would be back from Church shortly, and then all would be noise and excitement. He must join in and for a few hours forget about the industrial trouble in the pits, though he knew his brother expected a detailed account sometime of what had been happening during the last few weeks and how profits would be affected. But for the moment all was peace.

Alice came into the room. 'I thought you might be here, Papa.'

'Back already?'

'Yes. The others have gone upstairs, but they will be down soon.' She sat beside him on the sofa. 'It's lovely to see you having a rest. You're usually so busy, with the collieries and the dispute and everything. How long do you think it will go on for?'

'I don't know, my dear.' She was not usually so sociable these days, thought Sully, but he was pleased to talk to her. 'Let's talk about you. You haven't looked well for some weeks.'

He held her hand. They seldom had a quiet chat. Usually Hermione was present, and her large personality tended to overshadow them. But he cherished the occasions when he and Alice were alone together. He was sorry that somehow they had never been close and she had never confided her problems to him. But then he was not close to anyone these days, not even Hermione. He glanced at Alice. She seemed to be wanting to say something.

'Hubert proposed to me yesterday,' she said at last.

'I know. He told me he intended to.' Sully felt remiss he had not raised the subject with Alice first.

'He would like an answer tomorrow. Mama wants me to marry him.'

'Yes, I know.'

'I expect you want me to marry him, too.'

'Don't you want to?'

'You know I don't.'

It's this music teacher fellow, thought Sully; Hermione had spoken about him. 'Hubert Crawshay is a good, reliable man. He will make you

242

a fine husband. And he has great regard for you. I think you should accept him.'

'But I don't love him.'

'You will grow to love him when you are married.' That, thought Sully, would be better than being in love before marriage and falling out later. Like him and Hermione.

'I don't think so. He's kind and generous, I suppose. But, Papa, he is so boring.'

'There are worse faults in a husband than that.'

'You don't want a loveless marriage for me, do you, Papa?'

Sully did not reply. Perhaps, as Hermione said, she read too many romantic novels. But he must not judge her too harshly. He knew all about loveless marriages, or at least he knew about the agony and the resentment in his own marriage, how he tried to please Hermione yet saw, helplessly, how he annoyed her, how his smallest action would cause irritation. He knew also of the unhappiness of women who remained old maids. For years he had watched his sister longing for a proposal that never came, and saw her become skinny and hard and bitter as she waited.

He put his arm round Alice's waist. 'It would be for the best, I think. Your mother and I won't be here for ever, you know, and though I'll be able to leave you a good annuity to see you through later years, I should be happier to see you married and settled now and have children.'

He saw she was stifling tears. 'Do you want to tell me anything else?' he asked, hoping she would tell him something that would make him change his advice.

'No,' she said; but he waited. They sat in silence for several minutes.

Then her cousins burst into the room. 'Come on, Alice,' they shouted. 'Don't mope. It's Christmas and time for fun.'

Sully sat on after her cousins had swept Alice out of the room. This was not going to be a very happy Christmas. He was sorry for his daughter, of course, but she must be sensible and accept that her mother knew best. She must realise that girls did not have handsome young princes descend on them in places like Park End. He would give her a loving young prince if he could find one, though there was no guarantee, of course, that the prince would stay loving; he would certainly not remain young and handsome. Hermione had been a beautiful young princess when he had married her, but her beauty had diminished as she had grown older. He had vaguely realised that would happen, but he had not known that her love for him would vanish with her youth, and hardness would be substituted.

❧ ❧

Alice Sully and Hubert Crawshay were married a few weeks later at Park End Church. Because of the strike Sully would have preferred not to have the ceremony in the Forest, but Hermione insisted because she wanted the reception at home. She did not see why she should not have the wedding in their own village because of a lot of unruly colliers whom her husband should have brought to heel a long time ago.

The weather was not good and the Church was only half full. Sully's relations in Somerset had come by the dozen and some had had to be accommodated at the local inn. There were fewer Crawshays, the contingent from Merthyr Tydfil refusing to come and share anything with Eliza. Hermione had urged her husband to spare no expense, and indeed he had been generous.

The service over, the bride and groom emerged from the Church and walked down the path to the lych gate. A pale sun emerged, a token if unenthusiastic blessing for the occasion; but it disappeared immediately. A few villagers – mainly women who could not resist a good wedding – were waiting outside the churchyard. There were only a few because the Sullys were not liked in the village, and the strike had made them more unpopular than ever. Relations and friends followed the couple from the Church and threw rice over them as they climbed into their carriage, Hubert wearing the smug smile of a man who had achieved his aim, Alice smiling the sad resigned smile of someone who had not had the will to resist. She tossed her bouquet to the crowd, where it was caught by her chief bridesmaid, Lizzie.

It was but a few minutes ride to the house but Hubert wrapped a rug round Alice's knees to keep out the cold. The horses trotted off and the families and guests followed in their carriages. Outside the colliery offices was a group of colliers, their coat collars turned up against the wind, kicking their heels and waving their arms to keep warm. They glanced up as the wedding party appeared and scowled.

'Here come the lucky pair,' said one.

'Going to feed their guts until they bust, I suppose,' said another.

A third detached himself from the group and came over to the carriage. Hubert hoped he was not going to cause trouble. The collier's face though gaunt was kindly, his eyes were bright and generous.

244

He looked up at Alice. 'Good luck to you, miss,' he said, and reaching in his pocket he took out a small piece of coal and threw it to her. She caught it automatically and looked uncertainly at him. Then she smiled. It was Billy, young Billy who had helped her when she had slipped on the ground not far from here. The carriage moved on through the gates of Sully's house and up the drive.

Hubert looked questioningly at her, but she did not respond, just wiped away a tear.

CHAPTER 32

'I'm going to have a baby.'

'Oh my God, no. As if I haven't got enough trouble.' Adam put his head in his hands.

'Don't be so selfish. You've got trouble.' Martha glared at him. 'Don't you think having a baby which isn't your husband's isn't trouble – it's more than that, it's a calamity.'

It was Saturday night and Bert was in Gloucester. 'I gave him the money to get him out of the way.' Martha explained.

'I thought you were as hard up as the rest of us.'

'My aunt sends me a few shillings each week for food. He'll have to go hungry now he's taken some of it to see his woman. He knows that.'

Martha put down a loaf and some cheese in front of Adam. 'You look as if you could do with something to eat.'

He sat crushed and silent. Then, 'I'm sorry, Martha, but let's not quarrel. I love you still.'

'Yes, but don't just sit there. What shall we do?'

Adam sensed a hardening in Martha, but he knew her practical sense would rise to the top. He realised that he could take decisions based on hard logic, but not on emotion; she was the one for cutting the way through such matters, and would do so now. 'Are you sure you've got a baby?'

'I'm always regular. Now I've missed. Only once, but I know. I'm sick in the mornings.'

Adam did not understand such things. 'I suppose you could get rid of it.'

'Not if I can help it. You don't know what it's like to have a human life in your belly.'

'It couldn't possibly be Bert's could it?'

'No, it couldn't. It's yours.'

Adam was pleased she was so sure it wasn't Bert's. He was silent for a time. 'Supposing you slept with him just this once. Then he would think it was his.' He looked to see her reaction.

'No. I couldn't. It would make me feel ill. Anyway its a bit late for that. It would be a seven months' child. Bert's no good at arithmetic but he can count up to nine.'

Her remark eased the tension, and Adam smiled sadly. The smell of the bread and cheese made him realise he was hungry. Important though the subject was, his hunger, perpetual nowadays, demanded to be assuaged, and he cut himself a slice of bread and a piece of cheese and with one in each hand began to eat. But there was no pleasure in it. 'Only Bert would know when he slept with you, and he wouldn't let anybody know he wasn't the father.'

'Don't be so sure. He didn't mind who knew that he suspected me with going with Emrys.'

'But he was drunk and wasn't thinking what he was doing.' He drew her to him and put his hands round her waist, His hands wandered round her body, feeling her soft curves. Her hair glinted gold in the lamp light. The magic of her presence overcame his distress. 'We mustn't let this split us apart. There's been an edge to your voice this evening, my love.'

'That's not surprising. I'm worried.'

With his hands on her waist he drew her between his knees. She relaxed a little and smoothed his brown hair from his forehead. 'Your face is thinner these days,' said Martha, 'but I still love you.'

She turned away. 'If he tells everyone it's not his child, the whole village will think it's Emrys's. We couldn't let him take the blame for this as well as the other.' She looked at him. 'Could we?'

'No we couldn't, but what's the alternative? Even so I hate the idea of your body being mawled by him.'

'It's disgusting, but I've done it before and I can do it again.' She sat on his lap and picked up a piece of bread he had left on his plate and chewed it pensively. 'You know, our relationship – yours and mine – is cracking up. I knew it would sooner or later, and I'm surprised it's lasted so long with no-one suspecting. And the funny thing is, when someone said they spotted us together, it wasn't us!'

'No, Martha, we mustn't split up. I couldn't lose you. It would crucify me.'

'We all have our crosses to bear.' She sat with her arm round his neck, closed her eyes and thought. Then she made up her mind. 'All right. Give me a few days to warm him up and I'll sleep with him.'

∂ ∽

Cornelius said he would take Lennie up to bed, and would also go to bed himself, early though it was. Lennie clambered up the narrow staircase first, his great-grandfather following with a candle. He took off his trousers and climbed into the middle of his parents' bed, pushed to his mother's side the hot brick that Catrin had earlier placed there and, small and upright, sat expectant. Shadows from Cornelius's candle flickered down on him from the walls.

'Tell me a story, Grancher.'

Cornelius wet his finger tips and put out the candle. 'We needn't waste that if we be just going to talk.'

'Come in with me,' said Lennie.

Cornelius slowly lowered himself onto the bed. He pulled the bedclothes over them both, but left his legs and feet outside. Lennie snuggled up to him, and he put his arm round him.

'Tell me a story, Grancher.'

'What would you like?'

Lennie considered. 'Tell me how the giants were chased out of the Forest.'

'That be your favourite, I think.'

'Yes. Tell me, tell me now.'

Cornelius told him the story, as he had done a hundred times before. Lennie lay against him quietly, absorbing every word, with only an occasional wriggle. When the story was over Cornelius said, 'There, now you must go to sleep.'

'Tell me again, Grancher, tell me lots of times.'

So Cornelius told him the story again.

Then Lennie said, 'Let's say Humpty Dumpty together.'

'Do you know,' said Cornelius, 'they do say that Humpty Dumpty come from Gloucester when King Charles was fighting a battle there once.'

But Lennie had started to chant, and Cornelius joined in.

'Humpty Dumpty sat on a wall,

'Humpty Dumpty had a great fall.

'All the King's horses and all the King's men

'Couldn't put Humpty together again.'

At the end of the rhyme both paused in anticipation. Lennie wriggled and Cornelius held him tight against his body. Then Cornelius said, as he always said, 'Why not?'

'Because he was an egg,' shouted Lennie, and they both laughed.

'Now I do think you'm ready for sleep. Be you going on your back or side?'

'Side.'

Lennie lay down. Cornelius could feel his thin body relaxing and slipping away into sleep. He could not see him in the dark, but he imagined the boy's eyes closed with their long lashes, moist and black over the smooth, pale cheeks. He could hear his steady breathing, interrupted just occasionally by his cough.

He looked up at the outline of the window against the faint evening light from outside. He could go now to his own room if he wished. But he felt content lying close to Lennie. He was in no hurry. There was no need to hurry. He lay there content, for how long he didn't know, half asleep but aware of the boy's presence. Lennie meant so much to him and had occupied his thoughts so much in the last few years.

But the time had now come. He knew it.

He gently withdrew his arm. As he kissed him on the forehead he could smell his sweet body odour. He realised the lad was cold, and with an effort he lifted the rag mat from the floor and placed it over the blanket that covered him.

Then he got himself into his own room, and lay down on the bed. He was always tired these days – how his heart had pounded lately – but he was more tired than ever this evening. Talking to Lennie had exhausted him more than he would have expected. It was good to lie down and do nothing, not even to think. He felt so old, oh so old, and worn out. He coughed and panted a little, and felt his heart pound. He felt so alone. You are all alone when it comes to the end, he thought. He wanted to talk to someone about death, more now than ever before. But people never wanted to talk about it; they got upset if you mentioned it.

He thought of Lennie and the way he said 'Grancher'. Everyone called him Grancher nowadays. No-one could imagine that he had once been young with the juice of life in him and that he had run and laughed and, like all young people, had wasted his energy because there was always more.

He slipped into a dream. The sun was shining and the birds were singing on the tumps and he was running with a wench. He caught her and they tumbled laughing into the ferns. She looked seriously at him, kissed him full on the mouth and ran away, down the hill, laughing, her skirt round her knees, her heels twinkling, her golden hair bobbing in the sunlight. It had been Janie, and he had married her. How they had laughed together then. There was nothing to laugh about nowadays except with Lennie. Really there had been little to laugh about then. But just being alive was good, being alive and not aching, not being sore, not being half blind, not being deaf, not having a cough that racked your body.

He turned over and forgot the feel of the rough blanket against his face and the smell of sweat it exuded. The bed became soft and there were sheets, clean and white, soft and warm. Warm, too, was his mind with thoughts that swam before him, so varied, so inconsequential. He remembered things he had not thought about for years. He remembered Bill, the son who had died at the tin-plate works and how they had brought him home. He had not been a bad fellow in spite of what people had said. He saw himself making a rabbit hutch for young Harry, the son who had run away and died in the Crimea, and laughing as they put the rabbit in it. He saw his own face, so fixed and his eyes so sad and unblinking as he had carried Jim, his youngest boy, home from the pit. Light he had been in death, so still, so tender and relaxed, his arm hanging down loosely as he had carried him into the house.

Memories became quicker and more confused – the hooter of the pit, the clang of mattock on coal, the sweet, peculiar fragrance of his Janie, the laughter of his grandchildren, the chill of poverty, the despair of hunger. But none of it mattered any more. His sensations were gradually reduced to an amorphous feeling of calm and warmth and stillness. And then nothing.

When Adam came home that evening Emma had laid out Grancher's watch for him.

“”

Martha put her hands on Bert's shoulders and, leaning over, showed an interest in the newspaper he was reading. 'What are you reading about?'

He looked up in surprise. 'This Pole in Cinderford that have committed bigamy.'

She abandoned the small talk. 'Bert, I've been thinking we should make a better go of our marriage.'

Bert looked round. 'You be up to something? I thought it strange you gave me money to go to Gloucester last week. Wanted to get rid of me for the evening? Having it off with Emrys again, are you?'

'I've told you I never had it off with Emrys, as you crudely put it.'

'I'm not so sure about that. Anyway, why are you sucking up to me now?'

'I just thought we could be a bit more friendly.'

'We gets on all right outside the bed, just about. You does your job in the house, keeps the house clean and tidy and gets my meals, and I brings in the money – normally, that is, when we haven't this bloody strike. It's not much of a marriage, but there it is.'

'I thought we might get together more.'

'You mean go to bed, like?'

'Why not?'

'We ain't done that for a long time. I never forget that night you kicked me out of the bed and told me you found me rough and like an animal, and didn't want me near you. Why the change?'

'I don't like you going to Gloucester every week.'

'Jealous, eh? You spurned me and I made other arangements, as they say. Yes I do have a woman in Gloucester and she be a darn sight more sympathetic than you.'

'Can't we try again?'

'No, I be all right as I am.'

She turned on him in a fury. 'I try to mend our marriage and you refuse.'

'God, you do like your own way, don't you? Always did. And it be no use you getting in a temper. Since I'm stuck with you I'm content with things as they are.'

'You infuriating bugger!' she shouted and seizing her coat from a chair and her handbag from the mantelpiece flounced out of the cottage.

CHAPTER 33

Bert met Adam as he came up from Park End. 'I went down on the picket lines his afternoon. As I passed the colliery offices Gunter did call me over. He said Sully wants to let maintenance men down into the pits to shore up the roofs and that sort of thing, but they won't go down without our agreement. I said I'd see you.'

Adam was inclined to say no maintenance until the strike was over, but thought again. 'Sully's right,' he said slowly. 'There'll be no pits left to work when the men go back if they all cave in. Tell Gunter and the men we agree, will you? But we must tell the men on the picket line to watch that no blacklegs slip through.'

But Bert did not move, and Adam looked at him curiously. He was silent for a moment, then he began to unburden himself about Martha. He wants to confide in someone about his wife and chooses me, thought Adam. Me, his best friend! Adam encouraged him, but trod carefully.

'It wasn't just one of them ordinary rows. She was after something. What it was I don't know, something big, I suspect, and I was suspicious, like. She put her arms around my neck and I thought she wanted to kiss me – the first time she have done that for years – and I said to meself, 'Allo, 'allo, what's she after? Then, believe it or not, she wanted to get me into bed. And when I didn't rush to pick her up and carry her upstairs, she turned nasty and flounced out of the house.'

'Where's she gone?'

'Don't know. But this was two days ago and she ain't come back yet. But she will. They always do. I'm not worried, 'cept I has to get my own meals and there's not much in the cupboard and not likely to be until this bloody strike is over.'

Adam uttered a few vague words of commiseration – God how dishonest and despicable can you get – and put his arm, Judas like, round Bert's shoulder. But he was sorry for Bert even though he was the cause of his plight.

When Bert went off, Adam digested his news about Martha. So she had carried out his suggestion and tried to get Bert into bed with her so she could tell him that the child was his. And he had refused and she had left home in a rage. Was the rage against Bert or against him? Probably against him for making a revolting suggestion that had not worked.

Bert did not seem to know or care where she had gone; but Adam knew that he must search for her and bring her back home. Where would she have gone? As far as he knew she had no friends she could trust in Coalway or Park End. If he went off to look for her he would have to trust Bert to look after his union problems. What irony! The husband would do his job while he sought his wife! The alternative was to ask Joseph Cowmeadow to keep an eye on matters for him, but he wanted to keep him out of Park End business if he could.

He decided to wait a few days to see if she came back. When she did not, he wondered if she had gone off for ever. But where was she? Then it occurred to him she may have gone to her aunt in Gloucester. It was a big place, but he would go there next morning. He remembered she had said that her aunt's house was at Wootton. He decided to try there first.

He must find the fare money, otherwise he would have to walk, and that was twenty miles each way. He searched in his pockets and found but a shilling.

'George, I've got to go to Gloucester and I haven't enough money. Can you lend me tuppence?'

'Sorry, old butt, haven't a bean. Ask Mam.'

But Adam didn't want to tell his mother what the money was for. So at the first opportunity, his conscience gnawing him, he took tuppence from the mustard tin.

❧ ❧

He went to Wootton and found an avenue called Wootton Hill. He would try there. The houses were big, set in their own gardens. Each had a black railing fronting the road with a substantial decorative wrought-iron gate that led up a gravelled path to the house. He did not know the name of Martha's aunt or the name of the house so he started at one end and began to knock on the front doors.

'Excuse me I'm looking for a middle-aged lady who has a niece in the Forest of Dean.'

The stares of disapproval, going down to his shoes and back to his face, showed him that he was insufficiently well-dressed to dare to knock on the doors of such houses and ask such questions.

However, at the seventh house he received a positive answer.

'Are you Adam Turley?' The speaker was a large woman with rosy cheeks and dazzling white hair. Her face frowned when Adam said he was. 'Thought you might be.' She surveyed him, trying to make up her mind what to do.

Adam smiled at her, pleadingly. 'Please let me see Martha.'

With a sigh she said 'You'd better come in, I suppose.' She introduced herself as Mrs Spencer and led him upstairs to a bedroom. Adam entered and found Martha lying in bed. She looked weak and ill. Her golden hair, usually gleaming like gold, was dull and tired and straggled round her shoulders.

'My love.' He ran to her and embraced her. Seeing that Martha was pleased to see him, Mrs Spencer withdrew.

'What's happened to you? Why didn't you let me know you were here? And why are you so ill? Surely a row with Bert wouldn't have made you bad like this?'

Martha gave a smile and eased herself higher in the bed. 'I'd hoped you'd remember where my aunt lived and come. When you didn't I wrote and she posted the letter this morning.' She took Adam's hand and lifted it to her lips.

'But you look so ill.'

'It's gone.'

'What has?'

'The baby.'

'You got rid of it?'

'Yes.'

'For me?'

'Yes.'

He plunged his face into her breast and wept. He had never cried in her presence before. 'How did you –?'

'My aunt found someone who knew how to do it. She charged five pounds.'

'How – how did –?'

'She tried gin and a hot bath, and when that didn't work, a knitting needle.'

Horror struck his face. So crude a way, such an attack on her fair body. He clung to her and she cradled his head in her hands. They were silent until Mrs Spencer brought in tea and biscuits. 'You don't deserve this,' she said as she put the tray down. 'You men are all the same. Your own pleasure –'

'No, it wasn't like that,' Adam choked out.

'Yes, it's for your own pleasure and it doesn't help at all when the woman falls in love with you.'

Martha came to Adam's help. 'Yes, it does help, Aunt. And you know it does.'

Mrs Spencer unbent a trifle. 'She's told me all about it, you know. She's over the worst now but she can't go back home for a week or two. Then she can make it up with her husband. No-one will know what has happened.'

'But don't tell him I'm here. I'll go home in my own time.'

Adam opened the front door, and was annoyed to see Bert there. Since his visit to Martha he had not wanted to talk to him, and he had no intention of telling him where she was or about the abortion.

'Hallo, old butt,' said Bert amiably. He came in and his eyes darted round the room. He spotted Emrys sitting in the corner and decided to ignore him. Adam found him a chair. There was one fewer round the table now Grancher had gone.

'What about a cup of tea, Mam?'

Emma looked up, and was about to speak but changed her mind. She reached for the pot and caddy and made some tea.

'Swelp me bob,' said George as he looked into his cup. 'I can see the bottom.'

'There be no milk, and that's the last of the tea until someone gives me money to buy some more,' said Emma defiantly.

George laughed. 'With a bit more union pay, like, we could have a cup of decent tea, Adam.'

Adam smiled and shook his head. 'We've had one payout but there be no more cash in the kitty. We haven't had nothing from union headquarters and we've had precious little from other union branches, either.'

'Have we had anything from Wales?' asked Emrys. 'The Forest sent us three hundred pounds two years ago when we had our big strike and I lost my job.'

'They've sent us fifty shillings.'

'Fifty bob!' said Emrys, ashamed.

'I should send it back,' said George.

'No,' Bert grinned. 'It'll buy a lot of bread.'

Practicalities above principles, thought Adam. But he said, 'It'll help a bit.'

'Never fear,' said Emma from her seat by the fire. The others all looked at her. 'Never fear. We shall win. I have always thought the men was right in saying they wouldn't accept the cuts. My family, my grancher and his grancher, worked in the Park End pits for years. They often went hungry, even in the old days when they owned their own pits. And then when they foreigners like Sully come along it got worse. We've always had to fight and we had to make a stand this time. We've still all of us got reserves inside us. If the women stand behind their men we can last out, you can be sure.' She blushed at her temerity in speaking of such matters but carried on. 'As the good book says, every man should eat and drink and enjoy the good of all his labour. It is the gift of God.' Then she returned to sipping her tea.

Adam looked at his mother in amazement. She had never before offered any opinion on the strike one way or the other. He was proud of her. He glanced at Catrin sitting in the corner behind the table next to George to see how she reacted. Her face was impassive.

Bert left. The others began to make tracks for bed. Emrys and George, one candle between them, went upstairs together. When Cornelius had died Emrys had taken over his half of the double bed. Adam, without a word to Catrin, had already taken a candle and gone up.

Catrin collected the teacups and placed them in the bowl ready for washing next day, and put some sticks in the oven to dry for morning. Then she lit a candle and put out the oil lamp and followed Adam. He was lying on the bed, fully dressed, hands behind his head, silent and morose. He did not look up when she entered the room. He had no interest in her any longer, she decided; all his interest lay in Martha Preece now. She had not told him she had had a confrontation with her, and she doubted whether Martha Preece had told him either. But the fight hadn't changed anything; Adam acted the same towards her as before.

She raised her candle and glanced in the looking glass on the wall. Her face, once rosy as an apple, was now grey and haggard, and the healthy sparkle had gone from her eyes. No wonder Adam no longer cared for her. Her marriage was a failure and she was disagreeable, bitter and jealous. Then she told herself not to be stupid. Self pity, is it? There's a poor thing. Where's your courage?

256

Adam got off the bed and began to undress. She moved Lennie to the middle of the bed; these days he acted as a barrier between them. She was tired, not only from the talk of the evening, but tired of her existence. But though she was longing to go to sleep, she decided she would venture some conversation. She tried so hard nowadays to talk to him, using the uncontroversial small exchanges of everyday living to make life easier. But though he talked freely enough with other people, he answered her in monosyllables.

'Nice it was to have Bert round for a change. We don't see much of him these days.' She could not resist saying 'I hear his wife has left him.' She looked at Adam to see if she had drawn blood.

He turned on her. 'He's been busy working for the union.'

'Oh, yes the union.'

He pounced on her words. 'The union, the union. God, the way you say it!' She was surprised at the hostility in his voice. Her tiredness left her and she was impelled to confront him, bolstering her fear at speaking out with her pent-up emotions. 'Well, if you want to know, I think it wicked for the men to stay out like they do –'

'I gets more support from my mother.'

'– stay out and let their families go hungry. Look at Lennie, white and old beyond his years, getting thinner by the day through lack of food. Don't you care for him?'

'I can see what Lennie is going through. It's the same for all the colliers' children, but we'll be back at work soon.'

'You'll be driven back. And what will you all get out of it? ' Her voice, though kept low to avoid waking Lennie, pulsated with emotion and intensity. She felt she had to oppose him, even though his hostility was racking her and pushing her to the end of her emotional resources.

'A fine wife you've turned out to be. You don't support me. The opposite. Look at you and George, I've seen you.'

'Keep your voice down. You've seen nothing.'

'I saw you this evening, snuggling up tight against him, and him enjoying being close to you and patting your arm.'

'He did not. Though your attitude these days would be enough to make any woman go to someone else for a bit of warmth and comfort.'

'I shouldn't be surprised if you've done just that. And more.'

Did he really believe that she had been unfaithful to him? Or did his adultery with Martha Preece force him to accuse her of the same thing?

257

'I haven't forgot how you led me up to your bed at the farm many a time before we were married. And I've wondered how many men there were before me. I suppose none of them wanted to marry you because you couldn't conceive.'

Catrin burst into tears. 'It's not true, it's not true,' she whispered. 'There was only you. How can you say such hurtful things?' She sat on the bed, put both hands over her face and sobbed, her shoulders rounded and her thin frame showing through her dress. Then she drew a breath and, with it, fresh stimulation to clear her mind. She looked up at him.

'And what sort of a life do you think I've had since I came to Coalway? I would have put up with being poor and overcrowded in this place if I'd had your love. I'd have been happy to have more children but you didn't seem to want any more.'

'We don't want no more kids. They don't make you happy; they only make you poor.'

'They've got nine up the lane at the Dobbs's, and they're happy enough.'

'How do you know whether other people are happy? And how do you know you could have had more kids? You took long enough to produce the one we've got.'

Catrin found a handkerchief and wiped her face. Adam folded his arms as he leaned back against the wall, glowering at her. He had taken his coat off and in the flickering candle light his arms seemed to be brown, though she knew they were white. Those were the arms, strong and loving that had embraced her that day in the kitchen at the farm. The smiles he had given her then, lazy and sunny, now arose in her memory unbidden. There had been no sun in his face for many a month now. The memory of what had been softened her. 'What have I done to you?' she whispered. 'You used to love me once. Why have you gone so far from me?' But she knew the reason, and it wasn't her fault.

He turned with a shrug of his shoulders. 'It be no good crying over what might have been. We can't control what happens.'

His reply, though it showed he was wearying of the battle, only brought on her rage again. He has never seen me like this before, she thought. I've always been like a cushion, not reacting, not giving him the satisfaction of a response which he can pounce on and use to attack me again. Now he is getting a response and he doesn't like it.

Her temper was costing her dear, but now she had started her counter-attack she had to carry on. The dam to her thoughts had been removed and the river was in full flood. 'It's not surprising things have gone wrong,' she shouted, following him around the room. 'I wanted a house of my own. You promised me one, but I didn't get it. You had no intention. You took the £50 my father gave us and spent it.'

'I told you. I spent a lot of it on things for the pit. If we didn't have them, we wouldn't have been able to dig the coal. And I gave the rest to Mam for housekeeping when the strike started.'

Then she launched at him the deadliest weapon in her armoury. 'And who paid for the brooch you gave to Martha Preece?' The knowledge of Adam's gift to Martha had rankled inside her for so long, but it was out now.

Adam looked at her, chastened. 'So you know.'

'Of course I know.' She stood up and faced him, quite unafraid now. The candle flickered. Faint though his image was in its light, she could now see not hatred or dislike for her, not embarrassment at being found out, but only the agony that had lain long in his soul and now welled up within him. For a moment, in spite of the suffering he had inflicted on her, she wanted to take him in her arms and comfort him as she had in the early days of their marriage. But the mood passed quickly. She realised he would not come to her; the shade of Martha stood between them.

He was exhausted, she could see. She was exhausted, too, but if he would not yield, nor would she. They stood, one before the other, resolute. Then he gave in. 'I'll sleep downstairs,' he said and left the room.

When he had gone her exhaustion overcame her and she lay on the bed. She did not know if she had won this awful battle, did not even consider it in terms of winning or losing. But in her misery she needed comfort. She sought it by holding Lennie close to her, but gently, because she must not wake him up now he had slept through the tempest. As she held him close, the warmth of his body came to her, and her tears dropped on his tousled hair.

She lay wanting oblivion. Then with a start she realised that she had not blown out the light, and they could not afford to waste candles. But she could not worry about that now.

&~ ~&

Catrin was in her bedroom putting her family's washing away; Emma was visiting her sister; Lennie had gone up the lane to play with the twins; Emrys was out with a friend; George was downstairs having a bath; and Adam was out somewhere. Catrin wondered where. The knowledge of his squalid intrigue festered constantly inside her. Why had Martha Preece left her husband? Where was she now? Was she with Adam? The image of a dog panting round a bitch on heat, tongue lolling out, hit her and she felt sick. She was convinced he was sleeping with her, for he never made love to her nowadays. Only last Sunday the preacher at Pisgah had preached a sermon on adultery. Had he belatedly heard the rumours about Emrys and Martha and wanted to warn his flock of the possible consequences of their iniquity? The devil, he had told them, reserved the lowest pit in hell for adulterers, along with murderers. His tirade had supported Catrin's view of Adam's perfidy, but she would not go so far as to equate it with murder.

She put Lennie's socks in the drawer and wondered whether George had finished his bath. Earlier that afternoon when he had discovered that practically the whole family would be out of the way, he had announced that he fancied a bath. He wasn't dirty, he said, because he had not been in the pit for weeks, but he missed the refreshing feeling that his daily bath used to give him. A bath would help to ease the tedium of a long afternoon as well. So he had heated some water in the copper in the back kitchen, set the old tin bath in front of the fire and poured several bucketfuls of hot water into it.

Catrin had got out of his way while he enjoyed himself. After putting her washing away and rescuing a handkerchief of Emma's that had been mis-sorted, she sat on the bed and waited. Then, assuming that George had finished, she descended the stairs and pushed open the door at the bottom. George, she discovered, had not finished. He was just rising from the bath with his back to her, the water glistening on his shoulders and thighs as he straightened up, his broad back and buttocks gleaming white like marble. A strange feeling rose in her. She had glimpsed George taking his bath before – how could she have avoided it in this overcrowded house? – but, in her modesty, she had never examined his body as she was examining it now. She had never had any desire to touch him. Why did she have such a desire now? Why, indeed? Why this wickedness? For that was what it was. She had always been pure in heart and faithful to her husband. Was the devil tempting her? She shrugged her shoulders, but it was more a shiver, a revulsion from her thoughts than a simple dismissal of them.

He heard her and turned round. Had he seen her staring at him?

'Give us the towel, m'dear.' He indicated a towel on the fireguard beyond his reach. 'Don't want to make a mess on the floor.' He stood waiting, upright and open, and when she handed him the towel, he seemed to be in no hurry to take it. He stood looking at her.

Catrin turned away.

'Haven't you ever seen a man before?' he asked.

Grasping Emma's handkerchief she hurried into her room, and stood by the window, gazing out to the end of the garden towards the woods. She pondered on George's strange look, and his coarse remark.

Perhaps they had no significance. She went back into the kitchen. There was a tension in the air, but as she glanced at George she concluded that it was of her own creation. He had donned a clean shirt and trousers; his hair was glistening clean and his face was rosy from rubbing. He was sitting, ankle on knee, drying a foot.

She must behave normally. 'Cup of tea, is it, George?' As she took down the caddy from the mantelpiece she feared her voice sounded strange.

George rose and aproached her. 'You all right?' he asked.

She felt cornered, as indeed she was, between the fireplace and the dresser.

'It is all right, I am.'

'You upset, Catrin?' he said, raising an eyebrow; but he did not sound concerned.

'No.'

'You blushed when you came downstairs and saw me, my girl.'

'You had no clothes on.'

'Did you like that? Did you like that, Catrin?' He laughed and put his arms round her waist.

She pushed him away. 'It is the tea I am making, George.' She tried to push past him, but he would not move. She sensed his strength.

'Let's go upstairs, eh?'

'No, no!'

'I'm clean. Just had a bath.' He laughed again, and pulled her to him. 'I should think you'd like a bit. Adam's doing it you know. He's got himself a fancy woman. Didn't you know?' She did not answer. 'Oh, so you did know. And I were frightened to tell you the other day in case it hurt you. Well, well. If he can do it, why can't you?' He grabbed her by her arms and drew her towards him.

She struggled, pounding his shoulders with her fists, kicking his legs. 'George, let me go.' But he laughed. He was stronger than she was

261

and her blows had no effect. With his body he pushed her against the dresser. His face came nearer and she could see the stubble on it and the rawness of his neck closer than ever before.

'Let me go! I'll tell Adam.'

'You'll tell Adam! He won't believe you.' He held her close and frowned menacingly at her. She felt the hardness of his body against her. 'If you tells him anything, I'll say you led me on. He'll believe me, not you, you'll see.'

She burst into tears and her body slumped.

'Catrin –' but his advances were stopped. There was a scratching on the door outside as Lennie, his afternoon playing with the twins over, climbed onto the weather board and reached up for the catch.

CHAPTER 34

In mid-January the weather set in damp and cold. In the mornings when it became light, housewives went to the window and, pushing aside the curtains, searched the horizon for prospects of better weather. But day after day it remained cold and the clouds, heavy and motionless, pressed down and kept the gardens and woods subdued and dripping with moisture and, leaching their colour, obliged them to be almost as grey as themselves.

The damp in the houses could be dispelled only by heat, and the greyness banished only by colour from a fire in the grate; but the colliers could get no coal from the pits as they did when they were at work, and they had already gathered up all the dead timber left by the woodsmen after felling. Now it was necessary to go deeper into the woods to find any. Even when found it was damp and, put on the fire, would not burn. Green wood chopped down by the colliers when they were sure the woodsmen were not around would not burn, either.

Old men and women, living with no companions but their rheumatics, felt the weather most. They could not keep warm even though they took to their beds and piled high on them all the clothes they possessed. Some yielded to the horror they had always known might confront them in old age, and applied to go into the workhouse, where they exchanged cold nature for the bullying hand of authority.

The colliers asked the old men to tell them of places where coal broke through the surface of the earth, places where, in the days before the big collieries came, Foresters had sunk their own small pits. They searched the woods for these outcrops, pushing aside the brown, damp bracken, looking for the tell-tale black in the soil; and when they found what they were seeking they extracted all the coal they could carry and then covered their find with soil and bracken to keep it secret so that they could come back the next day for more.

Others took to walking the tumps, those heaps of slag from the pits, ugly and sterile, and cast unwanted on the hillside. They kicked the surface with their boots in search of tiny lumps of coal, and when they found any they bent down and picked them up gratefully and put them in their sacks. Sully, looking from his study window one morning, saw men searching on the distant tumps of his Catch-as-Catch-Can pit and realised what was happening. He ordered his pit managers to keep watch for this sort of thing – they had little else to do – and stop it. Many of the managers, so efficient in the pit, somehow never noticed strikers on the tumps. Others, and Gunter was the worst, confronted everyone they spotted.

'This is Mr Sully's land and he don't want none of you lot on it stealing his property.'

'Have a heart. Be your kids freezing like ours?'

'Those are my orders and I'm sticking to them. Move on.'

Every collier's household was hungry. The men set snares in the woods and occasionally came home with a rabbit to put in the pot with perhaps a few potatoes sifted from last summer's potato patch. But more men were setting snares than before, and rabbits were becoming either wiser or fewer.

The women eked out what food they could get. They were the hungriest, for they gave much of their share to their men and children. There had been but one issue of union pay, and that of only a few shillings, since the strike had started. After spending it and what savings they had managed to accrue, they asked for credit at the village store, fully aware of the deferred hardship it would cause when the men returned to work. Their shame was made bearable only by the thought that all the other collier families were in the same boat. But credit at the village shop became harder to get and stopped altogether when the shopkeeper himself could obtain no more credit.

'Not another penny,' shouted Joe Baldwin to a crowd of women outside his shop. He was inclined to give credit more readily to the younger, prettier wives, but there was no sign of that today. The women looked for a sign of pity in his eyes and when they found none they turned away, some with tears, some with curses. Baldwin went inside his shop and locked the door, fearful that some fool would throw a brick through his window and precipitate a riot.

The ugliness of the underfed – the lifeless hair, the anaemic flesh, the protruding bones – had become manifest. The children were listless and looked with uncomprehending eyes. The men made another hole in their belts and trudged around, hands deep in their pockets. There was nothing else in them so they could go deep.

Traders from Gloucester appeared, pushy and bright, and offered to buy household goods for cash – furniture, kitchen utensils, mattresses, pictures, anything. They jingled the pennies before the housewives and hastily threw the goods obtained in the back of their carts and whipped their horses on.

Though most colliers owned their own houses, the rent man continued to call on those that didn't. At the Tingle's house Nelly came to the door wiping tears from her eyes. She was not weeping from emotion; this was onions, the last of the year's crop, and she was peeling them to cook for supper. When she saw who it was she scowled, her eyes narrowed, her lips compressed.

'You'll get nothing from me.'

'You owe five weeks rent, Mrs Tingle. I've been told I must collect it.'

Nelly breathed in, and glared at him. Her bulk was still considerable, though the firmness of her cheeks and body had collapsed through lack of food. 'Not a penny till this trouble be over.'

'Just half a crown.'

'I've told you before, I've not enough money to feed my kids with, so I've certainly got none for rent.'

'I'll have to send the bailiffs in. You wouldn't like that.' His hard face became harder as he lifted his chin and looked at her.

'You try it. There be nothing worth taking, anyway.' She slammed the door.

The rent man sighed. It had been a frustrating day. It was always difficult screwing the rent out of these people, but today it was impossible. It was the same at every cottage his employer owned in the village. No-one would pay. It was a conspiracy, a rent strike as well as a coal strike. He decided to go home.

That night the Tingle family sat down to a hot meal. As well as the onions, there was a small serving of some sort of meat for everyone.

'This be lovely, Mam,' said Bessie. The other children echoed her.

'Tastes like mutton,' said Enoch. 'Though I don't think it is. Aren't you going to have none?'

'Don't fancy any,' said Nelly as she beamed at her brood. She did not tell them that in her desperation to feed them she had been out in the garden all morning collecting slugs.

❧ ❧

Martha came back to a village wracked with forebodings and despair. Adam said he would fetch her, but she would not tell him when she was fit and came on her own. She was pleased to discover Bert was out. Her walk from Park End station had exhausted her and she sat quietly for a few minutes recovering. Then, feeling cold, she cleared the ashes from the fireplace and lit a fire, and when it had burned up sufficiently she put the kettle on to make some tea.

She would have loved to have had Adam's child and her instincts were against having the abortion; but she had had it for his benefit, for his career and his well-being. She could see now, he had always taken first place in their relationship and she had always been second. His had not been love at first sight, as she had first thought. He needed someone to whom he could pour out his ambitions and share his hopes and fears. And because she, unlike that wife of his, could encourage him in these, he had been attracted to her and had then fallen in love.

As for herself, she realised it had not been love at first sight either, but, encouraged by his gentleness and need for support, she had gradually fallen in love. She knew now she had been ready for an affair and Adam had come at the right moment. He had offered her excitement, intellectual adventure, relief from boredom and sexual satisfaction. He had also offered her the opportunity to reject village morals and do what men did: control her actions and make decisions of her own.

What was going to happen now in her relationship with Adam? She did not know. She herself was tired, tired to the bone; her strength, which had previously been inexhaustible and had supported Adam so confidently, had disappeared – it had gone down the lavatory pan in her aunt's expensive new bathroom with the baby. She decided not to worry or try to influence happenings, but to sit back and see what happened. One thing, however, she was sure of. She still loved him. She would cuddle him and fondle him, but she would not risk falling for a child again, even if this separated them. The abortion she wanted to forget. It was a horror, private to her. Only her aunt and that little old woman with the warts and big nose who had known what to do had been present. She would never discuss it with anyone. It had been her agony and was for evermore her secret.

She was pouring herself a cup when irregular footsteps crunching up the garden path told her that Bert was returning.

'You back, then. Been with your aunt, I suppose.'

So he had guessed. 'Yes. Do you want something to eat and drink?'

She poured him a cup of tea and produced a meat pie and some bread and cheese which her aunt had supplied her with.

266

The prospect of the luxury of food seemed to soften Bert's hostility, but Martha fancied it was a show of hostility rather than the real thing. She could see he was glad she was back, even if only because he had missed her doing her household duties. She gave him a small timid smile. 'Yes, Bert, I'm back, and we can carry on as before, just as you wanted to.'

She sat in her chair at the side of the fire drinking her tea and eating bread and cheese, and Bert after a moment's hesitation sat on his side of the fireplace and did the same. She felt warmer towards him than she had for years, but she could not decide why. Was it because he had refused to be clay in her fingers and be manipulated according to her wish? He had indeed stood up to her; that, she had to admit, was good. She understood him better than before. It might be tolerable to lead an everyday life with him now. She would accept he had his woman in Gloucester. And she, of course, would have Adam.

Lennie was having a bad turn. His face sweated from the coughing and his thin body could hardly contain the convulsions that racked it. When he stopped for a moment he clung to Catrin for comfort, silently, his eyes closed. After a time he quietened. She settled him under the bedclothes, plumping them each side of his body to retain the heat, and kissed his forehead.

'Try to sleep, my love,' she said, and went downstairs.

'I think I shall leave Lennie in bed today,' she told Emma. 'Cold it is down here for him.'

'I could hear him coughing again, poor mite.' Emma had finished washing up the breakfast things. 'I think he be still grieving for Grancher.'

'And yesterday I was thinking he was getting a bit better. His face is rosier today than it was. But the coughs are fit to bring his heart up, and he's coughing blood again.'

'What about going to the doctor?'

Catrin turned away impatiently. 'You know we haven't money for that.'

Emma went to the dresser and reached down a vase from the top shelf. From it she took a half-crown piece and put it in Catrin's hand.

'It be all we have left, 'cept tuppence in the mustard tin. I've been saving it for something like this.'

'Oh, Mam,' said Catrin, and kissed her. It was the first time she had called her mother-in-law 'Mam' or had given her a kiss.

'Away with you. Go down to Park End and see the doctor. Dr Batten he be called, I think. I'll go up and sit with Lennie.'

Catrin knocked on the door of the doctor's house. Though he was the colliery doctor he saw colliers' families as well. A servant opened the door and stared at Catrin.

'Well?'

'Could I see Dr Batten, please?'

'What's it about?'

'My boy is ill, and needs –'

'Is your husband from the Park End pits?'

'Yes, but he's not working because of the strike.'

'Orders from Mr Sully not to treat colliers who won't go back, or their families.'

She was about to close the door, when Dr Batten appeared.

'It's my son, doctor. He's so ill.'

'Come in and tell me.'

'I can pay.' Catrin held out the half crown.

'We'll see about that.' He led her into his consulting room where she told him all Lennie's symptoms.

'Sounds like consumption. I'll look in. Better still, if you wait ten minutes you can come in my carriage.'

'Thank you.'

Half an hour later he was sitting on the bed examining Lennie. 'You must keep him warm. Feed him well. Give him warm milk, and chicken –.' He stopped and looked round the bedroom. Then he rummaged in his bag and produced a bottle of pink medicine. 'I brought this. I thought I might be prescribing it. Give him a teaspoonful every hour. It'll soothe his cough.'

Catrin thanked him with words which Emma, standing deferentially in the background, echoed.

'I'll call in a few days. Keep him warm.'

'Can I pay you, please?'

'No. No, thank you. Spend the money on food for the lad.' He paused. He wanted to say something, but the words would not come. As he left he said, 'You've taught me something today.'

That afternoon Catrin sat down at the kitchen table and wrote to her father and mother in Wales. The men were out and Emma had gone with the half-crown the doctor had refused to take to the shop to buy food for Lennie. Lennie was lying listlessly on her lap. George had found some wood and coal on the tumps that morning and the fire was warming the room. She wrote to her parents every few months to keep in touch. Her letters recently had been, as she admitted to herself, quite insincere, full of chatter, manufactured good news about Lennie's progress and how she and Adam were in good health. She had mentioned the strike in her last letter, but only in passing.

Now, at the end of her tether, she wrote pouring out her heart.

'Lennie is ill with consumption, and gets thinner and weaker by the day. I have suspected it for some time, and the doctor confirmed it this morning. I will tell Adam tonight when he comes in. The doctor says he needs good food and rest, but what chance have we got to give him good food in this terible place? Most of the villagers are cold and starving because the men won't accept the pay cut and go back to work. We, as a family, have not been as bad off as most others, since my mother-in-law kept some money in reserve, but now we have run out, and there is no sign of the men going back.

'I know I married my husband for better or for worse and should stay here at his side, but I have Lennie to think of, and it will break my heart if anything happens to him. Can I bring him back home? Please say yes. He needs good farm milk and fresh vegetables and meat, and we have none of these here.

'I am so miserable. Please answer soon and say we can come.'

Catrin posted the letter before Emma or the men came back.

CHAPTER 35

'Here they come,' said Adam. He and Billy were with the pickets at the pit-head of the Park End Royal Colliery, waiting for the maintenance men to arrive from the union offices.

'There be six more than yesterday,' said Billy.

'Blacklegs, I bet. They must have accepted Sully's reduction in pay, and he's slipping them in.'

They stood by the pit shaft along with the other pickets and barred the way. 'Only maintenance men allowed down. You're not on maintenance. You're blacklegging.'

The blacklegs replied belligerently.

'We've had enough.'

'We want to go back to work.'

'Better to have Sully's cuts than no wages at all.'

'We've got no money and our kids be starving for lack of food.'

Adam decided that this was not the time to argue and ignored them. Billy, with a more practical approach, went up close to them and glowered. 'You get back home. How are we going to win if you side with Sully?' He gave one a shove.

'Don't you dare push me.' He gave Billy a shove back.

Adam indicated to the overman to take his maintenance workers to the cages waiting to take them down. To the others he said, 'Go home. Drifting back to work like this is no help. You're letting your mates down when we've nearly won.'

But they shouted and raised their fists at him. 'You and your bloody union are the cause of all this trouble. Let us through.'

The pickets surrounded the blacklegs. 'Go on, bugger off, you scabs.'

There was a scuffle, and the would-be workers were pushed out of the gate. Defeated, and with a backward glance and a curse, they went off down the hill.

Adam went to the colliery offices and confronted Gunter. 'There were blacklegs among your maintenance men this morning.'

Gunter looked at him coldly 'Were there, now. They all reported for work. Why should I stop them?' And he turned and walked away.

Next day Adam and Billy, supported by Emrys and a considerably increased picket, arrived early to find police barring the entrance to the pit site. So Sully had called in the police to protect his blacklegs. Adam could see the maintenance men and about twenty blacklegs marching from the colliery offices under the escort of more police. As they approached, the pickets began to hiss the blacklegs, and shout abuse. 'Ratting on us are you, you buggers? You be bloody fine mates.'

Adam, Billy and Emrys stood firmly in the road in front of the procession; the police pushed them aside. But with the number of pickets threatening and the din they made the blacklegs doubted whether the cocoon of blue uniforms would protect them. They looked wildly around, turned heel and, pushing their way through the police, fled. The pickets cheered them with catcalls all the way down to the bottom of the hill and beyond. The police, with no-one left to protect, looked around surprised, then lined up outside the entrance and stared ahead.

The next morning the pickets found that the whole area in front of the pit had been fenced off with a barrier across the path. Police constables, their blue uniforms contrasting with the white of the snow that had fallen during the night, thronged around and watched out. The official maintenance men had decided not to go to work that morning – it was too dangerous to be mixed up with the blacklegs – but about thirty scabs were marching along the road from the colliery offices tightly protected by police with colliers running alongside shouting abuse at their former mates. At the approach to the pit their abuse became louder. Frustrated, because they could not lay their hands on the blacklegs, they began to throw stones. The objects of their hate looked straight ahead, their faces pale and tense.

Then Adam spotted Bert among the scabs. His face blanched. He went as near as he could and through the noise shouted his name. But Bert looked away.

Adam's attention was diverted by a horde of a hundred or so colliers running down from the woods above the pit-head. Past the stables they came, past the engine house, past the pit-head, whooping and shouting, 'traitors, blacklegs, scabs.' Billy had organised this surprise tactic. Head on, they confronted the column of police and blacklegs and surrounded it, gesticulating and shouting. The police drew their batons and lashed out, trying to slice a way through. The colliers picked

271

up stones and hurled them indiscriminately at both police and blacklegs, and with the stones went louder abuse. The police stepped aside to lunge at the demonstrators with their truncheons, swiping with venom and hatred. Some of the blacklegs, frightened by the situation they had caused by their desire to return to work and appalled at the sight of their fellow colliers lying on the ground groaning and bleeding, broke away and ran back down the hill. Only a few, including Bert, succeeded in reaching the pit-head, where surrounded by layers of police they were forced quickly into the cages and despatched below.

A policeman, hit on the head by a stone was lying unconscious by the gate, his arm against a picket streaming blood from his leg. The pickets picked up their man and withdrew. The police were intent on arrests and chased after them, but the colliers went in all directions and the police decided not to pursue them.

Adam, Emrys and Billy walked together and chewed over the battle.

'You know, I heard Bert tell someone last week he was fed up with the strike,' said Billy.

'But why did he decide to blackleg without saying a word to me about how he felt? When it gets out that he's gone back others will join him. He is, after all, the chairman of the lodge.'

'It seems he wasn't the only collier who wanted to go back,' said Emrys. 'We didn't realise how many.'

'We might have guessed,' said Billy. 'The trains leaving Park End these days have all got young colliers aboard, fed up and going north looking for work.'

'Sully must be sorry about that, especially as they are the young ones who can dig most coal,' said Emrys. 'He works on the theory that when you run a colliery you want more colliers that you actually need. It's always a good idea to have some unemployed around.'

But Adam was thinking about Bert. His desertion from the cause had hit him badly. His eyes crinkled up as if in pain. 'Well, we can't do much about him now. He's six hundred foot down.' Adam spoke calmly, but there was steel in his voice. 'But I'll get him when he comes up.'

'Aye,' said Billy, 'and best before boots go under the bed, too.'

Adam had seen Martha twice since she had returned home and his visit to Bert's cottage that evening was not to visit her but to confront Bert, who should by now have returned from the pit. Recently he had found it almost impossible to conceal his dislike for him. He realised that the cause of this dislike was his guilty feeling about his affair with his wife, and the situation had been worsened by the Judas-like, hypocritical relationship he had maintained towards him ever since the Emrys affair. This had tortured him, but he had consoled himself he was pretending to continue to be Bert's friend for the sake of Martha and the union. In any case he was sure Bert did not know the truth about him and Martha. Now there was this blacklegging, which increased his contempt for him.

As he walked up the garden path he could hear Martha playing her violin. It was a slow, mournful melody, one that she often played. He had always thought it sad, like their relationship, sad but beautiful; and the way she reluctantly progressed from one note to the next had always moved him. But this evening he had no such reaction.

She put her violin down in its case as he came in, and went to kiss him. But he brushed her aside. 'Bert have gone back to work.'

'I know.'

'You know!'

'He got up at the old time this morning and put his pit clothes on and asked for his bait. But he wouldn't say anything, was just more bad-tempered than usual.'

'Why didn't you come and tell me?'

'You know I can't go to your place.' She turned and shrugged her shoulders. Coolness and a take-it-or-leave-it attitude, he knew, was always her response to criticism.

'Is he in now?' he asked.

'Gone down to the Albion. A couple of his pals from the ironworks called ten minutes ago. They took him to buy him a beer to celebrate his going back.'

Without throwing her a word, he left and went to the Albion. As he reached the door of the inn he slowed his pace and stood for a few seconds relaxing his shoulders and arms; he must not provoke a fight for old times' sake, for Martha's sake, for the union's sake, for everyone's sake: he must not provoke a fight.

The pub was quiet. Dan Baglin sat as usual staring ahead, his opaque eyes sightless. 'Who's that?'

'Adam Turley. Just looking for someone right now, Dan.'

'You can have a drink on the five bar. I know you'll pay when you get back to work.'

Adam could hear voices in the inner room, and walked slowly to its door. Yes, there they were, the three of them, with their backs to him and warming their legs in front of the fire. On each side of Bert were his mates from the ironworks, hefty men with hard muscles and faces pitted by blasting. Bog Irish, by the looks of them, he thought, probably come via Merthyr Tydfil.

'Come on, me darlin',' one was saying to Bert. 'Sing us a song and cheer us up, will ye?' Bert shook his head with an amiable grin, and waited to be asked again.

'What about *The Jovial Foresters*?' The other belched and took a swig from his tankard.

Adam advanced slowly and stood behind Bert. 'Yes, let's have *The Jovial Foresters*, Bert.'

Bert turned round in his chair and looked up at Adam. At first he seemed frightened. Then he looked defiant. 'I ain't singing no songs tonight, and you bugger off.'

'What about the second verse of *The Jovial Foresters*?' Adam's voice was calm but menacing. 'You know how it do go, Bert, don't you?' And Adam half sang it and half declaimed it.

'Among mankind there miners are
'Of every degree.
'But he who undermines his friend
'Is far more black than we.
'He's black at heart without a doubt,
'And that's a stain will ne'er wash out. '

He grabbed Bert by the throat and forced him to rise. 'You hear that Bert Preece, you scab, "that's a stain will ne'er wash out". You bastard, if it wasn't for your leg I'd punch your face in.' He gave an extra twist to the clothes round Bert's neck and pushed him back into his chair. But Bert was up in a second.

'Don't you make no excuses because of my leg,' he shouted, and punched Adam in the stomach. Adam winced and his fist, white to the knuckles, took aim and hit him in the face. Bert received it full on the chin and crashed into a chair. Through the blindness of his passion Adam was not conscious of what he had done, but the tingle of pain that went up his arm made him feel good. He had not been in a fight since his teens, and the sensations he now experienced, the feelings of conquest and jubilation, exhilarated him as he had never been exhilarated before. He realised he had wanted to smash Bert's face in for a long time, not because he had doubted his allegiance to the colliers' cause but because he was Martha's husband and possessed something he coveted.

Bert's two mates rose menacingly, and took off their coats in anticipation of a good fight. 'You leave the man alone,' said one, 'or I'll knock you to Kingdom Come, so I will.' And without waiting to see if Adam was prepared to comply, he drew his fist back and, like a piston rod from one of his machines at the ironworks, hit him on the chin. Adam sprawled backwards onto the floor and slid through the sawdust until his head hit a corner of the room.

He got up, wiped the blood off his face, bent low and sidled up to the Irishman, feinted and took him with a right to the head. The Irishman shook his head in a daze and lumbered forward. Adam hooked him to the stomach and swung his hand to his jaw, missed it and hit him in the neck. He gave a cry of pain and staggered back. He looked up at Adam and assessed his next move, his coarse brown face sweating. 'I'll bloody do you, so help me God,' he snarled, and drunk with rage he charged like a bull. Adam, his heart thumping, stepped sideways, and the Irishman struck the air and stumbled forward. Adam put his foot out and sent him sprawling.

Meanwhile the other Irishman, coming on Adam from the side gave him a blow to the head which sent him again skidding across the floor.

In the other room two workmen, just arrived, were ordering drinks from Dan Baglin. On hearing the crack of knuckles against chin, they looked in. 'Come on Charlie,' said one. 'There's a fight,' and they came to the door to watch. Old Baglin, realising what was happening, called to his son in the cellar. 'Oliver. Trouble!'

Oliver arrived within seconds. Six foot tall and broad as the inn door, he took in the situation immediately.

'Adam,' said Dan. 'Throw him out. And get rid of those two mad Irishmen as well.'

Without a word Oliver grabbed Adam's feet and dragged him out of the room. With his coat gathering round his neck, his head bumping on the floor and sawdust clinging to the blood on his face, Adam regained consciousness as he reached the front door. Young Baglin heaved him to his feet and propelled him with his boot into the ditch on the other side of the road.

❧ ❧

The next day only twenty men turned up for work, and the police accompanied them as before. Bert was among them. He did not enjoy being escorted any more than he had the day before. He again averted his head to avoid the looks of contempt, the shouts of derision, the barbs of hate that assailed him from the picket line. It had more men on it than yesterday and they lined both sides of the path from the road to the barrier that Sully had had erected to keep the pickets out of the pit area. So he looked straight ahead at the big oaken frame over the pit-head as the procession marched through the picket line. A man called Duberley who was walking by Bert's side tried to attract his attention by pulling his sleeve, but Bert shook him off; he didn't want to talk to anyone. The atmosphere was calmer than on the day before. The police escort shot glances at the pickets and swung their truncheons, just a little, to keep them from coming too near.

Bert noticed that Adam was not among the pickets. Perhaps, he thought, he is still at home and in bed as a result of the thumps he had received last night. He hoped so and, feeling better at the thought, smiled. But Emrys and Billy were there again, men who had once been his friends, men with whom he had worked at the coal face and to whom he would have entrusted his life. Now they were snarling at him, calling him obscene names. Things could never be the same again. The tension would remain after the strike was over and, hard as it was to believe, he knew it would be over one day.

The procession reached the top of the slope and stopped near the pit office. Normally powdered with coaldust, the trees and grass round the pit-head were today white with snow. Bert looked round. He could see that Adam had now arrived at the barrier and was talking to Billy and glancing in his direction. He looked away and rubbed his chin, still sore from the blow Adam had dealt it the previous evening. Annoyance and shame rose in his throat as he recollected the indignity Adam had dealt him in front of his friends. The bastard! Adam had been a good friend and pleasant to work with in the union, pleasant, that was, until he had become so fanatical. But he couldn't see that friendship being repaired, ever.

At the pit-head there was no bustle, no urgency, none of the usual sense of purpose. Empty trams stood forlorn on their tracks, pushed so far and then forgotten. Outside the pit office Gunter was talking to a deputy. He crooked his finger at Bert and his companions and they went over to him.

'Right,' he said, surveying them as if they were recently captured animals, 'All on maintenance today. Mr Jones here will come down and tell you what to do.'

They pushed aside timber that was waiting in the trams to go down for maintenance work and climbed in. Joe, the engine man, watched them, but said nothing. He was not affected by the cut in rates and had no quarrel with his employer; but he clearly took a poor view of blacklegs. Well, bugger him as well, thought Bert.

'You be going to leave the union now?' Duberley asked as Joe sent them speeding down the shaft.

Bert looked at him with distaste. 'No. I still believes in the union.' The man shrugged his shoulders.

As he went down in the cage to pit bottom Bert comforted himself. Surely, he had the right to go back to work if he wanted to. The stoppage had gone on long enough, anyway. People were starving. The men, never fat, were getting as thin as mattock handles. The children, the first casualties in any industrial dispute, were like skeletons. One had died at Cinderford last week – from lack of food so the coroner said. At Park End a man had strung himself up in a barn, no longer able to bear the sight of his wife and children in distress. Poor devils, all of them. Well, the men had tried, but the masters had been stronger. Best that the men should recognise that they had been beaten.

He had not suffered as much as many. He had no children, and Martha had always come up with something to eat, meagre though it had been at times. He suspected she had some savings tucked away somewhere and was dipping into them. Her aunt was sending her money as well.

At pit bottom the large oil lamp had not been lit, and the only light was from a hand lamp perched high on a stone shelf. There was the usual smell of damp earth and horse manure. Bert and the others lit their candles, put them in their lanterns and looked at Jones for orders.

'Preece and Duberley to look for faults in the main roadway. The rest come with me,' and Jones led them away.

Bert and Duberley walked on. The lights from the candles in their lanterns gleamed on the damp walls as they went. Bert looked around, testing the roof with his mattock handle. The rock and earth was unstable, and saturated with water. The melted snow and heavy downpours of rain that they had experienced during the last few weeks were seeping through. Trickles of water, transparent and silent, came from fissures in the rock and fell on their heads.

'Maintenance have been skipped along here,' said Duberley.

'Same everywhere. Sully won't spend more than he has to on it in case it affects his profits.'

'Look how the floor have risen here because of the pressure on the earth round it. It be affecting all these props.' Duberley stopped to examine a roof arch that was twisted askew. 'Look at this one. We'd best replace it.'

Bert agreed. They fetched some new timber from pit bottom, cut it to size, propped the roof up temporarily and began to remove the faulty arch. It was embedded firmly in mud and stone, and as they strained their muscles to get the old timber away, they heard a crack, a sharp, ominous, whiplash sound that echoed along the road. The temporary support splintered like matchwood and the roof with a crunch settled lower and at an angle. Then came a noise like thunder, distant at first, then booming ever closer. The air shook, and stones and earth rained down. The whole roof was falling in.

The men turned and ran. Duberley got clear, but Bert turned awkwardly because of his leg and crashed to the ground face downwards, his hands above his head. A rock, pounding down on his back, crushed the air from his lungs, and earth and stones covered him. Fortunately his head had fallen into a small cavity, so he was able to breathe. But earth filled his mouth, and he tried to spit it out and shout, though the sound was no more than a moan. And the pain, oh the pain! He tried to move to relieve it, but couldn't shift an inch, and the attempt edged his nerves. The weight of the rubble above him pressed mercilessly on every part of his body. The ache across the back of his thighs, especially, was intense.

All was darkness but not as terrifying as the blackness that now descended on his mind. He fainted, but it was not into nothingness. In his unconsciousness rocks continued to pound his head and flail his body. All the malevolent powers of the devil combined to abuse him. He felt the icy touch of death.

The intensity of the pain revived him and he began to shout again, but once more the sound came out as a moan. He knew no-one could hear him. He decided he must try to relax to reduce the terrible pain in his legs. He sobbed in his agony, and mucus collected in his nose and mouth until he was nearly suffocated. And still he could not move to alleviate his pain.

Then he was aware of the silence, an awful silence, the silence of the grave. So this was what it was like to die in a pit accident. But he was not dead yet. Lying there was like being in hell, certainly, but he knew he was not dead. He would be rescued, surely. Men in pit disasters were usually rescued – but sometimes their bodies were brought up dead and mutilated.

He prayed, or tried to pray, but in his semi-conscious state he had difficulty in formulating the words. 'Please God, don't let me die. Don't let me die,' echoed through his mind again and again, unceasing, until with an effort he managed to stop them. He thought of his parents, of his friends, of the good times he had had, of Martha, of Molly in Gloucester. His mind dashed from one thing to another in a frenzy, and they all jumbled together and merged with the seering pain in his legs. He relapsed into unconsciousness again.

He was brought round by a sudden pain in his hand, a jab as if a knife were trying to hack it off; and he heard dimly a voice saying, 'Look out, look out, you fool. You've got his hand under your shovel – his hand!' Then there was scraping, and then he felt someone move his head, and there were fingers, dripping with blood from their rasping of earth and stones, clearing the debris from his face and smoothing his hair from his forehead.

'You'll be all right now,' said the voice. 'We've found you.'

Bert sobbed with relief and and tried to focus his eyes. Behind the speaker were several shadowy heads, all gazing at him, but he could not recognise them. The voice spoke again, kind and soothing, telling him that he was safe and they would soon get him to the top. They cleared away the earth and stones that covered him, and his rescuer put his arms round his shoulders and raised him up as gently as a woman. With the help of his companions he carried him to pit bottom. The pain was excruciating, and he sobbed again. But he screwed up his eyes to look at the man who had found him and was cradling him in his arms. At last he recognised him. It was Adam.

'Hallo, old butt,' he murmured.

They carried him on a board to the pit office and waited for Dr Batten, the colliery doctor. When he arrived he ordered some warm water and a clean cloth with which to wash Bert's body. But he should have remembered, there were no first aid facilities available. He was given a rusty bowl of cold water and a slimy cloth. He looked round in annoyance; and then he removed his own shirt and tore it into pieces and soaked one of them in the cold water. He cut away the clothing from Bert's body and washed him. It was impossible to clean his legs properly; they were smashed and twisted, clotted with blood and dirty with earth, and the lightest touch made him wince with pain. The doctor used the rest of his shirt to cover the wounds.

'It's his legs,' he said, brushing back his whiskers. 'I shouldn't be surprised if he loses both of them. But he may live if we can get him to hospital quickly.'

There was no hospital in the Forest: the nearest one was in Gloucester, twenty miles away. A train was about to leave shortly for Lydney, where a transfer could be made to the Gloucester train; and he was hurried to the station and loaded into the luggage van. Two of the pickets volunteered to accompany him.

❧   ❧

Sully did not sleep well that night. He was worried about the stoppage and the querulous letters he received from his brother about the handling of it. Charles seemed to think that he enjoyed industrial strife. In fact, he was sick with arguing with people, arguing with his staff, with the unions and with his wife. Now there was this roof-fall with a man nearly killed. What he needed was a period of calm and goodwill at the colliery and affection at home.

He got out of bed, put on his dressing gown and walked over to the window. Dawn was breaking. There was a stillness, a hushed feeling that a momentous day was about to be born. He looked over the village. The trees on the hills beyond were still black but the light from the sky was beginning to pick out their outline. All was silent, though workmen would soon be afoot to start the day's work in the ironworks and tin-plate works.

He glanced down at the garden and saw the dim outline of a pile of stones destined to be made into a sundial for Hermione. It would look well on the lawn, but why were the workmen taking so long to build it? He looked at the evergreen shrubbery. It was spreading and getting much too thick and high. He must tell the gardener to trim it back. He realised that he was critical, in a bad mood, and decided to go back to bed again. He was meeting the union for discussions in the morning, and needed to be fresh.

As he turned, he saw a shadow in the garden, a man walking stealthily away from the house along the lawn by the side of the path. He watched him, and saw him turn and wave up at the window of the next room, his wife's bedroom. The man's face was indistinct, but from his bearing Sully knew who it was. It was Gunter. What was Gunter doing in his garden at dawn? Had he spent the night in Hermione's bed? Had she committed adultery with Gunter in his own house? As he watched, Gunter continued by the side of the path, and went cautiously down the steps, through the gate and onto the road.

Shocked and quivering with rage, Sully was determined to have it out with her. He strode out of his room, but when he reached Hermione's door, he paused. Then he opened it quietly, and peered inside. The room was empty, though a candle flickered by the bedside. She must have gone into the dressing room that adjoined the bedroom, for he could see a light under the door and could hear the sound of water being poured into a bowl. Cleaning herself up, no doubt.

He looked at the bed, still hot with adultery. The sheets and underblanket were crumpled and revealed the blue-and-white tick cover of the mattress. Two pillows lay at the side of the bed, as if punched and exhausted by the night's happenings. Another pillow was on the floor. Then he recalled mysterious noises he had heard during the night – footsteps on the staircase, a hushed whisper – so faint that he put them down to his imagination. So it was true. He clenched his hands and turned to go after her. But then his fury gave way to caution, and he withdrew quietly to his own room. A confrontation now would not, perhaps, be wise. Or was he afraid to face her? She would deny it, of course, and she might even laugh in his face. But he determined he would confront her sometime. Better to remember the details – as if he could ever forget them – and await the opportunity of using them to best effect when it suited him.

After a troubled breakfast he went to the colliery offices and summoned Gunter. He told him he was discharging him and held out the salary he was due. He gave no reason, and Gunter did not ask for one. Sully knew now he had been right. His eyes dropped from Gunter's face and examined his body, his broad frame, his massive hands. These were the hands that had access to Hermione's body; this was the man who could do what he himself was not allowed to do.

Gunter stood in front of the desk, his eyes mocking; apart from the quick breaths which caused his chest to rise and fall beneath his shirt, his body was relaxed. He took the money and, without a word, turned and left the room.

CHAPTER 36

Later that morning Adam and his colleagues met Sully at the colliery offices to try to settle the dispute. Joseph Cowmeadow had tried again to attend as union agent, but Sully, to Adam's satisfaction, had flatly refused to have him as a member of the team.

Sully began by thanking Adam for rescuing Bert in the roof fall. 'I am told he is in Gloucester Hospital though his condition is serious.'

No mention of compensation for a man who had betrayed his friends to go back to work, thought Adam, but he blushed and murmured 'Thank you.' He blushed because he remembered his reaction when, on being summoned to come to Bert's rescue he had wondered whether he had wanted to rescue his enemy, his rival, Martha's husband. Why should he rescue him? Why not leave it to someone else? But when he realised there was no-one else – apart from Duberley who was apparently suffering from shock – with his knowledge of the gallery or ability to dig out the debris, he had hesitated only a second. No collier would under any circumstances refuse to help another collier hurt underground. He had accordingly seized a mattock and hurried to where the fall had taken place.

After this brief reference to the accident of the previous day, the meeting continued. Adam noticed that Gunter was not sitting at Sully's side. Sully seemed to miss him, for several times he turned to discuss a point, found no-one to help him and turned back with an expression of regret.

Once again Adam presented the case for a sliding scale and once again Sully would have none of it. 'However,' he said, 'all the coalmasters in the Forest have met and have agreed to compromise and accept a reduction of five per cent in rates now and another five per cent in two months time. I offer you the same. I consider it an extremely generous offer.'

Adam was annoyed by Sully's off-hand manner, but apart from his jaw becoming squarer he did not show it. He wanted to reject the offer and walk out of the meeting, but his colleagues after whispering urgently among themselves persuaded him to tell Sully he would consult the men first.

They left the colliery offices and gathered in the yard, sheltering by a wall from the bitter north wind.

'A lot of the men have had enough, man, and want to go back,' said Emrys.

'We must accept,' said Billy. 'Can't you see? We're pissing against the wind.'

Adam would not agree. 'Sully's weakening. You could see it in his face. We must keep up the pressure.' But he thought: he's ill, he's suffering torments of agony in his mind about something. But he's not suffering as much as the colliers and their families are.

'Let's go back right away and accept, Adam,' said Matthew Teague. 'The men can't take no more. You talk about Sully's face. Look at my face, look at your own face, skin stretched tight over your cheekbones, eyes sticking out. Think of your wife's and your child's faces. I look at my kids and I weep. We've all had enough.'

'No, we must go on. One more heave and I'm sure we'll win. But I agreed to consult the men, and we will.'

They fixed a meeting for that afternoon. The colliers of the Park End pits lived in many villages around, and numbered almost a thousand men. No hall in the area was big enough to accommodate them all, so it was decided that in spite of the cold weather they should meet on the open space outside Park End Church.

ॐ ॐ

'Give the rest of mine to Lennie.' Adam rose from the table at which they had shared a meagre meal.

'He won't eat it,' said Emma. 'Finish it yourself. You don't even eat what I gives you these days. You seem to exist on will-power alone.'

Adam ignored his mother. 'George, Emrys, you ready?' He put on his cap, muffler and coat.

'I'm not coming,' said George.

'Why not?'

'I want to stay home. Lennie be ill for one thing.'

Adam decided to ignore him. He looked at Catrin. 'I must go. Look after the lad. He doesn't seem too good today.'

'Anyroad,' continued George, 'I have no stomach any more for this bloody dispute if you want to know.'

283

'Leave him,' said Emrys. This was no time for an argument. Adam shot a look of dislike at George, and he and Emrys left the house.

'What is the matter with George?' asked Emrys. 'It is a strong supporter of the union he has always been.'

'He thinks this is a good opportunity with us out of the way to stay in with Catrin, I shouldn't wonder.'

Emrys looked up at him anxiously, the tip of his thin nose already blue with cold, but he said nothing.

At the gate they met Bessie Tingle.

'Letter for you, Adam.' She handed him a sealed envelope, and looked at him curiously. 'It be from Martha Preece.' She glanced scornfully at Emrys.

'About her husband in hospital, I 'spect,' said Adam, annoyed that Martha had sent him a letter by a neighbour. It would be all round the village in an hour. But he was pleased to hear from her.

He thanked Bessie, and read the letter. 'She be back from hospital and wants to see me right away. Emrys, you go on to the meeting. I'll follow.'

When Adam arrived Martha was standing by the fireplace with her back to the door. She did not move when Adam came in, though he was certain she knew it was him. He ran over to her and put his arms round her and kissed the back of her head. He sensed there was something wrong. 'Martha, what's the matter? Aren't you pleased to see me?'

'Of course.' She smiled at him, but it was a strained smile.

'I'm sorry I didn't see you before you went to Gloucester.'

'I had to hurry or I would have missed the train.'

He held her close to him. She did not resist, but her only response was, 'Aren't you going to ask how Bert is?'

'How is he?'

'The doctors say he will live, but they've had to amputate one of his legs. The other one won't be much good either. He won't be able to go down the pit again.'

'Oh.' There was a short silence. 'I'm sorry.'

'He's most thankful to you for rescuing him. He'll say so himself when he sees you.'

'I would have done the same for any pit-mate.' He drew her to the settle and took her hand. 'Bert's accident won't make no difference to us, will it? Sometime, not now, I want to talk again about us going away together.'

'I can't leave Bert now, whatever he's done in the past.'

Adam stiffened. 'So by losing a leg he has gained an advantage over me that he didn't have before?'

'Don't turn nasty. How can you be so mean and selfish?' She withdrew her hand from his. 'I never said I would go away with you, anyway.'

'Selfish! Is it selfish to love you, to want you all the time and not share you with someone who doesn't appreciate you, who has a woman in Gloucester?'

'He's finished with her. He told me.' She rose and fingered the leaves of the aspidistra plant.

'What difference does that make?' He got up and strode about the room. 'Martha, I love you. Can't you see that? I've told lies for you, I've degraded myself for you. I've sacrificed friends and family, and I've made Catrin's life hell.' He became quiet and sighed. 'You know, Martha, I married too early, and for the worst of reasons.'

'You loved Catrin when you married her. You told me. Don't say now you married her just because you'd made her pregnant.'

'It was my bad luck that after I got married I met the woman I should have met first; and fell in love with her, head over heels. I never dreamt I was capable of loving like that.' He sat down, despondent.

'You exaggerate.'

He looked over at her, pleading. 'Martha, did you really mean all these hateful things you said?'

She softened, and gave him a smile; but it was a weak one, and her eyes were searching him. 'Don't take it all so seriously. Our affair was bound to come to an end sooner or later. We couldn't have borne it much longer, either of us.'

She went over to him, to calm him. 'You know, Adam, quite seriously, if both of us had put as much effort into our marriages as we did into this affair, we wouldn't have needed to embark on it.'

He looked up at her, rejecting her attempt to soothe him. She was different now. No longer did her body seem soft and desirable. No longer did he want to hold her. Perhaps he would when this hateful encounter was over, when she had stopped saying horrible things to him. But he felt that if no reconciliation came before he left, if he went from the cottage now, it would all be over, for ever. But he did not want to give up. What could he say to placate her, make her withdraw all the remarks she had made? 'It's Bert's accident, isn't it, that's caused you to change?'

She distanced herself, and looked straight at him. 'I now want to devote myself to my husband, whatever has happened in the past.' She spoke slowly, deliberately. It was clearly a prepared speech. 'He won't be able to work again, but I can. I'll find work somewhere and I'll earn enough money to keep him. It'll be hard, but we'll manage.' Behind her determination there was just a hint of compassion. 'I'm sorry, Adam, but there it is.'

She tried to control herself, but tears sprang from her eyes. With a gesture of annoyance she turned away and wiped them. This was the first time that Adam had seen her cry. He realised the depth of her feelings; but the realisation did not stop his own reaction. Did she appreciate the depth of his feelings? Who was the selfish one now? His tension rose as he assimilated the enormity of the things she had said and realised that she was casting him aside.

He folded his arms and stared into the fire. She hadn't said she loved her husband. She was using Bert's disability as an opportunity to rid herself of him. His annoyance became rage and he wanted to shout to relieve the impotence he felt, the impotence to control the situation, the impotence to mend their differences. He wanted to shout at her, even to lay his hands on her to get his way.

Then he remembered his meeting, and took out his watch, Grancher's watch. 'I've got a meeting,' he stammered. He turned aside, exhausted, his shoulders bent. What could he do? Her reply determined him.

'Yes, you've got a meeting. You'd better go to it.'

Without another word he left the cottage.

He strode down the hill to Park End in anger, with energy that came from nowhere. 'I'll give them the speech of their lives,' he muttered to himself.

The meeting had already begun. The late afternoon was grey, and a mist was descending. Beyond the mass of colliers, the Church, withdrawn and unconcerned with what was happening in the open space beyond its churchyard, was blending into the darkening sky.

Adam went round the crowd to the back of a makeshift platform that had been erected, and climbed up onto it. Two paraffin torches had been lit and placed one at each end of the platform. Matthew Teague was making his predicted speech. 'And so I advocate acceptance of the master's terms,' he ended amid a sprinkling of cold applause.

286

'No,' shouted Adam, pushing his way to the front of the platform. 'No, don't throw away all you have suffered and fought for in the last eleven weeks.' He stood there, his arms raised towards them, the light from the torches flickering yellow on his body.

'Victory is near, I tell you. At the meeting this morning we could see that Sully was ready to yield. One more week of defiance will see us win. Do you want to give in now, when victory is nearly with us? Do you want to creep back in defeat like curs, whipped by their master?'

The crowd were silent, chastened by his words. They gazed at him as he stood with his hands on his hips, his jaw jutting forward, his authority over them complete. 'The coal that we are paid such a miserable pittance to dig and which Sully makes so much money from don't belong to him. Have you ever thought about that? That coal belongs to the people of Dean and always has done, just as the fish in the sea belong to the fishermen. God gave the coal to the people of Dean when he gave them the trees in the Forest and the air and the clouds in the sky. And even if the coal weren't yours by gift of God, I say that without doubt you and your ancestors have paid for it with the hundreds of years of blood and misery you have put in by your labour and suffering.'

The torches on each side of him flickered. With his arms outstretched, he held them spellbound. He stung them with his taunts, wooed them with his soft words, and made them feel ashamed with his accusations.

'The coalmasters tell us they can't afford to pay at the old rates, miserly though they are. They can't afford it! But they are making enormous profits, and have been for years. If they haven't, where did the money come from to build the mansions they live in, to dress their wives and daughters in the latest fashions and to drive them round the countryside in their luxurious carriages, looking down at us as they pass as if we was dirt? To maintain their position they'll use every means in their power, even the starvation of their workers and their families.'

His voice became more persuasive, more serious. 'Comrades, justice must be done. Don't forget, the coalowners will forever try to keep their feet on your necks, and they'll let your children die before they allow their profits to be reduced. But the day will come when the workers have the power and the wealth, not the masters. By stiffening our resistance to Sully and his cronies we can help that day to come. And remember, you are not alone. Colliers are struggling all over Dean, just as you are struggling. Don't let them down now by giving in. Only with unbroken ranks can we win.'

Adam's audience, whipped by his rhetoric, cheered. Their tiredness and the empty feeling in their bellies had disappeared.

'Let's pay Sully a visit,' shouted someone.

'You want to visit him and tell him what you think of him?' yelled Adam, his unabated anger with Martha upsetting his judgement. 'Come on then, follow me!' He grabbed a torch and jumped down from the platform. 'Victory or death!'

A mob of colliers followed him with a roar, a frightening roar that seemed to come out of the earth. Adam waved his torch aloft and led his supporters triumphantly down the road to Sully's house.

∾ ∾

There had been silence after Adam left the house, broken only by an occasional cough from Lennie. He was half-sitting half-lying in an armchair by the fire with one of Emma's warmest blankets round him. His large black eyes, round and bright in the pallor of his cheeks, had watched Adam close the door. 'Is Dadda coming back?' he asked Catrin who was sitting with the others at the table.

'Yes, dear. He'll be back later.' She picked him up and held him close to her breast. He looked up with his thin pale face, his eyes large and dark and filled with shadow, and his skin drawn tight over his cheekbones. She smiled down and wet her forefinger to smooth his eyebrows. 'There, there, my pet.' She held him against her face and felt his eyelashes fluttering against her cheek. So light and tender he seemed, a breath of wind would blow him away. She was waiting impatiently for a reply from her father about taking him home to Wales, but she wondered how he would stand up to the long journey in such weather. She had said nothing about the letter to anyone, knowing she was right and did not need anyone's backing, and fearful that any opposition to her idea of taking him back to Wales would weary her too much. 'I think he's better this evening. The doctor said this morning he would be a bit listless for some days, and we must keep hoping and praying.'

Emma got up to clear the table. 'We can only hope, my love.' She patted Catrin on the shoulder as she passed.

'I'll take him up to bed in a few minutes when he's had his medicine,' said Catrin.

'Would it be better to make a bed up by the fire for him tonight?' suggested Emma. 'You could sleep in an armchair.'

'Look, we has some more wood and coal, you know.' George wanted to be helpful. 'I was lucky to get some in the Forest this morning.'

'No, but if you take up the two bricks in the oven and put them in the middle of the bed that would be helpful.' Relations between Catrin and George had been strained since he had tried to force her after his bath that afternoon some weeks ago. She had told no-one, and he by his demeanour had shown he wanted her to forgive him. Now his eyes showed he was concerned with Lennie, and anyone who wanted to do something for him could not be wholly wicked and would receive her thanks. 'I'll go up with him and go to bed myself soon and hold him close to me to keep him warm. He likes to feel me close.'

To get out of Emma's way, she picked up Lennie and moved to the corner behind the table. As she did so Lennie began to cough. This time it was more severe than the hard, hollow cough that tore constantly at his lungs. A torrent of bright spumy blood, thick and scarlet, spurted from his lips and spluttered over his jersey. Catrin reached for a towel and wiped it away from his face. 'Come to Mummy, my pet.' She held him close, willing the coughing to cease. Her tears dropped on the blood. If enough tears would wash Lennie's lungs clean, she would provide them.

'Here, change his jersey.' Emma hurried over with a clean one. 'And George, go after Adam and get him back.'

'He must be at his meeting by now, but I'll get him.' He put on his cap and muffler and went off into the night.

CHAPTER 37

Sully was in his study writing a letter to his brother Charles, telling him what had happened at the morning's meeting. Edmunds, Sully's servant, burst in without knocking. 'I went to the meeting like you said, Sir,' he gasped. 'They're turning nasty and are heading this way.'

Sully was cool; but the lines of his face tautened. He had guessed that sooner or later something like this might happen. 'Go quickly to the police at the Fountain and tell Sergeant Bull to bring his men round right away.'

Edmunds hurried off. Sully paused for a moment and then reached for the bell rope. It seemed ages before a maid appeared. 'Tell the servants to close all the windows immediately and pull the curtains. Put out all the lights and lock the outside doors.' The servant hesitated. 'Come on, girl, do as you are told and don't ask questions. Quick, quick. It's urgent.'

The girl, mystified, scuttled away, and Sully hurried off in search of Hermione. He had said little to her since he had discovered her infidelity the previous night, and at the thought of it his annoyance and shame rose again in his throat. He did not know if Gunter had told her their secret had been discovered and that he had been discharged. At the moment he did not care; but he decided he must tell her of the approach of the rioters. She was in the small sitting room attached to her bedroom, looking bored and bad tempered. She glanced up at him languidly, but when he told her about the approaching colliers she became agitated, and jumped up and wrung her hands. She remembered the ugly scene some years back when strikers had stopped her carriage.

'Oh, dear, James. They'll murder us. We must get away.'

'Don't over-react, Hermione. I've sent for the police; they'll be here shortly and will drive them away. Just sit quietly and wait.'

But Hermione had no intention of sitting quietly and waiting. She summoned her maid and ran up to the loft where they sat in the pitch dark, unable to peep from any windows to see what was happening below, and shivering with fear.

Sully shrugged his shoulders. If that was what she wanted to do, she must do it. He had more important matters to attend to. He put out the lamps in Hermione's room and felt his way to his own bedroom. Cautiously he pulled the curtain back an inch and looked out. His eyes had now become used to the dark, but he could see no intruders. Then he heard noises at the back of the house and went across the corridor to Alice's old room.

The men had flung open the double gates used by the carriages and were flooding in like a stain spreading over a carpet. The torches they carried flickered and showed their distorted faces as they shouted obscenities. They fanned out, shouting and exploring everywhere, the outhouses, the sheds, the stables and the kitchen garden, which was now a sea of frost. They seized spades and garden forks for weapons. Soon the back garden was full but more pushed from outside to get in. They searched the windows of the house for signs of life, and spotted a light in the basement. The lamps in the kitchen had been extinguished when the cook and her assistant had fled, but in their haste they had not drawn the curtains and had left the candles burning. The glow from the kitchen range shone through the window, rosy and attractive and warm. On the top of the range the men could see saucepans of vegetables steaming, their lids agitating up and down, boiling water running over the sides. On the spit was a saddle of mutton, brown and succulent, the fat coursing down its sides, ready for eating, asking to be eaten. A groan arose at the sight, and the stomachs of the men tightened.

They were distracted by the approach of Edmunds, back from summoning the police. The moment he saw the crowd standing round the kitchen area, he realised his stupidity in returning that way. He turned and began to run; but they caught him and examined him under a torch.

'It be Sully's servant, the snotty bugger,' one of them shouted. They had often seen him about the village, nose aloft, assuming his master's superiority. But having made him their prisoner, they were uncertain what to do with him. Then someone spotted a water butt.

'In the butt with him. His face be a bit sweaty. That'll cool him down!'

'Wait a minute, don't spoil his nice new clothes. Take'em off first!'

So they pulled off his coat and trousers and began to lower him head first into the butt. But the surface of the water was frozen and his head slithered over it; and, push though they might, they could not get him into the tub.

'Not to do that sort of thing', said Emrys. 'It is a worker he is and deserves respect for that alone, whatever sort of a man he may be.'

'Let's go round to the front,' said Adam to divert them; and they threw Edmunds to the side and surged round to the front of the building. An oil lamp flickered outside the front door, and the light from it was sufficient to show the movement of a curtain in a room on the first floor.

A roar went up from the crowd. 'There he be!' 'Come on, Sully. Let's have you!' 'You've a nice dinner cooking, we see. Can we come in and have some?'

The curtain fell straight. Some of the men went to the front door with branches of a tree that they had broken off, and banged on it. 'Sully, Sully,' they cried.

The crowd were now bent on blood, and banging on the door and shouting were not enough. Just as their bellies were calling for food, their minds were demanding destruction. They discovered the pile of ornamental stones intended for Hermione's sundial, and began to throw them at the house. One went through a downstairs window and the tinkle of falling glass sent waves of alarm through the building. They smashed the lamp outside the front door, and left it swinging wildly with paraffin dripping onto the steps. Now the only light in the whole of the front garden was the twisting yellow flickerings of the torches the strikers had brought with them.

The mob sensed Sully was still there behind the curtains, and continued to throw stones and shout. Emrys started a chant, 'We want bread, we want bread,' which they took up. The sound increased in volume until villagers the other side of Park End heard it and came to their doors in wonder.

Adam consulted with Emrys about what should be done next. He knew the men would do anything he said, but he could see they were wavering, not least because they had little stamina from lack of food. He was against forcing an entry into the house. What would they do if they got in? What would they do to Sully if they caught him? He decided to call it a day. The fury that had beset him when Martha had told him, oh so brutally, that their relationship was over, the passion that had driven him while he made his speech, had been consumed, the frenzy that had impelled him to lead the attack on Sully's house had disappeared.

He was about to tell the men that they had made their point and should now go home when, at the far end of the garden, he saw a movement in the bushes. Within seconds some policemen, headed by Sergeant Bull, emerged and ran towards the strikers. Silently they advanced, their faces gleaming with resolve. They held their truncheons high, ready to flail the heads of the colliers. But there were only about two dozen of them, and there were nearly two hundred colliers. The two bands met. The police rained blows down on the heads of the colliers. The men, remembering they were Foresters and the police were aliens from outside, were stimulated by the attack and found strength to stand their ground and fight back. Sticks, stones and fists were the weapons they used, and their rage at being attacked kindled an upsurge of energy that was sufficient to repulse the police. They pushed them to the ground, seized their truncheons and beat them on their heads. Several of the colliers were also casualties, but the men won. The police, bloody and shaken, withdrew to the far end of the garden and tended their wounds.

The men waited for the police to make the next move, but they seemed in no hurry. Adam was uneasy. The whole business had gone further than he had intended, and he wished he had withdrawn his men before the police had arrived. The men, gathered in groups, were silent, eyeing the police warily and glancing in Adam's direction for guidance.

And still the police did not move. What were they waiting for? Some of the rioters had had enough and begun to retreat to the gate they had entered half an hour earlier. Others discovered the footpath that led through the shrubbery and left by the side gate onto the road.

Then the sound of horses' hooves, of many horses' hooves, loud and impatient, was heard galloping along the road from the village. At the same time the police sergeant yelled 'Charge' and his men, brandishing their truncheons, attacked. In closer formation than last time, they ran towards the colliers, and beat them without hesitation with blows intended to fell. Mounted policemen, appearing behind them, thundered down the lawn as well. The men staved off the foot police, but scattered on seeing the horses. One collier, shouting 'Adam', crossed in front of a police horse and was trampled down. The horse fell and his rider spread-eagled and slid towards Emrys, who clouted him on the head. But more mounted police were descending and they batonned Adam and Emrys. Emrys received a blow square on his head and dropped like a poleaxed bull, Adam twisted round to avoid the baton hurtling down on him and took the blow on his shoulder. His assailant rode on. 'Quick,' Adam whispered to Emrys, and dragged him semi-conscious into the shrubbery.

In the road more mounted police were charging along. They barred the road to the village, and chased the fleeing colliers in the opposite direction. They leaned over hard to administer their blows, encouraging their horses to wade through the bodies lying in their way.

It was soon over. The colliers were demoralised and frightened by the suddenness of the two-pronged attack. Most managed to get away, fleeing up the road or climbing over walls, the darkness helping them. Some, cornered by the police, were arrested, as were the wounded lying in the garden and on the road. The police removed the body of the collier who had been run down by a horse.

Adam and Emrys lay in the shrubbery, and escaped being found by the police when they came back searching for stray rioters. They heard the sergeant summon Sully to his front door and reassure him that the riot had been put down, that arrests had been made and that he and his wife could sleep safely in their bed that night.

Emrys had not been severely hurt, but he was frozen with cold. Even so, they thought it wise to wait until they were sure the police had departed; and it was not until the chimes of the church clock rang nine that they began to make their way home.

About midnight Catrin came downstairs. Emma tired out, had gone to bed, and George had not yet returned. She descended slowly, her feet unwilling to leave one step for the next. The door at the bottom of the staircase swung behind her as she went to the window. The living-room was empty and quiet. She put her candle down on the table, and placed her arm against the wall, leaning her head on it. She looked at the drawn curtains with unseeing eyes. Her face became suddenly convulsed, distorted with anguish into a strange, unrecognisable shape. A sob rose in her throat which she stifled by biting her arm; but the tears sprang unbidden, and insisted on falling onto her cheeks. She turned and gripped the back of a chair until the veins stood out on her arms.

He had gone quietly. She had sensed the moment he left. He had not protested, just slipped away without a murmur. Even as a baby he had not cried or whimpered as other babies did; nor had he cried when he was older and became frustrated or upset. It was not because he was brave, and he was certainly not robust. He did not seem to need to cry;

294

he just smiled that half smile, keeping his thoughts to himself and looking wonderingly, sometimes questioningly, with his big dark eyes; and his grief, for there was always grief in them, would shine through.

His lashes now lay over his cheeks, moistened by the sweat of his last ordeal. His hair was dishevelled and damp. His lips were grey. Oh, his lips! She had kissed them before she left the room. Though soft and moist, they were already cold.

He would not cough any more now. He was gone, and she was alone. She felt for a handkerchief and wiped her face. She sniffed. The noise seemed to reverberate round the room, but it made her remember where she was. She was glad she was alone, for she did not want to share her grief with anyone. Tomorrow would be soon enough. The person she would have wanted to be present with her when the end came had not been there. He had been out at his meeting.

She went upstairs again to see that he was comfortable and lying straight and covered.

❧ ❦

They made their way back to Coalway through the woods, avoiding the road because police patrols might be on the watch. Normally an enjoyable walk, it seemed a long journey this evening and tedious. Both men were tired, but Adam still had fire inside him that would not die down. As they were passing the Albion, he stopped.

'Let's have a drink.'

'Don't be silly, man. We've got no money.'

'Come on. Dan Baglin will give us something on the five barred. He told me the other night he would, anytime.'

Reluctantly Emrys went in with him.

'Evening, Dan.'

'Evening, Adam,' replied Baglin, without moving his head. 'What can I do for you?'

'Two pints. On tick, if you will.'

'I'll have rum and hot water,' said Emrys.' It's frozen I am, with this cold weather, see.'

They went into the inner room and sat by the fire. There were only a few other men there, ironworkers mostly, no colliers. Emrys shivered even more for a few seconds as he leaned forward and let the heat from the logs permeate his body. Adam fetched the drinks, heated his beer with a hot poker and sat staring into the fire.

'Oh, what a disaster! Why did I encourage the men to riot?'

'You made a first-class speech, man. Never heard you make a better one. And you had the men right behind you.'

'I was so buoyed up, I could hardly control myself.'

'What Martha said to you, was it?'

The heat from the fire thawed Adam out and made him more relaxed. He decided to tell Emrys the whole of the story of his love for Martha. He told him of his first taking her at the miners' rally at the Speech House, and then began to tell how Martha had led him upstairs to her bed – to Bert's bed – but paused. 'I've always regretted doing that, believe me,' he said, his emotions raging like a wild beast in its den.

The whole story came tumbling out: his inability to control his passion even though he could control all his other desires; his agony at the way he was treating Catrin; how he had neglected Lennie. He spared no detail.

Emrys held his glass of rum between his hands and looked down.

'Am I embarrassing you, Emrys?'

'No, no.' He looked Adam square in the face. 'It's not what you did that saddens me, though it's unfortunate that you did it. It's because you have been bottling it up all this time, man, and didn't tell anyone. You needed to tell someone so badly. No wonder you are in such a state. Why didn't you tell me?'

'Several times I nearly told you, but I thought you wouldn't understand, being –' He did not finish the sentence.

'I would have understood all right.'

'If only things would go as we want them to.'

Emrys smiled. 'No it wouldn't be better if things went as we wanted them to. Not in the long run.'

Adam pushed his hair from his forehead, rose and went for more drinks. As he walked to the counter he realised how stiff he was, how bone-tired. The day had been busy. Had the meeting with Sully happened only that morning? Had he had the quarrel with Martha only that afternoon? The lack of food since dinner time and the heart-pounding excitement of the evening were taxing even his constitution.

He returned with a beer for himself and a rum for Emrys. The second pint of beer began to make him feel queasy; but the alcohol freed his inhibitions and he carried on with his story. But he was getting maudlin and he knew it, though he could not help himself.

He went for more drinks. 'They say drink cheers you up, but I don't feel cheerful. They said it makes you forget your troubles, but I still remember mine.'

He emptied his glass. 'Emrys, get some more beer, there's a good chap.' But Emrys refused, so he staggered back to the counter and got another pint for himself.

Emrys drew nearer to him. 'You're determined to make yourself ill, Adam.'

'I be all right. Tell me about your troubles now for a change.' But he knew he did not want to hear them.

Emrys went to the counter and asked if Dan could let him have some food.

'Food is short, you know, but I might find you a bit of bread.' He disappeared into a back room and returned with a chunk.

Emrys looked at the bread lovingly as he handed it to Adam. 'Here eat this, man, and sop up some of the beer.'

But the bread did little for Adam. He sat staring into the fire, morbid and quite drunk. His eyes were bloodshot and his lips pale. The overall gnawing of disaster and defeat had overwhelmed him, and he was drained of any desire to think or move or do anything. He tried to proclaim to Emrys once again how fate had led him to the pit of his despair, but could not formulate the words.

'Come on, Adam, let's go home. It's late.'

'Yes, you'd better take him home,' said Dan. 'All the rest have gone and I want to shut up.'

Emrys, not sober himself, had a job to get Adam home, but succeeded in getting him into the house and up the stairs. He opened his bedroom door and pushed him inside.

CHAPTER 38

Next morning Adam awoke and screwed his face up in an attempt to ease the agony of his headache. He swallowed to try to remove the foul taste in his mouth and opened his eyes. Catrin was sitting by the window, looking out but seeing nothing. Her eyes were hollow and sad. He watched her for a few minutes, and then spoke.

'What be the matter, then?'

She turned her head slowly and examined his bloated appearance. Disgust spread over her face and she turned away.

'I know I look rough, but not as bad as that.' He lay back and pulled at his trousers, for he had slept in his clothes.

Catrin looked at him again. 'You don't know, do you?'

'Know what?'

'Lennie's dead.'

'What?'

Wide awake now, he looked around. On the other side of the bed was a bundle, something wrapped in a blanket. He leaned over and uncovered Lennie's face. 'Oh, my God! Little Lennie!'

'There was nowhere else in the room for me to put him.'

'When was it?'

'Last night. And you weren't here.'

'Oh, God.' He lay back and closed his eyes, exhausted. 'It was the consumption, then? I didn't think he was so bad.'

'It was sudden,' she conceded.

He rose and went to Lennie again, as if he did not believe what he had seen before. He touched Lennie's cheek with his finger but, usually soft, it was now hard and cold. He went over to Catrin and tried to put his arms round her. She shook him off and burst into tears. 'Don't touch me,' she screamed.

Uncertain what to do or say, he sat on the bed and put his head in his hands. Thoughts of his dead son banished everything else. Already

298

throbbing from the previous night's liquor, his head was straining to explode. 'I was late coming in last night,' was all he managed to stammer.

'You were drunk. I was lying in bed awake when Emrys pushed you through the door. I wanted to tell you then, but you fell on the bed and went straight to sleep.'

'I had a bad day yesterday.'

She turned on him. 'What sort of a day do you think I had?'

'Catrin,' he said, 'I didn't realise what was happening.'

'Rubbish. You knew he was worse.'

'I mean I didn't realise what I was doing to you and Lennie, how horrible I was being.'

'You say that now.'

He could see she despised him. 'Catrin, it be all over between me and Martha Preece, honest.'

She did not reply, but he sensed blearily that from the depth of her soul a glimmer of hope, almost of triumph, emerged.

'It be all over,' he repeated. 'I'm sorry.' He did not know what more to say.

She got up, her face swollen and pale, and went downstairs.

A few minutes later he followed her. As he descended the staircase he could hear voices in the kitchen, and he hesitated before he pushed open the door at the bottom. Emrys was speaking. 'George didn't come to bed last night. If he went to look for Adam he didn't find him.'

'Well, where is he?' asked Emma.

'A lot of colliers were beaten up by the police. Perhaps he got caught up with them. I expect he'll be home later.'

Emma turned impatiently from Emrys and regarded Adam. Her face, washed of emotion, was strained and fixed, but she said nothing. Emrys took a seat in the corner away from the others, for Lennie's death was a family matter and he would not want to intrude. He gave Adam a faint smile but said nothing. Adam looked at Catrin. There was no comfort there. Adam felt an intruder in his own house. God, it was not all his fault. He stifled a sob. 'Will no-one say anything, curse you?'

'You know then,' said Emma. 'Well, there it is.' She went on quietly, almost speaking to herself. 'We all owe God a death, but our times are in His hands and the number of our months is with Him.' She was silent for a moment. Then, in her usual way, she turned to practicalities. 'I'm afraid he'll have to be buried on the parish, poor mite. We've no money for a decent funeral. God bless his little soul.'

There was silence again. Adam wanted to say so much, but he knew they would not listen. But there was something he could do. He took Grancher's watch from his pocket and gave it to Emrys. 'See if you can sell this and buy a decent coffin for Lennie. He'll only want a small one. Grancher would have approved, I'm sure.'

The tension was broken by a knock on the door. 'We don't want anyone round here just now,' said Emma. She opened the door determinedly. It was Billy. She tried to bar his way, but he pushed in. 'Can I come in just a minute, Mrs Turley. It be about George. He was run down by a police horse last night outside Sully's house.'

'We saw it,' exclaimed Emrys. 'It happened within feet of where we were hiding.'

Adam turned away, stunned. So it had been George calling him.

'I'm afraid he be dead, Mrs Turley. They'll be bringing him home later this morning.'

Billy left immediately, and Emrys accompanied him, taking the opportunity to leave the Turleys to their grief.

'Sad about George,' said Billy. 'And he was never very keen on staying out.'

'Two deaths in one family from the strike. And a tottering marriage.'

'I don't know about Adam's marriage, though stories have been going round. But two casualties?'

'Lennie was a casualty of the strike as well, you know.'

They contemplated while they walked.

Billy broke the silence. 'Joseph Cowmeadow was down at Park End this morning when they told me about George. He'd heard about the attack on Sully's house, and had come to find out what had actually happened. Cutting about like a wild Irishman, he was, moaning about the effect it was going to have on the men and their relation to the union.'

'I expect he thought Adam should have accepted Sully's offer.'

'Yes. He reckons it's all over and the men'll be back at work in a few days.'

❧   ❧

Indeed, it was all over. Later that day, all round the Forest, the colliers met in their lodges. The riots at Park End had made them realise, even the hardheaded ones, that the end of the road had been reached. With little dissent they decided to accept their employers' compromise of a five per cent reduction now and five per cent later.

Adam took no part in negotiating the return of the men to the Park End pits the following morning. Billy, whose participation in union matters had grown since his jail sentence had given him a position of respect among the men, took his place. He went with Matthew Teague to wait on Sully.

Sully received them coldly. 'Very well. You can start work tomorrow. The butty men will have to re-register and I shall want a list of all day men working for them.' He waved his hand, indicating that the interview was over.

Billy hesitated and looked at Matthew Teague. 'There be just one thing, Mr Sully, Sir. We was wondering about a bit of advance pay, like.'

'Goodness, man, you haven't done any work yet.'

'No, Sir, but we haven't got no money, and under the usual rules we won't get no pay for a month, and our wives and kids be starving.' Then, as an added inducement, he added, 'The men will be able to work better with a bit o' food in their bellies, too.'

Sully considered. 'Very well. I'll ask the managers to see what they can arrange.'

They shuffled out, humiliated.

The rest of the day Sully spent in his office with his pit managers discussing arrangements for taking the men on again. He gave orders that if they applied for an advance of pay they should be given three days' money.

It was late when the managers left. Sully went over to the window and looked down on the square below. Early tomorrow morning it would be alive with colliers, pit managers and deputies, crossing and re-crossing it with purpose. The areas round the pit-heads would also be teeming with men. The engines would be belching smoke and hissing steam, the trams laden with coal would be clanging along their tracks, and the men, he hoped, would be working at the coal face with a will. He would be back in business. He was heartened by the prospect, and wanted it to be morning now.

He raised his eyes and sought in the gloom the vague outlines of his house on the other side of the road. Now the trouble with the men had been settled he would be able to devote more time to his private life. He would try to mend his relationship with Hermione. The shame and indignity of discovering that an employee of his had had access to her body still rankled with him, but his initial fury had now subsided into a sad acceptance of the fact of her adultery. But he still loved her, and he

301

decided not to confront her with it. He knew she would never return his love and be as close to him as she had been in the early days of their married life, but she might become more friendly. He would compromise on that.

He yawned, for he was tired and hungry, and decided to go home. He would put on his new suit, just arrived from the tailors, seek Hermione out, enquire whether she had recovered from the rioters' attack on their house, suggest that they had a bottle of their best wine with dinner and perhaps hint that he was proposing to buy her some new ear-rings.

He went straight to his room, washed and changed and went along the corridor to Hermione's sitting room. He looked round the door, ready to smile, indeed ready to kiss her if she would allow it. She wasn't there, so he went into her bedroom. She wasn't there, either. He was about to go downstairs when her maid entered.

'Where is my wife?'

The girl looked embarrassed. 'She's gone, Sir.'

'Gone? Where?'

'Gone. She went this morning. We thought you knew, and that was why you didn't come back at midday.'

'I don't understand.'

'She left about eleven, Sir. She had all her cases carried down and put in the carriage and then drove off.'

Sully dashed into the bedroom again and tore open the doors of the wardrobes. They were empty. He looked round. The top of the dressing table had been cleared, and her jewel case was gone. His face drained pale. He hurried downstairs and burst into the sitting room. She was not there. He sat down on the sofa, trembling.

The meaning of her absence hit him at last. She had left him. But where had she gone? Had she gone off with Gunter? That surely was not possible. He had no money, and Hermione needed a lot of money.

Then he realised she was indeed rich. Her father had entailed a considerable sum on her, and she had retained it on marriage. She must have loved Gunter a great deal to run off with him and be ready to support him. But had she gone off with him? Had she run off with anyone? Had she perhaps left her husband because she could not stand him any more? Had the rioting outside their house been the final happening that made it impossible for her to live with him? But women did not desert their husbands like that. Was Hermione, perhaps, the exception? He realised the dangers of allowing women control of their own money.

He sat alone in the lamplight. There was not a sound in the house. No servant came in to enquire if he wanted dinner. He sat thinking and thinking, wondering and hoping, churning the whole situation over in his mind again and again.

The door was not properly closed, and Sully's cat pushed it open and slid in. He rose, picked it up and held it tightly in his arms for comfort. But in his agony he squeezed the cat to his chest too hard. It hissed and gashed its claws across his face. Then it ran out of the room. Blood from the three lines that were scored in his flesh ran down his cheek.

CHAPTER 39

The colliers' wives did not welcome the early start next morning after so many weeks of lying in bed until dawn peeped over the bed clothes; but they rose with a grunt and went down to light the fire – if there was any fuel – and see what they could find for breakfast. Shortly afterwards the men came down, yawning and grumbling, and went into the backyard to sluice their faces with cold water to wake them up. Dry bread for breakfast, perhaps, and they were off. One after another the front doors in the village street opened and the men came out with their bait tins and containers of cold tea.

As they progressed towards their pits they met up with their mates. After initial greetings they were silent. For though they were glad there would be no more idle days to bore them and were eager to earn some money to enable them to repair the ravages the strike had brought, they had bitterness and resentment in their hearts for the coalmasters because they had forced them to yield. They also had bitterness and resentment for the union, the union that had promised them it would fight the masters and retain their wage rates, and had failed. They vowed they would no longer support it, for it had done nothing but bring hardship, poverty and debt to them. The union died the day they returned to work.

Adam and Emrys did not queue at the pit-head that morning to book in, for Lennie and George were being buried. But they attended the next morning, along with other stragglers.

'Name,' said the clerk at the desk.

'Adam Turley.'

The clerk referred to a list of names. 'No, not you. You're out.'

'What do you mean I'm out?'

'Mr Sully's orders. You're not to be taken on again.'

Adam stepped forward, put his hands wide on the desk and looked down at the clerk. 'So I be blacklisted, eh? Is that what you mean?'

The new pit manager, Gunter's replacement, a large untidy man, was sitting at the back of the shed, smoking. He cursed and heaved his weight and authority over to the desk. 'You heard what he said. There's no job for you at this pit. Or at any other pit in Dean, for that matter, either now or ever. And the same goes for your Welsh pal, there.'

Adam and Emrys stared at each other.

'Come on, get moving. There are other people waiting.'

Adam and Emrys returned home. On the way Emrys stopped to chat to a neighbour; Adam went on ahead, and found Catrin sitting at the kitchen table reading a letter. She looked up in surprise.

'You're back early.'

'Sully won't give me my job back, and it looks as if I won't be able to get one coalmining anywhere else in Dean. I'm blacklisted.'

Adam looked at her hard to see if there were any sign of jubilation in her face. But why should she rejoice at his misfortune? It was her misfortune as well. He sat down opposite her. He was still uncomfortable in her presence, his guilt still pressing down on him. 'Where be Mam?'

'Getting water.'

'Good thing water's still free. It's about the only thing that is.' He looked at her, his eyes questioning and afraid. For a moment his inner anxiety was revealed. 'Catrin, if I'm not working, what are we going to do for money?'

'Don't know,' she said, almost absentmindedly. She returned the letter to its envelope and placed it on the table before her.

'Letter from Wales?'

'Yes.' She indicated the letter with her hand as if inviting him to read it. Why did she do that? She knew he wouldn't be able to understand it because it was written in Welsh. But he did not show his annoyance. And he would not ask her what was in it. If she wanted to tell him she would do so.

She was quiet for a moment, thinking. Then she turned to him and looked at him properly for the first time since he had entered the room. 'Adam, I must tell you. A few days before Lennie died I wrote home and told them how unhappy I was with Lennie and how ill he was, and how we had no money and I wanted to bring Lennie home. I hated doing it, but it was desperate I was. No-one to share with, and Lennie being so ill.'

Tears began to form in her eyes, but she shook her head ever so slightly, and continued. 'In the letter today my father sent me some money – five pounds – to buy some food for Lennie and to pay the fare to the farm if we wanted to come and stay until the strike was over.'

'You didn't tell them about us?'

'No, just about Lennie being ill, and the strike.'

So she had not told her parents about their wrecked marriage; he had to be grateful for that, though he doubted whether it would be long before she told them if she went back. For their broken relationship was the only reason for her returning now. 'Do you want to go back? Even though the strike is over and Lennie has – gone?'

She did not reply.

'Go back if you want to.' But he hoped she would stay with him.

'I don't think I could stay in Coalway now with all its memories. I've never settled here.'

Adam tried to take her hands in his, but she shook him off and went over to the window. 'Your mother is coming with Emrys. No job for him either, is it?' She was glad of the diversion.

'So you can't get your jobs back, then,' said Emma when she came in. 'We can't manage with no wages, you know. You'll have to keep on trying. And George have gone, bless his soul. He won't bring anything in now.' She sighed. 'Well, there it is.' This was just another difficulty in a lifetime of difficulties. It would be overcome.

Emrys searched in his pocket and produced a florin.

'Where did you get that from?' asked Emma.

'I pawned some of my books, Mrs Turley. Catrin, go down to Baldwin's, will you, and get some tea for us and a bit of something for tomorrow.'

'No, no,' said Catrin. 'My father sent me some money in a letter that has just arrived. I'll pay for the food.' She put on her coat and hastened down to the shop.

                                              ❧ ❧

Adam and Emrys went out the next day to find work. They went to Sydney Trotter's pits at Coleford. But the clerk looked at his list and told them that on Trotter's instructions they were not to be given employment. They went further afield, to Brain's Trafalgar pit on the other side of the Forest, but the answer was the same. They went to Bilson and Crumpmeadow, to Cannop and Foxes Bridge, with the same result. Sully had done his work well.

Then they tried Crawshay's Lightmoor. 'We are not taking on any more men just now, and are not likely to for some time,' the clerk said. 'In any case Mr Crawshay's policy is to employ only local men.'

As they walked home exhausted, they realised that even if they had found jobs on the other side of the Forest there would have been a walk of up to six miles a day each way just to get to work and back.

'It be too far, anyway,' said Adam. 'It would kill us, what with slogging away all day as well.'

They announced their failure when the reached home. 'Tomorrow we'll try for something that has nothing to do with coalmining, the ironworks, perhaps, or timber cutting with the Office of Woods.'

They tried. They scoured the area within walking distance from home, but they could find nothing. For weeks they searched. 'We're ready to take anything,' Emrys told Catrin, 'but when they learn we're colliers, suspicious they are. And, truth to tell, we're unskilled at anything but winning coal, and there are plenty of others after the same jobs who are better at them than us.'

Adam sat down and put his head in his hands. 'The Forest of Dean is one big prison, and we are dying in it.'

'No, no,' said Emma. 'Something will turn up, for both of you. In the meantime we have to be patient.'

At this Adam looked up. Though his mother's remark had done nothing to lighten his despair, he was thankful that she still continued to regard Emrys as one of the family. But Emrys hurried to speak.

'Kind it is indeed, Mrs Turley, to imply that I shall be staying on. But I can't stay any longer without bringing money in. I must go.'

'But where will you go to? Back to Wales?'

'I think I might emigrate to America.'

'To America!' said Catrin.

'To Pittsburg. They say there's plenty of work there, and well paid, too, it is.'

'How do you emigrate?' asked Emma. 'I never knew nobody that did that.'

'There is a man in Bristol who can arrange it for you,' said Emrys. 'I've got his name and address. I'll go there and find a job, if I can, and stay until I have saved enough money to take me to America.'

'And if you can't find a job in Bristol?' asked Adam.

'I'll find a ship and persuade the captain to let me work my passage.' He looked round and smiled, but the smile was forced.

Adam went to bed first that night, with his bones weary, his heart sad and his pride in being able to earn a living shattered. As he lay waiting for Catrin to come up, he wondered whether in the last few days she had, perhaps, warmed to him a little. She had discussed his efforts to obtain work; responded to his chance remarks, for he chatted with her now in a way that he had not since Martha had arrived on the scene; and she did not seem to mind his physical proximity as much as she had immediately after Lennie's death. Perhaps their relationship was improving.

But Catrin still had no warmth for him, had not forgiven him even though he had told her his affair with Martha was over and apologised for all his slights and mean actions. But, his sense of fairness asked him, why she should forgive him? Apologies, kind words and well-meaning gestures were not enough. He realised how badly he needed her warmth. Indeed, he wanted her love, for he had become aware that he still loved her. Perhaps time would help. He must be patient.

Catrin came up and undressed quickly because the room was cold. She put out the candle and hurried into bed. There was a lot more space now Lennie did not share it with them. In the old days she would have snuggled up to Adam for warmth, but not now. He reached his hand out towards her back uncertainly, but withdrew it.

'Are you asleep?' she whispered.

He was immediately alert. She wanted to talk.

'No.'

She did not say anything more; but he felt that this was an auspicious moment. So he decided to say what was deepest in his heart. 'Catrin, we can't talk downstairs with the others around all the time, but I want to tell you again how bad I feel about things, how nasty I have been towards you.' He asked in a clear voice, humbly but directly, 'Will you forgive me, Catrin?' It was easier to say it in the dark.

She turned over on to her back, and then on to her other side so that she was facing him. 'I'd like to be how we were when we got married, Adam. It isn't easy, though, when you've had your heart torn out.'

He extended his arm and touched her. She did not move away. 'Catrin,' he said, and put his arm around her waist. 'Catrin, you be cold. Let me warm you.' He drew nearer to her.

But she was not ready for his embrace, and pushed him away. 'I want to talk.' She rolled on her back again. 'In his letter my father said things aren't too good at the farm. In trouble he is. Waldo has left home, but where he has gone they don't know. One of the farm hands has disappeared as well, and they think the two of them may have gone off together.'

Adam did not comment. Waldo had kept his promise to him, and he would keep his promise to Waldo.

'He said that now Waldo had gone he was too old to manage the farm on his own and that if you wanted you could come back with me and gradually take over from him.'

Adam was silent. This was surprising news. Telling him it surely meant that she was now better disposed towards him. But he did not know whether he wanted to leave the Forest and go to Wales, or indeed whether he fancied farming. He pondered what would happen if he refused to go to Wales, especially if he couldn't find a proper job in the Forest. Would she stay with him or would she insist on going home by herself? In his experience women always stayed with their husbands, however much they quarrelled. Was there something in women's nature that made them cling to their partners through thick and thin? Or was it because they had no alternative? But Catrin had an alternative. Would she take it? Did she care for him so little that she would leave him?

'I'll think about it,' he said, but Catrin had turned on her side with her back to him and gone to sleep.

&» «&

Adam went down to the station with Emrys to see him on a train for Bristol. It was a miserable day. The wind was keen and the sky was cloudy, a uniform grey, with no outline of clouds to be seen. Emrys had intended to walk to Bristol, but Catrin had insisted on giving him money for his fare and a few shillings to tide him over during the next few days; for she had kept control of the money her father had sent her.

'Remember coming up this road three years ago, Emrys?' Adam recalled how thin he had been then, what little flesh he had on his bones, all stripped away by the long weeks of the Welsh strike he had endured; and so weak that Adam had insisted on carrying his pathetic bundle of possessions up to Coalway for him. He was still thin, again as a result of a devastating stoppage of work, and his bundle of possessions was no bigger; but he carried it himself and he was more hopeful for the future.

'I be told they announced the profits for Bilson Colliery yesterday, and they're the highest ever in spite of the strike,' said Adam. 'And the coal market according to the paper is "buoyant".'

'Lovely word, "buoyant",' said Emrys, 'especially when attached to markets and profits.'

'And did you see that the Crawshays have issued notices that rates in their pits are to be cut too, to bring them into line with the rates of the other coalmasters in the Forest?'

'So much for being good employers. Let other coalmasters beat their employees down, and then cash in.'

'Can't do nothing about it now. The union's smashed. The men have shown that they have no faith in it. It's all over.'

'No, man, it's not all over.' Emrys's voice was impassioned. He stopped to make his point and, facing Adam, grabbed him by the shoulders. 'The union we worked for may be finished, but there'll be another. People will remember the struggle we put up, see. Working people will, anyway. Everywhere they'll remember the struggles us colliers have had trying to get a decent living, and they'll do something, sometime. Not next year, not in ten years time, perhaps, but sometime.'

'Maybe,' said Adam. 'At least I hope so.'

At the station Adam wished Emrys good luck. Now he was going, he appreciated to the full the preciousness and warmth of their friendship. He wanted to say once again how grateful he was to him for taking the blame when Martha's adultery had been discovered, how he regretted that he had allowed him to take the sneers and laughter of the villagers to protect him, how he wished he had confided in him about his feelings towards Martha earlier, how he appreciated that he had never asked questions about the affair, never said a word, had just shown by his friendship that he supported him.

But he could not say any of it. All he could do was grasp him to his chest and give him a hug. Then, as he began to disengage himself, Emrys, with a sob, hugged him more closely, strongly, violently, and kissed him on his cheek. Then he released his hold and turned away.

Adam did not know how to react. His mind cast round for something to say, anything. 'You'll be alone now,' was all he could find.

Emrys climbed into the train and slung his bundle onto a seat. 'You know, I think I've always been alone.'

The train pulled out, and Adam thrust his hands deep into his pockets and walked from the station, his emotions still unsettled. He did not feel like returning home yet, and decided he would have a look round Park End before going back. He went up the hill to Park End Royal pit. Leaning on the barrier erected to keep out the pickets and not yet removed, he contemplated the pit-head. They were busy up there, but how long would it last? How long would it be before Sully launched a further attack on the men's wages and provoked another strike? Why was such confrontation necessary? Wasn't there another way of exploiting the natural resources of the Forest? Emrys had said there was; Adam didn't know, wasn't certain. But he did know there were millions of tons of coal under the surface of the Forest of Dean, enough to provide riches for everyone; and there would always be colliers to dig it out.

From among the throng of men at the pit-head, the pit manager emerged and made his way down the slope. 'Here you,' he said. 'You clear off. We don't want the likes of you hanging round here.'

Another time Adam would have argued, would not have bowed to this abuse. But this time, sick in his heart, he shrugged his shoulders and slouched off without a word. Back down the road he went, and then up to the church. The platform outside the churchyard from which he had made his greatest and most fatal speech was still there. The area was deserted; only the sound of the sexton's spade as he dug a grave disturbed the peace. But in his head Adam could hear the cheers of the men as he had spoken. The recollection gave him little satisfaction. How different would things have been if he had not led the attack on Sully's house, if he had persuaded the men to hang on for just another week and forced a better concession out of Sully? And if he had, George would have lived. But remorse, though nagging in his heart, could not put things right, and he moved on.

He paused outside the gates of Sully's house and looked at one of the ground-floor windows. That's where he probably is, he thought, in his study, glorying that he has forced the men back to work on his terms, and celebrating with that haughty wife of his. May he get much joy from his victory. He walked on.

Two of his former comrades from the pit were approaching. One nudged the other as they came near. Adam looked at them in search of a glance of recognition but, stiff-faced, they stared ahead as they passed. His heart dropped heavy inside him. They had been brothers once, he thought, bound by a crumb of bread. Now they spurned him.

However, that was in the past, when he had been drunk on dreams. Now he had to decide whether to go to Wales and become a farmer. The affair with Martha was over and finished with. There was no doubt about that. Though he retained some pleasant memories of her company, there had always been an unhappy feeling of subterfuge and guilt, and he was ashamed he had allowed himself to be seduced as he had. So there was no one to keep him in Coalway – except his mother, of course. With George dead she would be alone if he went to Wales. But it should be possible for her to live with her married sister and family in Park End. There would be room and the sisters had always kept in touch.

If he went to Wales he would be in the territory of Catrin's parents. Did he want to live with them, be subject to their pressures? He conceded Catrin had willingly come over into his territory, and much heartache it had caused her. But he was loath to leave the Forest, to leave coalmining; it was in his blood. However, it was clear that Catrin was intent on returning. Going to Wales and becoming a farmer was part of the parcel if they were to stay together.

He remembered that it had been in Wales that he had given Lennie to Catrin. If he went to the farm they could start another baby, a son he hoped, to replace the one they had lost. And this time he would find time to be with him and not neglect him as he had Lennie.

Yes. He had decided. He knew now what he wanted. He would go to Wales with Catrin and restart his married life. He ached to make her happy again. If one had to choose, a wife and a family were more important than being a trade union leader lapping up applause from men who would abandon you when they thought you had failed them. He could see that now. Perhaps in time Catrin would learn to love him again as she used to.

Having made the decision he felt strong and whole again; his pride in himself had reasserted itself. He turned for home. The clouds, so heavy earlier, were clearing. The sun came out, thin and wintry, but sufficient to light up the frost still on the bare branches of the trees. With a turn of the path, the scene changed. In a copse he saw a faint mist of green, and stopped to wonder. Yes, it was the peculiar light green of the larch, tip-toeing on the edge of spring and ready with the encouragement of light and warmth to emerge. He looked again. The mist was gone. But it had been there; he had seen it.

He quickened his pace. Ahead, through the bare branches of a beech tree, he could see the first cottages of Coalway. But before he reached them he paused. In grass that shone moist in pale sunlight and was strewn with last year's leaves, he saw his first wild flowers of spring, tiny and white, shyly lifting their delicate heads and emerging before the trees put forth their leaves and deprived them of light. The earth was quickening to life, spring was coming to the Forest; it was the time of renewal.

Suddenly he saw a slim figure in the distance. Yes, it was Catrin, coming to meet him; she must have guessed he would return this way. She recognised him and waved.

His heart quickened as he raced towards her.